Douglas Hyde, Alfred T. Nutt

Beside the Fire

A Collection of Irish Gaelic Folk Stories

Douglas Hyde, Alfred T. Nutt

Beside the Fire
A Collection of Irish Gaelic Folk Stories

ISBN/EAN: 9783337117627

Printed in Europe, USA, Canada, Australia, Japan

Cover: Foto ©Andreas Hilbeck / pixelio.de

More available books at **www.hansebooks.com**

BESIDE THE FIRE

A COLLECTION OF

IRISH GAELIC FOLK STORIES.

EDITED, TRANSLATED, AND ANNOTATED

BY

DOUGLAS HYDE, LL.D., M.R.I.A.,

(ANCHRAOIBHÍN AOIBHINN.)

MEMBER OF THE COUNCIL OF THE GAELIC UNION; MEMBER OF THE PANCELTIC SOCIETY, ETC.

WITH ADDITIONAL NOTES

BY

ALFRED NUTT.

Tá pian map eóó aip oreaċt na h-oióće
Dheipéeap aip le gal beag gaoiée.—SCAN DAN.

"They are like a mist on the coming of night
That is scattered away by a light breath of wind."—OLD POEM.

LONDON:
DAVID NUTT, 270, 271 STRAND.
1890

PRINTED AT

THE FREEMANS JOURNAL, LIMITED

PRINTING & BOOKBINDING WORKS

DUBLIN.

DEDICATION.

To the memory of those truly cultured and unselfish
men, the poet-scribes and hedge-schoolmasters of the
last century and the beginning of this—men who may
well be called the last of the Milesians—I dedicate this
effort to preserve even a scrap of that native lore which
in their day they loved so passionately, and for the
preservation of which they worked so nobly, but in vain

CONTENTS.

———◆———

PREFACE.

IRISH and Scotch Gaelic folk-stories are, as a living form of literature, by this time pretty nearly a thing of the past. They have been trampled in the common ruin under the feet of the Zeitgeist, happily not before a large harvest has been reaped in Scotland, but, unfortunately, before anything worth mentioning has been done in Ireland to gather in the crop which grew luxuriantly a few years ago. Until quite recently there existed in our midst millions of men and women who, when their day's work was over, sought and found mental recreation in a domain to which few indeed of us who read books are permitted to enter. Man, all the world over, when he is tired of the actualities of life, seeks to unbend his mind with the creations of fancy. We who can read betake ourselves to our favourite novelist, and as we peruse his fictions, we can almost see our author erasing this, heightening that, and laying on such-and-such a touch for effect. His book is the product of his individual brain, and some of us or of our contemporaries have been present at its genesis.

But no one can tell us with certainty of the genesis of the folk-tale, no one has been consciously present at its inception, and no one has marked its growth. It is in many ways a mystery, part of the flotsam and jetsam of the ages, still beating feebly against the shore of the nineteenth century, swallowed up at last in England by the waves of materialism and civilization combined; but still surviving unengulfed on the western coasts of Ireland, where I gathered together some bundles of it, of which the present volume is one.

The folk-lore of Ireland, like its folk-songs and native literature, remains practically unexploited and ungathered. Attempts have been made from time to time during the present century to collect Irish folk-lore, but these attempts, though interesting from a literary point of view, are not always successes from a scientific one. Crofton Croker's delightful book, "Fairy Legends and Traditions of the South of Ireland," first published anonymously in 1825, led the way. All the other books which have been published on the subject have but followed in the footsteps of his; but all have not had the merit of his light style, his pleasant parallels from classic and foreign literature, and his delightful annotations, which touch, after a fascinating manner peculiarly his own, upon all that is of interest in his text. I have written the word "text," but that word conveys the idea of an original to be annotated upon; and Crofton Croker is, alas! too often his own original. There lies his weak point, and there, too, is the defect of all who have followed him. The form in which the stories are told is, of course, Croker's own; but no one who knows anything of fairy lore will suppose that his manipulation of the originals is confined to the form merely. The fact is that he learned the ground-work of his tales from conversations with the Southern peasantry, whom he knew well, and then elaborated this over the midnight oil with great skill and delicacy of touch, in order to give a saleable book, thus spiced, to the English public.

Setting aside the novelists Carleton and Lover, who only published some incidental and largely-manipulated Irish stories, the next person to collect Irish folk-lore in a volume was Patrick Kennedy, a native of the County Wexford, who published " Legendary Fictions of the Irish Celts," and in 1870 a good book, entitled, " The Fireside Stories of Ireland," which he had himself heard in Wexford when a boy. Many of the stories which he gives appear to be the detritus of genuine Gaelic folk-stories, filtered through an English idiom and much impaired and stunted in the process. He appears, however, not to have adulterated them very much. Two of the best stories in the book, " Jack, the Cunning Thief " and " Shawn an Omadawn," I heard myself in the adjoining county Wicklow, and the versions of them that I heard did not differ very widely from Kennedy's. It

is interesting to note that these counties, close to the
Pale as they are, and under English influence for so
long, nevertheless seem to have preserved a consider-
able share of the old Gaelic folk-tales in English dress,
while in Leitrim, Longford, Meath, and those counties
where Irish died out only a generation or two ago, there
has been made as clean a sweep of folk-lore and Gaelic
traditions as the most uncompromising " West Briton "
could desire. The reason why some of the folk-stories survive in the eastern counties is probably because the Irish
language was there exchanged for English at a time
when, for want of education and printed books, folk-
stories (the only mental recreation of the people) *had* to
transfer themselves rightly or wrongly into English.
When this first took place I cannot tell, but I have heard
from old people in Waterford, that when some of their
fathers or grandfathers marched north to join the Wexford Irish in '98, they were astonished to find English
nearly universally used amongst them.   Kennedy says
of his stories : "I have endeavoured to present them in
a form suitable for the perusal of both sexes and of all
ages"; and "such as they are, they may be received by
our readers as obtained from local sources." Unfortunately, the sources are not given by him any more than
by Croker, and we cannot be sure how much belongs to
Kennedy the bookseller, and how much to the Wexford
peasant.

After this come Lady Wilde's volumes—her "Ancient Legends," and her recently published "Ancient Cures, Charms, and Usages," in both of which books she gives us a large amount of narrative matter in a folk-lore dress; but, like her predecessors, she disdains to quote an authority, and scorns to give us the least inkling as to where such-and-such a legend, or cure, or superstition comes from, from whom it was obtained, who were her informants, whether peasant or other, in what parishes or counties the superstition or legend obtains, and all the other collateral information which the modern folk-lorist is sure to expect. Her entire ignorance of Irish, through the medium of which alone such tales and superstitions can properly, if at all, be collected, is apparent every time she introduces an Irish word. She astonishes us Irish speakers with such striking observations as this— "Peasants in Ireland wishing you good luck, say in Irish, 'The blessing of Bel and the blessing of Samhain be with you,' that is, of the sun and of the moon."* It

---

* Had Lady Wilde known Irish she might have quoted from a popular ballad composed on Patrick Sarsfield, and not yet forgotten :—

    A pádpuiᵹ Sáippéul ir buine le Dia cu,
    'S beannuiᵹée an calaṁ ap ṁúbail cu piaṁ aip,
    ᵹo mbeannuiᵹ an ᵹealaé ᵹeal 'r an ᵹpian buic,
    O éuᵹ cu an lá ap láṁ Ríᵹ 'Liaim leac.
                    Oé oéón.

—i.e.,

    Patrick Sarsfield, a man with God you are,
    Blessed the country that you walk upon,
    Blessing of sun and shining moon on you,
    Since from William you took the day with you.
                    Och, och hone.

would be interesting to know the locality where so
curious a Pagan custom is still practised, for I confess
that though I have spoken Irish in every county where it
is still spoken, I have never been, nor do I expect to be,
so saluted. Lady Wilde's volumes are, nevertheless, a
wonderful and copious record of folk-lore and folk customs, which must lay Irishmen under one more debt of
gratitude to the gifted compiler. It is unfortunate, however, that these volumes are hardly as valuable as they
are interesting, and for the usual reason—that we do not
know what is Lady Wilde's and what is not.

Almost contemporaneously with Lady Wilde's last
book there appeared this year yet another important
work, a collection of Irish folk-tales taken from the
Gaelic speakers of the south and north-west, by an
American gentleman, Mr. Jeremiah Curtin. He has
collected some twenty tales, which are told very well,
and with much less cooking and flavouring than

This would have made her point just as well. Unfortunately, Lady
Wilde is always equally extraordinary or unhappy in her informants
where Irish is concerned. Thus, she informs us that *bo-banna* (meant
for *bo-bainne*, a milch cow) is a " white cow " ; that tobar-na-bo (the
cow's well) is " the well of the white cow " ; that Banshee comes
from *van* " the woman " — (*bean* means " a woman ") ; that Leith
Brogan — *i.e.*, leprechaun—is "the artificer of the brogue," while it
really means the half or one-shoe, or, according to Stokes, is merely a
corruption of locharpan ; that tobar-na-dara (probably the " oak-well ') is.
the " well of tears," etc. Unfortunately, in Ireland it is no disgrace, but really
seems rather a recommendation, to be ignorant of Irish, even when writing on
Ireland.

his predecessors employed. Mr. Curtin tells us that he has taken his tales from the old Gaelic-speaking men; but he must have done so through the awkward medium of an interpreter, for his ignorance of the commonest Irish words is as startling as Lady Wilde's.* He follows Lady Wilde in this, too, that he keeps us in profound ignorance of his authorities. He mentions not one name, and except that he speaks in a general way of old Gaelic speakers in nooks where the language is still spoken, he leaves us in complete darkness as to where and from whom, and how he collected these stories. In this he does not do himself justice, for, from my own knowledge of Irish folk-lore, such as it is, I can easily recognize that Mr. Curtin has approached the fountain-head more nearly than any other. Unfortunately, like his predecessors, he has a literary style of his own, for

---

* Thus he over and over again speaks of a slumber-pin as *bar an suan*, evidently mistaking the *an* of *bioran*, "a pin," for *an* the definite article. So he has *slat an draoiachta* for *slaitin*, or *slatin draoigheachta*. He says *innis caol* (narrow island) means "light island," and that *gil an og* means "water of youth!" &c.; but, strangest of all, he talks in one of his stories of killing and boiling a stork, though his social researches on Irish soil might have taught him that that bird was not a Hibernian fowl. He evidently mistakes the very common word *sture*, a bullock, or large animal, or, possibly, *torc*, "a wild boar," for the bird stork. His interpreter probably led him astray in the best good faith, for *sturck* is just as common a word with English-speaking people as with Gaelic speakers, though it is not to be found in our wretched dictionaries.

which, to say the least of it, there is no counterpart in the Gaelic from which he has translated.[*]

We have as yet had no[,] folk-lorist in Ireland who could compare for a moment with such a man as Iain Campbell, of Islay, in investigative powers, thoroughness of treatment, and acquaintance with the people, combined with a powerful national sentiment, and, above all, a knowledge of Gaelic. It is on this last rock that all our workers-up of Irish folk-lore split. In most circles in Ireland it is a disgrace to be known to talk Irish; and in the capital, if one makes use of an Irish word to express one's meaning, as one sometimes does of a French or German word, one would be looked upon as positively outside the pale of decency; hence we need not be surprised at the ignorance of Gaelic Ireland displayed by littérateurs who write for the English public, and foist upon us modes of speech which we have not got, and idioms which they never learned from us.

This being the case, the chief interest in too many of our folk-tale writers lies in their individual treatment of the skeletons of the various Gaelic stories obtained through English mediums, and it is not devoid of in-

---

[*] Thus: " Kill Arthur went and killed Ri Fohin and all his people and beasts—didn't leave one alive;" or, " But that instant it disappeared—went away of itself;" or, " It won all the time—wasn't playing fair," etc., etc.

terest to watch the various garbs in which the sophisticated minds of the ladies and gentlemen who trifled
in such matters, clothed the dry bones. But when the
skeletons were thus padded round and clad, although
built upon folk-lore, they were no longer folk-lore themselves, for folk-lore can only find a fitting garment in
the language that comes from the mouths of those whose
minds are so primitive that they retain with pleasure
those tales which the more sophisticated invariably
forget. For this reason folk-lore is presented in an un-
certain and unsuitable medium, whenever the contents
of the stories are divorced from their original expression
in language. Seeing how Irish writers have managed it
hitherto, it is hardly to be wondered at that the writer
of the article on folk-lore in the "Encyclopedia Bri-
tanica," though he gives the names of some fifty authorities on the subject, has not mentioned a single Irish
collection. In the present book, as well as in my
Leaḃaɼ Sgeuluiġeaċta, I have attempted—if nothing
else—to be a little more accurate than my predecessors,
and to give the *exact language* of my informants, together
with their names and various localities—information
which must always be the very first requisite of any
work upon which a future scientist may rely when he
proceeds to draw honey (is it always honey?) from the
flowers which we collectors have culled for him.

It is difficult to say whether there still exist in Ireland many stories of the sort given in this volume. That is a question which cannot be answered without further investigation. In any other country the great body of Gaelic folk-lore in the four provinces would have been collected long ago, but the " Hiberni incuriosi suorum" appear at the present day to care little for anything that is Gaelic; and so their folk-lore has remained practically uncollected.

Anyone who reads this volume as a representative one of Irish folk-tales might, at first sight, imagine that there is a broad difference between the Gaelic tales of the Highlands and those of Ireland, because very few of the stories given here have parallels in the volumes of Campbell and MacInnes. I have, however, particularly chosen the tales in the present volume on account of their dissimilarity to any published Highland tales, for, as a general rule, the main body of tales in Ireland and Scotland bear a very near relation to each other. Most of Mr. Curtin's stories, for instance, have Scotch Gaelic parallels. It would be only natural, however, that many stories should exist in Ireland which are now forgotten in Scotland, or which possibly were never carried there by that section of the Irish which colonized it; and some of the most modern—especially of the kind whose genesis I have called conscious—must have arisen amongst the Irish since then, while on the other

hand some of the Scotch stories may have been be-
queathed to the Gaelic language by those races who
were displaced by the Milesian Conquest in the fifth
century.

Many of the incidents of the Highland stories have
parallels in Irish MSS., even incidents of which I have
met no trace in the folk-lore of the people. This is
curious, because these Irish MSS. used to circulate
widely, and be constantly read at the firesides of the
peasantry, while there is no trace of MSS. being in use
in historical times amongst the Highland cabins. Of
such stories as were most popular, a very imperfect list
of about forty is given in Mr. Standish O'Grady's excellent preface to the third volume of the Ossianic Society's
publications. After reading most of these in MSS. of
various dates, and comparing them with such folk-lore
as I had collected orally, I was surprised to find how
few points of contact existed between the two. The
men who committed stories to paper seem to have
chiefly confined themselves to the inventions of the
bards or professional story-tellers—often founded, however, on folk-lore incidents—while the taste of the people
was more conservative, and willingly forgot the bardic
inventions to perpetuate their old Aryan traditions, of
which this volume gives some specimens. The discrepancy in style and contents between the MS. stories
and those of the people leads me to believe that the

stories in the MSS. are not so much old Aryan folk-tales written down by scholars as the inventions of individual brains, consciously inventing, as modern novelists do. This theory, however, must be somewhat modified before it can be applied, for, as I have said, there are incidents in Scotch Gaelic folk-tales which resemble those of some of the MS. stories rather nearly. Let us glance at a single instance—one only out of many—where High-land tradition preserves a trait which, were it not for such preservation, would assuredly be ascribed to the imaginative brain of an inventive Irish writer.

The extraordinary creature of which Campbell found traces in the Highlands, the Fáchan, of which he has drawn a whimsical engraving,* is met with in an Irish MS. called ꞇoꞁꞁᴀ̇ɴɴ ᴀ̇ꞃᴜ-ᴅᴇᴀꞁᵹ. Old MacPhie, Camp-bell's informant, called him the "Desert creature of Glen Eite, the son of Colin," and described him as having "one hand out of his chest, one leg out of his haunch, and one eye out of the front of his face;" and again, "ugly was the make of the Fáchan, there was one hand out of the ridge of his chest, and one tuft out of the top of his head, and it were easier to take a mountain from the root than to bend that tuft." This one-legged, one-handed, one-eyed creature, unknown, as Campbell re-marks, to German or Norse mythology, is thus described

---

* Campbell's "Popular Tales of the West Highlands." Vol. iv. p. 327.

in the Irish manuscript: "And he (Iollann) was not long
at this, until he saw the devilish misformed element, and
the fierce and horrible spectre, and the gloomy disgust-
ing enemy, and the morose unlovely churl (moɣꞅ); and
this is how he was: he held a very thick iron flail-club
in his skinny hand, and twenty chains out of it, and fifty
apples on each chain of them, and a venomous spell on
each great apple of them, and a girdle of the skins of
deer and roebuck around the thing that was his body,
and one eye in the forehead of his black-faced countenance, and one bare, hard, very hairy hand coming out
of his chest, and one veiny, thick-soled leg supporting him
and a close, firm, dark blue mantle of twisted hard-thick
feathers, protecting his body, and surely he was more
like unto devil than to man." This creature inhabited
a desert, as the Highlander said, and were it not for this
corroborating Scotch tradition, I should not have hesi-
tated to put down the whole incident as the whimsical
invention of some Irish writer, the more so as I had
never heard any accounts of this wonderful creature in
local tradition. This discovery of his counterpart in the
Highlands puts a new complexion on the matter. Is
the Highland spectre derived from the Irish manuscript
story, or does the writer of the Irish story only embody
in his tale a piece of folk-lore common at one time to
all branches of the Gaelic race, and now all but extinct.
This last supposition is certainly the true one, for it is

borne out by the fact that the Irish writer ascribes no name to this monster, while the Highlander calls him a Fáchan,* a word, as far as I know, not to be found elsewhere.

But we have further ground for pausing before we ascribe the Irish manuscript story to the invention of some single bard or writer. If we read it closely we shall see that it is largely the embodiment of other folk-tales. Many of the incidents of which it is composed can be paralleled from Scotch Gaelic sources, and one of the most remarkable, that of the prince becoming a journey-man fuller, I have found in a Connacht folk-tale. This diffusion of incidents in various tales collected all over the Gaelic-speaking world, would point to the fact that the story, as far as many of the incidents go, is not the invention of the writer, but is genuine folk-lore thrown by him into a new form, with, perhaps, added incidents of his own, and a brand new dress.

But now in tracing this typical story, we come across another remarkable fact—the fresh start the story took on its being thus recast and made up new. Once the order and progress of the incidents were thus stereo-typed, as it were, the tale seems to have taken a new

---

* Father O'Growney has suggested to me that this may be a diminutive of the Irish word *fathach*, "a giant." In Scotch Gaelic a giant is always called "famhair," which must be the same word as the *fomhor* or sea-pirate of mythical Irish history.

lease of its life, and gone forth to conquer; for while it continued to be constantly copied in Irish manuscripts, thus proving its popularity as a written tale, it continued to be recited verbally in Scotland in something like the same bardic and inflated language made use of by the Irish writer, and with pretty nearly the same sequence of incidents, the three adventurers, whose Irish names are Ur, Artuir, and Iollann, having become transmogrified into Ur, Athairt, and Iullar, in the mouth of the Highland reciter. I think it highly improbable, however, that at the time of this story being composed—largely out of folk-tale incidents—it was also committed to paper. I think it much more likely that the story was committed to writing by some Irish scribe, only after it had gained so great a vogue as to spread through both Ireland and Scotland. This would account for the fact that all the existing MSS. of this story, and of many others like it, are, as far as I am aware, comparatively modern.* Another argument in favour of this

---

* The manuscript in which I first read this story is a typical one of a class very numerous all over the country, until O'Connell and the Parliamentarians, with the aid of the Catholic prelates, gained the ear and the leadership of the nation, and by their more than indifference to things Gaelic put an end to all that was really Irish, and taught the people to speak English, to look to London, and to read newspapers. This particular MS. was written by one Seorsa MacEincircineadh, whoever he was, and it is black with dirt, reeking with turf smoke, and worn away at the corners by repeated reading. Besides this story it contains a number of others, such as "The Rearing of Cuchulain," "The Death of Conlaoch," "The King of Spain's Son," etc., with many Ossianic and elegiac poems. The people used to gather in at night to hear these read, and, I am sure, nobody who understands the contents of these MSS., and the beautiful

supposition, that bardic tales were only committed to writing when they had become popular, may be drawn from the fact that both in Ireland and the Highlands we find in many folk-lore stories traces of bardic compositions easily known by their poetical, alliterative, and inflated language, of which no MSS. are found in either country. It may, of course, be said, that the MSS. have perished; and we know how grotesquely indifferent the modern Irish are about their literary and antiquarian remains; yet, had they ever existed, I cannot help thinking that some trace of them, or allusion to them, would be found in our surviving literature.

There is also the greatest discrepancy in the poetical passages which occur in the Highland oral version and the Irish manuscript version of such tales as in incident are nearly identical. Now, if the story had been propagated from a manuscript written out once for all, and then copied, I feel pretty sure that the resemblance between the alliterative passages in the two would be much closer. The dissimilarity between them seems to show that the incidents and not the language were the things to be remembered, and that every wandering bard who picked up a new story from a colleague, stereotyped the incidents in his mind, but uttered them whenever he recited

---

alliterative language of the poems, will be likely to agree with the opinion freely expressed by most of our representative men, that it is better for the people to read newspapers than study anything so useless.

the story, in his own language ; and whenever he came
to the description of a storm at sea, or a battle, or
anything else which the original poet had seen fit to
describe poetically, he did so too, but not in the same
way or the same language, for to remember the language of his predecessor on these occasions, from merely
hearing it, would be well-nigh impossible. It is likely,
then, that each bard or story-teller observed the places
where the poetical runs should come in, but trusted to
his own cultivated eloquence for supplying them. It
will be well to give an example or two from this tale of
Iollann. Here is the sea-run, as given in the Highland
oral version, after the three warriors embark in their
vessel :—

" They gave her prow to sea and her stern to shore,
  They hoisted the speckled flapping bare-topped sails,
  Up against the tall tough splintering masts,
  And they had a pleasant breeze as they might chose themselves,
  Would bring heather from the hill, leaf from grove, willow from 's roots.
  Would put thatch of the houses in furrows of the ridges,
  The day that neither the son nor the father could do it,
  That same was neither little nor much for them,
  But using it and taking it as it might come.
  The sea plunging and surging,
  The red sea the blue sea lashing,
  And striking hither and thither about her planks,
  The whorled dun whelk that was down on the floor of the ocean,
  Would give a *snag* on her gunwale and a crack on her floor,
  She would cut a slender oaten straw with the excellence of her going.

It will be observed how different the corresponding
run in the Irish manuscript is, when thrown into verse,

for the language in both versions is only measured prose :—

" Then they gave an eager very quick courageous high-spirited flood-leap
  To meet and to face the sea and the great ocean.
  And great was the horror • • • • •
  Then there arose before them a fierceness in the sea,
  And they replied patiently stoutly strongly and vigorously,
  To the roar of the green sided high-strong waves,
  Till they made a high quick very-furious rowing
  Till the deep-margined dreadful blue-bordered sea
  Arose in broad-sloping fierce-frothing plains
  And in rushing murmuring flood-quick ever-deep platforms.
  And in gloomy horrible swift great valleys
  Of very terrible green sea, and the beating and the pounding
  Of the strong dangerous waves smiting against the decks
  And against the sides of that full-great full-tight bark."

It may, however, be objected that sea-runs are so common and so numerous, that one might easily usurp the place of another, and that this alone is no proof that the various story-tellers or professional bards, contented themselves with remembering the incidents of a story, but either extemporised their own runs after what flourish their nature would, or else had a stock of these, of their own composing, always ready at hand. Let us look, then, at another story of which Campbell has preserved the Highland version, while I have a good Irish MS. of the same, written by some northern scribe, in 1762. This story, " The Slender Grey Kerne," or "Slim Swarthy Champion," as Campbell translates it, is full of alliterative runs, which the Highland reciter has retained in their proper places, but couched in different language, while he introduces a run of his own which the Irish has not got, in describing the swift movement of the kerne. Every time the kerne is asked where he comes from, the Highlander makes him say—

> " I came from hurry-skurry,
> From the land of endless spring,[*]
> From the loved swanny glen,
> A night in Islay and a night in Man,
> A night on cold watching cairns
> On the face of a mountain.
> In the Scotch king's town was I born,
> A soiled sorry champion am I
> Though I happened upon this town."

In the Irish MS. the kerne always says—

> " In Dun Monaidh, in the town of the king of Scotland,
> I slept last night,
> But I be a day in Islay and a day in Cantire,
> A day in Man and a day in Rathlin,
> A day in Fionncharn of the watch
> Upon Slieve Fuaid,
> A little miserable traveller I,
> And in Aileach of the kings was I born.
> And that," said he, " is my story."

Again, whenever the kerne plays his harp the Highlander says :—

> " He could play tunes and *oirts* and *orgain*,
> Trampling things, tightening strings,
> Warriors, heroes, and ghosts on their feet,
> Ghosts and souls and sickness and fever,

* Campbell has mistranslated this. I think it means "from the bottom of the well of the deluge."

> That would set in sound lasting sleep
> The whole great world,
> With the sweetness of the calming* tunes
> That the champion would play."

The Irish run is as follows :—

> " The kerne played music and tunes and instruments of song,
> Wounded men and women with babes,
> And slashed heroes and mangled warriors,
> And all the wounded and all the sick,
> And the bitterly-wounded of the great world,
> They would sleep with the voice of the music,
> Ever efficacious, ever sweet, which the kerne played."

Again, when the kerne approaches anyone, his gait is thus described half-rythmically by the Scotch narrator :—" A young chap was seen coming towards them, his two shoulders through his old coat, his two ears through his old hat, his two squat kickering tatter-y shoes full of cold roadway-ish water, three feet of his sword sideways in the side of his haunch after the scabbard was ended."

The Irish writer makes him come thus :—" And he beheld the slender grey kerne approaching him straight, and half his sword bared behind his haunch, and old shoes full of water sousing about him, and the top of his ears out through his old mantle, and a short butt-burned javelin of holly in his hand."

These few specimens, which could be largely multi-

---

* Campbell misunderstood this also, as he sometimes does when the word is Irish. *Siogaidh* means " fairy."

plied, may be sufficient for our purpose, as they show that
wherever a run occurs in the Irish the same occurs in
the Gaelic, but couched in quite different language,
though preserving a general similarity of meaning. This
can only be accounted for on the supposition already
made, that when a professional bard had invented a
successful story it was not there and then committed to
paper, but circulated *viva voce*, until it became the pro-
perty of every story-teller, and was made part of the
stock-in-trade of professional *filès*, who neither remembered nor cared to remember the words in which the
story was first told, but only the incidents of which it
was composed, and who (as their professional training
enabled them to do) invented or extemporised glowing
alliterative runs for themselves at every point of the
story where, according to the inventor of it, a run
should be.

It may be interesting to note that this particular story
cannot—at least in the form in which we find it disseminated both in Ireland and Scotland—be older than
the year 1362, in which year O'Connor Sligo marched
into Munster and carried off great spoil, for in both the
Scotch and Irish versions the kerne is made to accompany that chieftain, and to disappear in disgust because
O'Connor forgot to offer him the first drink. This story
then, and it is probably typical of a great many others,
had its rise in its present shape—for, of course, the germ

of it may be much older—on Irish ground, not earlier
than the end of the fourteenth or the beginning of the
fifteenth century, and was carried by some Irish bard or
professional story-teller to the Gaeldom of Scotland,
where it is told to this day without any great variations,
but in a form very much stunted and shortened. As to
the Irish copy, I imagine that it was not written down
for a couple of centuries later, and only after it had
become a stock piece all over the Scotch and Irish
Gaeldom ; that then some scribe got hold of a story-teller
(one of those professionals who, according to the Book
of Leinster, were obliged to know seven times fifty stories), and stereotyped in writing the current Irish varia-
tion of the tale, just as Campbell, two, three, or four centuries afterwards, did with the Scotch Gaelic version.

It may, of course, be alleged that the bombastic and
inflated language of many of the MS. stories is due not
to the oral reciter, but to the scribe, who, in his pride of
learning, thought to himself, *nihil quod tango non orno ;*
out though it is possible that some scribes threw in ex-
traneous embellishments, I think the story-teller was
the chief transgressor. Here, for instance, is a verbally
collected specimen from a Connemara story, which contains all the marks of the MS. stories, and yet it is
almost certain that it has been transmitted purely *vivâ
voce* :—" They journeyed to the harbour where there was
a vessel waiting to take them across the sea. They

struck into her, and hung up the great blowing, bellying, equal-long, equal-straight sails, to the tops of the masts, so that they would not leave a rope without straining, or an oar without breaking, plowing the seething, surging sea ; great whales making fairy music and service for them, two-thirds going beneath the wave to the one-third going on the top, sending the smooth sand down below and the rough sand up above, and the eels in grips with one another, until they grated on port and harbour in the Eastern world." This description is probably nothing to the glowing language which a professional story-teller, with a trained ear, enormous vocabulary, and complete command of the language, would have employed a couple of hundred years ago. When such popular traces of the inflated style even still exist, it is against all evidence to accredit the invention and propagation of it to the scribes alone.

The relationship between Ireland and the Scottish Gaeldom was of the closest kind, and there must have been something like an identity of literature, nor was there any break in the continuity of these friendly relations until the plantation of Ulster cut off the high road between the two Gaelic families. Even during the fifteenth and sixteenth centuries it is probable that no sooner did a bardic composition win fame in Ireland than it was carried over to try its fortune in Scotland too, just as an English dramatic company will come over from London to Dublin. A story which throws great light on the dispersion of heroic tales amongst the Gaelic-speaking peoples, is Conall Gulban, the longest of all Campbell's tales. On comparing the Highland version with an Irish MS., by Father Manus O'Donnell, made in 1708, and another made about the beginning of this century, by Michael O'Longan, of Carricknavar, I was surprised to find incident following incident with wonderful regularity in both versions. Luckily we have proximate data for fixing the date of this renowned story, a story that, according to Campbell, is " very widely spread in Scotland, from Beaulay on the east, to Barra on the west, and Dunoon and Paisley in the south." Both the Irish and Gaelic stories relate the exploits of the fifth century chieftain, Conall Gulban, the son of Niall of the Nine Hostages, and his wars with (amongst others) the Turks. The Irish story begins with an account of Niall holding his court, when a herald from the Emperor of Constantinople comes forward and summons him to join the army of the emperor, and assist in putting down Christianity, and making the nations of Europe embrace the Turkish faith. We may fairly surmise that this romance took its rise in the shock given to Europe by the fall of Constantinople and the career of Mahomet the Great. This would throw back its date to the latter end of the fifteenth century at the earliest; but one might almost suppose that Constantinople had been long enough held

by the Turks at the time the romance was invented to
make the inventor suppose that it had always belonged to
them, even in the time of Niall of the Nine Hostages.*
We know that romances of this kind continued to be
invented at a much later date, but I fancy none of these
ever penetrated to Scotland. One of the most popular
of romantic tales with the scribes of the last century and
the first half of this, was " The Adventures of Torolbh Mac
Stairn, and again, the "Adventures of Torolbh MacStairn's
Three Sons," which most of the MSS. ascribe to Michael
Coiminn, who lived at the beginning of the eighteenth
century,† and whose romance was certainly not propagated by professional story-tellers, as I have tried to prove
was the case with the earlier romances, but by means of
numerous manuscript copies; and it is also certain that
Coiminn did not relate this tale as the old bards did, but

---

* In a third MS., however, which I have, made by a modern Clare
scribe, Domhnall Mac Consaidin, I find "the Emperor Constantine," not
the "Emperor of Constantinople," written. O'Curry in his "Manuscript
Materials," p. 319, ascribes "Conall Gulban" with some other stories, to a date
prior to the year 1000; but the fighting with the Turks (which motivates the
whole story, and which cannot be the addition of an ignorant Irish scribe, since
it is also found in the Highland traditional version), shows that its date, in its
present form, at least, is much later. There is no mention of Constantinople in
the Scotch Gaelic version, and hence it is possible—though, I think, hardly
probable—that the story had its origin in the Crusades.

† I find the date, 1749, attributed to it in a voluminous MS. of some 600
closely written pages, bound in sheepskin, made by Laurence Foran of Waterford, in 1812, given me by Mr. W. Doherty, C.E.

wrote it down as modern novelists do their stories. But this does not invalidate my surmise, or prove that Conall Gulban, and forty or fifty of the same kind, had their origin in a written manuscript; it only proves that in the eighteenth century the old order was giving place to the new, and that the professional bards and story-tellers were now a thing of the past, they having fallen with the Gaelic nobility who were their patrons. It would be exceedingly interesting to know whether any traces of these modern stories that had their rise in written manuscripts, are to be found amongst the peasantry as folklore. I, certainly, have found no remnant of any such; but this proves nothing. If Ireland had a few individual workers scattered over the provinces we would know more on the subject; but, unfortunately, we have hardly any such people, and what is worse, the present current of political thought, and the tone of our Irish educational establishments are not likely to produce them. Until something has been done by us to collect Irish folk-lore in as thorough a manner as Highland tales have already been collected, no deductions can be made with certainty upon the subject of the relationship between Highland and Irish folk-tales, and the relation of both to the Irish MSS.

Irish folk-stories may roughly be divided into two classes, those which I believe never had any *conscious* genesis inside the shores of Ireland, and those which

had. These last we have just been examining. Most of
the *longer* tales about the Fenians, and all those stories
which have long inflated passages full of alliterative
words and poetic epithets, belong to this class. Under
the other head of stories that were never consciously
invented on Irish ground, we may place all such simple
stories as bear a trace of nature myths, and those which
appear to belong to our old Aryan heritage, from the fact
of their having parallels amongst other Aryan-speaking
races, such as the story of the man who wanted to learn to
shake with fear, stories of animals and talking birds, of
giants and wizards, and others whose directness and
simplicity show them to have had an unconscious and
popular origin, though some of these may, of course,
have arisen on Irish soil. To this second class belong
also that numerous body of traditions rather than tales,
of conversational anecdotes rather than set stories, about
appearances of fairies, or "good people," or Tuatha De
Danann, as they are also called ; of pookas, leprechauns,
ghosts, apparitions, water-horses, &c. These creations
of folk-fancy seldom appear, as far as I have observed,
in the folk-tale proper, or at least they only appear as
adjuncts, for in almost all cases the interest of these
regular tales centres round a human hero. Stories about
leprechauns, fairies, &c., are very brief, and generally
have local names and scenery attached to them, and are
told conversationally as any other occurrence might be

told, whereas there is a certain solemnity about the repe-
tition of a folk-tale proper.

After spending so much time over the very latest
folk-tales, the detritus of bardic stories, it will be well to
cast a glance at some of the most ancient, such as bear
their pre-historic origin upon their face. Some of these
point, beyond all doubt, to rude efforts on the part of
primitive man to realize to himself the phenomena of
nature, by personifying them, and attaching to them
explanatory fables. Let us take a specimen from a story
I found in Mayo, not given in this volume—"The Boy
who was long on his Mother." * In this story, which in
Von Hahn's classification would come under the heading
of "the strong man his adventures," the hero is a
veritable Hercules, whom the king tries to put to death
by making him perform impossible tasks, amongst other
things, by sending him down to hell to drive up the
spirits with his club. He is desired by the king to drain
a lake full of water. The lake is very steep on one side
like a reservoir. The hero makes a hole at this side,
applies his mouth to it, and sucks down the water of the
lake, with boats, fishes, and everything else it contained,
leaving the lake ċoṁ ṫiṁ le boir̄ ꝺo láiṁe, "as dry as
the palm of your hand." Even a sceptic will be likely to
confess that this tale (which has otherwise no meaning)

---

* an buaċaill ꝺo bi a bꝼaoꝼaiꝛ a ṁáċaiꝛ.

is the remains of a (probably Aryan) sun-myth, and personifies the action of the warm sun in drying up a lake and making it a marsh, killing the fishes, and leaving the boats stranded. But this story, like many others, is suggestive of more than this, since it would supply an argument for those who, like Professor Rhys, see in Hercules a sun-god. The descent of our hero into hell, and his frightening the spirits with his club, the impossible tasks which the king gives him to perform in the hopes of slaying him, and his successful accomplishment of them, seem to identify him with the classic Hercules. But the Irish tradition preserves the incident of drying the lake, which must have been the work of a sun-god, the very thing that Hercules—but on much slighter grounds—is supposed to have been.* If this story is not the remains of a nature myth, it is perfectly unintelligible, for no rational person could hope to impose upon even a child by saying that a man drank up a lake, ships, and all ; and yet this story has been with strange conservatism repeated from father to son for probably thousands of years, and must have taken its rise at a time when our ancestors were in much the same rude and mindless

---

* Prof. Rhys identifies Cuchulain with Hercules, and makes them both sun-gods. There is nothing in our story, however, which points to Cuchulain, and still less to the Celtic Hercules described by Lucian.

condition as the Australian blacks or the Indians of California are to-day.

Again, in another story we hear of a boat that sails equally swiftly over land and sea, and goes straight to its mark. It is so large that if all the men in the world were to enter it there would remain place for six hundred more; while it is so small that it folds up into the hand of the person who has it. But ships do not sail on land, nor grow large and small, nor go straight to their mark; consequently, it is plain that we have here another nature myth, vastly old, invented by pre-historic man, for these ships can be nothing but the clouds which sail over land and sea, are large enough to hold the largest armies, and small enough to fold into the hand, and which go straight to their mark. The meaning of this has been forgotten for countless ages, but the story has survived.

Again, in another tale which I found, called "The Bird of Sweet Music," * a man follows a sweet singing bird into a cave under the ground, and finds a country where he wanders for a year and a day, and a woman who befriends him while there, and enables him to bring back the bird, which turns out to be a human being. At the end of the tale the narrator mentions quite casually that it was his mother whom he met down there.

---

* An c éun ceól-binn.

But this touch shows that the land where he wandered was the Celtic Hades, the country of the dead beneath the ground, and seems to stamp the tale at once as at least pre-Christian.

Even in such an unpretending-looking story as "The King of Ireland's Son" (the third in this volume), there are elements which must be vastly old. In a short Czech story, "George with the Goat," we find some of the prince's companions figuring, only slightly metamorphosed. We have the man with one foot over his shoulder, who jumps a hundred miles when he puts it down; while the gun-man of the Irish story who performs two parts—that of seeing and shooting—is replaced in the Bohemian tale by two different men, one of whom has such sight that he must keep a bandage over his eyes, for if he removed it he could see a hundred miles, and the other has, instead of a gun, a bottle with his thumb stuck into it for a stopper, because if he took it out it would squirt a hundred miles. George hires one after the other, just as the prince does in the Irish story. George goes to try to win the king's daughter, as the Irish prince does, and, amongst other things, is desired to bring a goblet of water from a well a hundred miles off in a minute. "So," says the story,* "George said to the man who had the foot on his

---

* Wratislaw's Folk-Tales from Slavonic Sources.

shoulder, 'You said that if you took the foot down you could jump a hundred miles.' He replied : 'I'll easily do that.' He took the foot down, jumped, and was there ; but after this there was only a very little time to spare, and by this he ought to have been back. So George said to the second. 'You said that if you removed the bandage from your eyes you could see a hundred miles ; peep, and see what is going on.' 'Ah, sir, goodness gracious ! he's fallen asleep.' 'That will be a bad job,' said George ; 'the time will be up. You third man, you said if you pulled your thumb out you could squirt a hundred miles. Be quick, and squirt thither, that he may get up ; and you, look whether he is moving, or what.' 'Oh, sir, he's getting up now ; he's knocking the dust off ; he's drawing the water.' He then gave a jump, and was there exactly in time." Now, this Bohemian story seems also to bear traces of a nature myth ; for, as Mr. Wratislaw has remarked : "the man who jumps a hundred miles appears to be the rainbow, the man with bandaged eyes the lightning, and the man with the bottle the cloud." The Irish story, while in every other way superior to the Bohemian, has quite obscured this point ; and were it not for the striking Sclavonic parallel, people might be found to assert that the story was of recent origin. This discovery of the the Czech tale, however, throws it at once three thousand years back ; for the similarity of the Irish and Bohemian

story can hardly be accounted for, except on the supposition, that both Slavs and Celts carried it from the
original home of the Aryan race, in pre-historic times,
or at least from some place where the two races were in
contiguity with one another, and that it, too—little as it
appears so now—was at one time in all probability a
nature myth.

Such myth stories as these ought to be preserved,
since they are about the last visible link connecting
civilized with pre-historic man; for, of all the traces
that man in his earliest period has left behind him, there
is nothing except a few drilled stones or flint arrow-
heads that approaches the antiquity of these tales, as
told to-day by a half-starving peasant in a smoky
Connacht cabin.

It is time to say a word about the narrators of these
stories. The people who can recite them are, as far as
my researches have gone, to be found only amongst the
oldest, most neglected, and poorest of the Irish-speaking
population. English-speaking people either do not
know them at all, or else tell them in so bald and con-
densed a form as to be useless. Almost all the men
from whom I used to hear stories in the County Roscommon are dead. Ten or fifteen years ago I used to
hear a great many stories, but I did not understand their
value. Now when I go back for them I cannot find
them. They have died out, and will never again be

heard on the hillsides, where they probably existed for a
couple of thousand years; they will never be repeated
there again, to use the Irish phrase, while grass grows
or water runs.   Several of these stories I got from an old
man, one Shawn Cunningham, on the border of the
County Roscommon, where it joins Mayo.   He never
spoke more than a few words of English till he was fifteen years old.   He was taught by a hedge schoolmaster
from the South of Ireland out of Irish MSS.   As far as I
could make out from him the teaching seemed to consist
in making him learn Irish poems by heart.   His next
schoolmaster, however, tied a piece of stick round his
neck, and when he came to school in the morning the
schoolmaster used to inspect the piece of wood and pretend that it told him how often he had spoken Irish
when at home.   In some cases the schoolmasters made
the parents put a notch in the stick every time the child
failed to speak English.   He was beaten then, and always
beaten whenever he was heard speaking a word of Irish,
even though at this time he could hardly speak a word of
English.   His son and daughter now speak Irish, though
not fluently, his grandchildren do not even understand
it.   He had at one time, as he expressed it, "the full of
a sack of stories," but he had forgotten them.   His
grandchildren stood by his knee while he told me one
or two, but it was evident they did not understand a
word.   His son and daughter laughed at them as non-

sense.   Even in Achill where, if anywhere, one ought to
find folk-stories in their purity, a fine-looking dark man
of about forty-five, who told me a number of them, and
could repeat Ossian's poems, assured me that now-a-
days when he went into a house in the evening and the
old people got him to recite, the boys would go out;
"they wouldn't understand me," said he, " and when they
wouldn't, they'd sooner be listening to ʒéimneaċ na mbó,"
"the lowing of the cows."   This, too, in an island where
many people cannot speak English.   I do not know
whether the Achill schoolmasters make use of the notch
of wood to-day, but it is hardly wanted now.   It is
curious that this was the device universally employed
all over Connacht and Munster to kill the language.
This took place under the eye of O'Connell and the Parliamentarians, and, of course, under the eye and with
the sanction of the Catholic priesthood and prelates,
some of whom, according to Father Keegan, of
St. Louis, distinguished themselves by driving the
Irish teachers out of their dioceses and burning their
books.   At the present day, such is the irony of fate if
a stranger talks Irish he runs a good chance of being
looked upon as an enemy, this because some attempts
were made to proselytize " natives " by circulating Irish
bibles, and sending some Irish scripture-readers amongst
them.   Surely nothing so exquisitely ludicrous ever
took place outside of this island of anomalies, as that a

stranger who tries to speak Irish in Ireland runs the
serious risk of being looked upon a proselytizing Eng-
lishman. As matters are still progressing gaily in this
direction, let nobody be surprised if a pure Aryan language which, at the time of the famine, in '47, was spoken
at least four million souls (more than the whole population of Switzerland), becomes in a few years as extinct
as Cornish. Of course, there is not a shadow of necessity,
either social or economical, for this. All the world
knows that bi-linguists are superior to men who know
only one language, yet in Ireland everyone pretends to
believe the contrary. A few words from the influential
leaders of the race when next they visit Achill, for instance, would help to keep Irish alive there in *sæcula
sæculorum*, and with the Irish language, the old Aryan
folk-lore, the Ossianic poems, numberless ballads, folk-
songs, and proverbs, and a thousand and one other interesting things that survive when Irish is spoken, and
die when it dies. But, from a complexity of causes which
I am afraid to explain, the men who for the last sixty
years have had the ear of the Irish race have persistently
shown the cold shoulder to everything that was Irish and
racial, and while protesting, or pretending to protest,
against West Britonism, have helped, more than anyone
else, by their example, to assimilate us to England and
the English, thus running counter to the entire voice of
modern Europe, which is in favour of extracting the best

from the various races of men who inhabit it, by helping
them to develop themselves on national and racial
lines.   The people are not the better for it either, for one
would fancy it required little culture to see that the man
who reads Irish MSS., and repeats Ossianic poetry, is a
higher and more interesting type than the man whose
mental training is confined to spelling through an
article in *United Ireland.**

I may mention here that it is not as easy a thing as
might be imagined to collect Irish stories.   One hears
that tales are to be had from such and such a man,
generally, alas ! a very old one.   With difficulty one
manages to find him out, only to discover, probably, that
he has some work on hand.   If it happens to be harvest
time it is nearly useless going to him at all, unless one

* It appears, unfortunately, that all classes of our Irish politicians alike
agree in their treatment of the language in which all the past of their race—
until a hundred years ago—is enshrined. The inaction of the Parliamentarians,
though perhaps dimly intelligible, appears, to me at least, both short-sighted
and contradictory, for they are attempting to create a nationality with one hand
and with the other destroying, or allowing to be destroyed, the very thing
that would best differentiate and define that nationality. It is a making of
bricks without straw.   But the non-Parliamentarian Nationalists, in Ireland at
least, appear to be thoroughly in harmony with them on this point. It is
strange to find the man who most commands the respect and admiration of that
party advising the young men of Gaelic Cork, in a printed and widely-circu-
lated lecture entitled : " What Irishmen should know," to this effect :—" I
begin by a sort of negative advice. You all know that much has been written
in the Irish language. This is of great importance, especially in connection
with our early history, hence must ever form an important study for scholars
But you are, most of you, not destined to be scholars,and so I should simply

is prepared to sit up with him all night, for his mind is sure
to be so distraught with harvest operations that he can tell
you nothing. If it is winter time, however, and you fortu-
nately find him unoccupied, nevertheless it requires some
management to get him to tell his stories. Half a glass of
ishka-baha, a pipe of tobacco, and a story of one's own
are the best things to begin with. If, however, you
start to take down the story *verbatim* with pencil and
paper, as an unwary collector might do, you destroy all,
or your shanachie becomes irritable. He will not wait
for you to write down your sentence, and if you call out,
"Stop, stop, wait till I get this down," he will forget
what he was going to tell you, and you will not get a
third of his story, though you may think you have it all.
What you must generally do is to sit quietly smoking

---

advise you—especially such of you as do not already know Irish—to leave all
this alone, or rather to be content with what you can easily find in a translated
shape in the columns of Hardiman, Miss Brooke, Mangan, and Sigerson." So
that the man whose most earnest aspiration in life is Ireland a nation, begins by
advising the youth of Ireland *not* to study the language of their fathers, and to
read the gorgeous Gaelic poetry in such pitiful translations as Hardiman and
Miss Brooke have given of a few pieces. The result of this teaching is as
might be expected. A well-known second-hand book-seller in Dublin assured
me recently that as many as 200 Irish MSS. had passed through his hand
within the last few years. Dealers had purchased them throughout the
country in Cavan, Monaghan, and many other counties for a few pence, and
sold them to him, and he had dispersed them again to the four winds of heaven,
especially to America, Australia, and New Zealand. Many of these must have
contained matter not to be found elsewhere. All are now practically lost, and
nobody in Ireland either knows or cares. In America, however, of all coun-
tries in the world, they appreciate the situation better, and the fifth resolution
passed at the last great Chicago Congress was one about the Irish language.

your pipe, without the slightest interruption, not even when he comes to words and phrases which you do not understand. He must be allowed his own way to the end, and then after judiciously praising him and discussing the story, you remark, as if the thought had suddenly struck you, "buḋ ṁaiṫ liom ꝑin a ḃeiṫ aᵹam aiꝱ ꝑáiꝑeuꝱ," "I'd like to have that on paper." Then you can get it from him easily enough, and when he leaves out whole incidents, as he is sure to do, you who have just heard the story can put him right, and so get it from him nearly in its entirety. Still it is not always easy to write down these stories, for they are full of old or corrupted words, which neither you nor your narrator understand, and if you press him too much over the meaning of these he gets confused and irritable.

The present volume consists of about half the stories in the *Leabhar Sgeuluigheachta*, translated into English, together with some half dozen other stories given in the original together with a close English translation. It is not very easy to make a good translation from Irish into English, for there are no two Aryan languages more opposed to each other in spirit and idiom. Still, the English spoken by three-fourths of the people of Ireland is largely influenced by Gaelic idioms, for most of those expressions which surprise Englishmen are really translations from that Irish which was the language of the

speaker's father, grandfather, or great-grandfather—
according to the part of the country you may be in—and
there have perpetuated themselves, even in districts
where you will scarce find a trace of an Irish word.
There are, however, also hundreds of Gaelic idioms not
reproduced in the English spoken by the people, and it
is difficult to render these fitly. Campbell of Islay has
run into rather an extreme in his translations, for in
order to make them picturesque, he has rendered his
Gaelic originals something too literally. Thus, he invariably translates *bhain se an ceann deth*, by "he reaped
the head off him," a form of speech which, I notice, a
modern Irish poet and M.P. has adopted from him ; but
bain, though it certainly means "reap" amongst other
things, is the word used for taking off a hat as well as a
head. Again, he always translates *thu* by "thou,"
which gives his stories a strange antique air, which is
partly artificial, for the Gaelic "thou" corresponds to
the English "you," the second person plural not being
used except in speaking of more than one. In this way,
Campbell has given his excellent and thoroughly reliable
translations a scarcely legitimate colouring, which I have
tried to avoid. For this reason, I have not always translated the Irish idioms quite literally, though I have used
much unidiomatic English, but only of the kind used all
over Ireland, the kind the people themselves use. I do
not translate, for instance, the Irish for "he died," by

" he got death," for this, though the literal translation, is not adopted into Hibernian English ; but I do translate the Irish *ghnidheadh se sin* by "he used to do that," which is the ordinary Anglo-Irish attempt at making—what they have not got in English—a consuetudinal tense. I have scarcely used the pluperfect at all. No such tense exists in Irish, and the people who speak English do not seem to feel the want of it, and make no hesitation in saying, "I'd speak sooner if I knew that," where they mean, "if I had known that I would have spoken sooner." I do not translate (as Campbell would), " it rose with me to do it," but " I succeeded in doing it ;" for the first, though the literal translation of the Irish idiom, has not been adopted into English ; but I do translate "he did it and he drunk," instead of, "he did it while he was drunk ; " for the first phrase (the literal translation of the Irish) is universally used throughout English-speaking Ireland. Where, as sometimes happens, the English language contains no exact equivalent for an Irish expression, I have rendered the original as well as I could, as one generally does render for linguistic purposes, from one language into another.

In conclusion, it only remains for me to thank Mr. Alfred Nutt for enriching this book as he has done, and for bearing with the dilatoriness of the Irish printers, who find so much difficulty in setting Irish type, that many good Irishmen have of late come round to the idea of printing our language in Roman characters; and to express my gratitude to Father Eugene O'Growney for the unwearying kindness with which he read and corrected my Irish proofs, and for the manifold aid which he has afforded me on this and other occasions.

———

POSTSCRIPT BY ALFRED NUTT.

I HAD hoped to accompany these tales with as full a commentary as that which I have affixed to the Argyllshire *Märchen*, collected and translated by the Rev. D. MacInnes. Considerations of business and health prevent me from carrying out this intention, and I have only been able to notice a passage here and there in the Tales ; but I have gladly availed myself of my friend, Dr. Hyde's permission, to touch upon a few points in his Introduction.

Of special interest are Dr. Hyde's remarks upon the relations which obtain between the modern folk-tale current among the Gaelic-speaking populations of Ireland and Scotland, and the Irish mythic, heroic, and romantic literature preserved in MSS., which range in date from the eleventh century to the present day.

In Ireland, more than elsewhere, the line of demarcation between the tale whose genesis is conscious, and that of which the reverse is true, is hard to draw, and students will, for a long while to come, differ concerning points of detail. I may thus be permitted to disagree at times with Dr. Hyde, although, as a rule, I am heartily at one with him.

Dr. Hyde distinguishes between an older stratum of folk-tale (the "old Aryan traditions," of p. xix.) and the newer stratum of "bardic inventions." He also establishes a yet younger class than these latter, the romances of the professional story-tellers of the eighteenth century, who "wrote them down as modern novelists do their stories." Of these last he remarks (p. xxxiv.), that he has found no remnant of them among the peasantry of to-day ; a valuable bit of evidences, although, of course, subject to the inconclusiveness of all merely negative testimony. To revert to the second class, he looks upon the tales comprised in it as being rather the inventions of individual brains than as old Aryan folk-tales (p. xx.) It must at once be conceded, that a great number of the tales and ballads current in the Gaelic-speaking lands undoubtedly received the form under which they are now current, somewhere between the twelfth and the sixteenth centuries ; that the authors of that form were equally undoubtedly the professional bards and story-tellers attached to the court of every Gaelic chieftain ; and that the method of their transmission was oral, it being the custom of the story-tellers both to teach their tales to pupils, and to travel about from district to district.

The style of these stories and ballads enables us to date them with sufficient precision.   Dr. Hyde also notes historical allusions, such as the reference to O'Connor Sligo, in the story of the " Slim Swarthy Champion," or to the Turks in the story of " Conall Gulban." I cannot but think, however, that it is straining the evidence to assert that the one story was invented after 1362, or the other after the fall of Constantinople.   The fact that " Bony " appears in some versions of the common English mumming play does not show that it originated in this century, merely that these particular versions have passed through the minds of nineteenth century peasants ; and in like manner the Connaught fourteenth century chieftain may easily have taken the place of an earlier personage, the Turks in " Conall Gulban," of an earlier wizard-giant race. If I cannot go as far as Dr. Hyde in this sense, I must equally demur to the assumption (p. xl.), that community of incident between au Irish and a Bohemian tale necessarily establishes the pre-historic antiquity of the incident. I believe that a great many folk-tales, as well as much else of folk-lore, has been developed *in situ*, rather imported from the outside ; but I, by no means, deny importation in principle, and I recognise that its agency has been clearly demonstrated in not a few cases.

The main interest of Irish folk-literature (if the expression be allowed) centres in the bardic stories.   I think that Dr. Hyde lays too much stress upon such external secondary matters as the names of heroes, or allusions to historical events ; and, indeed, he himself, in the case of Murachaidh Mac-Brian, states what I believe to be the correct theory, namely, that the Irish bardic story, from which he derives the Scotch Gaelic one, is, as far as many of its incidents go, not the invention of the writer, but genuine folklore thrown by him into a new form (p. xxii.)

Had we all the materials necessary for forming a judgment, such is, I believe, the conclusion that would in every case be reached.   But I furthermore hold it likely that in many cases the recast story gradually reverted to a primitive folk-type in the course of passing down from the court storyteller to the humbler peasant reciters, that it sloughed off the embellishments of the *ollamhs*, and reintroduced the older, wilder conceptions with which the folk remained in fuller sympathy than the more cultured bard.   Compare, for instance, as I compared ten years ago, " Maghach Colgar," in Campbell's version (No. 36), with the " Fairy Palace of the Quicken Trees."   The one tale has all the incidents in the wildest and most fantastic form possible ; in the other they are rationalised to the utmost possible extent and made to appear like a piece of genuine history. I do not think that if this later version was *invented* right out by a thirteenth or fourteenth century *ollamh*, it could have given rise to the former one. Either "Maghach Colgar" descends from the folk-tale which served as the basis of the Irish story, or, what s more likely, the folk, whilst appreciating and preserving the new arrangement of certain well-known incidents, retained the earlier form of the incidents themselves, as being more consonant with the totality of its conceptions, both moral and æsthetic. This I hold to be the vital lesson the folklorist may learn from considering the relations of Gaelic folk-tale and Gaelic romance (using the latter term in the sense of story with a conscious genesis): that romance, to live and propagate itself among the folk, must follow certain rules, satisfy certain conceptions of life, conform to certain conventions. The Irish bards and story-tellers had little difficulty, I take it, in doing this ; they had not outgrown the creed of their countrymen, they were in substantial touch with the intellectual and artistic laws that govern their subject-matter. Re-arrange, rationalise somewhat, deck out with the questionable adornment of their scanty and ill-digested book-learning—to this extent, but to this extent only, I believe, reached their influence upon the mass of folk-conceptions and presentments which they inherited from their fathers, and which, with these modifications and additions, they handed on to their children.

But romance must not only conform to the conventions, it must also fit in with the *ensemble* of conditions, material, mental and spiritual, which constitute the culture (taking this much-abused word in its widest sense) of a race. An example will make this clear.

Of all modern, consciously-invented fairy tales I know but one which conforms fully to the folk-tale convention—"The Shaving of Shagpat." It follows the formula as closely and accurately as the best of Grimm's or of Campbell's tales. To divine the nature of a convention, and to use its capabilities to the utmost, is a special mark of genius, and in this, as in other instances, whatever else be absent from Mr. Meredith's work, genius is indubitably present. But I do not think that "The Shaving of Shagpat" could ever be acclimatised as a folk-tale in this country. Scenery, conduct of story, characterisation of personages, are all too distinctively Oriental. But let an Eastern admirer of Mr. Meredith translate his work into Arabic or Hindi, and let the book fall into the hands of a Cairene or Delhi story-teller (if such still exist), I can well imagine that, with judicious cuts, it should win praise for its reciter in market-place or bazaar. Did this happen, it would surely be due to the fact that the story is strictly constructed upon traditional lines, rather than to the brilliant invention and fancy displayed on every page. Strip from it the wit and philosophy of the author, and there remains a fairy tale to charm the East; but it would need to be reduced to a skeleton, and reclothed with new flesh before it could charm the folk of the West.

To bring home yet more clearly to our minds this necessity for romance to conform to convention, let us ask ourselves, what would have happened if one of the Irish story-tellers who perambulated the Western Isles as late as the seventeenth century, had carried with him a volume of Hakluyt or Purchas, or, supposing one to have lingered enough, Defoe or Gil Blas? Would he have been welcomed when he substituted the new fare for the old tales of " Finn and the Fians?" and even if welcomed, would he have gained currency for it? Would the seed thus planted have thriven, or would it not rather, fallen upon rocky places, have withered away?

It may, however, be objected that the real difference lies not so much in the subject-matter as in the mode of transmission; and the objection may seem to derive some force from what Dr. Hyde notes concerning the prevalence of folk-tales in Wicklow, and the nearer Pale generally, as contrasted with Leitrim, Longford, and Meath (p. xii.). It is difficult to over-estimate the interest and importance of this fact, and there can hardly be a doubt that Dr. Hyde has explained it correctly. It may, then, be urged that so long as oral transmission lasts the folk-tale flourishes; and only when the printed work ousts the story-teller is it that the folk-tale dies out. But this reasoning will not hold water. It is absurd to contend that the story-teller had none but a certain class of materials at his disposal till lately. He had the whole realm of intellect and fancy to draw upon; but he, and still more his hearers, knew only one district of that realm; and had it been possible for him to step outside its limits his hearers could not have followed him. I grant folk fancy has shared the fortunes of humanity together with every other manifestation of man's activity, but always within strictly defined limits, to transgress which has always been to forfeit the favour of the folk.

What, then, are the characteristic marks of folk-fancy? The question is of special interest in connection with Gaelic folk-lore. The latter is rich in transitional forms, the study of which reveal more clearly than is otherwise possible the nature and workings of the folk-mind.

The products of folk-fancy (putting aside such examples of folk-wisdom and folk-wit as proverbs, saws, jests, etc.), may be roughly divided among two great classes:

Firstly, stories of a quasi-historical or anecdotic nature, accepted as actual fact (of course with varying degrees of credence) by narrator and hearer. Stories of this kind are very largely concerned with beings (supernatural, as we should call them) differing from man, and with their relations to and dealings with man. Not infrequently, however, the actors in the stories are wholly human, or human and animal. Gaelic folk-lore is rich in such stories, owing to the extraordinary tenacity of the fairy belief. We can hardly doubt that the Gael, like all other races which have passed through a certain stage of culture, had at one time an organised hierarchy of divine beings. But we have to piece together the Gaelic god-saga out of bare names, mere hints, and stories which have evidently suffered vital change. In the earliest stratum of Gaelic mythic narrative we find beings who at some former time had occupied divine rank, but whose relations to man are substantially, as therein presented, the same as those of the modern fairy to the modern peasant. The chiefs of the Tuatha de Danann hanker after earthly maidens ; the divine damsels long for and summon to themselves earthly heroes. Though undying, very strong, and very wise, they may be overpowered or outwitted by the mortal hero. As if conscious of some source of weakness we cannot detect, they are anxious, in their internecine struggles, to secure the aid of the sons of men. Small wonder that this belief, which we can follow for at least 1,200 years, should furnish so many elements to the folk-fancy of the Gael.

In stories of the second class the action is relegated to a remote past— once upon a time—or to a distant undefined region, and the narrative is not necessarily accepted as a record of actual fact. Stories of this class, whether in prose or verse, may again be subdivided into—humorous, optimistic, tragic ; and with regard to the third sub-division, it should be noted that the stories comprised in it are generally told as having been true once, though not in the immediate tangible sense of stories in the first class.

These different narrative groups share certain characteristics, though in varying proportions.

Firstly, the fondness for and adherence to a comparatively small number of set formulas. This is obviously less marked in stories of the first class, which, as being in the mind of the folk a record of what has actually happened, partake of the diversity of actual life. And yet the most striking similarities occur ; such an anecdote, for instance, as that which tells how a supernatural changeling is baffled by a brewery of egg-shells being found from Japan to Brittany.

Secondly, on the moral side, the unquestioning acceptance of fatalism, though not in the sense which the Moslem or the Calvinist would attach to the word. The event is bound to be of a certain nature, provided a certain mode of attaining it be chosen. This comes out well in the large group of stories which tell how a supernatural being helps a mortal to perform certain tasks, as a rule, with some ulterior benefit to itself in view. The most disheartening careless-ness and stupidity on the part of the man cannot alter the result ; the skill and courage of the supernatural helper are powerless without the mortal co-operation. In what I have termed the tragic stories, this fatalism puts on a moral form, and gives rise to the conception of Nemesis.

Thirdly, on the mental side, animism is prevalent, *i.e.*, the acceptance of a life common to, not alone man and animals, but all manifestations of force. In so far as a distinction is made between the life of man and that of nature at large, it is in favour of the latter, to which more potent energy is ascribed.

Just as stories of the first class are less characterised by adherence to formula, so stories of the humorous group are less characterised by fatalism and animism. This is inevitable, as such stories are, as a rule, concerned solely with the relations of man to his fellows.

The most fascinating and perplexing problems are those connected with the groups I have termed optimistic and tragic. To the former belong the almost entirety of such nursery tales as are not humorous in character. "They were married and lived happily ever afterwards;" such is the almost invariable end formula. The hero wins the princess, and the villain is punished.

This feature the nursery tale shares with the god-saga ; Zeus confounds the Titans, Apollo slays the Python, Lug overcomes Balor, Indra vanquishes Vritra. There are two apparent exceptions to this rule. The Teutonic god myth is tragic; the Anses are ever under the shadow of the final conflict. This has been explained by the influence of Christian ideas ; but although this influence must be unreservedly admitted in certain details of the passing of the gods, yet the fact that the Iranian god-saga is likewise undecided, instead of having a frankly optimistic ending, makes me doubt whether the drawn battle between the powers of good and ill be not a genuine and necessary part of the Teutonic mythology. As is well known, Rydberg has established some striking points of contact between the mythic ideas of Scandinavia and those of Iran.

In striking contradiction to this moral, optimistic tendency are the great heroic sagas. One and all well-nigh are profoundly tragic. The doom of Troy the great, the passing of Arthur, the slaughter of the Nibelungs, the death of Sohrab at his father's hands, Roncevalles, Gabhra, the fratricidal conflict of Cuchullain and Ferdiad, the woes of the house of Atreus ; such are but a few examples of the prevailing tone of the hero-tales. Achilles and Siegfried and Cuchullain are slain in the flower of their youth and prowess. Of them, at least, the saying is true, that whom the gods love die young. Why is it not equally true of the prince hero of the fairy tale ? Is it that the hero tale associated in the minds of hearers and reciters with men who had actually lived and fought, brought down to earth, so to say, out of the mysterious wonderland in which god and fairy and old time kings have their being, becomes thereby liable to the necessities of death and decay inherent in all human things? Some scholars have a ready answer for this and similar questions. The heroic epos assumed its shape once for all among one special race, and was then passed on to other races who remained faithful to the main lines whilst altering details. If this explanation were true, it would still leave unsolved the problem, why the heroic epos, which for its fashioners and hearers was at once a record of the actual and an exemplar of the ideal, should, among men differing in blood and culture, follow one model, and that a tragic one. Granting that Greek and Teuton and Celt did borrow the tales which they themselves conceived to be very blood and bone of their race, what force compelled them all to borrow one special conception of life and fate?

Such exceptions as there are to the tragic nature of the heroic saga are apparent rather than real. The Odyssey ends happily, like an old-fashioned novel, but Fénélon long ago recognised in the Odyssey—"un amas de contes de vieille."

Perseus again has the luck of a fairy-tale prince, but then the story of his fortunes is obviously a fairy-tale, with named instead of anonymous personages.

Whilst the fairy-tale is akin in tone to the god saga, the ballad recalls the heroic epos. The vast majority of ballads are tragic. Sir Patrick Spens must drown, and Glasgerion's leman be cheated by the churl ; Clerk Saunders comes from the other world, like Helge to Sigrun ; Douglas dreams his dreary dream, " I saw a dead man win a fight, and that dead man was I." The themes of the ballad are the most dire and deadly of human passions ; love scorned or betrayed, hate, and revenge. Very seldom, too, do the plots of ballad and märchen cross or overlap. Where this does happen it will, as a rule, be found that both are common descendants of some great saga.

We find such an instance in the Fenian saga, episodes of which have lived on in the Gaelic folk memory in the double form of prose and poetry. But it should be noted that the poetry accentuates the tragic side—the battle of Gabhra, the death of Diarmaid—whilst the prose takes rather some episode of Finn's youth or manhood, and presents it as a rounded and complete whole, the issue of which is fortunate.

The relations of myth and epos to folk-lore may thus be likened to that of trees to the soil from which they spring, and which they enrich and fertilise by the decay of their leaves and branches which mingle indistinguishably with the original soil. Of this soil, again, rude bricks may be made, and a house built ; let the house fall into ruins, and the bricks crumble into dust, it will be hard to discriminate that dust from the parent earth. But raise a house of iron or stone, and, however ruined, its fragments can always be recognised.

In the case of the Irish bardic literature the analogy is, I believe, with soil and tree, rather than with soil and edifice.

Reverting once more to the characteristics of folk-fancy, let us note that they appear equally in folk-practice and folk-belief. The tough conservatism of the folk-mind has struck all observers : its adherence to immemorial formulas; its fatalistic acceptance of the mysteries of nature and heredity, coupled with its faith in the efficacy of sympathetic magic ; its elaborate system of custom and ritual based upon the idea that between men and the remainder of the universe there is no difference of kind.

A conception of the Cosmos is thus arrived at which, more than any religious creed, fulfils the test of catholicity ; literally, and in the fullest significance of the words, it has been held *semper, ubique et ab omnibus.* And of this conception of the universe, more universal than any that has as yet swayed the minds of man, it is possible that men now living may see the last flickering remains ; it is well-nigh certain that our grandchildren will live in a world out of which it has utterly vanished.

For the folk-lorist the Gospel saying is thus more pregnant with meaning than for any other student of man's history—" the night cometh wherein no man may work." Surely, many Irishman will take to heart the example of Dr. Hyde, and will go forth to glean what may yet be found of as fair and bounteous a harvest of myth and romance as ever flourished among any race.

le h-ais na teineaḋ.

an Cailiur agus na Cri béitiġeaċ.

Bí táiliúp son uaip amáin i nĠoillim, agus bí ré ag fuaigeál eudaig. Connaipc re opeancuid ag éipiġe amaċ ap an eudaċ, agus ċait re an cpnácad léiċe agus maptb ré an opeancuid. Oubaipc re ann pin "Naċ bpeáġ an gaipgideaċ mipe nuaip a bí mé abalta aip an opeancuid pin do maptbad!"

Oubaipc ré ann pin go gcaitfead ré dul go b'L'acliaċ go cúipt an piġ, go bfeicfead ré an dtiucpad leir a deunam. Bí an cúipt pin 'ġá deunam le fada, aċt an méad dí do gnitíde ann pan lá do leagaide ann pan oidċe é, agus níop feud duine aip biċ a cup ruas map ġeall aip pin. 'S iad cpi fátaċ a tigead 'pan oidċe a bidead 'ġá leagad. O'imtiġ an táiliúp an lá aip na mápac, agus do tug re leir an uipliр, an ppád agus an cpluapad.

Níop bpada ċuaid ré gup cappad capall bán dó, agus ċuip re popán aip. "Go mbeannuiġ Oia duit," ap ran capall, "cá bfuil tu dul?" "Tá mé dul go b'L'acliaċ," ap ran táiliúp, "le deunam cúipte an piġ, go bfáġ' mé bean-uapal, má tig liom a deunam," map do ġeall an piġ go dtiúbpad ré a ingean féin agus a lán aipgid léiċe don té pin a tiucpad leir an cúipt pin do cup ruas. "An ndeunpá poll dam?" ap ran pean-ġeappán bán, "paċainn i bfolaċ ann nuaip atá na daoine mo ċabaipt ċum an muilinn agus ċum an áca i pioċt naċ bfeicpíd riad mé, óip tá mé cpáíte aca, ag deunam oibpe dóib."

THE TAILOR AND THE THREE BEASTS.

THERE was once a tailor in Galway, and he was sewing cloth. He saw a flea springing up out of the cloth, and he threw his needle at it and killed it. Then he said : "Am I not a fine hero when I was able to kill that flea?"

Then he said that he must go to Blackleea (Dublin), to the king's court, to see would he be able to build it. That court was a' building for a long time ; but as much of it as would be made during the day used to be thrown down again during the night, and for that reason nobody could build it up. It was three giants who used to come in the night and throw it. The day on the morrow the tailor went off, and brought with him his tools, the spade and the shovel.

He had not gone far till he met a white horse, and he saluted him.

"God save you," said the horse. " Where are you going?"

"I am going to Dublin," said the tailor, "to build a court for the king, and to get a lady for a wife, if I am able to do it ; " for the king had promised that he would give his own daughter, and a lot of money with her, to whoever would be able to build up his court.

"Would you make me a hole," said the old white garraun (horse) "where I could go a' hiding whenever the

"Deunfaiḋ mé ṡin go deiṁin," aṙ ṡan táiliúr, "aguṡ
fáilte." Ṫug ṙé an ráḋ leiṡ aguṡ an trluaṡaḋ, aguṡ
ṗinne ṙé poll, aguṡ duḃairt ṙé leiṡ an g-capall bán dul
ṡíoṡ ann, go ḃfeicṙeaḋ ṙé an ḃróiṁreaḋ ṙé ḋó. Ċuaiḋ an
capall bán ṡíoṡ ann ṡan bpoll, aċt nuair d'ḟeuċ ṙé do
ṫeaċt ruaṡ aríṡ aṙ, níoṙ ḟeud ṙé.

"Deun áit ḋam anoiṡ," aṙ ṡan capall bán, "a ṫiucfaṡ
mé aníoṡ aṙ an bpoll ro nuair a ḃéiḋeaṡ ocaṡaṡ orm."
"Ní ḋeunfaḋ," aṙ ṡan táiliúr, "fan ann ṡin go dtigiḋ
mé aṙ m'aiṡ, aguṡ tógfaiḋ mé aníoṡ ṫu."

D'imṫiġ an táiliúr an lá aṙ na máraċ, aguṡ caṡaḋ
ḋó an rionnaċ, "Go mbeannuiġ Dia ḋuit," aṙ ṡan
rionnaċ. "Go mbeannuiġ Dia 'guṙ Muire ḋuit."   "Cá
ḃfuil tu dul?" "Tá mé dul go B'l'acliaṫ go ḃfeuḋaiḋ
mé an dtiucfaiḋ liom cúirt ḃeunaṁ do'n ríġ." "An
ndeunfá áit ḋam, a raċfainn i bfolaċ innti," aṙ ṡan
rionnaċ, "tá an ċuid eile de na rionnaiġiḃ dom' ḃualaḋ
aguṡ ní leigeann riaḋ ḋam aon niḋ iṫe 'nnṡ g-cuiḋeaċta."
"Deunfaiḋ mé ṡin duit," "aṙ ṡan táiliúr. Ṫug ṙé leiṡ
a ṫuaġ aguṡ a fáḃ, aguṡ ḃain re rlata, go ndeaṙnaiġ
ṙé, maṙ ḋeurfá, cliaḃ ḋó, aguṡ duḃairt ṙé leiṡ an trionn-
naċ dul ṡíoṡ ann, go ḃfeicṙeaḋ re an ḃróiṁreaḋ ṙé ḋó.
Ċuaiḋ an rionnaċ ann, aguṡ nuair fuair an táiliúr ṡíoṡ
é, leag ṙé a ṫóin aṙ an bpoll a ḃí ann. Nuair a ḃí an
rionnaċ ṡárta faoi ḃeirreaḋ go raiḃ áit ḃeaṡ aige d'iarr
ṙé aṙ an táiliúr a leigean amaċ, aguṡ d'ḟreagair an
táiliúr naċ leigfeaḋ; "Fan ann ṡin go dtigiḋ miṡe aṙ
m'aiṡ," aṙ ṙé.

D'imṫiġ an táiliúr an lá aṙ na máraċ, aguṡ ní faḋa
ḃí ṙé riúḃal guṙ caṡaḋ maḋr'-alla ḋó, aguṡ ċuir an
máḋr'-alla forán aiṙ, aguṡ d'ḟiarruiġ ṙé ḋé cá raiḃ ṙé
aġ triall. "Tá me dul go B'l'acliaṫ go ndeunfaiḋ mé
cúirt do'n ríġ má ṫiġ liom ṙin ḃeunaṁ," aṙ ṡan táiliúr."
"Dá ndeunfá ceuċt ḋam," aṙ ṡan maḋr'-alla, "ḃeiḋeaḋ

people are for bringing me to the mill or the kiln, so that they won't see me, for they have me perished doing work for them?"

"I'll do that, indeed," said the tailor, "and welcome."

He brought the spade and shovel, and he made a hole, and he said to the old white horse to go down into it till he would see if it would fit him. The white horse went down into the hole, but when he tried to come up again he was not able.

"Make a place for me now," said the white horse, "by which I'll come up out of the hole here, whenever I'll be hungry."

"I will not," said the tailor; "remain where you are until I come back, and I'll lift you up."

The tailor went forward next day, and the fox met him.

"God save you," said the fox.

"God and Mary save you."

"Where are you going?"

"I'm going to Dublin, to try will I be able to make a court for the king."

"Would you make a place for me where I'd go hiding?" said the fox. "The rest of the foxes do be beating me, and they don't allow me to eat anything along with them."

"I'll do that for you," said the tailor.

He took with him his axe and his saw, and he cut rods, until he made, as you would say, a thing like a cleeve (creel), and he desired the fox to get into it till he would see whether it would fit him. The fox went into it, and when the tailor got him down, he clapped his thigh on the hole that the fox got in by. When the fox was satisfied at last that he had a nice place of it within, he asked the tailor to let him out, and the tailor answered that he would not.

mire agus na maoir-alla eile ag treasḃaḋ agus ag
forraḋ, go mbeiḋeaḋ greim againn le n-iṫe ann ran
ḃróġṁar." "Deunfaiḋ mé rin duit," ar ran táiliúir.
Ċug ré leir a ṫuaġ 'r a ráḃ, agus rinne ré ceuċt. Nuair
ḃí an ceuċt deunta ċuir ré poll ann ran mbéam (rail)
agus duḃairt re leir an maoir-alla dul arteaċ raoi an
g-ceuċt go ḃfeicfeaḋ ré an raiḃ treasḃaḋ mait ann. Ċuir
ré a earball arteaċ ann ran bpoll a rinne ré, agus ċuir
ré "peg" ann-rin ann, agus níor ṫáinig leir an maoir-
alla a earball ṫarraing amaċ ar arír. "Sgaoil mé
anoir," ar ran maoir-alla, agus dearóċamaoiḋ féin agus
treasḃramaoiḋ." Duḃairt an táiliúir naċ rgaoilfeaḋ ré
é no go dtiucfaḋ ré féin air air. D'ḟág ré ann rin é agus
ċuaiḋ ré go ḃ'l'alciaṫ.

Nuair ṫáinig ré go ḃ'l'acliaṫ ċuir ré páipeur amaċ an
méaḋ luċd' céirde do ḃí ag tóġḃáil na cúirte do ṫeaċt
ċuige·rean, agus go n-íocfaḋ reirean iad —— agus ní
ḃíḋeaḋ daoine ag rágail 'ran am rin aċt ríġin 'ran lá.
Do ċruinniġ a lán luċd céirde an lá air na ṁárac, agus
ṫorraiġ riad ag obair dó.   Ḃí riad ag dul a ḃaile anḋú-
aiġ an laé nuair duḃairt an táiliúir leó "an ċloċ ṁór
rin do ċur ruar air bárr na h-oiḃre a ḃí deunta aige."
Nuair d' árduiġeaḋ ruar an ċloċ ṁór rin, ċuir an táiliúir
rliġe éigin rúṁċa go leagfaḋ ré anuar i nuair a ṫiucfaḋ
an raṫaċ ċoṁ rada léiṫe. D'imṫiġ an luċd oiḃre a ḃaile
ann rin, agus ċuaiḋ an táiliúir i ḃfolaċ air ċúl na cloiċe
móire. Nuair ṫáinig dorċadar na h-oiḋċe ċonnairc ré na
tri raṫaiġ ag teaċt, agus ṫorraiġ riad ag leagáḋ na
cúirte no go dtáinig riad ċoṁ rada leir an áit a raiḃ an
táiliúir ruar, agus ḃuail fear aca buille d'á oro air
an áit a raiḃ ré i ḃfolaċ. Leag an táiliúir an ċloċ
anuar air, agus, ċuit rí air, agus ṁarḃ rí é. D'imṫiġ
riad a ḃaile ann rin, agus d'ḟág riad an méaḋ a ḃí ann
gan leagan, ó ḃí fear aca féin marḃ.

" Wait there until I come back again," says he.

The tailor went forward the next day, and he had not walked very far until he met a modder-alla (lion?) and the lion greeted him, and asked him where was he going.

" I'm going to Dublin till I make a court for the king if I'm able to make it," said the tailor.

" If you were to make a plough for me," said the lion, " I and the other lions could be ploughing and harrowing until we'd have a bit to eat in the harvest."

" I'll do that for you," said the tailor.

He brought his axe and his saw, and he made a plough. When the plough was made, he put a hole in the beam of it, and he said to the lion to go in under the plough till he'd see was he any good of a ploughman. He placed the tail in the hole he had made for it, and then clapped in a peg, and the lion was not able to draw out his tail again.

" Loose me out now," said the lion, " and we'll fix ourselves and go ploughing."

 The tailor said he would not loose him out, until he came back himself. He left him there then, and he came to Dublin.

When he came to Dublin he put forth a paper, desiring all the tradesmen that were raising the court to come to him, and that he would pay them ; and at that time workmen used only to be getting one penny in the day. A number of tradesmen gathered the next day, and they began working for him. They were going home again after their day, when the tailor said to them "to put up that great stone upon the top of the work that they had done." When the great stone was raised up, the tailor put some sort of contrivance under it, that he might be able to throw it down as soon as the giant would come as far as it. The work people went home then, and the tailor went in hiding behind the big stone.

Táinig an luċt céirde orír, an lá air na máraċ, agus
bí riad ag obair go dtí an oiḋċe, agus nuair a bí riad
dul aḃaile duḃairt an táiliúr leó an ċloċ mór do ċur
ruar air ḃárr na h-oiḃre mar bí rí an oiḋċe roiṁe rin.
Rinne riad rin dó, agus d'imṫiġ riad aḃaile, agus cuaiḋ
an táiliúr i ḃrolaċ, mar bí ré an tratnóna roiṁe rin.
Nuair bí na daoine uile imṫiġṫe 'nna ruaiṁnear, táinig
an dá ṗataċ, agus bí riad ag leagan an méid a bí
rompa; agus nuair toruiġ riad, ċuir riad dá ġlaoḋ orta.
Bí an táiliúr air rúḃal agus é ag obair no gur leag ré
anuar an ċloċ mór gur ṫuit rí air ċloigionn an ṗataiġ a
bí rúiṫ agus marḃ rí é.   Ní raiḃ ann rin aċt an t-aon
ṗataċ amáin ann, agus ní táinig reirean go raiḃ an
ċúirt criroċnuiġṫe.

Cuaiḋ an táiliúr cum an riġ ann rin, agus duḃairt ré
leir, a ḃean agus a ċuid airgid do ṫaḃairt dó, mar do
bí an ċúirt déanta aige, aċt duḃairt an riġ leir naċ
dtiúḃraḋ ré aon ḃean dó, no go marḃraḋ ré an ṗataċ
eile, agus naċ dtiúḃraḋ ré dadaṁ dó anoir no go
marḃraḋ ré an fear deireannaċ.   Duḃairt an táiliúr
ann rin go marḃraḋ ré an ṗataċ eile dó, agus ráilte,
naċ raiḃ aon ṁaille air biṫ air rin.

D'imṫiġ an táiliúr ann rin, go dtáinig ré cum na
h-áite a raiḃ an ṗataċ eile, agus d'fiarruiġ air ṫeartuiġ buaċaill uaiḋ.   Duḃairt an ṗataċ gur ṫeartuiġ,
dá ḃfáġaḋ ré buaċaill a ḋeunraḋ an rud a deunraḋ ré
féin.   "Rud air biṫ a ḋeunfar tura, deunraiḋ mire é,"
ar ran táiliúr.

Cuaiḋ riad cum a noinéir ann rin, agus nuair bí ré
itte aca duḃairt an ṗataċ leir an táiliúr an dtiucfaḋ
leir an oiread anḃruiṫ ól agus é féin, aníor ar a fiucaḋ.
"Tiucfaiḋ," ar ran táiliúr, "aċt go dtiúḃraiḋ tu uair
dam rul a ċoróċamaoid air."   "Béarfaiḋ mé rin duit,"
ar ran ṗataċ.   Cuaiḋ an táiliúr amaċ ann rin, agus

When the darkness of the night was come he saw the
three giants arriving, and they began throwing down the
court until they came as far as the place where the tailor
was in hiding up above, and a man of them struck a blow
of his sledge on the place where he was. The tailor threw
down the stone, and it fell on him and killed him.   They
went home then, and left all of the court that was remaining without throwing it down, since a man of themselves was dead.

The tradespeople came again the next day, and they
were working until night, and as they were going home
the tailor told them to put up the big stone on the top of
the work, as it had been the night before.   They did
that for him, went home, and the tailor went in hiding
the same as he did the evening before.

When the people had all gone to rest, the two giants
came, and they were throwing down all that was before
them, and as soon as they began they put two shouts out
of them.   The tailor was going on manœuvring until he
threw down the great stone, and it fell upon the skull of
the giant that was under him, and it killed him. There was
only the one giant left in it then, and he never came
again until the court was finished.

Then when the work was over he went to the king
and told him to give him his wife and his money, as
he had the court finished, and the king said he would
not give him any wife, until he would kill the other
giant, for he said that it was not by his strength he
killed the two giants before that, and that he would
give him nothing now until he killed the other one
for him.   Then the tailor said that he would kill the
other giant for him, and welcome ; that there was no
delay at all about that.

The tailor went then, till he came to the place where

ꝼuaiꞃ ꞃe cꞃoicionn caoꞃaċ aguꞅ ꝺ'ꝼuaiġ ꞃé ꞃuaꞅ é, ꞃo
nꝺeaꞃnaiġ ꞃé mála ꝺé aguꞅ ꝺeaꞃuiġ ꞃé ꝼíoꞃ ꝼaoi na ċóta
é. Táinig ꞃé aꞃteaċ ann ꞃin, aguꞅ ꝺubaiꞃt ꞃé leiꞅ an
ḃꝼaċaċ galún ꝺe'n anḃꞃuiṫ ól i ꝺtoꞃaċ. Ꝺ'ól an ꝼaċaċ
ꞃin aníoꞅ aꞃ a ꞃiuċaḋ.

"Ꝺeunꝼaiḋ miꞅe ꞃin," aꞃ ꞃanc áiliúꞃ. Ḃí ꞃé aiꞃ
ꞃiúbal guꞃ ḃóiꞃc ꞃé aꞃteaċ ꞃan g-cꞃoicionn é, aguꞅ ꝼaoil
an ꝼaċaċ go ꞃaiḃ ꞃé ólta aige. Ꝺ'ól an ꝼaċaċ galún
eile ann ꞃin, aguꞅ leig an táiliúꞃ galún eile ꝼíoꞃ 'ꞃan
g-cꞃoicionn, aċt ꝼaoil an ꝼaċaċ, go ꞃaiḃ ꞃé 'ġá ól. "Ꝺéan-
ꝼaiḋ miꞅe ꞃuꝺ anoiꞅ naċ ꝺtiucꝼaiḋ leat-ꞃa ḋeunaṁ," aꞃ
ꞃan táiliúꞃ. "Ní ḃéanꝼá," aꞃ ꞃan ꝼaċaċ, "cꞃeuꝺ é ꞃin
ꝺo ḃéanꝼá?"

"Poll ꝺo ḃeunaṁ, aguꞅ an t-anḃꞃuiṫ ꝺo leigean
amaċ aiꞃꞅ," aꞃ ꞃan táiliúꞃ. "Ꝺéan tu ꝼéin i ꝺtoꞃaċ é,"
aꞃ ꞃan ꝼaċaċ. Tug an táiliúꞃ "pꞃaꝺ" ꝺe'n ꞅgín, aguꞅ
leig ꞃé amaċ an t-anḃꞃuiṫ aꞃ an g-cꞃoicionn. "Ꝺéan,
ṫuꞃa, ꞃin," aꞃ ꞃé leiꞅ an ḃꝼaċaċ. "Ꝺéanꝼaꝺ," aꞃ ꞃan
ꝼaċaċ ag tabaiꞃt pꞃaꝺ ꝺe'n ꞅgín 'nna ḃuilg ꝼéin guꞃ
ṁaꞃḃ ꞃé é ꝼéin. Sin é an ċaoi a ṁaꞃḃ ꞃé an tꞃíoṁaḋ
ꝼaċaċ.

Ċuaiḋ ꞃé ꝺo'n ꞃíġ ann ꞃin, aguꞅ ꝺubaiꞃt ꞃé leiꞅ, an
bean aguꞅ a ċuiꝺ aiꞃgiꝺ ꝺo ċuꞃ amaċ ċuige, aguꞅ go
leagꝼaḋ ꞃe an ċúiꞃc muna ḃꝼáġaḋ ꞃé an bean. Ḃí ꝼaic-
ċíoꞅ oꞃꞃa ann ꞃin go leagꝼaḋ ꞃé an ċúiꞃc aiꞃꞅ, aguꞅ
ċuiꞃ ꞃiaꝺ an bean amaċ ċuige.

Nuaiꞃ ḃí ꞃé lá imċiġṫe, é ꝼéin aguꞅ a bean, ġlac ꞃiaꝺ
aiṫpeaċáꞃ aguꞅ lean ꞃiaꝺ é, go mbainꝼeaḋ ꞃiaꝺ an bean
ꝺé aiꞃꞅ. Ḃí an ṁuinntiꞃ ꝺo bí 'nna ḃiaiġ 'ġá leanaṁaint
no go ꝺtáinig ꞃiaꝺ ꞃuaꞅ ꝺo'n áit a ꞃaiḃ an maꝺꞃ'-alla,
aguꞅ ꝺubaiꞃt an maꝺꞃ'-alla leó. "Ḃí an táiliúꞃ aguꞅ
a bean ann ꞃo anꝺé, connaiꞃc miꞅe iaꝺ ag ꝺul ṫaꞃt,
aguꞅ má ꞃgaoileann ꞃiḃ miꞅe anoiꞅ tá mé níoꞅ luaiṫe 'ná
ꞃiḃ-ꞅe, aguꞅ leanꝼaiḋ mé iaꝺ go mbéaꞃꝼaiḋ mé oꞃꞃa."

the other giant was, and asked did he want a servant-
boy. The giant said he did want one, if he could get one
who would do everything that he would do himself.

"Anything that you will do, I will do it," said the
tailor.

They went to their dinner then, and when they had it
eaten, the giant asked the tailor " would it come with him
to swallow as much broth as himself, up out of its boiling.' The tailor said : " It will come with me to do that,
but that you must give me an hour before we begin on
it." The tailor went out then, and he got a sheepskin,
and he sewed it up till he made a bag of it, and he
slipped it down under his coat. He came in then and
said to the giant to drink a gallon of the broth himself first. The giant drank that, up out of its boiling.
" I'll do that," said the tailor. He was going on until
he had it all poured into the skin, and the giant thought
he had it drunk. The giant drank another gallon then,
and the tailor let another gallon down into the skin, but
the giant thought he was drinking it.

" I'll do a thing now that it won't come with you to
do," said the tailor.

" You will not," said the giant. "What is it you
would do ? "

" Make a hole and let out the broth again," said the
tailor.

" Do it yourself first," said the giant.

The tailor gave a prod of the knife, and he let the
broth out of the skin.

"Do that you," said he.

" I will," said the giant, giving such a prod of the knife
into his own stomach, that he killed himself. That is the
way he killed the third giant.

He went to the king then, and desired him to send

Nuair ċualaiḋ riaḋ rin rgaoil riaḋ amaċ an maor' alla.

D'imtiġ an maor'-alla agus muinntir Ḃ'l'acliaṫ, agus bí riaḋ ḋá leanaṁaint go oáiníg riaḋ ḋo'n áit a raiḃ an rionnaċ, agus ċuir an rionnaċ foṗán oṗṗa, agus ḋuḃairt ré leó, "bi an táiliúr agus a bean ann ro air maoin anoiú, agus má rgaoilrió riḃ amaċ mé tá mó níor luaite 'ná riḃ agus leanfaió mé iaḋ agus béaṗṗaió mé oṗṗa." Sgaoil riaḋ amaċ an rionnaċ ann rin.

D'imtiġ an maor'-alla agus an rionnaċ, agus arm Ḃ'l'acliaṫ ann rin, ag feuċaint an ngaḃaḋ riaḋ an táiliúr, agus, táiníg riaḋ ḋo'n áit a raiḃ an fean-ġearrán bán, agus ḋuḃairt an fean-ġearrán bán leó, gu raiḃ an táiliúr, agus a bean ann rin air maoin, "agus rgaoiligiḋe amaċ mé," ar ré, "tá mé níor luaite 'ná riḃ-re agus béaṗṗaió mé oṗṗa." Sgaoil riaḋ amaċ an fean ġearrán bán, agus lean an fean-ġearrán bán, an rionnaċ, an maor'-alla, agus arm Ḃ'l'acliaṫ an táiliúr 'r a bean, i g-cuiḋeaċt a ċéile, agus níor ḃfaḋa go oáiníg riaḋ ruar leir an táiliúr, agus ċonnairc riaḋ é féin 'r a bean amaċ rompa.

Nuair ċonnairc an táiliúr iaḋ ag tiġeaċt ċáiníg ré féin 'r a bean amaċ ar an g-cóirte, agus fuió ré ríor air an talaṁ.

Nuair ċonnairc an fean-ġearrán bán an táiliúr ag ruiḋe ríor ḋuḃairt ré, "Sin é an cuma a bí ré nuair rinne ré an poll ḋaṁra, nár feuḋ mé teaċt amaċ ar, nuair ċuaiḋ mé arteaċ ann; ní raċfaió mé níor foigre ḋó."

"Ní h-eaḋ," ar ran rionnaċ, "aċt ir mar rin, ḋo bí ré nuair bí re ḋéanaṁ an ruiḋ ḋaṁ-ra, agus ní raċfaió mire níor foigre ḋó."

"Ní h-eaḋ!" ar ran maor'-alla, "aċt ir mar rin ḋo

him out his wife and his money, for that he would throw
down the court again, unless he should get the wife.
They were afraid then that he would throw down the
court, and they sent the wife out to him.

When the tailor was a day gone, himself and his wife,
they repented and followed him to take his wife off him
again. The people who were after him were following
him till they came to the place where the lion was, and
the lion said to them: "The tailor and his wife were
here yesterday. I saw them going by, and if ye loose
me now, I am swifter than ye, and I will follow them
till I overtake them." When they heard that they
loosed out the lion.

The lion and the people of Dublin went on, and they
were pursuing him, until they came to the place where
the fox was, and the fox greeted them, and said: "The
tailor and his wife were here this morning, and if ye
will loose me out, I am swifter than ye, and I will
follow them, and overtake them." They loosed out the
fox then.

The lion and the fox and the army of Dublin went on
then, trying would they catch the tailor, and they were
going till they came to the place where the old white
garraun was, and the old white garraun said to them that
the tailor and his wife were there in the morning, and
"loose me out," said he; "I am swifter than ye, and I'll
overtake them." They loosed out the old white garraun
then, and the old white garraun, the fox, the lion, and
the army of Dublin pursued the tailor and his wife together, and it was not long till they came up with him,
and saw himself and the wife out before them.

When the tailor saw them coming he got out of the
coach with his wife, and he sat down on the ground.

When the old white garraun saw the tailor sitting

ḃí ṛé nuaiṛ ḃí ṛé ṽéanaṁ an ceuċta 'nna ṛaiḃ miṛe
ᵹaḃċa. Ni ṛaċṛaiṽ miṛe níoṛ ṛoiᵹṛe ṽó."

D'imċiᵹ ṛaṽ uile uaiṽ ann ṛin, aᵹuṛ ṽ'ḟill ṛaṽ. Ċáiniᵹ
an táiliúṛ aᵹuṛ a ḃean a ḃaile ᵹo Ƨailliṁ. Ċuᵹ ṛaṽ
ṽam ṛtocaiṽ páipéiṛ aᵹuṛ ḃṛóᵹa ḃainne ṛaṁaiṛ—ċaill
mé iaṽ ó ṛoin. Ḟuaiṛ ṛaṽ-ṛan an t-áċ aᵹuṛ miṛe an
loċán, ḃáiteaṽ iaṽ-ṛan aᵹuṛ ċáiniᵹ miṛe.

ḃRꝊN.

ḃí cú ḃṛeáᵹ aᵹ Ḟionn. Sin ḃṛan. Ċualaiṽ tu caint
aiṛ ḃṛan. Seó an ṽaċ a ḃí aiṛ.

>　Coṛa ḃuiṽe a ḃí aiṛ ḃṛan
>　Ṽá ċaoiḃ ṽuḃa aᵹuṛ táṛṛ ᵹeal,
>　Ṽṛuim uaine aiṛ ṽaċ na ṛeilᵹe
>　Ṽá ċluaiṛ cṛuinne cóṁ-ṽeaṛᵹa.

ḃéaṛṛaṽ ḃṛan aiṛ na ᵹaċtiḃ-ṛiaṽna ḃí ṛí cóṁ luaċ ṛin.

down on the ground, he said: "That's the position he had when he made the hole for me, that I couldn't come up out of, when I went down into it. I'll go no nearer to him."

"No!" said the fox, "but that's the way he was when he was making the thing for me, and I'll go no nearer to him."

"No!" says the lion, "but that's the very way he had, when he was making the plough that I was caught in. I'll go no nearer to him."

They all went from him then and returned. The tailor and his wife came home to Galway. They gave me paper stockings and shoes of thick milk. I lost them since. They got the ford, and I the flash;* they were drowned, and I came safe.

———

BRAN.

FINN had a splendid hound. That was Bran. You have heard talk of Bran. This is the colour was on him:

> Yellow feet that were on Bran,
> Two black sides, and belly white,
> Grayish back of hunting colour,
> Two ears, red, round, small, and bright.

Bran would overtake the wild-geese, she was that swift,

* Flash, in Irish, *lochán*, i.e., little lake, or pool of water. Most story-tellers say, not, "I got the *lochán*," but the "*clochán*," or stepping-stones.

Nuaıṙ bí ṡí 'nna coıleán d'éıṙıġ ımṗeaṡ no ṫṙoıd éıġın ameaṡg na g-con a bí ag an ḃféın, aguṡ

Tṙí ṡıċe cu aguṡ ṡıċe coıleán
Maṙḃ Bṙán aguṡ í 'nna coıleán,
Dá ġé-ṡaḋáın, aguṡ an oıṙeaḋ leó uıle.

Sé Fıonn ṡéın a ṁaṙḃ Bṙán. Ċuaıḋ ṡıad amaċ ag ṡıaḋaċ aguṡ ṗınneaḋ eılıt de ṁáṫaıṙ Fınn. Bí Bṙán dá tóṙuıġeaċt.

" Eılıt ḃaoṫ ṡáġ aıṙ ṡlıaḃ
aṙ Fıonn.
" A ṁıc óıg," aṙ ṡıṙe, " Cá ṡaċṡaıḋ mé aṙ ?"

Má ṫéıḋım ann ṡan ḃṙaıṙṙıge ṡíoṙ
Coıḋċe nı ṡıllṡınn aıṙ m'aıṡ,
S má ṫéıḋım ann ṡan aeṙ ṡuaṡ
Nı ḃeuṙṡaıḋ mo luaṫaṡ aıṙ Bṙán.

" Gaḃ amaċ eıdıṙ mo ḋá ċoıṡ," aṙ Fıonn. Ċuaıḋ ṡıṙe amaċ eıdıṙ a ḋá ċoıṡ, aguṡ lean Bṙán í, aguṡ aıṙ ngaḃáıl amaċ dı, d'ṡáıṙg Fıonn a ḋá ġlúın uıṙṙı aguṡ ṁaṙḃ ṡé í.

Bí ınġean ag Bṙán. Cu duḃ a bí ann ṡan g-coıleán ṡın, aguṡ tóg na Fıanna í, aguṡ duḃaıṙt ṡıad leıṡ an mnaoı a bí taḃaıṙt aıṙe do'n ċoıleán, baınne bó gan aon ḃall do ċaḃaıṙt do'n ċoıleán, aguṡ gaċ aon deóṙ do ċaḃaıṙt dó, aguṡ gan aon ḃṙaon ċongḃáıl uaıḋ. Nı ḋeaṙnaıḋ an bean ṡın, aċt ċongḃuıg cuıd de'n baınne gan a ċaḃaıṙt uıle do'n ċoıleán. An ċeud lá do ṡgaoıl na Fıanna an cu óg amaċ bí gleann lán de ġéaḋaıḃ ṡıaḋaıne aguṡ d' eunṡéaıḃ eıle, aguṡ nuaıṙ ṡgaoıleaḋ an cú duḃ 'nna meaṡg, do ġaḃ ṡı ıad uıle aċt ṡíoṙ-beagán aca a ċuaıḋ amaċ aıṙ beaṙna a bí ann. Aguṡ aċt guṙ ċong-

There arose some quarrel or fighting between the hounds that the Fenians had, when she was only a puppy, and

> Three score hounds and twenty puppies
> Bran did kill, and she a puppy,
> Two wild-geese, as much as they all.

It was Finn himself who killed Bran. They went out hunting, and there was made a fawn of Finn's mother. *Who made a fawn of her ? Oh, how do I know ? It was with some of their pishtrogues.*) Bran was pursuing her.

> "Silly fawn leave on mountain,"

said Finn. "Oh, young son," said she, "how shall I escape ?—

> "If I go in the sea beneath
> I never shall come back again,
> And if I go in the air above
> My swiftness is no match for Bran.

"Go out between my two legs," said Finn.

She went between his two legs, and Bran followed her; and as Bran went out under him, Finn squeezed his two knees on her and killed her.

Bran had a daughter. That pup was a black hound, and the Fenians reared it; and they told the woman who had a charge of the pup to give it the milk of a cow without a single spot, and to give it every single drop, and not to keep back one tint* from her. The woman did not do that, but kept a portion of the milk without giving it to the pup.

The first day that the Fenians loosed out the young hound, there was a glen full of wild-geese and other birds; and when the black hound was loosed amongst them, she caught them all except a very few that went

---

† Tint, means a drop, or small portion of liquid, amongst English speaking persons in Connacht and most other parts of Ireland.

buıġ an bean cuıd de'n baınne uaıċ do ṁaıbfad ṙí ıad uıle.

Bí fear de na fıannaıb 'nna ḋall, aguṙ nuaıṙ leıgead an cu amaċ d'fıaṙṙuıġ ṙé de na daoınıb a bí anaıce leıṙ, cıa an ċaoı a ṙınne an cú óg. Dubaıṙt ṙıad-ṙan leıṙ guṙ ṁaṙb an cu óg an meud ġé ṙıaḋáın aguṙ eun a bı ann ṙan ngleann, aċt beaġán aca a ċuaıd amaċ aıṙ ḃeaṙna, aguṙ ġo ṙaıb ṙí ceaċt a baıle anoıṙ. "Dá bṙáġad ṙí an baınne uıle a ċáınıg de'n bo ġan aon ḃall," aṙ ṙan dall, "nı leıġṙead ṙí d'eun aıṙ bıċ ımċeaċt uaıdı," aguṙ d'fıaṙṙuıġ ṙé, ann ṙın, cad é an ċaoı a ṙaıb ṙí cıġeaċt a baıle. "Cá ṙí ceaċt anoıṙ," aṙ ṙıad "aguṙ, ṙġáıl' laṙta aṙ a muıneul aguṙ ı aıṙ buıle."

"Cabaıṙ m'ımṙıde ḋam anoıṙ," aṙ ṙan dall, "aguṙ cuıṙ mé 'mo ṙuıḋe ann ṙan g-cáċaoıṙ aguṙ cuıṙ ġual ann mo láıṁ, óıṙ muna maṙbaım í anoıṙ maṙbṙaıd ṙí muıd (ṙınn) uıle. Cáınıg an cú, aguṙ ċaıt ṙé an ġual léıċe aguṙ ṁaṙb ṙé í, aguṙ é dall.

Aċt dá bṙáġad an coıleán ṙın an baınne uıle do ċıucfad ṙí aguṙ luıḋead ṙí ṙíoṙ ġo ṙocaıṙ, maṙ luıḋead Bṙan.

Mac Ríġ Éıreann.

Bí mac ríġ ı n-É.ṙınn, fad ó ṙoın, aguṙ ċuaıd ṙé amaċ aguṙ tuġ ṙé a ġunna 'ṙ a ṁadad leıṙ. Bí ṙneaċta amuıġ. Ṁaṙb ṙé ṙıaċ dub. Cuıt an ṙıaċ dub aıṙ an tṙneaċta. Ní facaıd ṙé aon ṙıud buḋ ġıle 'ná an ṙneaċta,

out on a gap that was in it. (*And how could she catch the wild-geese? Wouldn't they fly away in the air? She caught them, then. That's how I heard it.*) And only that the woman kept back some of the milk from her, she would have killed them all.

There was a man of the Fenians, a blind man, and when the pup was let out, he asked the people near him how did the young hound do. They told him that the young hound killed all the wild-geese and birds that were in the glen, but a few that went out on a gap. "If she had to get all the milk that came from the cow without spot," says the blind man, "she wouldn't let a bird at all go from her." And he asked then "how was the hound coming home?" "She's coming now," said they, "and a fiery cloud out of her neck," (*How out of her neck? Because she was going so quick.*) "and she coming madly."

"Grant me my request now," said the blind man. "Put me sitting in the chair, and put a coal* (?) in my hand; for unless I kill her she'll kill us."

The hound came, and he threw the coal at her and killed her, and he blind.

But if that pup had to get all the milk, she'd come and she'd lie down quietly, the same as Bran used to lie ever.

THE KING OF IRELAND'S SON.

THERE was a king's son in Ireland long ago, and he went out and took with him his gun and his dog. There was snow out. He killed a raven. The raven fell on the snow. He never saw anything whiter than the snow,

---

* Gual.

ná buḋ ḋuiḃe 'ná cloıġıonn an ꝼıaċ ḋuiḃ, ná buḋ ḋeıꞃġe 'ná a ċuıꝺ ꝼola ḃí 'ġá ḋóꞃcaḋ amaċ.

Ċuıꞃ ꞃé ꝼaoı ġeaꞃaıḃ aġuꞃ ꝺeımúġ (*sic*) na bliaḋna naċ n-ıoꞃaḋ ꞃé ḋá ḃıaḋ ı n-aon ḃoꞃꝺ, ná ḋá oıḋċe ꝺo ċoꝺlaḋ ann aon teaċ, Ɡo ḃꝼáġaḋ ꞃé bean a ꞃaıḃ a cloıġıonn ċoṁ ꝺuḃ leıꞃ an ḃꝼıaċ ꝺuḃ, aꞬuꞃ a cꞃoıcıonn ċoṁ Ɡeal leıꞃ an tꞃneaċta, aꞬuꞃ a ḋá ġꞃuaıḋ ċoṁ ꝺeaꞃꞬ le ꝼuıl.

Ní ꞃaıḃ aon ḃean ann ꞃan ꝺoṁan maꞃ ꞃın, aċt aon ḃean aṁáın a bí ann ꞃan ꝺoṁan ꞃoıꞃ.

Lá aıꞃ na ṁáꞃaċ ġaḃ ꞃé amaċ, aꞬuꞃ ní ꞃaıḃ aıꞃꞬıoꝺ ꝼaıꞃꞃınꞬ, aċt ċuꞬ ꞃé leıꞃ ꝼıce púnta. Ní ꞃaꝺa ċuaıḋ ꞃé Ɡuꞃ caꞃaḋ ꞃoċꞃaoıꝺ ꝺó, aꞬuꞃ ꝺuḃaıꞃt ꞃé Ɡo ꞃaıḃ ꞃé ċoṁ maıt ḋó tꞃí ċoıꞃċéım ḋul leıꞃ an Ɡ-coꞃꞃán. Ní ꞃaıḃ na tꞃí ċoıꞃċéım ꞃıúḃalta aıꞬe Ɡo ꝺtáınıꞬ ꝼeaꞃ aꞬuꞃ leaꞬ ꞃé a ꞃeaꞃta aıꞃ an Ɡ-coꞃꞃ, aıꞃ ċúıꞬ púnta. Ḃí ꝺlıġeaḋ ı n-Eıꞃınn an t-am ꞃın, ꝺuınea ıꞃ bıt a ꞃaıḃ ꝼıaċa aıꞬe aıꞃ ꝼeaꞃ eıle, naċ ꝺtıucꝼaḋ le muınntıꞃ an ꝼıꞃ ꞃın a ċuꞃ, ꝺá mbeıḋeaḋ ꞃé maꞃḃ, Ɡan na ꝼıaċa ꝺ'ıoc, no Ɡan ceaꝺ ó'n ꝺuıne a ꞃaıḃ na ꝼıaċa ꞃın aıꞬe aıꞃ an ḃꝼeaꞃ maꞃḃ. Nuaıꞃ ċonnaıꞃc Mac ꞂíꞬ Éıꞃeann mıc aꞬuꞃ ınġeana an ꝺuıne ṁaıꞃḃ aꞬ caoıneaḋ, aꞬuꞃ ıaꝺ Ɡan an t-aıꞃꞬıoꝺ aca le taḃaıꞃt ꝺo 'n ꝼeaꞃ, ꝺuḃaıꞃt ꞃé leıꞃ ꝼeın, "ıꞃ móꞃ an ċꞃuaġ é naċ ḃꝼuıl an t-aıꞃꞬıoꝺ aꞬ na ꝺaoınıḃ boċta," aꞬuꞃ ċuıꞃ ꞃé a láıṁ ann a póca aꞬuꞃ ꝺ'ıoc ꞃé ꝼéın na cúıꞬ púnta, aıꞃ ꞃon an ċuıꞃp. Ꝺuḃaıꞃt ꞃé Ɡo ꞃaċꝼaḋ ꞃé cum an teampoıll ann ꞃın, Ɡo ḃꝼeıcꝼeaḋ ꞃé cuꞃċa é. ĊáınıꞬ ꝼeaꞃ eıle ann ꞃın, aꞬuꞃ leaꞬ ꞃé a ꞃeaꞃta aıꞃ an Ɡ-coꞃꞃ aıꞃ ꞃon cúıꞬ púnta eıle. "Maꞃ ċuꞬ mé na ceuꝺ cúıꞬ púnta," aꞃ Mac ꞂíꞬ Éıꞃeann leıꞃ ꝼéın, "tá ꞃé ċoṁ maıt ḋam cúıꞬ púnta eıle taḃaıꞃt anoıꞃ, aꞬuꞃ an ꝼeaꞃ boċt ꝺo leıꞬean ꝺul 'ꞃan uaıġ," Ꝺ'ıoc ꞃé na cúıꞬ púnta eıle. Ní ꞃaıḃ aıꞬe ann ꞃın aċt ꝺeıċ bpúnta.

or blacker than the raven's skull, or redder than its share
of blood,* that was a'pouring out.

He put himself under *gassa*† and obligations of the
year, that he would not eat two meals at one table, or
sleep two nights in one house, until he should find a
woman whose hair was as black as the raven's head, and
her skin as white as the snow, and her two cheeks as
red as the blood.

There was no woman in the world like that; but one
woman only, and she was in the eastern world.

The day on the morrow he set out, and money
was not plenty, but he took with him twenty
pounds. It was not far he went until he met a
funeral, and he said that it was as good for him to
go three steps with the corpse. He had not the three
steps walked until there came a man and left his writ
down on the corpse for five pounds. There was a law in
Ireland at that time that any man who had a debt upon
another person (*i.e.*, to whom another person owed a
debt) that person's people could not bury him, should he
be dead, without paying his debts, or without the leave
of the person to whom the dead man owed the debts.
When the king of Ireland's son saw the sons and daughters of the dead crying, and they without money to
give the man, he said to himself: "It's a great pity that
these poor people have not the money," and he put his
hand in his pocket and paid the five pounds himself for
the corpse. After that, he said he would go as far as
the church to see it buried. Then there came another
man, and left his writ on the body for five pounds more.

* This is an idiom in constant use in Gaelic and Irish; but to translate it
every time it occurs would be tedious. In Gaelic we say, my share of money,
land, etc., for my money, my land.

In Irish, *geasa*—mystic obligations.

Níor ḃfada cuaiḋ sé gur casaḋ fear gearr glas ḋó
agus ḋ'ḟiafruiġ sé ḋé cá raiḃ sé ḋul. Duḃairt sé go
raiḃ sé ḋul ag iarraiḋ mná 'san ḋoṁan soir. Ḋ'ḟiafruiġ
an fear gearr glas ḋé, an raiḃ buacaill teastál uaiḋ,
agus ḋuḃairt sé go raiḃ, agus caḋ é an páiḋe ḃeiḋeaḋ
sé ag iarraiḋ. Duḃairt seisean "an céud póg air a
ṁnaoi, ḋá ḃfáġaḋ sé í." Duḃairt Mac Ríg Éireann go
g-caitfeaḋ sé sin fáġail.

Níor ḃfada cuaiḋ siad gur casaḋ fear eile ḋóiḃ agus
a ġunna ann a láiṁ, agus é ag "leibléaracḋ" air an
londuḃ a ḃí tall 'san ḋoṁan soir, go mbeiḋeaḋ sé aige
le n-aġaiḋ a ḃínéir. Duḃairt an fear gearr glas le
Mac Ríg Éireann gó raiḃ sé coṁ maiṫ ḋó an fear sin
ġlacaḋ air aimsir, ḋa racfaḋ sé air aimsir leis.
Ḋ'ḟiafruiġ Mac Ríg Éireann an ḋtiucfaḋ sé air aimsir
leis.

"Racfaḋ," ar san fear, "má ḃfáġ' mé mo ṫuarastal."

"Agus caḋ é an tuarastal ḃeiḋeas tu 'g iarraiḋ?"

"Áit tiġe agus garḋa."

"Ġeoḃaiḋ tu sin uaim, má éiriġeann mo ṫurus liom."

Ḋ'imṫiġ Mac Ríg Éireann leis an ḃfear glas agus
leis an ngunnaire, agus ní fada cuaiḋ siad gur casaḋ
fear ḋóiḃ, agus a ċluas leagṫa air an talaṁ, agus é
ag éisteacḋ leis an ḃfeur ag fás.

"Tá sé coṁ maiṫ ḋuit an fear sin ġlacaḋ air
aimsir," ar san fear gearr glas.

Ḋ'ḟiafruiġ Mac Ríg Éireann de 'n fear an ḋtiucfaḋ
sé leis air aimsir.

"Tiucfaḋ má ḃfáġ mé áit tiġe agus garḋa."

"Ġeoḃaiḋ tu sin uaim má éiriġeann an ruḋ atá ann
mo ċeann liom."

"As I gave the first five pounds," said the king of Erin's son to himself, "it's as good for me to give the other five, and to let the poor man go to the grave." He paid the other five pounds. He had only ten pounds then.

Not far did he go until he met a short green man, and he asked him where was he going. He said that he was going looking for a woman in the eastern world. The short green man asked him did he want a boy (servant), and he said he did, and [asked] what would be the wages he would be looking for? He said: "The first kiss of his wife if he should get her." The king of Ireland's son said that he must get that.

Not far did they go until they met another man and his gun in his hand, and he a' levelling it at the blackbird that was in the eastern world, that he might have it for his dinner. The short green man said to him that it was as good for him to take that man into his service if he would go on service with him. The son of the king of Ireland asked him if he would come on service with him.

"I will," said the man, "if I get my wages."

"And what is the wages you'll be looking for?"

"The place of a house and garden."

"You'll get that if my journey succeeds with me."

The king of Ireland's son went forward with the short green man and the gunner, and it was not far they went until a man met them, and his ear left to the ground, and he listening to the grass growing.

"It's as good for you to take that man into your service," said the short green man.

The king's son asked the man whether he would come with him on service.

"I'll come if I get the place of a house and garden."

"You will get that from me if the thing I have in my head succeeds with me."

Ċuaiḋ Mac Ríg Éireann, an ḟear ġearr ġlas, an ġunnaire, aguſ an cluaſaire, aguſ ní faḋa ċuaiḋ ſiaḋ gur caſaḋ ḟear eile ḋóiḃ aguſ a leaṫ-ċoſ air a ġualainn, aguſ é aſ conġḃáil páirce ġeiṁ́ríaḋ ġan aon ġeiṁ́ríaḋ leigean aſteaċ ná amaċ. Ḃí ionġantaſ air Mac Ríg Éireann aguſ ḃ'iaḟ́ruiġ ſé caḋ é an ċiall a raiḃ a leaṫ-ċoſ air a ġualainn mar ſin.

"O," aſ ſeiſean, "ḋá mbeiḋeaḋ mo ḋá ċoiſ aġam air an talam ḃeiḋinn ċoṁ luaṫ ſin ġo raċfainn aſ aṁarc."

"An ḋtiucfaiḋ tu air aimſir liom," aſ ſan Mac Ríg.

"Tiucfaḋ, má ḃfáġ' mé áit tiġe aguſ ġaoiḋa."

"Ġeoḃaiḋ tu ſin uaim," aſ Mac Ríg Éireann, "má éiriġeann an ruḋ atá ann mo ċeann, liom."

Ċuaiḋ Mac Ríg Éireann, an ḟear ġearr ġlas, an ġunnaire, an cluaſaire, aguſ an coirre air aġaiḋ, aguſ níor ḃfaḋa ġo ḋtáncaḋar ġo ḟear aguſ é aſ cur muilinn ġaoiṫe ṫart le na leaṫpolláire, aguſ a ṁeur leaġṫa aige air a ṡrón aſ ḋruiḋim na polláire eile.

"Caḋ ċuiġe ḃfuil do ṁeur aġaḋ air do ṡrón ?" aſ Mac Ríg Éireann leiſ.

"O," aſ ſeiſean, "ḋá ſéiḋfinn aſ mo ḋá polláire ḋo ſguaḃfainn an muileann amaċ aſ ſin ſuaſ 'ſan aeir."

"An ḋtiucfaiḋ tu air aimſir ?"

"Tiucfaḋ, má ḃfáġ' mé áit tiġe aguſ ġaoiḋa."

"Ġeoḃaiḋ tu ſin, má éiriġeann an ruḋ atá ann mo ċeann liom."

Ċuaiḋ Mac Ríg Éireann, an ḟear ġearr ġlas, an ġunnaire, an cluaſaire, an coirre, aguſ an ſéiḋire ġo ḋtáncaḋar ġo ḟear a ḃí 'nna ṡuiḋe air taoiḃ an ḃóṫair, aguſ é aſ briſeaḋ cloċ le na leaṫ-ṫóin aguſ ní raiḃ caſúr ná daḋaṁ aige. Ḋ'fiaḟruiġ an Mac Ríg ḋé, caḋ ċuiġe a raiḃ ſé aſ briſeaḋ na g-cloċ le na leaṫ-ṫóin.

The son of the king of Ireland, the short green man, the gunman, and the earman, went forward, and it was not far they went until they met another man, and his one foot on his shoulder, and he keeping a field of hares, without letting one hare in or out of the field. There was wonder on the king's son, and he asked him "What was the sense of his having one foot on his shoulder like that."

"Oh," says he, "if I had my two feet on the ground I should be so swift that I would go out of sight."

"Will you come on service with me?" says the king's son.

"I'll come if I get the place of a house and garden."

"You'll get that if the thing I have in my head succeeds with me."

The son of the king of Ireland, the short green man, the gunman, the earman, and the footman, went forward, and it was not far they went till they came to a man and he turning round a wind-mill with one nostril, and his finger left on his nose shutting the other nostril.

"Why have you your finger on your nose?" said the king of Ireland's son.

"Oh," says he, "if I were to blow with the two nostrils I would sweep the mill altogether out of that up into the air."

"Will you come on hire with me?"

"I will if I get the place of a house and garden."

"You'll get that if the thing I have in my head succeeds with me."

The son of the king of Ireland, the short green man, the gunman, the earman, the footman, and the blowman went forward until they came to a man who was sitting on the side of the road and he a' breaking stones with one thigh, and he had no hammer or anything else.

"O," ap peipean, "dá mbualpainn leip an tóin úúbalta
1ao úeunpainn púgoap diob."

"An otiucpaiú tu aip aimpip liom?"

"Tuicpad, má bpag' mé áit tíge agup gapúa."

D'imtig piad uile ann pin, Mac Ríg Eipeann, an peap
geapp glap, an gunnaipe, an cluapaipe, an coipipe, an
péidipe, agup peap bpipte na g-cloc le taoib a tóna
agup beuppaú piad aip an ngaoit Mápta a bí pompa
agup an gaot Mápta a bí 'nna n-diaig ní beuppaú pí
oppa-pan go dtáinig tpatnóna agup deipeaú an· laé.

Úeapc Mac Ríg Éipeann uaiú agup ní pacaiú pé aon
teac a mbeiúeaú pé ann an oiúce pin. Úeapc an peap
geapp glap uaiú agup connaipc pe teac nac paib bonn
cleite amac aip, ná bápp cleite apteac aip, act aon
cleite amáin a bí ag congbáil divinn agup papgaiú aip.
Dubaipt mac píg Éipeann nac paib piop aige cá caitpeaú
piad an oiúce pin, agup dubaipt an peap geapp glap go
mbeiúeaú piad i dteac an pataig tall an oiúce pin.

Táinig piad cum an tige, agup tappaing an peap geapp
glap an cuaille cómpaic agup níop pág pé leanb i mnaoi
peappac i g-capall, pigín i muic, ná bpoc i ngleann náp
iompuig pé tapt tpí uaipe iad le méad an topain do bain
pé ap an g-cuaille cómpaic. Táinig an patac amac
agup dubaipt pé "motuigim bolaú an Éipeannaig binn
bpeugaig paoi m'póidín úútaig."

"Ní Éipeannac binn bpeugac mipe," ap pan peap geapp
glap, "act tá mo máigiptip amuig ann pin ag ceann an
bótaip agup má tagann pé bainpiú pé an ceann diot."
Bí an peap geapp glap ag meudugaú, agup ag meudugaú
go paib pé paoi deipeaú cóm móp leip an g-caipleán. Bí
paitcíop aip an bpatac agup dubaipt pé, "bpuil do
máigiptip cóm móp leat péin?"

The king's son asked him why it was he was breaking stones with his half (*i.e.*, one) thigh.

"Oh," says he, "if I were to strike them with the double thigh I'd make powder of them."

"Will you hire with me?"

"I will if I get the place of a house and garden."

"You'll get that if the thing I have in my head succeeds with me."

Then they all went forward together—the son of the king of Ireland, the short green man, the gunman, the earman, the footman, the blowman, and the man that broke stones with the side of his thigh, and they would overtake the March wind that was before them, and the March wind that was behind them would not overtake them, until the evening came and the end of the day.

The king of Ireland's son looked from him, and he did not see any house in which he might be that night. The short green man looked from him, and he saw a house, and there was not the top of a quill outside of it, nor the bottom of a quill inside of it, but only one quill alone, which was keeping shelter and protection on it. The king's son said that he did not know where he should pass that night, and the short green man said that they would be in the house of the giant over there that night.

They came to the house, and the short green man drew the *coolaya-coric* (pole of combat), and he did not leave child with woman, foal with mare, pigeen with pig, or badger in glen, that he did not turn over three times with the quantity of sound he knocked out of the *coolaya-coric*. The giant came out, and he said: "I feel the smell of the melodious lying Irishman under (*i.e.*, in) my little sod of country."

"I'm no melodious lying Irishman," said the short green man;" but my master is out there at the head of

"Tá," ar ʼsan fear zearr zlas, "azus níos mó."

"Cuir i brolac mé zo maioin zo n-imtizeann oo móizirtir," ar ʼsan fatac.

Cuir ré an fatac faoi zlas, ann sin, azus cuaio sé
cum a móizirtir

Táinig macríz Éireann, an fear zearr zlas, an zunnaire
an cluasaire, an réioire, an coirre, azus fear buirte na
z-cloc le taoib a tóna, arteac ʼsan z-cairleán, azus cait
siao an oioce sin, trian oíle fiannaízeact azus trian le
rzeuluízeact, azus trian le roinm (sic.) róim ruain azus
fíor-cooalta.

Nuair oʼ éiriz an lá air na mórac tuz sé leir a
móizirtir azus an zunnaire, azus an cluasaire, azus an
coirre, azus an réioire, azus fear buirte na z-cloc le
taoib a tóna, azus oʼfáz sé amuiz az ceann an bótair
iao, azus táinig sé féin air air azus bain sé an zlas oe
ʼn fatac. Oubairt sé leir an bfatac zur cuir a móizirtir air air é i z-coinne an birréio ouib a bí faoi colba
a leabuio. Oubairt an fatac zo otiubrao sé hata oó nór
cait sé féin ariam, act zo raib náire air, an fean-birreuo
oo tabairt oó. Oubairt an fear zearr zlas muna
otiubrao sé an birreuo oó zo otiucfao a móizirtir air
air, azus zo mbainfeao sé an ceann oé.

"Is fearr oam a tabairt ouit," ar ʼsan fatac, "azus
uair air bit a cuirfear tu air oo ceann ó, feicfió tu uile
ouine azus ni feicfió ouine air bit tu." Tuz sé oó an
birreuo ann sin, azus cuaio an fear zearr zlas azus tuz
sé oo mac ríz Éireann é.

Bí siao az imteact ann sin. Oo béarfao siao air
an nzaoit Márta oo bí rómpa, azus an zaot Márta
oo bí ʼnna noiaiz ní béarfao sí orra-san, az oul

the avenue, and if he comes he will whip the head off
you." The short green man was growing big, growing
big, until at last he looked as big as the castle. There
came fear on the giant, and he said : "Is your master as
big as you ?"

" He is," says the short green man, " and bigger."

" Put me in hiding till morning, until your master
goes," said the giant.

Then he put the giant under lock and key, and
went out to the king's son. Then the king of Ireland's
son, the gunman, the earman, the footman, the blowman, and the man who broke stones with the side
of his thigh, came into the castle, and they spent that
night, a third of it a' story-telling, a third of it with
Fenian tales, and a third of it in mild enjoyment (?)
of slumber and of true sleep.

When the day on the morrow arose, the short green
man brought with him his master, the gunman, the
earman, the footman, the blowman, and the man who
broke stones with the side of his thigh, and he left them
outside at the head of the avenue, and he came back
himself and took the lock off the giant. He told the
giant that his master sent him back for the black cap
that was under the head of his bed. The giant said that
he would give him a hat that he never wore himself, but
that he was ashamed to give him the old cap. The short
green man said that unless he gave him the cap his
master would come back and strike the head off him.

" It's best for me to give it to you," said the giant; "and
any time at all you will put it on your head you will see
everybody and nobody will see you." He gave him the
cap then, and the short green man came and gave it to
the king of Ireland's son.

" They were a'going then. They would overtake the

do'n domȧn ṡoiṙ. Nuaiṙ ṫáiniġ tṙaṫnóna aġuṡ deiṙeaḋ
an lae ḃeaṙc mac ṙíġ Éireann uaiḋ aġuṡ ní ḟacaiḋ ṙé aon
áit a mbeiḋeaḋ ṙé ann an oiḋċe ṡin. Ḃeaṙc an ṡeaṙ
ġeaṙṙ ġlaṡ uaiḋ, aġuṡ ċonnaiṙc ṙé caiṙleán, aġuṡ duḃaiṙt ṙé, "an ṡaṫaċ atá ann ṡan ġ-caiṙleán ṡin, iṡ deaṙ-
ḃṙáṫaiṙ do'n ṡaṫaċ a ṙaḃamaṙ aṙéiṙ aiġe, aġuṡ béiḋmíd
ann ṡan ġ-caiṙleán ṡin anoċt." Ṫáiniġ ṙiad, aġuṡ d'ḟáġ
ṙé mac ṙíġ Éireann aġuṡ a ṁuinntiṙ aġ ceann an ḃóṫaiṙ,
aġuṡ ċuaiḋ ṙé ċum an ċaiṙleáin, aġuṡ ṫaṙṙaing ṙé an
cuaille cómṗaic, aġuṡ níoṙ ḟáġ ṙé leanḃ i mnaoi ná
ṙeaṙṙaċ i ġ-capall ná piġin i muic ná bṙoc i nġleann, i
ḃṙoiġṙe ṙeaċt míle ḋó, náṙ ḃain ṙé tṙí iompóḋ aṙta leiṙ
an méaḋ toṙain a ṫuġ ṙé aṙ an ġ-cuaille cómṗaic.

Ṫáiniġ an ṡaṫaċ amaċ, aġuṡ duḃaiṙt ṙé, "Moṫuiġim
bolaḋ an Éireannaiġ ḃinn ḃṙeuġaiġ ṡaoi m'ḟóiḋin dúṫaiġ."

"Ní Éireannaċ binn ḃṙeuġaċ miṡe," aṙ ṙan ṡeaṙ ġeaṙṙ
ġlaṡ, "aċt tá mo ṁáiġiṡtiṙ amuiġ ann ṡin aġ ceann an
ḃóṫaiṙ, aġuṡ má ṫaġann ṙé baiṙṙúḋ ṙé an ceann díot."

"Iṡ móṙ liom ḃe ġṙeim tu, aġuṡ iṡ beaġ liom de ḃá
ġṙeim tu "aṙ ṡan ṡaṫaċ.

"Ní ḃṙuiġṙiḋ tu mé de ġṙeim aiṙ biṫ," aṙ ṡan ṡeaṙ ġeaṙṙ
ġlaṡ, aġuṡ ṫoiṙiġ ṙé aġ meuḋuġaḋ ġo ṙaiḃ ṙé ċoṁ móṙ
leiṙ an ġ-caiṙleán.

Ṫáiniġ ṡaitċíoṡ aiṙ an ḃṙaṫaċ aġuṡ duḃaiṙt ṙé,
"bṙuil do ṁáiġiṡtiṙ ċoṁ móṙ leat-ṡa?"

"Tá aġuṡ níoṡ mó," aṙ ṡan ṡeaṙ beaġ ġlaṡ.

"Cuiṙ i bṙolaċ mé ġo maiḋin ġo n-imṫiġeann do
ṁáiġiṡtiṙ," aṙ ṡan ṡaṫaċ, "aġuṡ ṙud aiṙ biṫ atá tu aġ
iaṙṙaiḋ caiṫṙúḋ tu a ḟáġail."

Ṫuġ ṙé an ṡaṫaċ leiṙ, aġuṡ ċaiṫ ṙé ṡaoi ḃeul daḃaiċ
é. Ċuaiḋ ṙe amaċ aġuṡ ṫuġ ṙé aṙteaċ mac ṙíġ Éireann,
an ġunnaiṙe, an cluaṡaiṙe, an ṙéiḋiṙe, an coiṙṙe, aġuṡ
ṡeaṙ bṙuṙte na ġ-cloċ le taoiḃ a ṫóna, aġuṡ ċaiṫ ṙiad
au oiḋċe ann ṡin, tṙian le ṙiannuiġeaċt tṙian le ṙġeu-

March wind that was before them, and the March wind that was behind them would not overtake them, going to the eastern world. When evening and the end of the day came, the king of Ireland's son looked from him, and he did not see any house in which he might be that night. The short green man looked from him, and he saw a castle, and he said : "The giant that is in that castle is the brother of the giant with whom we were last night, and we shall be in this castle to-night.' They came to the castle, and he left the king's son and his people at the head of the avenue, and he went to the door and pulled the *coolaya-coric*, and he did not leave child with woman, foal with mare, pigeen with pig, or badger in glen, within seven miles of him, that he did not knock three turns out of them with all the sound he knocked out of the *coolaya-coric*.

The giant came out, and he said, "I feel the smell of a melodious lying Irishman under my sod of country. "

"No melodious lying Irishman am I," says the short green man ; " but my master is outside at the head of the avenue, and if he comes he will whip the head off you."

"I think you large of one mouthful, and I think you small of two mouthfuls," said the giant.

"You won't get me of a mouthful at all," said the short green man, and he began swelling until he was as big as the castle. There came fear on the giant, and he said :

"Is your master as big as you ?"

" He is, and bigger."

" Hide me," said the giant, " till morning, until your master goes, and anything you will be wanting you must get it."

He brought the giant with him, and he put him under

laiġeaċt, aguſ cuan le ſoipin ſáṁ ſuain aguſ ſíop-
ċoḋalta, ɼo ḋtí an ṁaiḋin.

Aip maiḋin, lá aip na ṁápaċ, tuɼ an ſeap ɼeapp ɼlaſ
mac ríġ Éireann aguſ a ṁuinntip amaċ aſ an ɼ-caiſleán
aguſ ḋ'ſáɼ ſé aɼ ceann an ḃótaip iaḋ, aguſ táiniɼ ſé
ſéin aip aip aguſ ḋ'iaſp ſé na ſean-ſlipéapaiḋ a ḃí ſaoi
ċolḃa an leaḃuiḋ, aip an ḃſaċaċ. Duḃaipt an ſaċaċ ɼo
ḋtiúḃpaḋ ſé péipe ḃútaip ċoṁ maiṫ aguſ ċaiṫ ſé apuaṁ
ḋ'a ṁáiɼiptip, aguſ caḋ é an maiṫ a ḃí ann ſna ſean-
ſlipéapaiḃ! Duḃaipt an ſeap ɼeapp ɼlaſ muna ḃſáɼaḋ
ſé na ſlipeapaiḋ ɼo ſaċſaḋ ſé i ɼ-coinne a ṁáiɼiptip,
leiſ an ceann ḋo ḃaint ḋé. Duḃaipt an ſaċaċ ann ſin
ɼo ḋtiúḃpaḋ ſé ḋó iaḋ, aguſ tuɼ. "Am aip ḃiṫ," aſ ſeiſean, "a ċuipſeaſ tu na ſlipeapaiḋ ſin opt, aguſ "haiɼ
óiḃip" ḋo ſáḋ, áit aip ḃiṫ a ḃſuil ſúil aɼaḋ ḋo ḋul ann,
béiḋ tu innti."

D'imṫiɼ mac ríġ Éireann aguſ an ſeap ɼeapp ɼlaſ,
aguſ an ɼunnaipe, aguſ an cluaſaipe, aguſ an coippe
aguſ an ſéiḋipe, aguſ ſeap ḃpipte na ɼ-cloċ le taoiḃ a
tóna, ɼo ḋtáiniɼ tpaṫnóna aguſ ḋeipeaḋ an laé; aguſ
ɼo paiḃ ancapall aɼ ḋul ſaoi ſɼáṫ na copóiɼe aguſ ní
ſanſaḋ an copóɼ leiſ. D'ſiaſpuiɼ mac ríġ Éireann ḋe'n
ſeap ɼeapp ɼlaſ ann ſin, cá ḃeiḋeaḋ ſiaḋ an oiḋċe ſin,
aguſ ḋuḃaipt an ſeap ɼeapp ɼlaſ ɼo mḃeiḋeaḋ ſiaḋ i
ḋteaċ ḋeapḃpátap an ſaċaiɼ aɼ a paiḃ ſiaḋ apeip.
Ḋeapc mac ríġ Éireann uaiḋ aguſ ni ſacaiḋ ſé ḋaḋaṁ.
Ḋeapc an ſeap ɼeapp ɼlaſ uaiḋ aguſ ċonnaipc ſé
caiſleán móp. D'ſáɼḃaiɼ ſé mac ríġ Éireann aguſ a
ṁuinntip ann ſin aguſ ċuaiḋ ſé ċum an ċaiſleáin leiſ
ſéin, aguſ ċappuiinɼ ſé an cuaille cóṁpaic, aguſ níop
ſáɼḃaiɼ ſé leanḃ i mnaoi, ſeappaċ i láip, piɼín i muic, na
bpoc i nɼleann, nóp ċionntuiɼ ſé tapt tpí uaipe leiſ
an méaḋ topain a ḃain ſé aſ an ɼ-cuaille cóṁpaic.
Táiniɼ an ſaċaċ amaċ aguſ ḋuḃaipt ſé "moṫuiɼim

the mouth of a *douac* (great vessel of some sort). He went out and brought in the son of the king of Ireland, the gunman, the earman, the footman, the blowman, and the man who broke stones with the side of his thigh, and they spent that night, one-third of it telling Fenian stories, one-third telling tales, and one-third in the mild enjoyment of slumber and of true sleep until morning.

In the morning, the day on the morrow, the short green man brought the king's son and his people out of the castle, and left them at the head of the avenue, and he went back himself and asked the giant for the old slippers that were left under the head of his bed.

The giant said that he would give his master a pair of boots as good as ever he wore ; and what good was there in the old slippers ?

The short green man said that unless he got the slippers he would go for his master to whip the head off him.

Then the giant said that he would give them to him, and he gave them.

" Any time," said he, " that you will put those slippers on you, and say 'high-over !' any place you have a mind to go to, you will be in it."

The son of the king of Ireland, the short green man, the gunman, the earman, the footman, the blowman, and the man who broke stones with the side of his thigh, went forward until evening came, and the end of the day, until the horse would be going under the shade of the docking, and the docking would not wait for him. The king's son asked the short green man where should they be that night, and the short green man said that they would be in the house of the brother of the giant with whom they spent the night before. The king's son looked from him and he saw nothing. The short green man looked from him and he saw a

4

boladh an Éireannaig binn breugaig faoi m'ḟóidín dú-
taig."

"Ní Éireannać binn breugać mire," ar ran fear
gearr glar, "ać tá mo ṁáigirtir 'nna fearaṁ ann rin,
ag ceann an búṫair, agur má ṫagann ré bainfiú ré an
ceann díot."

Agur leir rin ṫoruig an fear gearr glar ag méadu-
gaḋ go raiḃ ré coṁ mór leir an g-cairleán faoi ṫeireaḋ.

Ṫáinig faiṫćior air an ḃfaṫać, agur duḃairt ré, "ḃfuil
do ṁáigirtir ćoṁ mór leat féin?"

"Tá," ar ran fear gearr glar, "agur níor mó."

"O cuir mé a ḃfolać, cuir me i ḃfolać," ar ran faṫać,
"go n-imṫigeann do ṁáigirtir, agur rud air biṫ a béiḋear
tu ag iarraiḋ caiṫfiḋ tu a ḟágail."

Ṫug ré an faṫać leir agur cuir ré faoi ḃeul dabaiċ é,
agur glar air.

Ṫáinig ré air air agur ṫug ré mac ríg Éireann, an
gunnaire, an cluaraire, an coirire, an réidire, agur
fear bririte na g-cloć le taoiḃ a ṫóna airteać leir,
agur ćaiṫ riad an oiḋće rin go rúgać, trian dí le
riannuigeaċt, agur trian dí le rgeuluigeaċt, agur trian
dí le roirir ráiṁ ruain agur fíor ċodalta.

Air maidin, lá air na ṁárać, ṫug ré mac ríg Éireann
agur a ṁuinntir amać agur d'ḟágḃuig ré ag ceann an
búṫair iad agur ṫáinig ré féin air air, agur leig ré
amać an faṫać, agur duḃairt re leir an ḃfaṫać an cloi-
ḋeaṁ meirrgeać a bí faoi ċolḃa a leabuiḋ do ṫaḃairt dó.

great castle. He left the king's son and his people there, and he went to the castle by himself, and he drew the *coolaya-coric*, and he did not leave child with woman, foal with mare, pigeen with pig, or badger in glen, but he turned them over three times with all the sound he struck out of the *coolaya-coric*. The giant came out, and he said: "I feel the smell of a melodious lying Irishman under my sod of country."

"No melodious lying Irishman am I," said the short green man; "but my master is standing at the head of the avenue, and if he comes he shall strike the head off you."

And with that the short green man began swelling until he was the size of the castle at last. There came fear on the giant, and he said: "Is your master as big as yourself?"

"He is," said the short green man, "and bigger."

"Oh! put me in hiding; put me in hiding," said the giant, "until your master goes; and anything you will be asking you must get it."

He took the giant with him, and he put him under the mouth of a *douac*, and a lock on him. He came back, and he brought the king of Ireland's son, the gunman, the earman, the footman, the blowman, and the man who broke stones with the side of his thigh, into the castle with him, and they spent that night merrily—a third of it with Fenian tales, a third of it with telling stories, and a third of it with the mild enjoyment of slumber and of true sleep.

In the morning, the day on the morrow, he brought the son of the king of Ireland out, and his people with him, and left them at the head of the avenue, and he came back himself and loosed out the giant, and said to him, that he must give him the rusty sword that was

Oubaıрc an ɼасас nаċ осıúbрaʋ ɼé an ɼеаn-сlоıʋеaṁ ɼın o' аоn ouınе, аċс ʒо осıúbрaʋ ɼé ʋó сlоıʋеaṁ nа срı ɼаоbaр, náр ɼáʒ ɼuıʒеal buılle 'nnа ʋıaıʒ, аʒuɼ ʋá bɼáʒ-ɼаʋ ɼé ʒо осıubрaʋ ɼé leıɼ an oaɼа buılle é.

"Nı ʒlaсɼaıʋ mé ɼın," aɼ ɼan ɼеaɼ ʒеaɼɼ ʒlaɼ, "саıċɼıʋ mé an сlоıʋеaṁ mеıрʒеaċ ɼáʒaıl, аʒuɼ munа bɼáʒ' mé é ɼаċɼаıʋ mе ı ʒ-соmnе mo ṁáıʒıɼсıɼ аʒuɼ baıɼɼıʋ ɼé an сеann ʋіос."

"Іɼ ɼеaɼɼ oam a ċabaıрс ouіс," aɼ ɼan ɼасас, "аʒuɼ сıa bé áıс a buaılɼеaɼ cu buılle leıɼ an ʒ-сlоıʋеaṁ ɼın ɼаċɼаıʋ ɼé ʒо ouí an ʒaınеaṁ ʋá mbuıʋ ıaɼann a bı ɼоıṁе." Cuʒ ɼé an сlоıʋеaṁ mеıрʒеaċ ʋó ann ɼın.

Cuaıʋ mac ɼíʒ Eıреann аʒuɼ an ɼеaɼ ʒеaɼɼ ʒlaɼ, аʒuɼ an ʒunnaıре, аʒuɼ an сluaɼaıре, аʒuɼ an соıɼɼе, аʒuɼ an ɼéıʋıре, аʒuɼ ɼеaɼ bɼıɼсе nа ʒ-сlоċ le саоıb a ċónа ann ɼın, ʒо осáının срaċnónа аʒuɼ ʋеıреaʋ an laé, ʒо ɼaıb an сapall аʒ oul ɼаоı ɼʒáċ nа сuɼóıʒе аʒuɼ nı ɼanɼaʋ an ċоɼóʒ leıɼ. Nı béaɼɼaʋ an ʒaoċ Máɼса a bı ɼоmpa оɼɼа аʒuɼ an ʒaoċ Máɼса a bı 'nnа noıaıʒ nı ɼuʒ ɼı оɼɼа-ɼan, аʒuɼ bı ɼıaʋ an oıʋċе ɼın ann ɼan oоṁan ɼоıɼ, an áıс a ɼaıb an bеan-uaɼal.

O' ɼıaɼɼuıʒ an bеan oе mac ɼíʒ Eıреann сɼеuʋ oo bı ɼé аʒ ıaɼɼaıʋ аʒuɼ oubaıрc ɼеıреan ʒо ɼaıb ɼé аʒ ıaɼɼaıʋ íɼéın maɼ ṁnaoı. "Саıċɼıʋ cu m'ɼáʒaıl," aɼ ɼıɼе, "má ɼuaɼʒlann cu mo ʒеaɼɼa ʋіom."

Fuaıɼ ɼé a lóıɼсın le nа ċuıʋ buaċaıll ann ɼan ʒ-саıɼleán an oıʋċе ɼın, аʒuɼ ann ɼan oıʋċе ċáını ɼıɼе аʒuɼ oubaıрc leıɼ, "ɼеó ɼоɼúɼ аʒao, аʒuɼ munа bɼuıl an ɼоɼúɼ ɼın аʒao aıɼ maıoın amáɼaċ baınɼıʒеaɼ an сеann ʋіос."

under the corner of his bed. The giant said that he would not give that old sword to anyone, but that he would give him the sword of the three edges that never left the leavings of a blow behind it, or if it did, it would take it with the second blow.

"I won't have that," said the short green man, "I must get the rusty sword; and if I don't get that, I must go for my master, and he shall strike the head off you."

"It is better for me to give it to you," said the giant, "and whatever place you will strike a blow with that sword, it will go to the sand (*i.e.*, cut to the earth) though it were iron were before it." Then he gave him the rusty sword.

The son of the king of Ireland, the gunman, the ear-man, the footman, the blowman, and the man who broke stones with the side of his thigh, went forward after that, until evening came, and the end of the day, until the horse was going under the shade of the docking, and the docking would not wait for him. The March wind that was behind them would not overtake them, and they would overtake the wind of March that was before them, and they were that night (arrived) in the eastern world, where was the lady.

The lady asked the king of Ireland's son what it was he wanted, and he said that he was looking for herself as wife.

"You must get me," said she, "if you loose my geasa * off me."

He got lodging with all his servants in the castle that evening, and in the night she came and said to him, "Here is a scissors for you, and unless you have that scissors for me to-morrow morning, the head will be struck off you."

---

* Geasa, pronounced *gassi*, means "enchantment" in this place.

Cuir ʃí biorán-ʃuain faoi na ceann, aguʃ tuit ʃé
'nna chodladh, aguʃ chom luat aʃ tuit ʃé nna chodladh
ʃug ʃí an ʃorúp uaidh aguʃ d'fágbuig ʃí é. Tug ʃí an
ʃorúp do'n ʃíg mine, aguʃ dubairt ʃí leiʃ an ʃíg.
an ʃorúp do beit aige aʃ maidin di. D'imtig ʃí ann ʃin.
Nuair bi ʃí imtigte tuit an ʃíg mine 'nna chodladh
aguʃ nuair a bí ʃé 'nna chodladh táinig an fear geaʃ
glaʃ aguʃ na ʃean-ʃliréaʃaid aiʃ, aguʃ an birreud
aiʃ a ceann, aguʃ an clordeaṁ meirgeac ann a láiṁ,
aguʃ cia bé ait a d'fágbuig an ʃíg an ʃorúp fuaiʃ
ʃeiʃean é. Tug ʃé do ṁac ʃíg Éireann é, aguʃ nuair
táinig ʃiʃe aiʃ maidin d'fiaʃruig ʃí " a ṁic ʃíg Éireann
bfuil an ʃorúp agad ?"

"Tá," aʃ ʃeiʃean.

Bi tʃí ʃíce cloigionn na ndaoine a táinig 'gá h-iarraid
aiʃ ʃpicib timcioll an caiʃleáin aguʃ faoil ʃí go mbeidead
a clogionn aiʃ ʃpíce aici i g-cuideact leó.

An oidce, an lá aiʃ na ṁáraʃ, táinig ʃí aguʃ tug ʃí
ciaʃ dó, aguʃ dubairt ʃí leiʃ muna mbeidead an ciaʃ
aige aiʃ maidin nuair a tiucʃad ʃí go mbeidead an ceann
bainte dé. Cuir ʃí biorán-ʃuain faoi na ceann aguʃ tuit
ʃé 'nna chodladh maʃ tuit ʃé an oidce ʃoiṁe, aguʃ goid
ʃiʃe an ciaʃ léite. Tug ʃí an ciaʃ do'n ʃíg mine aguʃ
dubairt ʃí leiʃ gan an ciaʃ do caillead maʃ caill ʃé an
ʃorúp. Táinig an fear geaʃ glaʃ aguʃ na ʃean-ʃléiʃa-
ʃaid aiʃ a corʃaib, an ʃean-birreud aiʃ a ceann aguʃ an
clordeaṁ meirgeac ann a láiṁ, aguʃ ní facaid an ʃíg é
go dtáinig ʃe taob ʃiaʃ dé aguʃ tug ʃé an ciaʃ leiʃ
uaid.

Nuair táinig an maidin, dúiʃig mac ʃíg Éireann aguʃ
toʃuig ʃé ag caoinead na ciaʃe a bi imtigte uaid. " Ná

She placed a pin of slumber under his head, and he fell into his sleep, and as soon as he did, she came and took the scissors from him and left him there. She gave the scissors to the King of Poison,* and she desired the king to have the scissors for her in the morning. Then she went away. When she was gone the King of Poison fell into his sleep; and when he was in his sleep the short green man came, and the old slippers on him, and the cap on his head, and the rusty sword in his hand, and wherever it was the king had left the scissors out of his hand, he found it. He gave it to the king of Ireland's son, and when she (the lady) came in the morning, she asked: "Son of the king of Ireland, have you the scissors?"

"I have," said he.

There were three scores of skulls of the people that went to look for her set on spikes round about the castle, and she thought that she would have his head on a spike along with them.

On the night of the next day she came and gave him a comb, and said to him unless he had that comb for her next morning when she would come, that the head should be struck off him. She placed a pin of slumber under his head, and he fell into his sleep as he fell the night before, and she stole the comb with her. She gave the comb to the King of Poison, and said to him not to lose the comb as he lost the scissors. The short green man came with the old slippers on his feet, the old cap on his head, and the rusty sword in his hand; and the king did not see him until he came behind him and took away the comb with him.

When the king of Ireland's son rose up the next morning he began crying for the comb, which was gone

* Or "the King of N'yiv.

bac leir rin," ap ran feap geapp glar, "cá pé agam-ra."
Nuair táinig rire tug ré an ciap di, agur bi iongantar
uippi.

Táinig rí an tríomad oidce, agur dubaipt rí le mac pig
Eipeann an ceann do ciapad leir an g-ciap rin do beit
aige uí, ap maidin amárac. Noir," ap rire, "ni paib
baogal opt go dti anoct, agur má cailleann tu an t-am
ro i, tá do cloigionn imtigte."

Bi an biopán-ruain faoi na ceann, agur tuit ré
'nna cool ad. Táinig rire agur goid rí an ciap uaid.
Tug rí do'n pig mine i, agur dubaipt rí leir nár feud
an ciap imteact uaid no go mbampide an ceann dé."
Tug an pig mine an ciap leir, agur cuip ré artead i i
g-cappaig cloice, agur trí pice glar uippi, agur fand
an pig taoib amuig de na glaraib uile ag dopar na
cappaige, 'gá faire. Táinig an fear geapp glar, agur
na rlipeuraid agur an bippeud aip, agur an cloideam
meipgead ann a láim, agur buail ré buille aip an
g-cappaig cloice agur d'forgail ruar i, agur buail ré
an dapa buille aip an pig mine, agur bain ré an ceann
dé. Tug ré leir an ciap cuig (do) mac pig Eipeann ann
rin, agur fuair ré é ann a búireact, agur é ag caoinead
na ciapa. "Súd i do ciap duit," ap reirean, "tiucraid
rire aip ball, agur rarródaid rí úfot an bruil an ciap
agad, agur abaip léite go bruil, agur an ceann do
ciapad léite, agur cait cuici an cloigionn.

Nuair táinig rire ag rarruig an paib an ciap aige,
dubaipt ré go paib, agur an ceann do ciapad léite, agur
cait ré ceann an pig mine cuici.

Nuair connaipc rí an cloigionn bi fearg mór uippi, agur
dubaipt rí leir nac bruigread ré i le pórad go brágad
ró coippe a rúbalfad le na coippe féin i g-coinne trí
buideul na h-íocrláinte ar tobap an domain foip, agur

from him. "Don't mind that," said the short green man: "I have it." When she came he gave her the comb, and there was wonder on her.

She came the third night, and said to the son of the king of Ireland to have for her the head of him who was combed with that comb, on the morrow morning. "Now," said she, "there was no fear of you until this night ; but if you lose it this time, your head is gone."

The pin of slumber was under his head, and he fell into his sleep. She came and stole the comb from him. She gave it to the King of Poison, and she said to him that he could not lose it unless the head should be struck off himself. The King of Poison took the comb with him, and he put it into a rock of stone and three score of locks on it, and the king sat down himself outside of the locks all, at the door of the rock, guarding it. The short green man came, and the slippers and the cap on him, and the rusty sword in his hand, and he struck a stroke on the stone rock and he opened it up, and he struck the second stroke on the King of Poison, and he struck the head off him. He brought back with him then the comb to the king's son, and he found him awake, and weeping after the comb. "There is your comb for you," said he ; "she will come this now,* and she will ask you have you the comb, and tell her that you have, and the head that was combed with it, and throw her the skull."

When she came asking if he had the comb, he said he had, and the head that was combed with it, and he threw her the head of the King of Poison.

When she saw the head there was great anger on her, and she told him he never would get her to marry until he got a footman (runner) to travel with her runner for three bottles of the healing-balm out of the well of the

---

* An ordinary Connacht expression, like the Scotch " the noo."

vó mbuv luaite a táinig a coirpe féin 'ná an coirpe
oige-rean, go raib a ceann imtigte.

Fuair rí rean-cailleac (buitre éigin), agus tug rí trí
buiveula ói. Dubairt an fear gearr glar trí buiveula
vo tabairt vo'n fear a bí ag congbáil páirce na ngeirr-
riav, agus tugav vó iav. D'imtig an cailleac agus an
fear, agus trí buivéala ag gac aon aca, agus bí coirpe
mic ríg Éireann ag tígeact leat-ealaig air air, rul a
bí an cailleac imtigte leat-bealaig ag vul ann. "Suiv
ríor," ar ran cailleac leir an g-coirpe, "agus leig vo
rgít, tá an beirt aca pórta anoir, agus ná bí bpireav
vo croive ag rit." Tug rí léite cloigionn capaill agus
cuir rí raoi na ceann é, agus biorán-ruain ann, agus
nuair leag ré a ceann air, tuit ré 'nna covlav.

Vóirt ríre an t-uirge a bí aige amac, agus v'imtig rí.

b'rava leir an brear gearr glar go raib riav ag
tígeact, agus dubairt ré leir an g-clurraire, "Leag vo
clúar air an talam, agus reuc an bruil riav ag teáct."
"Cluinim," ar reirean, "an cailleac ag teáct, agus tá
an coirpe 'nna covlav, agus é ag rranurairtig."

"Veare uait," ar ran fear gearr glar leir an ngunnaire "go breicriv tu ca bruil an coirpe."

Dubairt an gunnaire go raib ré ann a leitiv rin v'áit,
agus cloigionn capaill raoi na ceann, agus é 'nna
covlav."

"Cuir vo gunna le vo rúil," ar ran fear gearr glar,
"agus cuir an cloigionn ó na ceann."

Cuir ré an gunna le na rúil agus rguaib ré an cloigionn
ó na ceann. Vúirig an coirpe, agus ruair ré na buiveula
a bí aige rolam, agus b'éigin vó rilleav cum an tobair
arír.

bí an cailleac ag teáct ann rin agus ní raib an coirpe le reiceál (reicrint). Ar ran fear gearr glar ann

western world ; and if her own runner should come back more quickly than his runner, she said his head was gone.

She got an old hag—some witch—and she gave her three bottles. The short green man bade them give three bottles to the man who was keeping the field of hares, and they were given to him. The hag and the man started, and three bottles with each of them ; and the runner of the king's son was coming back half way on the road home, while the hag had only gone half way to the well. " Sit down," said the hag to the foot-runner, when they met, " and take your rest, for the pair of them are married now, and don't be breaking your heart running." She brought over a horse's head and a slumber-pin in it, and laid it under his head, and when he laid down his head on it he fell asleep. She spilt out the water he had and she went.

The short green man thought it long until they were coming, and he said to the earman, " Lay your ear to the ground and try are they coming."

"I hear the hag a' coming," said he ; " but the foot-man is in his sleep, and I hear him a' snoring."

" Look from you," said the short green man to the gunman, " till you see where the foot-runner is."

The gunman looked, and he said that the footman was in such and such a place, and a horse's skull under his head, and he in his sleeping.

" Lay your gun to your eye," said the short green man, " and put the skull away from under his head."

He put the gun to his eye and he swept the skull from under his head. The footman woke up, and he found that the bottles which he had were empty, and it was necessary for him to return to the well again.

The hag was coming then, and the foot-runner was

rin, leir an bpear a bí ag cup an muilinn-gaoiċe ċapt
le na polláipe, "éipiġ puar agur peuċ an g-cuippeó an
ċailleaċ aip a h-aip." Cuip ré a meup aip a rpón agur
nuaip bí an ċailleaċ ag teaċt ċuip ré réipeóg gaoiċe
rúici a rguaib aip a h-aip í. Bí rí teaċt aprír agur pinne
ré an píio ceuona léiċe. Gaċ am a bíoeaó pire ag teaċt
a bpogar oúib oo bíoeaó peirean oá cup aip a h-aip aprír
leir an ngaoiċ oo réioeaó ré ar a polláipe. Aip oeipeaó
réio re leir an oá polláipe agur rguaib ré an ċailleaċ
ċum an oomain roip aprír. Táinig coirpe mac píg Eireann
ann rin, agur bí an lá rin gnóċuigċe.

Bí reapg móp aip an mnaoi nuaip ċonnaipc rí naċ oċái-
nig a coirpe rém aip aip i oturaċ, agur oubaipt rí le
mac píg Eireann, "ní bruiġriú tu mire anoir no go
púbailriú tu tpí míle gan bpóig gan rtoca, aip rnáċaioib
ċruaioe."

Bí lóċap aici tpí míle aip rao, agur rnáċaioe geupa
ċruaioe ċpaiċte aip, ċóm tiug leir an bpeur. Ap ran reap
geapp glar le reap-bpuiċte na g-cloċ le na leaċ-ċóm,
"téiú agur maol iao rin." Cuaió an reap rin oppa le
na leaċ-ċóm agur pinne ré rtumparó víob. Oubaipt an
reap geapp glar leir oul oppa le na ċóm vúbalta. Cuaió
ré oppa ann rin le na ċóm vúbalta, agur pinne ré
púġvap agur ppaireaċ víob. Táinig mac píg Eireann
agur rúbail ré na tpí míle, agur bí a bean gnóċuigċe
aige.

Pórraó an beipt ann rin, agur bí an ċéuo póg le rágail
ag an bpeap geapp glar. Rug an reap geapp glar an
bean leir rém airteaċ i reompa, agur ċorruig ré uippi.
Bí rí lán oe naiċpeaċaib mine, agur beiúeaó mac píg
Eireann mapb aca, nuaip a raċraó ré 'nna ċoolaó, aċt
gup pinc an reap geapp glar airti iao.

Táinig ré go mac píg Eireann ann rin, agur oubaipt ré
leir, "Tig leat oul le oo mnaoi anoir. Ir mire an reap

not to be seen. Says the short green man to the man who was sending round the windmill with his nostril: "Rise up and try would you put back that hag." He put his finger to his nose, and when the hag was coming he put a blast of wind under her that swept her back again. She was coming again, and he did the same thing to her. Every time she used to be coming near them he would be sending her back with the wind he would blow out of his nostril. At last he blew with the two nostrils and swept the hag back to the western world again. Then the foot-runner of the king of Ireland's son came, and that day was won.

There was great anger on the woman when she saw that her own foot-runner did not arrive first, and she said to the king's son: "You won't get me now till you have walked three miles, without shoes or stockings, on steel needles." She had a road three miles long, and sharp needles of steel shaken on it as thick as the grass, and their points up. Said the short green man to the man who broke stones with the side of his thigh: "Go and blunt those." That man went on them with one thigh, and he made stumps of them. He went on them with the double thigh, and he made powder and *prashuch* of them. The king of Ireland's son came and walked the three miles, and then he had his wife gained.

The couple were married then, and the short green man was to have the first kiss. The short green man took the wife with him into a chamber, and he began on her. She was full up of serpents, and the king's son would have been killed with them when he went to sleep, but that the short green man picked them out of her.

He came then to the son of the king of Ireland, and he told him, "You can go with your wife now. I am the man who was in the coffin that day, for whom you paid

a bí ann ʃan ʒ-cómpa an lá ʃin, a v'íoc ʇu na veiɕ
bpúnʇa aiʁ a ʃon, aʒuʃ an múinnʇiʁ ʁeó a bí leaʇ iʃ
ʁeiʁbíʃíʒe iaʋ ʋo ɕuiʁ Ʋia ɕuʒaʋ-ʃa."

Ʋ'imɕiʒ an ʃeaʁ ʒeaʁʁ ʒlaʃ aʒuʃ a múinnʇiʁ ann ʃin
aʒuʃ ní ʃacaiʋ macʁíʒ Éiʁeann apíʃ é. ʁuʒ ʃé a bean
abaile leiʃ, aʒuʃ ɕaiʇ ʃiaʋ beaɕa ʃona le céile.

———

an alp-luachra.

Bhí ʃeolóʒ ʃaiʋbiʁ a ʒ-Connaɕʇaib aon uaiʁ amáin, aʒuʃ
bí maoin ʒo leóʁ aiʒe, aʒuʃ bean maiɕ aʒuʃ muiʁiʒin
bʁeáʒ aʒuʃ ní ʁaib vaʋaiɕ aʒ cuʁ buaiʋʁeaʋ ná ʇʁiob-
lóiʋe aiʁ, aʒuʃ veaʁʁʃá ʃéin ʒo ʁaib ʃé 'nna ʃeaʁ compóʁ-
ʇamail ʁáʃʇa, aʒuʃ ʒo ʁaib an ʇ-áʋ aiʁ, cóm maiɕ aʒuʃ
aiʁ vuine aiʁ biɕ a bí beó. Bhí ʃé maʁ ʃin ʒan bʁón ʒan
buaiʋʁeaʋ aiʁ ʃeaʋ móʁáin bliaʋain i ʃláinʇe maiɕ aʒuʃ
ʒan ʇinneaʃ ná aiciʋ aiʁ ʃéin ná aiʁ a ɕloinn, no ʒo
vʇáiniʒ lá bʁeáʒ annʃan bʁóʒmaʁ, a ʁaib ʃé veaʃpeaʋ
aiʁ a ɕuiʋ vaoine aʒ veunaṁ ʃéiʁ annʃan moinʃeuʁ a bí
a n-aice le na ɕeaɕ ʃéin, aʒuʃ maʁ bí an lá ʁo ɕeiɕ v'ól
ʃé veoɕ bláɕaiɕe aʒuʃ ʃín ʃé é ʃéin ʁiaʁ aiʁ an bʃeuʁ úʁ
bainʇe, aʒuʃ maʁ bí ʃé ʁápuiʒɕe le ʇeaʃ an laé aʒuʃ
leiʃ an obaiʁ a bí ʃé aʒ veunaṁ, vo ɕuiʇ ʃé ʒan ṁoill
'nna ɕoʋlaʋ, aʒuʃ v'ʃan ʃé maʁ ʃin aiʁ ʃeaʋ ʇʁí no
ceiɕʁe uaiʁ no ʒo ʁaib an ʃeuʁ uile cʁapɕa aʒuʃ ʒo ʁaib
a ʋaoine oibʁe imɕiʒɕe aʁ an bpáiʁc.

Nuaiʁ ʋúiʃiʒ ʃé ann ʃin, ʃuiʋ ʃe ʃuaʃ aiʁ a ɕóin, aʒuʃ
ní ʁaib ʃioʁ aiʒe cia an áiʇ a ʁaib ʃé, no ʒuʁ ɕuiṁniʒ ʃe ʃaoi
 veiʁe ʒuʁ annʃan bpáiʁc aiʁ cúl a ɕiʒe ʃéin vo bí ʃé 'nna
luiʋe. V'éiʁiʒ ʃé ann ʃin aʒuʃ ɕuaiʋ ʃé aiʁ aiʁ cum a
ɕiʒe ʃéin, aʒuʃ aiʁ n-imɕeaɕʇ vó, ṁoɕaiʒ ʃé maʁ ʃian no

the ten pounds; and these people who are with you,
they are servants whom God has sent to you."

The short green man and his people went away then,
and the king of Ireland's son never saw them again.
He brought his wife home with him, and they spent a
happy life with one another.

———

THE ALP-LUACHRA.

THERE was once a wealthy farmer in Connacht, and he
had plenty of substance and a fine family, and there was
nothing putting grief nor trouble on him, and you would
say yourself that it's he was the comfortable, satisfied
man, and that the luck was on him as well as on e'er a
man alive. He was that way, without mishap or misfortune, for many years, in good health and without sickness or sorrow on himself or his children, until there
came a fine day in the harvest, when he was looking at
his men making hay in the meadow that was near his
own house, and as the day was very hot he drank a
drink of buttermilk, and stretched himself back on the
fresh cut hay, and as he was tired with the heat of the
day and the work that he was doing, he soon fell asleep,
and he remained that way for three or four hours, until
the hay was all gathered in and his workpeople gone
away out of the field.

When he awoke then, he sat up, and he did not know
at first where he was, till he remembered at last that it
was in the field at the back of his own house he was
lying. He rose up then and returned to his house,
and he felt like a pain or a stitch in his side. He made

maꞃ ġꞃeim ann a ḃoilg. Níoꞃ ċuiꞃ ꞃé ꞃuim ann, aċt ꞃuiꝺ
ꞃé ꞃíoꞃ ag an teine aguꞱ ċoꞃuig ꞃé 'gá ċéigeaꝺ ꝼéin.

"Cá ꞃaiḃ tu?" aꞃꞱ an ingean leiꞱ.

"Ḃhí mé mo ċoꝺlaꝺ," aꞃ ꞃeiꞃean, "aiꞃ 'an ḃꞃeuꞃ úꞃ
ann ꞃa' ḃꞃáꞃꞃ 'nna ꞃaiḃ ꞃiaꝺ ag ꝺeunaṁ an ꝼéiꞃ."

"Cꞃeuꝺ a ḃain ꝺuit," aꞃ ꞃiꞃꞱ, "ní ꝼéuċann tu go
maiṫ."

"Muꞃꞃe! maiꞃeaꝺ! ni'l ꝼioꞃ agam," aꞃ ꞃeiꞃean, "aċt
tá ꞃaitċioꞃ oꞃm go ḃꝼuil ꞃuꝺ éigin oꞃm, iꞱ aiꞃteaċ a
ṁoċaigim mé ꝼéin, ní ꞃaiḃ mé maꞃ ꞃin aꞃiaṁ ꞃoiṁe ꞃeó,
aċt béiꝺ mé níoꞱ ꞃeaꞃꞃ nuaiꞃ a ḃꝼuigꞃiꝺ mé ċoꝺlaꝺ
maiṫ."

Chuaiꝺ ꞃé ꝺ'á leaḃuiꝺ aguꞱ luiꝺ ꞃé ꞃíoꞃ, aguꞱ ċuit ꞃé
ann a ċoꝺlaꝺ, aguꞱ níoꞃ ḋúiꞱiġ ꞃé go ꞃaiḃ an ġꞃian áꞃꝺ.
Ꝺ'éꞃꞃiġ ꞃé ann ꞃin aguꞱ ꝺuḃaiꞃt a ḃean leiꞱ, "Cꞃeuꝺ ꝺo
ḃi oꞃt nuaiꞃ ꞃinn' tu coꝺlaꝺ ċoṁ ꝼaꝺa ꞃin?"

"Níl ꝼioꞃ agam," aꞃ ꞃeiꞃean.

Chuaiꝺ ꞃé annꞱan g-ciꞃteanaċ, n'áit a ḃi a ingean ag
ꝺeunaṁ cáca le h-aġaiꝺ an ḃꞃeáċ-ꝼaꞃt (biaꝺ na maiꝺne),
aguꞱ ꝺuḃaiꞃt ꞃiꞱe leiꞱ, "Cia an ċaoi ḃꝼuil tu anꝺiú, ḃꝼuil
aon ḃꞃeaċ oꞃt a Ʇtaiꞃ?"

"Ꝼuaiꞃ mé coꝺlaꝺ maiṫ," aꞃ ꞃeiꞃean, "aċt ni'l mé
bLaꞃ níoꞱ ꞃeaꞃꞃ 'ná ḃi mé aꞃéiꞃ, aguꞱ go ꝺeiṁin ꝺá
g-cꞃeiꝺꞱeá mé, ꞃaoilim go ḃꝼuil ꞃuꝺ éigin aꞱtiġ ionnam,
ag ꞃꞃċ anonn 'Ʇ anall ann mo ḃoilg o ċaoiḃ go taoiḃ."

"Aꞃa ní ꝼéiꝺiꞃ," aꞃ Ʇ an ingean, "iꞱ Ʇlaiġꝺeáꞃ a ꝼuaiꞃ
tu aꝺ' luiġe amuiġ ané aiꞃ an ḃꞃeuꞃ úꞃ, aguꞱ muna
ḃꝼuil tu níoꞱ ꞃeaꞃꞃ annꞱan tꞃaċꞃóna cuiꞃꞃꞱü ꝼioꞃ aiꞃ
an ꝺoċtúiꞃ."

nothing of it, sat down at the fire and began warming himself.

"Where were you?" says the daughter to him.

"I was asleep a while," says he, "on the fresh grass in the field where they were making hay."

"What happened to you, then?" says she, "for you don't look well."

"Muirya,* musha, then," says he, "I don't know; but it's queer the feeling I have. I never was like it before; but I'll be better when I get a good sleep."

He went to his bed, lay down, and fell asleep, and never awoke until the sun was high. He rose up then and his wife said to him: "What was on you that you slept that long?"

"I don't know," says he.

He went down to the fire where the daughter was making a cake for the breakfast, and she said to him:

"How are you to-day, father; are you anything better?"

"I got a good sleep," said he, "but I'm not a taste better than I was last night; and indeed, if you'd believe me, I think there's something inside of me running back and forwards."

"Arrah, that can't be," says the daughter, "but it's a cold you got and you lying out on the fresh grass; and if you're not better in the evening we'll send for the doctor."

* "Oh, Mary," or "by Mary," an expression like the French "dame!"

Ċáinig an tráċnóna, aċt bí an ouine boċt annran gcaoi ċeuona, agur b'éigin vóib rior ċur air an voċtúir. Bhi ré ag ráv go raib pian air, agur naċ raib fior aige go ceart cao é an áit ann a raib an pian, agur nuair naċ raib an voċtúir teaċt go luaṫ bí rgannruġav mór air. Bhi muinntir an tiġe ag veunam uile fóir v'ḟeua riao veunam le meirneaċ a ċur ann.

Ċáinig an voċtúir raoi veire, agur v'ḟiarruiġ ré vé creuv vo bí air, agur vubairt reirean air go raib riav éigin mar émin ag léimniġ ann a bolg. Noċtuiġ an voċtúir é agur rinne ré breaċnuġav maiṫ air, aċt ni facaiv ré vavam a bí ar an m-bealaċ leir. Chuir ré a ċluar le na ċaoib agur le na ṫraim, aċt níor ċualaiv ré riav air biṫ ċiv gó raib an ouine boċt é féin ag ráv—"Anoir! Noir! naċ g-cluinn tu é? Noir! naċ naċ bfuil tu 'g éirteaċt leir, ag léimniġ?" Aċt níor ċug an voċtúir riav air biṫ raoi veara, agur f'aoil ré raoi veire go raib an rear ar a ċéill, agur naċ raib vavam air.

Dubairt ré le mnaoi an tiġe nuair ċáinig ré amaċ, naċ raib aon riav air a rear, aċt gur ċreiv ré féin go raib ré tinn, agur go g-cuirreav ré vriuganna ċuige an lá air na máraċ a béarrav coolav maiṫ vó, agur a roċ-róċav tear a ċuirp. Rinne ré rin, agur ḟluig an ouine boċt na vriuganna uile agur ruair ré coolav mór air aċt nuair vúirġ ré air maivin bí ré níor meara 'ná 'riam, aċt vubairt ré náir ċualaiv ré an riav ag léimniġ taob artiġ vé anoir.

Chuir riav fior air an voċtúir air, agur ċáinig re aċt níor feuo ré riav air biṫ veunam. O'ḟág ré vriuganna eile leir an bfear, agur vubairt ré go vtiucrav ré air i g-ceann reaċṫmuine eile le na feicrint. Ni bruair an ouine boċt fóiriġin air biṫ ar an ḟág an voċtúir leir, agur nuair váinig an voċtúir air riar ruair ré é

He was saying then that there was a pain on him, but that he did not know rightly what place the pain was in. He was in the same way in the evening, and they had to send for the doctor, and when the doctor was not coming quickly there was great fright on him. The people of the house were doing all they could to put courage in him.

The doctor came at last, and he asked what was on him, and he said again that there was something like a *birdeen* leaping in his stomach. The doctor stripped him and examined him well, but saw nothing out of the way with him. He put his ear to his side and to his back, but he heard nothing, though the poor man himself was calling out: "Now! now! don't you hear it? Now, aren't you listening to it jumping?" But the doctor could perceive nothing at all, and he thought at last that the man was out of his senses, and that there was nothing the mattter with him.

He said to the woman of the house when he came out, that there was nothing on her husband, but that he believed himself to be sick, and that he would send her medicine the next day for him, that would give him a good sleep and settle the heat of his body. He did that, and the poor man swallowed all the medicines and got another great sleep, but when he awoke in the morning he was worse than ever, but he said he did not hear the thing jumping inside him any longer.

They sent for the doctor again, and he came; but he was able to do nothing. He left other medicines with them, and said he would come again at the end of a week to see him. The poor man got no relief from all that the doctor left with him, and when he came again he found him to be worse than before; but he was not

níoɾ meaɾa na ɾoiṁe ɾin; aċt níoɾ ḟeuɓ ɾé aon ɾuɓ ɓéanaṁ aguɾ ní ɾaiḃ ḟioɾ aiɾ biṫ aige caɓ é'n cineál tinniɾ
ɓo bí aiɾ. "Ní béiɓ mé aɢ glacaɓ ɓ'aiɾɢiɓ uait ḟeaɾta,"
aɾ ɾeiɾean, le mnaoi an tíġe, "maɾ naċ ɓtiɢ liom ɾuɓ
aiɾ biṫ ɓéanaṁ annɾan ɢ-cúiɾ ɾeó; aguɾ maɾ naċ
ɓtuiɢim cɾeuɓ atá aiɾ, ní leiɢfiɓ mé oɾm ó ɓo ċuiɢɾint.
Tiucɾaiɓ mé le na ḟeicɾint ó am ɢo h-am aċt ní ġlacɾaiɓ
mé aon aiɾɢioɓ uait."

Iɾ aiɾ éiɢin ɓ'ḟeuɓ an bean an ḟeaɾɢ ɓo bí uiɾɾi ɓo
ċonɢṁáil aɾteaċ. Nuaiɾ bí an ɓoċtúiɾ imṫiġte ċɾuinniġ
ɾí muinntiɾ an tiġe le ċéile aguɾ ġlac ɾiaɓ cóṁaiɾle,
"An ɓoċtúiɾ bɾaɓaċ ɾin," aɾ ɾiɾe, "ní ɾú tɾaiṫnín é.
Ḃfuil ḟioɾ aguiḃ cɾeuɓ ɓuḃaiɾt ɾé? naċ nɢlacɾaɓ ɾé
aon aiɾɢioɓ uainn ḟeaɾta, aguɾ ɓuḃaiɾt ɾé naċ ɾaiḃ
eólaɾ aiɾ biṫ aige aiɾ ɓaɓaṁ. "Suɾ," aiɾ! an bɾċeaṁnaċ!
ní tiucɾaiɓ ɾé taɾ an taiɾɾeaċ ɾó ɢo bɾáṫ. Ɍaċḟamaoiɓ
ɢo ɓtí an ɓoċtúiɾ eile, má tá ɾé níoɾ ḟaiɓe uainn, ḟéin, iɾ
cuma liom ɾin, caiṫɾimiɓ a ḟáġail." Ḃhi uile ɓuine a bí
annɾa teaċ aiɾ aon ḟocal léiṫe, aguɾ ċuiɾ ɾiaɓ ḟioɾ aiɾ
an ɓoċtúiɾ eile, aguɾ nuaiɾ táiniɢ ɾé ní ɾaiḃ aon eólaɾ
ɓo b' ḟeaɾɾ aige-ɾean 'ná ɓo bí aɢ an ɢ-ceuɓ-ɓoċtúiɾ aċt
aṁáin ɢo ɾaiḃ eólaɾ ɢo leóɾ aige aiɾ a n-aiɾɢioɓ ɓo
ġlacaɓ. Táiniɢ ɾé leiɾ an ɓuine tinn ɓ'ḟeicɾint, ɢo
minic, aguɾ ɢaċ am a táiniɢ ɾe ɓo bí ainm eile aige níoɾ
ḟaiɓe 'na a ċéile aiɾ a ṫinneaɾ, aimmneaċa (anmanna)
náɾ ċuiɢ ɾé ḟéin, ná ɓuine aiɾ biṫ eile, aċt bí ɾiaɓ aige le
ɾɢannɾuġaɓ na n-ɓaoine.

Ɓ'ḟan ɾiaɓ maɾ ɾin aiɾ ḟeaɓ ɓá ṁí, ɢan ḟioɾ aɢ ɓuine
aiɾ biṫ cɾeuɓ ɓo bí aiɾ an ḃḟeaɾ boċt, aguɾ nuaiɾ naċ
ɾaiḃ an ɓoċtúiɾ ɾin aɢ ɓéanaṁ maiṫ aiɾ biṫ ɓó, ḟuaiɾ
ɾiaɓ ɓoċtúiɾ eile, aguɾ ann ɾin ɓoċtúiɾ eile, no ɢo ɾaiḃ
uile ɓoċtúiɾ a bí annɾa' ɢ-conɓaċ aca, ḟaoi ɓeiɾe, aguɾ

able to do anything, and he did not know what sort of sickness was on him. "I won't be taking your money from you any more," says he to the woman of the house, "because I can do nothing in this case, and as I don't understand what's on him, I won't let on * to be understanding it. I'll come to see him from time to time, but I'll take no money from you."

The woman of the house could hardly keep in her anger. Scarcely ever was the doctor gone till she gathered the people of the house round her and they took counsel. "That doctor *braduch*," says she, "he's not worth a *trancen*; do you know what he said—that he wouldn't take any money from me any more, and he said himself he knew nothing about anything; *suf* on him, the *behoonuch*, he'll cross this threshold no more; we'll go to the other doctor; if he's farther from us, itself, I don't mind that, we must get him." Everybody in the house was on one word with her, and they sent for the other doctor; but when he came he had no better knowledge than the first one had, only that he had knowledge enough to take their money. He came often to see the sick man, and every time he would come he would have every name longer than another to give his sickness; names he did not understand himself, nor no one else but he had them to frighten the people.

They remained that way for two months, without anyone knowing what was on the poor man; and when that doctor was doing him no good they got another doctor, and then another doctor, until there was not a doctor in the county, at last, that they had not got, and they

---

* To "let on" is universally used in Connacht, and most parts of Ireland for to "pretend." It is a translation of the Irish idiom.

ċaill ṗiad a lán aiṗġid leó, aġuṗ b'éiġin dóiḃ cuid d'á
n-callaċ ḋíol le h-aiṗġiod ḟáġail le na n-íoc.

Ḃí ṗiad maṗ ṗin le leiṫ-ḃliaḋain aġ conġṁáil doċtuiṗ
leiṗ, aġuṗ na doċtúiṗiḃ aġ taḃaiṗt druġanna ḋó, aġuṗ
an duine boċt a ḃí ṗaṁaṗ beaṫaiġṫe ṗoiṁe ṗin, aġ
éiṗiġe lom aġuṗ tana, ġo naċ ṗaiḃ unṗa ḟeóla aiṗ, aċt
an cṗoicion aġuṗ na cnáṁa aṁáin.

Ḃí ṗé ṗaoi ḋeiṗe cóṁ dona ṗin ġuṗ aiṗ éiġin d'ḟeud ṗé
ṗúḃal, aġuṗ d'imṫiġ a ġoile uaiḋ, aġuṗ buḋ ṁóṗ an
ṫṗoḃloṗ leiṗ, ġṗeim aṗáin buiġ, no deoċ bainne úiṗ do
ṗluġaḋ aġuṗ ḃí uile ḋuine aġ ṗáḋ ġo m-b'ḟeaṗṗ dó báṗ
ḟáġail, aġuṗ buḋ ḃeaġ an t-ionġnaḋ ṗin, maṗ naċ ṗaiḃ
ann aċt maṗ beiḋeaḋ ṗġáile i mbuiḋeul.

Aon lá aṁáin, nuaiṗ ḃí ṗé 'nṗa ṗuiḋe aiṗ cáṫaoiṗ aġ
doṗaṗ an tiġe, 'ġá ġṗianuġaḋ ḟéin ann ṗan teaṗ, aġuṗ
muinntiṗ an tiġe uile imṫiġṫe amaċ, aġuṗ ġan duine ann
aċt é ḟéin, ċáiniġ ṗeanduine boċt a ḃí aġ iaṗṗaiḋ ḋéiṗce
o áit ġo h-áit ṗuaṗ ċum an doṗaiṗ, aġuṗ d'aiṫiġ ṗé ḟeaṗ
an tiġe 'nna ṗuiḋe annṗa' ġ-cáṫaoiṗ, aċt ḃí ṗé cóṁ
h-aṫṗuiġṫe ṗin aġuṗ cóṁ caiṫte ṗin ġuṗ aiṗ éiġin d'aiṫ-
neóċaḋ duine é. "Tá mé ann ṗó aṗiṗ aġ iaṗṗaiḋ ḋéiṗce
ann ainm Dé," aṗ an ḟeaṗ boċt, "aċt ġlóiṗ do Ḋia
a ṁáiġiṗtiṗ cṗeud do ḃain duit ní tuṗa an ḟeaṗ céudna
a ċonnaiṗc mé leiṫ-ḃliaḋain ó ṗoin nuaiṗ ḃí mé ann ṗó,
ġo ḃṗóinṗ Dia oiṗt."

"Aṗa a Sheumaiṗ," aṗ ṗan ḟeaṗ tinn, "iṗ miṗe naċ
ḃṗeudṗaḋ innṗint duit cṗeud do ḃain dam, aċt tá ḟioṗ
aġam aiṗ aon ṗud, naċ mbéiḋ mé ḃṗad aiṗ an t-ṗaoġal
ṗo."

"Aċt tá bṗón oṗm d'ḟeiċṗint maṗ tá tu," aṗ ṗan déiṗ-
ceaċ, "naċ dtiġ leat innṗint dam cia an éaoi aiṗ ṫoṗuiġ
ṗé leat? cṗeud a duḃaiṗt na doċtúiṗiḃ?"

"Na doċtúiṗiḃ!" aṗ ṗan ḟeaṗ tinn, "mo ṁallaċt
oṗṗa! ní'l ḟioṗ aiṗ dadaṁ aca, aċt ní cóiṗ dam beiṫ aġ

lost a power of money over them, and they had to sell a portion of their cattle to get money to pay them.

They were that way for half a year, keeping doctors with him, and the doctors giving him medicines, and the poor man that was stout and well-fed before, getting bare and thin, until at last there was not an ounce of flesh on him, but the skin and the bones only.

He was so bad at last that it was scarcely he was able to walk. His appetite went from him, and it was a great trouble to him to swallow a piece of soft bread or to drink a sup of new milk, and everyone was saying that he was better to die, and that was no wonder, for there was not in him but like a shadow in a bottle.

One day that he was sitting on a chair in the door of the house, sunning himself in the heat, and the people of the house all gone out but himself, there came up to the door a poor old man that used to be asking alms from place to place, and he recognised the man of the house sitting in the chair, but he was so changed and so worn that it was hardly he knew him. "I'm here again, asking alms in the name of God," said the poor man; "but, glory be to God, master, what happened to you, for you're not the same man I saw when I was here half a year ago; may God relieve you!"

"Arrah, Shamus," said the sick man, "it's I that can't tell you what happened to me; but I know one thing, that I won't be long in this world."

"But I'm grieved to see you how you are," said the beggarman. "Tell me how it began with you, and what the doctors say."

"The doctors, is it?" says the sick man, "my curse on them; but I oughtn't to be cursing and I so near the grave; *suf* on them, they know nothing."

caṛcuine aguṛ miṛe ċoṁ ḟogaṛ ṛin ḋom' ḃáṛ, "ṛúḟ" oṗṛa ní'l eólaṛ aiṛ biṫ aca."

"b'éiḋiṛ," aṛ ṛan ḋéiṛceaċ, "go ḃḟeuḋḟainn ḟéin biṛeaċ ṫaḃaiṛt ḋuit, ḋá n-inneóṛá ṫám cṛeuḋ atá oṛt. Deiṛ ṛiaḋ go mḃíḋim eólaċ aiṛ aicíḋiḃ, aguṛ aiṛ na luiḃeannaiḃ atá maiṫ le na leiġeaṛ."

Rinne an ḟeaṛ tinn gáiṛe. "Ní'l ḟeaṛ-leiġiṛ ann ṛa' g-conḋaé," aṛ ṛé, "naċ ṛaiḃ ann ṛó liom ; naċ ḃḟuil leaṫ an callaiġ a ḃí agam aiṛ an ḃḟeilm ḋíolta le na n-íoc ! aċt ní ḃḟuaṛ mé ṛóṛṛiġin ḋá laġaḋ ó ḋuine aiṛ biṫ aca, aċt inneóṛaiḋ mé ṫuit-ṛe maṛ ḋ'éiṛiġ ṛé ṫam aiṛ ḋtúṛ." Aguṛ ann ṛin ṫug ṛé cúntaṛ ḋó aiṛ uile ṗian a ṁoṫuiġ ṛé, aguṛ aiṛ uile ṛuḋ a ḋ'oṛḋuiġ na ḋoéctúṛiḋ.

D'éiṛt an ḋéiṛceaċ leiṛ go cúṛamaċ, aguṛ nuaiṛ ċṛíoċ- nuiġ ṛé an ṛgeul uile, ḋ'ḟiaṛṛuiġ ṛé ṫé, "caḋ é an ṛóṛt páiṛce í aiṛ aṛ ṫuit tu ḋo ċoḋlaḋ?"

"Iṛ móinḟeuṛ a ḃí ann," aṛ ṛan ḋuine tinn, "aċt ḃí ṛé go ḋíṛeaċ bainte, ann ṛan am ṛin."

"Raiḃ ṛé ḟliuċ," aṛṛ an ḋéiṛceaċ.

"Ní ṛaiḃ," aṛ ṛeiṛean.

"Raiḃ ṛṛoċán uiṛge no caiṛe a' ṛit ċṛíoṛ?" aṛṛ an ḋéiṛceaċ.

"bhi," aṛ ṛeiṛean.

"An ḋtig liom an páiṛc ḟeicṛint?"

"Tig go ḋeiṁin, aguṛ taiṛḃéunḟaiḋ mé ṫuit anoiṛ é."

D'éiṛiġ ṛé aṛ a ċáṫaoiṛ aguṛ ċoṁ ḋona aguṛ ḃí ṛé, ṛtṛáċ- ail ṛé é ḟéin aiṛ aġaiḋ, no go ḋtáinig ṛé ċum na h-áite ann aiṛ luiḋ ṛé 'nna ċoḋlaḋ an tṛaṫnóna ṛin. Bḃṛeaṫ- nuiġ ḟeaṛ-na-ḋéiṛce aiṛ an áit, tamall ḟaḋa, aguṛ ann ṛin ċṛom ṛé aiṛ an ḃḟeuṛ aguṛ ċuaiḋ ṛé anonn 'ṛ anall aguṛ a ċoṛṛ lúḃta aguṛ a ċeann cṛomta ag ṛmeuṛṫaċt ann ṛna luiḃeannaiḃ, aguṛ amcaṛg an luiḃeaṛnaiġ ḋo ḃí ag ḟáṛ go tiuġ ann.

D'éiṛiġ ṛé ḟaoi ḋeiṛe, aguṛ ḋubaiṛt ṛé, "Tá ṛé maṛ ḟaoil mé," aguṛ ċṛom ṛé é ḟéin ṛíoṛ aṛíṛ, aguṛ ṫoṛuiġ

" Perhaps," says the beggerman, " I could find you a relief myself, if you were to tell me what's on you. They say that I be knowledgable about diseases and the herbs to cure them."

The sick man smiled, and he said: "There isn't a medicine man in the county that I hadn't in this house with me, and isn't half the cattle I had on the farm sold to pay them. I never got a relief no matter how small, from a man of them ; but I'll tell you how it happened to me first." Then he gave him an account of everything he felt and of everything the doctors had ordered.

The beggarman listened to him carefully, and when he had finished all his story, he asked him : " What sort of field was it you fell asleep in ? "

"A meadow that was in it that time," says the sick man ; " but it was just after being cut."

" Was it wet," says the beggarman.

" It was not," said he.

" Was there a little stream or a brook of water running through it?" said the beggarman.

" There was," says he.

" Can I see the field ? "

" You can, indeed, and I'll show it to you."

He rose off his chair, and as bad as he was, he pulled himself along until he came to the place where he lay down to sleep that evening. The beggarman examined the place for a long time, and then he stooped down over the grass and went backwards and forwards with his body bent, and his head down, groping among the herbs and weeds that were growing thickly in it.

He rose at last and said : " It is as I thought," and he stooped himself down again and began searching as be-

aʒ cuaptuʒaḋ map poiṁe pin. Tóʒ pé a ċeann an ḋapa
uaip, aʒup ḃí luiḃ ḃeaʒ ʒlap ann a láiṁ. "An ḃpeiceann
tu pin," ap pé, " áit aip biḋ ann Éipinn a ḃpáʒann an luiḃ
peó ann, bíonn alp-luaċpa anaice leip, aʒup ƒluiʒ tu
alp-luaċpa."

"Caḋ é an ċaoi ḃƒuil píop aʒaḋ pin?" app an ḋuine
tinn, "ḋá mbuḋ map pin ḋo ḃí pe, ip ḋóiʒ ʒo n-inneúpaḋ
na ḋoċtúipiḋ ḋam é poiṁe peo."

"Ʒo ḋtuʒaiḋ Dia ciall ḋuit, na bac leip na ḋoċtúipiḃ,"
app an ḋéipceaċ, "ni'l ionnta aċt callta amaḋán. A
ḋeipim leat ap p, aʒup cpeiḋ mipe, ʒup Alp-luaċpa a
ƒluiʒ tu; naċ ḋuḃaipt tu féin ʒup ṁoċuiʒ tu puḋ éiʒin
aʒ léimniʒ ann ḋo ḃolʒ an ċéaḋ lá 'péip tu ḃeit tinn.
Ḃ'é pin an alp-luaċpa, aʒup map ḋo ḃí an áit pin ann
ḋo ḃolʒ pcpaipceupaċ leip i ḋtopaċ, ḃí pé mí-ƒuaiṁneaċ
innti, aʒ ḋul anonn'p anall, aċt nuaip ḃí pé cúpla lá innti,
ƒocuiʒ pé é féin, aʒup puaip pé an áit compóptaṁail
aʒup pin é an t-áḋḃap pá ḃƒuil tu aʒ conʒṁáil ċoṁ tana
pin: map uile ʒpeim ḋ'á ḃƒuil tu aʒ iċe bíonn an alp-
luaċpa pin aʒ páʒail an ṁait ap. Aʒup ḋuḃaipt tu féin
liom ʒo paiḃ ḋo leat-taoḃ aċta, ip í pin an taoḃ 'n áit a
ḃƒuil an puḋ ʒpánna 'nna ċóṁnuiḋe."

Ṁop ċpeiḋ an feap é, a ḋtopaċ, aċt lean an ḋéipceaċ
ḋá ċóṁpáḋ leip, aʒ cpuṫuʒaḋ ḋó, ʒup b' é an ƒípinne a
ḃí pé aʒ páḋ, aʒup nuaip táiniʒ a ḃean aʒup a iŋean aip
aip apíp ḋo'n teaċ, laḃaip pé leó-pan an ċaoi ċeuḋna
aʒup ḃí piaḋ péiḋ ʒo leóp le na ċpeiḋeaṁaint.

Níop ċpeiḋ an ḋuine tinn, é féin, é, aċt ḃí piaḋ uile aʒ
laḃaipt leip, ʒo ḃƒuaip piaḋ buaiḋ aip, paoi ḋeipe; aʒup
tuʒ pé ceaḋ ḋóiḃ tpí ḋoċtúipḋe ḋo ʒlaoḋaċ apteaċ le
ċéile, ʒo n-inneópaḋ pe an pʒeul nuaḋ po ḋóiḃ. Táiniʒ
an tpiúp le ċéile, aʒup nuaip ḋ'éipt piaḋ leip an méaḋ
a ḃí an ḋéipceaċ aʒ páḋ, aʒup le cóṁpáḋ na mban,
pinne piaḋ ʒáipe aʒup ḋuḃaipt piaḋ naċ paiḃ ionnta aċt

fore. He raised his head a second time, and he had a little green herb in his hand. "Do you see this?" said he. "Any place in Ireland that this herb grows, there be's an alt-pluachra near it, and you have swallowed an alt-pluachra."

"How do you know that?" said the sick man. "If that was so, sure the doctors would tell it to me before now."

"The doctors!" said the beggarman. "Ah! God give you sense, sure they're only a flock of *omadawns*. I tell you again, and believe me, that it's an alt-pluachra you swallowed. Didn't you say yourself that you felt something leaping in your stomach the first day after you being sick? That was the alt-pluachra; and as the place he was in was strange to him at first, he was uneasy in it, moving backwards and forwards, but when he was a couple of days there, he settled himself, and he found the place comfortable, and that's the reason you're keeping so thin, for every bit you're eating the alt-pluachra is getting the good out of it, and you said yourself that one side of you was swelled; that's the place where the nasty thing is living."

The sick man would not believe him at first, but the beggarman kept on talking and proving on him that it was the truth he was saying, and when his wife and daughter came back again to the house, the beggarman told them the same things, and they were ready enough to believe him.

The sick man put no faith in it himself, but they were all talking to him about it until they prevailed on him at last to call in three doctors together until he should tell them this new story. The three came together, and when they heard all the *boccuch* (beggarman) was saying, and all the talk of the women, it is what they laughed, and

amaoáin uile go léir, aguf gurb'é rud eile amaċ 'r amaċ
a bi air fear-an-tiġe, aguf gaċ ainm a bi aca air a ċin-
neaf an t-am fo, bí fé oá uair, 'r trí huaire níor faioe 'ná
roime fin. O'fág fiao buioéul no cúpla buioeul le n-ól
ag an bfear boċt, aguf o'imċiġ fiao leó, ag magaó faoi
an rud a oubairt na mná gur fluig fé an alp-luaċra.

Oubairt an óéirceaċ nuair bí fiao imċiġċe. "Ni'l
iongantaf air biċ orm naċ bfuil tu fágail beirġ má'r
amaoáin mar iao fin atá leat. Ni'l aon ooctúir ná
fear-leiġif i n-Éirinn anoif a ċeanfaf aon maiṫ ċuit-fe
aċt aon fear amáin, aguf if fé fin Mac Diarmaoa,
Prionnfa Chúil-Ui-Bfinn air brúaċ Loċa-Ui-Ġeaóra
an ooctúir if fearr i g-Connaċtaib ná 'ma cúig cúigib.
"Cá bfuil Loċ-Ui-Ġeaóra?" arf an ouine tinn. "Shíor
i g-conoaé Shligiġ; if loċ mór é, aguf tá an Prionnfa
'ma ċómnuióe air a brúaċ," ar fé, "aguf má ġlacann
tu mo ċómairle-fe raċfaió tu ann, mar 'r é an caoi
óeireannaċ atá agao, aguf buó ċóir ouit-fe, a máiġif-
treaf," ar fé ag tiontóú le mnaoi an tiġe, "oo ċur iaċ
(o'fiaċaib) air, oul ann, má'r maiṫ leat o'fear a beiṫ
beó."

"Maireaó," arf an bean, "óeunfainn rud air biċ a
flánóċaó é."

"Mar fin, cuir go oti Prionnfa Chúil-Ui-Bfinn é,"
ar feirean.

"Oheunfainn féin rud air biċ le mo flánuġaó," arf an
fear tinn "mar tá'f agam naċ bfuil a bfao agam le
mairtain air an t-faoġal fo, muna noeuntar rud éigin
oam a ċearfaf conġnaṁ aguf fóiriġin oam."

"Mar fin, téió go oti an Prionnfa," ar fan óéirceaċ.

"Rud air biċ a meafann tu go noeunfaió fé maiṫ ċuit
buó ċóir ċuit a ċeanaṁ, a ataif," arf an inġean.

"Ni'l oaoaṁ le óéanaṁ maiṫ óó aċt oul go oti an
Prionnfa," arf an óéirceaċ.

said they were fools altogether, and that it was something else entirely that was the matter with the man of
the house, and every name they had on his sickness this
time was twice—three times—as long as ever before.
They left the poor man a bottle or two to drink, and they
went away, and they humbugging the women for saying
that he had swallowed an alt-pluachra.

The boccuch said when they were gone away: "I
don't wonder at all that you're not getting better, if
it's fools like those you have with you. There's not a
doctor or a medicine-man in Ireland now that'll do you
any good, but only one man, and that's Mac Dermott
the Prince of Coolavin, on the brink of Lough Gara, the
best doctor in Connacht or the five provinces."

"Where is Lough Gara?" said the poor man.

"Down in the County Sligo," says he; "it's a big
lake, and the prince is living on the brink of it; and if
you'll take my advice you'll go there, for it's the last hope
you have; and you, Mistress," said he, turning to the
woman of the house, "ought to make him go, if you
wish your man to be alive."

"Musha!" says the woman, "I'd do anything that
would cure him."

"If so, send him to the Prince of Coolavin," says he.

"I'd do anything at all to cure myself," says the sick
man, "for I know I haven't long to live on this world
if I don't get some relief, or without something to be
done for me."

"Then go to the Prince of Coolavin," says the beggarman.

"Anything that you think would do yourself good,
you ought to do it father," says the daughter.

"There's nothing will do him good but to go to the
Prince of Coolavin," said the beggarman.

Iſ maɾ ſin ḃí ſiad aɜ áɾɜúinꞇ aɜuſ aɜ cuiḃlinꞇ ɜo ꝺꞇí
an oiꝺċe, aɜuſ ꝼuaiɾ an ꝺéiɾceaċ leaḃuiꝺ ꞇuiɡe annſa'
ſɜioḃól aɜuſ ċoɾuiɜ ſé aɜ áɾɜúinꞇ aɾíſ aiɾ maiꝺin ɜo
mḃuꝺ ċóiɾ ꝺul ɜo ꝺꞇí an Pʰɾionnſa, aɜuſ ḃí an ḃean aɜuſ
an inɡean aiɾ aon ꝼocal leiſ, aɜuſ ꝼuaiɾ ſiad ḃuaiꝺ aiɾ
an ḃɾeaɾ ꞇinn, ſaoi ḃeiɾe; aɜuſ ꝺuḃaiɾꞇ ſé ɜo ɾaċꝼaꝺ
ſé, aɜuſ ꝺuḃaiɾꞇ an inɡean ɜo ɾaċꝼaꝺ ſiſe leiſ, le
ꞇaḃaiɾꞇ aiɾe ꝺó, aɜuſ ꝺuḃaiɾꞇ an ꝺéiɾceaċ ɜo ɾaċꝼaꝺ
ſeiɾean leó-ſan le ꞇaiɾḃéanꞇ an ḃóċaiɾ ꝺóiḃ. "Aɜuſ
ḃeiꝺ miſe" aɾſ an ḃean, "aiɾ ſonc an ḃáiɾ le h-imniꝺe
aɜ ſanaṁainꞇ liḃ, ɜo ꝺꞇiucꝼaiꝺ ſiḃ aiɾ aiſ."

Ꝺ'úɜṁuiɜ ſiad an capall aɜuſ ċuiɾ ſiad ſaoi an ɜeaɾɾc
é, aɜuſ ɡlac ſiad lón ɾeaċꞇṁuine leó, aɾán aɜuſ baɜún
aɜuſ uiḃeaċa, aɜuſ ꝺ'imꞇiɜ ſiad leó. Níoɾ ꝼeuꝺ ſiad
ꝺul ɾú ꝼaꝺa an ċeuꝺ lá, maɾ ḃí an ꝼeaɾ ꞇinn ċoṁ laɜ ſin
náɾ ꝼeuꝺ ſé an cɾaꞇaꝺ a ḃí ſé ꝼáɡail annſa' ɜ-caɾɾc
ꝼeaɾſiṁ, aċꞇ ḃí ſé níoſ ꝼeaɾɾ an ꝺaɾa lá, aɜuſ ꝺ'ꝼan ſiad
uile i ꝺꞇeaċ ꝼeilméaɾa aiɾ ċaoiḃ an ḃóċaiɾ an oiꝺċe ſin
aɜuſ ċuaiꝺ ſiad aiɾ aɜaiꝺ aɾíſ aiɾ maiꝺin, aɜuſ an
ꞇɾíoṁaꝺ lá annſan ꞇɾaċnóna ċáiniɜ ſiad ɜo h-áiꞇ-ċóṁ-
nuiꝺe an Pʰɾionnſa. Ḃí ꞇeaċ ꝺeaſ aiɜe aiɾ ḃɾuaċ an
loċa, le cúṁꝺaċ ꞇuiɡe aiɾ, ameaɾɜ na ɜ-cɾann.

Ꝺ'ꝼáɜ ſiad an capall aɜuſ an caiɾꞇ i mḃaile ḃeaɜ a
ḃí anaice le háiꞇ an Pʰɾionnſa, aɜuſ ſiúḃail ſiad uile le
ċéile ɜo ꝺ-ꞇáiniɜ ſiad ċum an ꞇiɡe. Chuaiꝺ ſiad aɾꞇeaċ
'ſan ɜ-ciɾꞇeanaċ aɜuſ ꝺ'ꝼiaꝼɾuiɜ ſiad, "aɾ ꝼeuꝺ ſiad an
Pʰɾionnſa ꝺ'ꝼeicſinꞇ." Ꝺuḃaiɾꞇ an ɾeaɾḃꝼóɜanꞇa ɜo
ɾaiḃ ſé aɜ iꞇe a ḃéile aċꞇ ɜo ꝺꞇiucꝼaꝺ ſé, b'éiꝺiɾ, nuaiɾ
ḃeiꝺeaꝺ ſé ɾéiꝺ.

Ċáiniɜ an Pʰɾionnſa ꝼéin aɾꞇeaċ aiɾ an móimiꝺ ſin
aɜuſ ꝺ'ꝼiaꝼɾuiɜ ſé úioḃ cɾeuꝺ ꝺo ḃí ſiad aɜ iaɾɾaiꝺ.
Ꝺ'éiɾiɜ an ꝼeaɾ ꞇinn aɜuſ ꝺuḃaiɾꞇ ſé leiſ ɜuɾ aɜ iaɾɾaiꝺ
coinɡnaṁ ó na onóiɾ ꝺo ḃí ſé, aɜuſ ꝺ'inniſ ſé an ſɜeul

So they were arguing and striving until the night came, and the beggarman got a bed of straw in the barn, and he began arguing again in the morning that he ought to go to the prince, and the wife and daughter were on one word with him; and they prevailed at last on the sick man, and he said that he would go, and the daughter said that she would go with him to take care of him, and the boccuch said that he would go with them to show them the road; "and I'll be on the pinch of death, for ye, with anxiety," said the wife, "until ye come back again."

They harnessed the horse, and they put him under the cart, and they took a week's provision with them—bread, and bacon, and eggs, and they went off. They could not go very far the first day, for the sick man was so weak, that he was not able to bear the shaking he was getting in the cart; but he was better the second day, and they all passed the night in a farmer's house on the side of the road, and they went on again in the morning; but on the third day, in the evening, they came to the dwelling of the prince. He had a nice house, on the brink of the lake, with a straw roof, in among the trees.

They left the horse and the cart in a little village near the prince's place, and they all walked together, until they came to the house. They went into the kitchen, and asked, "Couldn't they see the prince?" The servant said that he was eating his meal, but that he would come, perhaps, when he was ready.

The prince himself came in at that moment, and asked what it was they wanted. The sick man rose up and told him, that it was looking for assistance from his honour he was, and he told him his whole story. "And

uile vó. " 'Noiſ an oṫiġ le v'onóiſ aon ḟóiſiġin ṫaḃaiſt vam?" aſ ſé, nuaiſ ċríoċnuiġ ſé a ſġéul.

"Tá ſúil aġam ġo vṫiġ liom," aſ ſan Pſionnſa, " aiſ móv aiſ biṫ véanſav mé mo ḃiṫċioll aiſ vo ſon, maſ ṫáiniġ tu cóṁ ſava ſin le m'ḟeicſint-ſe. b'olc an ceaſt vam ġan mo ḃiṫċioll ṁeunaṁ. Taſ ſuaſ annſa bſáſlúiſ· iſ ſíoſ an ſiuv a vuḃaiſt an ſean vuine atá ann ſin leat. Shluiġ tu alp-luaċſa, no ſiuv éiġin eile. Taſ ſuaſ 'ſa' bſáſlúiſ liom."

Tuġ ſé ſuaſ leiſ é, aġuſ iſ é an béile a ḃí aiġe an lá ſin ġiota móſ ve ṁaiſtſeóil ſaillte. Ġheaſſ ſé ġſeim móſ aġuſ cuſ ſé aiſ pláta é, aġuſ tuġ ſé vo'n vuine boċt le n-iṫe é.

" Óſó! Cſéav atá v' onóiſ aġ véanaṁ ann ſin anoiſ," aſſ an vuine boċt, " níoſ ſluiġ mé oiſeav aġuſ toiſt uiſe v'ḟeóil aiſ biṫ le ſáiṫ ċe, ní'l aon ġoile aġam, ní ṫiġ liom vavaṁ iṫe."

" bí vo ṫoſt a ṁuine," aſſ an Pſionnſa, " iṫ é ſin nuaiſ a veiſim leat é."

V'iṫ an ſeaſ boċt an oiſeav aġuſ v'ḟeuv ſé, aċ nuaiſ leiġ ſé an ſġian aġuſ an ġablóġ aſ a láiṁ cuſ an Pſionnſa iav (v'ḟiaċaiḃ) aiſ iav vo ṫóġḃáil aſíſ, aġuſ vo ṫoſuġav aſ an nuav. Congḃuiġ ſé ann ſin é aġ iṫe, ġo ſaiḃ ſe ſéiv le pleuſġav, aġuſ níoſ ſeuv ſé ſaoi ḃeiſe aon ġſeim eile ſluġav vá ḃſáġav ſe ceuv púnta.

Nuaiſ connaiſc an Pſionnſa naċ vtiucſav leiſ tuil-leav vo ſluġav, tuġ ſé amaċ aſ an teaċ é, aġuſ vuḃaiſt ſé leiſ an inġin aġuſ leiſ an t-ſean-ḃeiſceaċ iav vo leanaṁaint, aġuſ ſuġ ſé an ſeaſ leiſ, amaċ ġo móinſeuſ bſeáġ ġlaſ vo ḃí oſ coinne an tiġe, aġuſ ſſoṫán beaġ uiſġe aġ ſi tſív an móinſeuſ.

Tuġ ſé ġo bſuaċ an t-ſſoṫáin é, aġuſ vuḃaiſt ſé leiſ, luiṫe ſíoſ aiſ a bolġ aġuſ a ċeann congḃáil oſ cionn

now can your honour help me?" he said, when he had finished it.

"I hope I can," said the prince; "anyhow, I'll do my best for you, as you came so far to see me. I'd have a bad right not to do my best. Come up into the parlour with me. The thing that old man told you is true. You swallowed an alt-pluachra, or something else. Come up to the parlour with me."

He brought him up to the parlour with him, and it happened that the meal he had that day was a big piece of salted beef. He cut a large slice off it, and put it on a plate, and gave it to the poor man to eat.

"Oro! what is your honour doing there?" says the poor man; "I didn't swallow as much as the size of an egg of meat this quarter,* and I can't eat anything."

"Be silent, man," says the prince; "eat that, when I tell you."

The poor man eat as much as he was able, but when he left the knife and fork out of his hand, the Prince made him take them up again, and begin out of the new (over again). He kept him there eating until he was ready to burst, and at last he was not able to swallow another bit, if he were to get a hundred pounds.

When the Prince saw that he would not be able to swallow any more, he brought him out of the house, and he said to the daughter and the old beggarman to follow them, and he brought the man out with him to a fine green meadow that was forenent † the house, and a little stream of water running through it.

He brought him to the brink of the stream, and told him to lie down on his stomach over the stream, and to hold his face over the water, to open his mouth as wide

---

* *i.e.*, this quarter of a year.

† forenent, or forenenst = over against.

an uirge, aguṡ a ḃeul d'ḟorgailt ċoṁ mór aguṡ d'ḟeuvfaḋ
ṛé, aguṡ a ċongḃáil, beag-naċ, ag baint leiṛ an uirge,
" aguṡ fan ann ṛin go ciúin aguṡ na corṛuiġ, aiṛ v'anam,"
aṛ ṛé, " go ḃfeicfiḋ tu creuv éiṛeóċaṛ vuit."

Ġheall an feaṛ boċt go mbeiḋeaḋ ṛé ṛocaiṛ, aguṡ ṡín
ṛé a ċoṛp aiṛ an ḃfeuṛ, aguṡ ċongḃuiġ ṛé a ḃeul foṛ-
gailte oṛ cionn an t-ṛṛioċáin uirge, aguṡ d'ḟan ṛé ann
ṛin gan corṛuġaḋ.

Chuaiḋ an Pṛionnṡa timċioll cúig ṛlata aiṛ aiṛ, aiṛ a
ċúl, aguṡ ċarṛaing ṛé an inġean aguṡ an ṛean-feaṛ leiṛ,
aguṡ iṡ é an ṛocal veiṛeannaċ a vubaiṛt ṛé leiṛ an
ḃfeaṛ tinn, "bí cinnte" aṛ ṛé, " aguṡ aiṛ v'anam na
cuiṛ coṛ aṛaḋ, cia ḃé aiṛ biṫ ṛuv éiṛeóċaṛ vuit."

Ni ṛaiḃ an vuine boċt ceaṫṛaṁaḋ uaiṛe 'nna luiḋe maṛ ṛin
nuaiṛ ċoṛuiġ ṛuv éigin ag corṛuġaḋ taob aṛtiġ ṿé aguṡ ṁo-
ċaiġ ṛé ṛuv éigin ag teaċt ṛuaṛ ann a ṛgoṛnaċ, aguṡ ag
vul aiṛ aiṛ aṛiṛ. Táinig ṛé ṛuaṛ, aguṡ ċuaiḋ ṛé aiṛ aiṛ tṛí
no ceiṫṛe uaiṛe anḋuaiġ a ċéile. Táinig ṛé faoi ḃeiṛe go
vtí a ḃeul, aguṡ feaṛ ṛé aiṛ ḃáṛṛ a ṫeanga aċt ṛgann-
ṛuiġ ṛé aguṡ ċuaiḋ ṛé aiṛ aiṛ aṛiṛ, aċt i gceann tamaill
biġ táinig ṛé ṛuaṛ an vaṛa uaiṛ, aguṡ feaṛ ṛé aiṛ ḃáṛṛ
a ċeanga, aguṡ léim ṛé ṛíoṛ faoi ḃeiṛe annṛan uirge.
Ḃhi an Pṛionnṡa ag ḃṛeaṫnuġaḋ go geuṛ aiṛ, aguṡ
ġlaoḋ ṛé amaċ, "na corṛuiġ ṛóṛ," maṛ bí an feaṛ vul
ag éiṛiġe.

Ḃ'éigin vo'n vuine boċt a ḃeul foṛgailt aṛíṡ aguṡ
v'ḟan ṛé an ċaoi ċeuvna, aguṡ ni ṛaiḃ ṛé móimiv ann, no
go vtáinig an vaṛa ṛuv ṛuaṛ ann a ṛgoṛnaċ an ċaoi
ċeuvna, aguṡ ċuaiḋ ṛé aiṛ aiṛ aṛiṛ cúpla uaiṛ, aṁail a'ṛ
maṛ bí ṛé ṛgannṛuiġte, aċt faoi ḃeiṛe táinig ṛeiṛean maṛ
an ċeuv-ċeann ṛuaṛ go vtí an ḃeul aguṡ feaṛ ṛé aiṛ ḃáṛṛ
a ṫeanga, aguṡ faoi ḃeiṛe nuaiṛ ṁoċuiġ ṛé bolaḋ an uirge
faoi, léim ṛé ṛíoṛ annṛan tṛṛioċán.

as he could, and to keep it nearly touching the water, and "wait there quiet and easy," says he; "and for your life don't stir, till you see what will happen to you."

The poor man promised that he would be quiet, and he stretched his body on the grass, and held his mouth open, over the stream of water, and remained there without stirring.

The prince went backwards, about five yards, and drew the daughter and the old man with him, and the last word he said to the sick man was: "Be certain, and for your life, don't put a stir out of you, whatever thing at all happens to you."

The sick man was not lying like that more than a quarter of an hour, when something began moving inside of him, and he felt something coming up in his throat, and going back again. It came up and went back three or four times after other. At last it came to the mouth, stood on the tip of his tongue, but frightened, and ran back again. However, at the end of a little space, it rose up a second time, and stood on his tongue. and at last jumped down into the water. The prince was observing him closely, and just as the man was going to rise, he called out: "Don't stir yet."

The poor man had to open his mouth again, and he waited the same way as before; and he was not there a minute until the second one came up the same way as the last, and went back and came] up two or three times, as if it got frightened; but at last, it also, like the first one, came up to the mouth, stood on the tongue, and when it felt the smell of the water below it, leaped down into the little stream.

Choɣaiʁ an Pʁionnʁa, aɣuʁ oubaiʁc ʁé "Noiʁ cá 'n capc aɣ ceacc oʁʁa, o'oibʁiɣ an ʁalann a bí 'ʁa' maiʁcʁeóil iao; noiʁ ciucʁaió ʁao amac." Aɣuʁ ʁul oo bí an ʁocal aʁ a beul cuic an cʁʁomaó ceann le "plop" annʁan uiʁɣe, aɣuʁ móinʋo 'nna úiaiɣ ʁin, léim ceann eile ʁíoʁ ann, aɣuʁ ann ʁin ceann eile, no ɣuʁ cómaiʁiɣ ʁao, cúiɣ, ʁé, ʁeacc, occ, naoi, oeic ɣ-cinn, aon ceann oeuɣ, oá ceann oeuɣ.

"Sin ouiʁín aca anoiʁ" aʁ ʁ an Pʁionnʁa, "Sin é an c-ál, níoʁ cáiniɣ an c-ʁean-mácaiʁ ʁóʁ."

bhí an ʁeaʁ bocc oul 'ɣ eiʁiɣe aʁíʁ, acc ɣlaoú an Pʁionnʁa aiʁ. "Fan maʁ a bʁuil cu, níoʁ cáiniɣ an mácaiʁ."

"O'ʁan ʁé maʁ oo bí ʁé, acc níoʁ cáiniɣ aon ceann eile amac, aɣuʁ o'ʁan ʁé níoʁ mó ʁá ceacʁaʁaó uaiʁe. bhí an Pʁionnʁa ʁéin aɣ eiʁiɣe mí-ʁuaimneac, aiʁ eaɣla nac ɣ-coʁʁócaó an ʁean-Alc-pluacʁa coʁ aiʁ bic. bhí an ouine bocc cóm ʁáʁuiɣce ʁin aɣuʁ cóm laɣ ʁin ɣo m' b'ʁeaʁʁ leiʁ eiʁiɣe 'ná ʁanamainc maʁ a ʁaib ʁé, aɣuʁ ann ainúcóin ɣac ʁuio a oubaiʁc an Pʁionnʁa bí ʁé aɣ ʁeaʁam ʁuaʁ, nuaiʁ ʁuɣ an Pʁionnʁa aiʁ a leac-cóiʁ aɣuʁ an úéiʁiceac aiʁ an ɣ-coiʁ eile, aɣuʁ oo conɣbuiɣ ʁao ʁíoʁ é ɣan buiúeacaʁ oó.

O'ʁan ʁao ceacʁaʁaó uaiʁe eile, ɣan ʁocal oo ʁáó, aɣuʁ i ɣ-ceann an ama ʁin mocuiɣ an ouine bocc ʁuio éiɣin aɣ coʁʁuɣaó aʁíʁ ann a caoib, acc ʁeacc n-uaiʁe níoʁ meaʁa 'na ʁoiʁe ʁeó, aɣuʁ iʁ aiʁ éiɣin o'ʁeuo ʁé é ʁéin oo conɣbáil o ʁɣʁeaoac. bhí an ʁuio ʁin aɣ coʁʁuɣaó le camall maic ann, aɣuʁ ʁaoil ʁé ɣo ʁaib a coʁʁ ʁeubca an caob aʁcíɣ leiʁ. Ann ʁin coʁuiɣ an ʁuio aɣ ceacc ʁuaʁ, aɣuʁ cáiniɣ ʁé ɣo ocí a beul aɣuʁ cuaió ʁé aiʁ aiʁ aʁíʁ. Cáiniɣ ʁé ʁaoi úeiʁe cóm ʁaoa ʁin ɣuʁ cuiʁ an ouine bocc a oá méuʁ ann a beul aɣuʁ ʁaoil ʁé ɣʁeim ʁáɣail uiʁʁi. Acc má'ʁ obann cuiʁ ʁé a méuʁa

The prince said in a whisper: "Now the thirst's coming on them; the salt that was in the beef is working them; now they'll come out." And before the word had left his mouth, the third one fell, with a plop, into the water; and a moment after that, another one jumped down, and then another, until he counted five, six, seven, eight, nine, ten, eleven, twelve.

"There's a dozen of them now," said the prince; "that's the clutch; the old mother didn't come yet."

The poor sick man was getting up again, but the prince called to him: "Stay as you are; the mother didn't come up."

He remained as he was, but no other one came out, though he stayed there more than a quarter of an hour. The prince himself was getting uneasy for fear the old alt-pluachra might not stir at all. The poor man was so tired and so weak that he wished to get up; and, in spite of all the prince told him, he was trying to stand on his feet, when the Prince caught him by one leg, and the boccuch by the other, and they held him down in spite of him.

They remained another quarter of an hour without speaking a word, or making a sound, and at the end of that time the poor man felt something stirring again in his side, but seven times worse than before; and it's scarcely he could keep himself from screeching. That thing kept moving for a good while, and he thought the side was being torn out of himself with it. Then it began coming up, and it reached the mouth, and went back again. At last it came up so far that the poor man put the two fingers to his mouth and thought to catch

'ɼteaċ iɼ luaiťe 'ná ɼin ċuaiḋ an tɼean alt-pluaċɼa aiɼ
aiɼ.

" 'Óɼ ! a ḃiťeaṁnaiġ !" aɼ ɼan Pɼionnɼa, "caḋ ċuiʒe
ɼinn' ʈu ɼin ? Naċ ᴅuḃaiɼʈ mé leaʈ ʒan coɼ ᴅo
ċuɼ aɼaᴅ. Má ťiʒ ɼé ɼuaɼ aɼíɼ ɼan ʒo ɼocaɼɼ."
ḃ' éiʒin ᴅóiḃ ɼanaṁainʈ le leaċ-uaiɼ maɼ ᴅo ḃí
ɼean-ṁáťaiɼ na n-alp-luaċɼa ɼʒannɼuiġťe, aʒuɼ ḃí
ɼaiċċioɼ uɼɼɼɼ ťeaċʈ amaċ. Aċʈ ťáiniʒ ɼí ɼuaɼ aɼíɼ, ɼaoi
ḋeiɼe ; ḃ'éiᴅiɼ ʒo ɼaiḃ an iomaɼcuiḋ ʈaɼʈ' uɼɼɼ aʒuɼ
níoɼ ɼeuᴅ ɼí ḃolaḋ an uiɼʒe a ḃí aʒ cuɼ caťuiʒťe uɼɼɼ
ɼeaɼaṁ, no ḃ'éiᴅiɼ ʒo ɼaiḃ ɼí uaiʒneaċ 'ɼ éiɼ a clainne
ᴅ'imťeaċʈ uaiťi. Aɼ ṁóḋ aɼ biʈ ťáiniʒ ɼí amaċ ʒo ḃáɼɼ
á ḃéil aʒuɼ ɼeaɼ ɼí aɼ a ťeanʒa ċoṁ ɼaᴅ aʒuɼ ḃeiťeá
aʒ cóṁaiɼeaṁ ceiťɼe ɼéiᴅ, aʒuɼ ann ɼin léim ɼí maɼ
ᴅo léim a h-ál ɼoimɼi, aɼʈeaċ 'ɼan uiɼʒe, aʒuɼ ḃuᴅ ċɼuinne
toɼan a ʈuiʈim' ɼeaċʈ n-uaiɼe, 'ná an plaɼ a ɼinne a
clann.

ḃhí an Pɼionnɼa aʒuɼ an ḃeiɼʈ eile aʒ bɼeaťnuʒaᴅ
aiɼ ɼin, ʒo h-iomlán, aʒuɼ ḃuᴅ ḃeaʒ naċ ɼaiḃ ɼaiċċioɼ
oɼɼɼa, a n-anál ᴅo ťaɼɼaing, aɼ eaʒla ʒo ɼʒannɼóċaᴅ
ɼiaᴅ an ḃeiťiḋeaċ ʒɼánna. Ċoṁ luaʈ aʒuɼ léim ɼí aɼʈeaċ
'ɼan uiɼʒe ťaɼɼaing ɼiaᴅ an ɼeaɼ aɼ aiɼ, aʒuɼ ċuiɼ ɼiaᴅ
aɼ a ḋá ċoiɼ aɼíɼ é.

ḃhí ɼe ʈɼí huaiɼe ʒan ɼocal ᴅo laḃaiɼʈ, aċʈ an ċeuᴅ
ɼocal a ᴅuḃaiɼʈ ɼé, ḃuᴅ h-é "iɼ ᴅuine nuaᴅ mé."

Ċonʒḃuiʒ an Pɼionnɼa ann a ťeaċ ɼéin le coiɼíḋeaɼ é,
aʒuɼ ʈuʒ ɼe aiɼe ṁóɼ aʒuɼ beaťuʒaᴅ maiʈ ḋó. Leiʒ ɼé
ḋó imťeaċʈ ann ɼin, aʒuɼ an inʒean aʒuɼ an ᴅéiɼceaċ
leiɼ, aʒuɼ ḃúlʈuiʒ ɼé oiɼeaᴅ aʒuɼ ɼiʒin ᴅo ġlacaᴅ uaťa.

"ḃ'ɼeaɼɼ liom 'ná ᴅeiċ bɼúnʈa aɼ mo láiṁ ɼein," aɼ
ɼé, "ʒuɼ ťionnʈuiʒ mo leiʒeaɼ amaċ ċoṁ maiʈ ɼin ; náɼ
leiʒɼiᴅ Dia ʒo nʒlacɼainn ɼiʒin no leiċ-ɼi'n uaiʈ. Ċaill
ʈu ʒu leóɼ le ᴅoċʈúɼɼiḃ ċeana."

hold of it. But if he put in his fingers quick, the old alt-pluachra went back quicker.

"Oh, you *behoonach!*" cried the prince, "what made you do that? Didn't I tell you not to let a stir out of you? Remain quiet if she comes up again."

They had to remain there for half an hour, because the old mother of the alt-pluachras was scared, and she was afraid to come out. But she came up at last, perhaps, because there was too much thirst on her to let her stand the smell of the water that was tempting her, or perhaps she was lonesome after her children going from her. Anyhow, she came up to his mouth, and stood there while you would be counting about four score; and when she saw nothing, and nothing frightened her, she gave a jump down into the water, like her clutch before her; and the plop of her into the water was seven times heavier than theirs.

The prince and the other two had been watching the whole, and they scarcely dared to breathe, for fear of startling the horrid beast. As soon as ever she jumped down into the water, they pulled back the man, and put him standing again on his two feet.

He was for three hours before he could speak a word; but the first thing he said was: "I'm a new man."

The prince kept him in his own house for a forthight, and gave him great care and good feeding. He allowed him to go then, and the daughter and the boccuch with him; and he refused to take as much as a penny from them.

"I'm better pleased than ten pounds on my own hand," said he, "that my cure turned out so well; and I'd be long sorry to take a farthing from you; you lost plenty with doctors before."

Táiniġ ſiad a baile ʒo ſábálca, aʒuſ d'éiriġ ſé ſlán ſپir aʒuſ ſaṁار. Bhí ſé coṁ buiḋeać de'n deiſceać boċc ʒuſ conʒbuiġ ſé ann a ċeać ſéin ʒo dcí a báſ é. Aʒuſ coṁ ſad a'ſ bí ſé ſéin beó níoſ luıú ſé ſíoſ aıſ an bſeaſ ʒLaſ aپſſ. Aʒuſ, ſıad eile ; dá mbeıḋeaḋ cınneaſ no caſLáınce aıſ, ní h-ıad na doċcúıſıḋ a ġLaoḋáḋ ſé aſceać.

Buḋ beaʒ an c-ıonʒnaḋ ſın !

Páidín O'Ceallaiġ aʒus an easóg.

A bſad ó ſoın bí ſeaſ d'aſ' b'aınm Páidín O'Ceallaiġ 'nna cóṁnuıḋe ı nʒaſ do Tuaım ı ʒcondaé na ʒaıllıṁe. Aon ṁaıdın aṁáın d'éıſıġ ſé ʒo moċ aʒuſ ní ſaıb ſıoſ aıʒe cıa an c-am a bí ſé, maſ bí, ſoları bſeáġ ó'n nʒealaıġ. Bí dúıl aıʒe Le dul ʒo h-aonać Cátaſ-na-maſc Le ſcoſc aſaıl do ḋíol.

Ní ſaıb ſé níoſ mó 'na cſí ṁıle aıſ an mbócaſ ʒo dcáıniʒ doſċaḋaſ móſ aıſ, aʒuſ coſuıġ cıċ cẛom aʒ cuıcım. Connaıſc ſé ceać móſ ameaſʒ cſann cımċıoll cúıʒ ċeud ſLac ó'n mbócaſ aʒuſ dubaıſc ſé Leıſ ſéin, " ſaċſaıḋ mé cum an cíġe ſın, ʒo dcéıḋ an cıc ċaſc." Nuaıſ ċuaıḋ ſé cum an cíġe, bí an doſaſ ſoſʒaılce, aʒuſ aſceać Leıſ. Connaıſc ſé ſeompa móſ aıſ caoıb a Láıṁe ċLé, aʒuſ ceıne bſeáġ 'ſan nʒſáca. Suıḋ ſé ſíoſ aıſ ſcol Le coıſ an balla, aʒuſ níoſ bſada ʒuſ coſuıġ ſé aʒ cuıcım 'nna ċodLaḋ, nuaıſ connaıſc ſé easóg ṁóſ aʒ ceać cum na ceıneaḋ aʒuſ Leaʒ ſı ʒınıḋ aıſ Leıc an ceaʒLaıġ aʒuſ d'ımċıġ. Níoſ bſada ʒo dcáıniʒ ſı aıſ aıſ Le ʒınıḋ eıle aʒuſ Leaʒ aıſ Leıc an ceaʒLaıġ é, aʒuſ d'ımċıġ. Bí ſı aʒ ımċeać aʒuſ aʒ ceać ʒo ſaıb cáſnán móſ ʒınıḋ aıſ

They came home safely, and he became healthy and fat. He was so thankful to the poor boccuch that he kept him in his own house till his death. As long as he was alive he never lay down on green grass again; and another thing, if there was any sickness or ill-health on him, it isn't the doctors he used to call in to him.

That was small wonder!

***

PAUDYEEN O'KELLY AND THE WEASEL.

A LONG time ago there was once a man of the name of Paudyeen O'Kelly, living near Tuam, in the county Galway. He rose up one morning early, and he did not know what time of day it was, for there was fine light coming from the moon. He wanted to go to the fair of Cauher-na-mart to sell a *sturk* of an ass that he had.

He had not gone more than three miles of the road when a great darkness came on, and a shower began falling. He saw a large house among trees about five hundred yards in from the road, and he said to himself that he would go to that house till the shower would be over. When he got to the house he found the door open before him, and in with him. He saw a large room to his left, and a fine fire in the grate. He sat down on a stool that was beside the wall, and began falling asleep, when he saw a big weasel coming to the fire with something yellow in its mouth, which it dropped on the hearth-stone, and then it went away. She soon

an teaġlaċ. Aċt faoi ḃeireaſ nuair ḃ'imṫiġ rí ḃ'éiriġ
Páiḋín, aguſ ċuir ſé an méaſ óir a ḃí ċruinniġṫe aici ann
a póca, aguſ amaċ leiſ.

Ní raiḃ ſé a ḃ-faḃ imṫiġṫe gur ċualaiſ ſé an easóg
aġ teaċt 'nna ḃiaiġ aguſ i aġ rġreaſaoil ċoṁ h-áro le
píobaiḃ. Cuaiſ rí rioṁ Páiḋín air an mbóċar aguſ ſ aġ
luḃarnuiġ anonn 'r anall aguſ aġ iarraiſ ġreim rġornaiġ ḃ'fáġail air. Ḃí maiḋe maiṫ ḃaraċ aġ Páiḋín aguſ
ċonġḃuiġ ſé í uaiſ go ḃṫáiniġ beirt fear ruar. Ḃí maḃaſ
maiṫ aġ fear aca, aguſ ruaiġ ſé airteaċ i bpoll 'ran
mballa í.

Cuaiſ Páiḋín ċum an aonaiġ, aguſ ann áit é ḃeiṫ tíġ-
eaċt a baile leiſ an airgioſ a ruair ſé air a ḟean-aſal,
mar faoil ſé air maiḋin go mbeiſeaſ ſé aġ ḃeanaiṁ,
ċeannuiġ ſé capall le cuiſ ḃe'n airgioſ a ḃain ſé ḃe'n
easóiġ, aguſ ṫáiniġ ſé a baile aguſ é aġ marcuiġeaċt.
Nuair ṫáiniġ ſé ċoṁ faḋa leiſ an áit air ċuir an maḃaſ an
easóg ann ran bpoll, ṫáiniġ ſí amaċ roiṁe, ṫug léim ruar,
aguſ ruair ġreim rġornaiġ air an ġ-capall. Ṫoruiġ an
capall aġ riṫ, aguſ nior feuḃ Páiḋín a ċeaparſ, no go
ḃṫug ſé léim airteaċ i ġ-claiſ ṁóir a ḃí líonta ḃ'uirġe
aguſ ḃe ṁúlaċ. Ḃi ſé 'ġá báṫaſ aguſ 'ġá ċaċtaſ go
luaṫ, go ḃṫáiniġ rir ruar a ḃí teaċt air Ġailliṁ aguſ
ṫiḃir riaḃ an easóg.

Ṫug Páiḋín an capall a baile leiſ, aguſ ċuir ſé airteaċ i ḃteaċ na mbó é, aguſ ċuit ſé 'nna ċoḃlaſ.

Air maiḋin, lá air na ṁárac, ḃ'éiriġ Páiḋín go moċ, aguſ
ċuaiſ ſé amaċ le uirġe aguſ fear taḃairt ḃo'n ċapall.
Nuair ċuaiſ ſé amaċ ċonnairc ſé an easóg aġ teaċt
amaċ air teaċ na mbó, aguſ i foluiġṫe le ruil. "Mo

came back again with the same thing in her mouth, and he saw that it was a guinea she had. She dropped it on the hearth-stone, and went away again. She was coming and going, until there was a great heap of guineas on the hearth. But at last, when he got her gone, Paudyeen rose up, thrust all the gold she had gathered into his pockets, and out with him.

He was not gone far till he heard the weasel coming after him, and she screeching as loud as a bag-pipes. She went before Paudyeen and got on the road, and she was twisting herself back and forwards, and trying to get a hold of his throat. Paudyeen had a good oak stick, and he kept her from him, until two men came up who were going to the same fair, and one of them had a good dog, and it routed the weasel into a hole in the wall.

Paudyeen went to the fair, and instead of coming home with the money he got for his old ass, as he thought would be the way with him in the morning, he went and bought a horse with some of the money he took from the weasel, and he came home and he riding. When he came to the place where the dog had routed the weasel into the hole in the wall, she came out before him, gave a leap up and caught the horse by the throat. The horse made off, and Paudyeen could not stop him, till at last he gave a leap into a big drain that was full up of water and black mud, and he was drowning and choking as fast as he could, until men who were coming from Galway came up and banished the weasel.

Paudyeen brought the horse home with him, and put him into the cows' byre and fell asleep.

Next morning, the day on the morrow, Paudyeen rose up early and went out to give his horse hay and oats. When he got to the door he saw the weasel coming out

ſeaċt mile mallaċt oſit," aſi Páiḋín, "tá ſaitċioſ oſim
ġo ḃſuil anaċain ḋéanta aġaḋ." Cuaiḋ ſé aſteaċ, aġuſ
ſuaiſi ſé an capall, péiſie bó-bainne, aġuſ ḋá laoġ maſiḃ.
Ċáiniġ ſé amaċ aġuſ ċuiſi ſé maḋaḋ a ḃí aiġe anúiaiġ na
h-eaſóiġe. Fuaiſi an maḋaḋ ġſieim uſiſiſi aġuſ ſuaiſi
ſiſie ġſieim aiſi an maḋaḋ. Buḋ maḋaḋ mait é, ſéc
b'éiġin ḋó a ġſieim ẛġaoileaḋ ſul ċáiniġ Páiḋín ſuaſi; ſéc
conġḃuiġ ſé a ſúil uſiſiſi ġo ḃſacaiḋ ſé í aġ ḋul aſteaċ i
mbotán beaġ a ḃí aiſi ḃſuaċ loċa. Ċáiniġ Páiḋín aġ
ſiic, aġuſ nuaiſi ḃí ſé aġ an mbotáinín beaġ tuġ ſé cſia-
ċaḋ ḋo'n maḋaḋ aġuſ ċuiſi ſé ſeaſiġ aiſi, aġuſ ċuiſi ſé
aſteaċ ſioſiie é. Nuaiſi ċuaiḋ an maḋaḋ aſteaċ ċoſiuiġ
ſé aġ taċſanc. Cuaiḋ Páiḋín aſteaċ aġuſ connaiſie ſé
ſean-ċailleaċ ann ſan ġ-coiſinéul. D'ſiaſſiuiġ ſé úi an
ḃſacaiḋ ſí eaſóġ aġ teaċt aſteaċ.

"Ní ſacaiḋ mé," aſi ſan ċailleaċ, "tá mé bſieóiḋte le
ġalaſi millceaċ aġuſ muna ḋtéiḋ tu amaċ ġo tapa ġlac-
ſaiḋ tu uaim é."

Coṁ ſaḋ aġuſ ḃí Páiḋín aġuſ an ċailleaċ, aġ caint, ḃí
an maḋaḋ aġ teannaḋ aſteaċ, no ġo ḋtuġ ſé léim ſuaſi
ſaoi ḃeiſieaḋ, aġuſ ſiuġ ſé ġſieim ẛġoſinaiġ aiſi an ġ-cail-
liġ.

Sġſieaḋ ſiſie, aġuſ ḋuḃaiſic, "túġ ḋíom ḋo ṁaḋaḋ a
Páiḋín Ui Ċeallaiġ, aġuſ ḋeunſaiḋ mé ſeaſi ſaiḋḃiſi
ḋíot."

Chuiſi Páiḋín iaċ (ḋ'ſiaċaiḃ) aiſi an maḋaḋ a ġſieim
ẛġaoileaḋ, aġuſ ḋuḃaiſic ſé, "Inniſ ḋam cia tu, no caḋ
ſáċ aſi ṁaſiḃ tu mo ċapall aġuſ mo ḃa?"

"Aġuſ caḋ ſáċ ḋtuġ tuſa leat an t-óſi a ſiaiḃ mé cúiġ
ċeuḋ bliaḋain 'ġá ċſiuinniuġaḋ ameaſġ cnoc aġuſ ġleann
an ḋoṁain."

"Ṡaoil mé ġuſi eaſóġ a ḃí ionnaḋ," aſi Páiḋín, "no ni
ḃainſinn le ḋo ċuiḋ óiſi; aġuſ niḋ eile, má tá tu cúiġ

of the byre and she covered with blood. "My seven thousand curses on you," said Paudyeen, "but I'm afraid you've harm done." He went in and found the horse, a pair of milch cows, and two calves dead. He came out and set a dog he had after the weasel. The dog got a hold of her, and she got a hold of the dog. The dog was a good one, but he was forced to loose his hold of her before Paudyeen could come up. He kept his eye on her, however, all through, until he saw her creeping into a little hovel that was on the brink of a lake. Paudyeen came running, and when he got to the little hut he gave the dog a shake to rouse him up and put anger on him, and then he sent him in before himself. When the dog went in he began barking. Paudyeen went in after him, and saw an old hag (cailleach) in the corner. He asked her if she saw a weasel coming in there.

"I did not," said she; "I'm all destroyed with a plague of sickness, and if you don't go out quick you'll catch it from me."

While Paudyeen and the hag were talking, the dog kept moving in all the time, till at last he gave a leap up and caught the hag by the throat. She screeched, and said:

"Paddy Kelly take off your dog, and I'll make you a rich man."

Paudyeen made the dog loose his hold, and said: "Tell me who are you, or why did you kill my horse and my cows?"

"And why did you bring away my gold that I was for five hundred years gathering throughout the hills and hollows of the world?"

"I thought you were a weasel," said Paudyeen, "or I wouldn't touch your gold; and another thing," says

céud bliadhain air an tsaoghal so tá sé i n-am duit im-
theacht cum suaimhnis."

"Rinne mé coir mhór i m'óige, agus táim le beit sgaoilte
óm' fulaing má tig leat fiche púnta íoc air son ceud agus
trí fichid airgionn dam."

"Cá bfuil an t-airgiod?" ar Páidín.

"Éirigh agus pómair faoi sgeich atá os cionn tobair
big i g-coirneul na páirce sin amuigh, agus geobaid tu
pota líonta d'ór. Íoc an fiche púnta air son na n-air-
gionn agus béid an cuid eile agad féin. Nuair a bain-
fear tu an leac de'n pota, feicfid tu madadh mór dub ag
teacht amach, act ná bíod aon faitcíos ort; is mac damh-
sa é. Nuair a gheobar tu an t-ór, ceannuig an teach ann
a bfacaid tu mire i dtorach, geobaid tu saor é, mar tá
sé faoi cáil go bfuil taidhbre ann. Béid mo mhac-sa físor
ann san troiléar," ní béansaid sé aon dochar duit, act
béid sé 'nna chairaid mait duit. Béid mire maib mi ó'n
lá so, agus nuair gheobar tu maib mé cuir rplanc faoi
an mbotán agus dóig é. Ná h-innir d'aon neach beó aon
niú air bit de m'éasoib-se, agus béid an t-áu ort."

"Cad é an t-ainm atá ort?" ar Páidín.

"Máire ní Ciarbáin," ar san cailleach.

Cuaid Páidín a baile agus nuair táinig dorcadar na
h-oidce tug sé láidhe leir agus cuaid sé cum na sgeice a
bí i g-coirneul na páirce agus tosuig sé ag pómair. Mór
bfada go bfuair sé an pota agus nuair bain sé an leac
dé léim an madadh mór dub amach, agus ar go bráth leir,
agus madadh Páidín 'nn a dhiaig.

Tug Páidín an t-ór a baile agus cuir sé i brolac i
dteach na mbó é. Timcioll mí 'nna dhiaig sin, cuaid sé go
h-aonac i ngaillimh agus ceannuig sé péire bó, capall

he, " if you're for five hundred years in this world, it's time for you to go to rest now."

" I committed a great crime in my youth," said the hag, "and now I am to be released from my sufferings if you can pay twenty pounds for a hundred and three score masses for me."

" Where's the money ? " says Paudyeen.

" Go and dig under a bush that's over a little well in the corner of that field there without, and you'll get a pot filled with gold. Pay the twenty pounds for the masses, and yourself shall have the rest. When you'll lift the flag off the pot, you'll see a big black dog coming out ; but don't be afraid before him ; he is a son of mine. When you get the gold, buy the house in which you saw me at first. You'll get it cheap, for it has the name of there being a ghost in it. My son will be down in the cellar. He'll do you no harm, but he'll be a good friend to you. I shall be dead a month from this day, and when you get me dead put a coal under this little hut and burn it. Don't tell a living soul anything about me—and the luck will be on you."

" What is your name ? " said Paudyeen.

" Maurya nee Keerwaun " (Mary Kerwan), said the hag.

Paudyeen went home, and when the darkness of the night came on he took with him a loy,* and went to the bush that was in the corner of the field, and began digging. It was not long till he found the pot, and when he took the flag off it a big black dog leaped out, and off and away with him, and Paudyeen's dog after him.

Paudyeen brought home the gold, and hid it in the

---

* Narrow spade used all over Connacht.

agus duirín caora. Ní raiḃ fíos ag na cómharsannaiḃ cia an áit a ḃfuair sé an t-airgiod. Duḃairt cuid aca go raiḃ roinn aige leir na daoiniḃ maiṫe.

Aon lá amáin ġleus Páidín é féin agus ċuaiḋ sé ċum an duine-uasail ar leir an teaċ mór, agus d'iarr air, an teaċ agus an talaṁ do ḃí 'nna ṫimcioll, do ḋíol leis.

"Tiġ leat an teaċ beiṫ agad gan cíos, aċt tá taiḋḃre ann, agus níor ṁaiṫ liom tu dul do ċóṁnuiḋe ann, gan a innsint; aċt ní sgarfainn leis an talaṁ gan ceud púnta níor mó 'ná tá agad-sa le tairgsint dam."

"B'éidir go ḃfuil an oiread agam-sa 's atá agad féin," ar Páidín, "béiḋ mé ann so amáraċ leir an airgiod má tá tusa réiḋ le reilḃ do ṫaḃairt dam."

"Béiḋ mé réiḋ," ar san duine-uasal.

Ċuaiḋ Páidín aḃaile agus d'innis d'á ṁnaoi go raiḃ teaċ mór agus gaḃáltas talṁan ceannuiġṫe aige.

"Cia an áit a ḃfuair tu an t-airgiod?" ar san bean.

"Naċ cuma ḋuit?" ar Páidín.

Lá ar na ṁáraċ, ċuaiḋ Páidín ċum an duine-uasail, tug ceud púnta ḋó, agus fuair reilḃ an tiġe agus na talṁan, agus d'ḟág an duine-uasal an spurcán aige asteaċ leir an margaḋ.

D'ḟan Páidín ann san teaċ an oiḋċe sin, agus nuair ṫáinig an dorċadas ċuaiḋ sé síos ann san tsoiléar, agus ċonnairc sé fear beag le na ḋá ċoir sgarṫa air báirille.

" 'Diú Dia ḋuit, a ḋuine ċóir," ar san fear beag.

"Go mbuḋ h-é ḋuit," ar Páidín.

"Ná bioḋ aon faitċíos ort róṁam-sa," ar san fear beag, "béiḋ mé mo ċaraid maiṫ ḋuit-se má tá tu ionnán run do ċonġḃáil."

cow-house.   About a month after that he went to the
fair of Galway, and bought a pair of cows, a horse, and
a dozen sheep.   The neighbours did not know where he
was getting all the money; they said that he had a share
with the good people.

One day Paudyeen dressed himself, and went to the
gentleman who owned the large house where he first
saw the weasel, and asked to buy the house of him, and
the land that was round about.

" You can have the house without paying any rent at
all; but there is a ghost in it, and I wouldn't like you to
go to live in it without my telling you, but I couldn't
part with the land without getting a hundred pounds
more than you have to offer me."

" Perhaps I have as much as you have yourself," said
Paudyeen.   " I'll be here to-morrow with the money, if
you're ready to give me possession."

" I'll be ready," said the gentleman.

Paudyeen went home and told his wife that he had
bought a large house and a holding of land.

" Where did you get the money?" says the wife.

" Isn't it all one to you where I got it?" says
Paudyeen.

The day on the morrow Paudyeen went to the gentleman, gave him the money, and got possession of the
house and land; and the gentleman left him the furniture and everything that was in the house, in with the
bargain.

Paudyeen remained in the house that night, and when
darkness came he went down to the cellar, and he saw
a little man with his two legs spread on a barrel.

"God save you, honest man," says he to Paudyeen.

"The same to you," says Paudyeen.

7

"Táim go deiṁin. Conġḃuiġ mé pún do ṁáṫair, aguſ conġḃóċaiḋ mé do pún-ſa mar an g-ceudna."

"b'éidir go ḃfuil tart ort," ar ſan fear beag.

"Níl mé ſaor uaiḋ," air Páidín.

Cuir an fear beag láṁ ann a ḃrolláċ, aguſ ṫarraing ſé corn óir amaċ, aguſ tug do Ṗáidín é, aguſ duḃairt leiſ, "tarraing fíon ar an mbáirille ſin ſúm."

Ṫarraing Páidín lán coirn aguſ ſeaċaid do'n fear beag é. "Ól, tu féin, i dtoſaċ," ap ſeiſean. D'ól Páidín, ṫarraing corn eile aguſ tug dón fear beag é, aguſ d'ól ſé é.

"Líon ſuaſ aguſ ól ariſ," ar ſan fear beag, "iſ mian liom-ſa beiṫ go ſúgaċ anoċt."

Ḃí an beirt ag ól go raḃadar leaṫ air meiſge. Ann ſin tug an fear beag léim anuaſ air an urlár, aguſ duḃairt le Páidín, "naċ ḃfuil dúil agad i g-ceól?"

"Tá go deiṁin," ar Páidín, "aguſ iſ maiṫ an daṁ-ſóir mé."

"Tóg ſuaſ an leac ṁór atá 'ſan g-coirneul úd, aguſ geoḃaiḋ tu mo píobaiḋ fúiṫi."

Tóg Páidín an leac, fuair na píobaiḋ, aguſ tug do 'n fear beag iad. D'fáiſg ſé na píobaiḋ air, aguſ ṫoruig ſé ag ſeinm ceóil binn. Ṫoruig Páidín ag daṁſa go raiḃ ſé tuirſeaċ. Ann ſin ḃí deoċ eile aca, aguſ duḃairt an fear beag:

"Dean mar duḃairt mo ṁáṫair leat, aguſ tairḃeanfaiḋ miſe ſaiḋḃreaſ mór duit. Tig leat do bean ċaḃairt ann ſo, aċt ná h-innir di go ḃfuil miſe ann, aguſ ni feicfiḋ ſí mé. Am air biṫ a ḃéiḋeaſ líonn nó fíon ag teaſtail uait tar ann ſo aguſ tarraing é. Slán leat

"Don't be afraid of me at all," says the little man. I'll be a friend to you, if you are able to keep a secret."

"I am able, indeed; I kept your mother's secret, and I'll keep yours as well."

"May-be you're thirsty?" says the little man.

"I'm not free from it," said Paudyeen.

The little man put a hand in his bosom and drew out a gold goblet. He gave it to Paudyeen, and said: "Draw wine out of that barrel under me."

Paudyeen drew the full up of the goblet, and handed it to the little man, "Drink yourself first," says he. Paudyeen drank, drew another goblet, and handed it to the little man, and he drank it.

"Fill up and drink again," said the little man. "I have a mind to be merry to-night."

The pair of them sat there drinking until they were half drunk. Then the little man gave a leap down to the floor, and said to Paudyeen:

"Don't you like music?"

"I do, surely," says Paudyeen, "and I'm a good dancer, too."

"Lift up the big flag over there in the corner, and you'll get my pipes under it."

Paudyeen lifted the flag, got the pipes, and gave them to the little man. He squeezed the pipes on him, and began playing melodious music. Paudyeen began dancing till he was tired. Then they had another drink, and the little man said:

"Do as my mother told you, and I'll show you great riches. You can bring your wife in here, but don't tell her that I'm there, and she won't see me. Any time

anoir, agus téiḋ ann do ċodlaḋ, agus tar ċugam-sa an oíḋċe amáraċ."

Ċuaiḋ Páiḋín 'nna leabuiḋ, agus níor ḃfada go raiḃ sé 'nna ċodlaḋ.

Air maidin, lá air na máraċ, ċuaiḋ Páiḋín a baile agus tug a ḃean agus a ċlann go dtí an teaċ mór, agus ḃíodar go sona. An oíḋċe sin ċuaiḋ Páiḋín síos ann san troiléas. Ċuir an fear beag fáilte roiṁe, agus d'iarr air "raiḃ fonn daṁsa air?"

"Níl go bráġ' mé deoċ," ar Páiḋín.

"Ól do ṡáiċ," ar san fear beag, "ní béiḋ an báirille sin folaṁ fad do ḃeaṫa."

D'ól Páiḋín lán an ċoirn agus tug deoċ do 'n fear beag; ann sin duḃairt an fear beag leis.

"Táim ag dul go Dún-na-ríḋ anoċt, le ceól do ṡeinm do na daoiniḃ maiṫe, agus má ṫagann tu liom feicfiḋ tu gleann breáġ. Béarfaiḋ mé capall duit naċ ḃfacaiḋ tu a leiṫeid ariaṁ roiṁe."

"Raċfad agus fáilte," ar Páiḋín, "aċt cia an leis-sgeul a ḃéunfas mé le mo ṁnaoi?"

"Téiḋ do ċodlaḋ léiṫe, agus béarfaiḋ mise amaċ ó n-a taoiḃ tu, a gan fios di, agus béarfaiḋ mé air ais tu an ċaoi ċeudna," ar san fear beag.

"Táim úmal," ar Páiḋín, "béiḋ deoċ eile agam sul a dtéiḋ mé ar do láṫair."

D'ól sé deoċ anuisiġ ḃiġe, go raiḃ sé leaṫ air meirge agus ċuaiḋ sé 'nn a leabuiḋ ann sin le na ṁnaoi.

Nuair ḋúisiġ sé fuair sé é féin ag marcuiġeaċt air sguaib i ngar do Dún-na-ríḋ, agus an fear beag ag marcuiġeaċt air sguaib eile le na ṫaoiḃ. Nuair ṫáinig siad ċoṁ fada le cnoc glas an Dúin, labair an fear beag

at all that ale or wine are wanting, come here and
draw. Farewell now; go to sleep, and come again to
me to-morrow night."

Paudyeen went to bed, and it wasn't long till he fell
asleep.

On the morning of the day on the morrow, Paudyeen
went home, and brought his wife and children to the big
house, and they were comfortable. That night Paudyeen
went down to the cellar; the little man welcomed him
and asked him did he wish to dance?"

"Not till I get a drink," said Paudyeen.

"Drink your 'nough," said the little man; "that barrel
will never be empty as long as you live."

Paudyeen drank the full of the goblet, and gave a
drink to the little man. Then the little man said to
him :

"I am going to Doon-na-shee (the fortress of the
fairies) to-night, to play music for the good-people, and
if you come with me you'll see fine fun. I'll give you
a horse that you never saw the like of him before."

"I'll go with you, and welcome," said Paudyeen;
"but what excuse will I make to my wife?"

"I'll bring you away from her side without her knowing it, when you are both asleep together, and I'll bring
you back to her the same way," said the little man.

"I'm obedient," says Paudyeen; "we'll have another
drink before I leave you."

He drank drink after drink, till he was half drunk, and
he went to bed with his wife.

When he awoke he found himself riding on a besom
near Doon-na-shee, and the little man riding on another

cúpla ḟocal náṗ ċuiġ Páiḋín ; ḃ'ḟoṗġail an cnoc ġloṗ, aguṡ ċuaiḋ Páiḋín aṗteaċ i ṗeomṗa ḃṗeáġ.

Ní ḟacaiḋ Páiḋín aon ċṗuinniuġaḋ aṗiaṁ maṗ ḃí ann ṗan dún. Ḃí an áit líonta ḋe ḋaoiniḃ ḃeaġa, ḃí ḟiṗ aguṡ mná ann, ṗean aguṡ óġ. Cḣuiṗeaḋaṗ uile ḟáilte ṗoiṁ Dóṁnal aguṡ ṗoiṁ Páiḋín O Ceallaiġ. Ḃ'é Dóṁnal ainm an ṗíoḃaiṗe ḃiġ. Ṫáiniġ ṗíġ aguṡ ḃainṗíoġan na ṗíú 'nna láṫaiṗ aguṡ duḃaiṗt ṗiaḋ :

"Ṫámaoiḋ uile aġ ḋul ġo Cnoc Maċa anoċt, aṗ cuaiṗt ġo h-áṗd-ṗíġ aguṡ ġo ḃainṗíoġain áṗ nḋaoine."

Ḋ'eiṗiġ an t-iomlán aca, aguṡ ċuaiḋ ṗiaḋ amaċ. Ḃí capaill ṗéiḋ aġ ġaċ aon aca, aguṡ an Cóiṗte ḃoḋaṗ le h-aġaiḋ an ṗíġ aguṡ na ḃainṗíoġna. Ċuaḋaṗ aṗteaċ 'ṗan ġ-cóiṗte. Léim ġaċ duine aṗ a ċapall ṗéin, aguṡ ḃí cinnte naċ ṗaiḃ Páiḋín aṗ ḋeiṗeaḋ. Ċuaiḋ an ṗio-ḃaiṗe amaċ ṗompa, aguṡ ċoṗuiġ aġ ṗeinm ceóil ḋóiḃ, aguṡ aṗ ġo ḃṗáċ leó. Móṗ ḃṗaḋa ġo ḋtángaḋaṗ ġo Cnoc Maċa. Ḋ'ḟoṗġail an cnoc aguṡ ċuaiḋ an ṗluaġ ṗíú aṗteaċ.

Ḃí Finḃeaṗa aguṡ Nuala ann ṗin, áṗd-ṗíġ aguṡ ḃain-ṗíoġan Sluaiġ-ṗíú Connaċt, aguṡ milte ḋe ḋaoiniḃ ḃeaġa. Ṫáiniġ Finḃeaṗa a láṫaiṗ aguṡ tuḃaiṗt :

"Ṫámaoiḋ dul báiṗe ḃualaḋ ann aġaiḋ ṗluaiġ-ṗíú Miúṁan anoċt, aguṡ muna mḃuailṗimíḋ iaḋ tá áṗ ġ-clú imtiġte ġo ḋeó. Tá an báiṗe le ḃeiṫ ḃuailte aṗ Máiġ-Ṫúṗa ḟaoi ṡliaḃ Belġaḋáin."

"Ṫámaoiḋ uile ṗéiḋ," aṗ ṗluaġ-ṗíú Connaċt, "aguṡ ní'l ṡiṁṗaṗ aġainn naċ mḃuailṗimíḋ iaḋ."

"Amaċ liḃ uile," aṗ ṗan t-áṗd-ṗíġ "ḃéiḋ ḟiṗ Cnuic Néiṗin aṗ an talaṁ ṗómainn."

Ḋ'imṫiġeaḋaṗ uile amaċ, aguṡ Dóṁnal ḃeaġ aguṡ ḋá 'ṗ ḋeuġ ṗíoḃaiṗe eile ṗómpa aġ ṗeinm ceóil ḃinn. Nuaiṗ

besom by his side. When they came as far as the green
hill of the Doon, the little man said a couple of words
that Paudyeen did not understand.   The green hill
opened, and the pair went into a fine chamber.

Paudyeen never saw before a gathering like that which
was in the Doon.   The whole place was full up of little
people, men and women, young and old.   They all welcomed little Donal—that was the name of the piper—and
Paudyeen O'Kelly.   The king and queen of the fairies
came up to them, and said :

"We are all going on a visit to-night to Cnoc Matha,
to the high king and queen of our people."

They all rose up then and went out.   There were
horses ready for each one of them and the *coash-t'ya
bower* for the king and the queen.   The king and queen
got into the coach, each man leaped on his own horse,
and be certain that Paudyeen was not behind.   The
piper went out before them and began playing them
music, and then off and away with them.   It was not
long till they came to Cnoc Matha.   The hill opened
and the king of the fairy host passed in.

Finvara and Nuala were there, the arch-king and
queen of the fairy host of Connacht, and thousands of
little persons.   Finvara came up and said :

"We are going to play a hurling match to-night
against the fairy host of Munster, and unless we beat
them our fame is gone for ever.   The match is to be
fought out on Moytura, under Slieve Belgadaun.

The Connacht host cried out : "We are all ready,
and we have no doubt but we'll beat them."

" Out with ye all," cried the high king; "the men of
the hill of Nephin will be on the ground before us."

They all went out, and little Donal and twelve pipers
more before them, playing melodious music.   When

tángadar go Mág-Tuire bí sluag-píð Ulúṁan agus ríṁ-ṁir Cnuic Néiṁin pompa. Anoiṁ, iṁ éigin do'n tsluag-píð beiṁt ṁeaṁ beó do beiṫ i láṫaiṁ nuaiṁ a bíonn ṁiad ag tṁoiḋ no ag bualaḋ báiṁe, agus ṁin é an ṁáṫ ṁug Dóṁnal beag Páidín O Ceallaig leiṁ. Bí ṁeaṁ daṁ ab ainm an Stangaiṁe buiḋe ó Innṁ i g-conndaé an Chláiṁ le sluag-píð Ulúṁan.

Níoṁ ḃṁada guṁ glac an dá ṁluag taoḃa, caiteaḋ ṁuaṁ an liaṫṁóiḋ agus toṁuig an gṁeann dá ṁṁiḃ.

Bí ṁiad ag bualaḋ báiṁe agus na píoḃaiṁiḋe ag ṁeinm ceóil, go ḃṁacaiḋ Páidín O Ceallaig ṁluag Ulúṁan ag ṁágail na láiṁe láiḋṁe, agus toṁuig ṁé ag cuiḋeaċtaiṁ le ṁluag-píð Connaċt. Táinig an Stangaiṁe i láṫaiṁ agus d'ionnṁuig ṁé Páidín O Ceallaig, aċt níoṁ ḃṁada guṁ ċuiṁ Páidín an Stangaiṁe buiḋe aiṁ a ṫaṁ-an-áiṁde. Ó bualaḋ-báiṁe, toṁuig an dá ṁluag ag tṁoiḋ, aċt níoṁ ḃṁada guṁ buail ṁluag Connaċt an ṁluag eile. Ann ṁin ṁinne ṁluag Ulúṁan pṁiompollám díoḃ ṁéin, agus toṁuig ṁiad ag iṫe uile niḋ glaṁ d'á dtáinig ṁiad ṁuaṁ leiṁ. Bíodaṁ ag ṁgṁioṁ na tíṁe pompa, go dtangadar cóṁ ṁada le Conga, nuaiṁ d'éiṁiġ na milte colam aṁ Poll-móṁ agus ṁluig ṁiad na pṁiompollám. Níl aon ainm aiṁ an bpoll go dtí an lá ṁo aċt Poll-na-gcolam.

Nuaiṁ ġnóṫuiġ ṁluag Connaċt an caṫ, tángadar aiṁ aiṁ go Cnoc Maċa, luċġáiṁeaċ go leóṁ, agus tug an ṁíġ Finbeaṁa ṁopán óiṁ do Páidín O Ceallaig, agus tug an píoḃaiṁe beag a ḃaile é, agus ċuiṁ ṁé 'nna ċoulaḋ le na ṁnaoi é.

Cuaiḋ mi ṫaṁt ann ṁin, agus ní ṫáṁla aon niḋ do b'ṁiú a innṁint; aċt aon oiḋċe aṁáin cuaiḋ Páidín ṁíoṁ 'ṁan tṁoiléaṁ agus dubaiṁt an ṁeaṁ beag leiṁ, "Tá mo ṁáṫaiṁ maṁḃ, agus dóġ an boṫán oṁ a cionn."

they came to Moytura, the fairy host of Munster and
the fairy men of the hill of Nephin were there before
them. Now, it is necessary for the fairy host to have
two live men beside them when they are fighting or at
a hurling-match, and that was the reason that little
Donal took Paddy O'Kelly with him. There was a man
they called the " *Yellow Stongirya*," with the fairy host
of Munster, from Ennis, in the County Clare.

It was not long till the two hosts took sides ; the ball
was thrown up between them, and the fun began in
earnest. They were hurling away, and the pipers playing music, until Paudyeen O'Kelly saw the host of Munster getting the strong hand, and he began helping the
fairy host of Connacht. The *Stongirya* came up and
he made at Paudyeen O'Kelly, but Paudyeen turned him
head over heels. From hurling the two hosts began at
fighting, but it was not long until the host of Connacht
beat the other host. Then the host of Munster made
flying beetles of themselves, and they began eating every
green thing that they came up to. They were destroying the country before them until they came as far as
Cong. Then there rose up thousands of doves out of the
hole, and they swallowed down the beetles. That hole
has no other name until this day but Pull-na-gullam,
the dove's hole.

When the fairy host of Connacht won their battle, they
came back to Cnoc Matha joyous enough, and the king
Finvara gave Paudyeen O'Kelly a purse of gold, and
the little piper brought him home, and put him into bed
beside his wife, and left him sleeping there.

A month went by after that without anything worth
mentioning, until one night Paudyeen went down to the
cellar, and the little man said to him : "My mother is
dead ; burn the house over her."

"Is fíor duit," ar Páidín, "duḃairt sí naċ raiḃ sí le beiṫ air an t-saoġal so aċt mí, agus tá an mí suas anois."

Air maidin, an lá air na ṁáraċ, ċuaiḋ Páidín cum an boṫán agus fuair sé an ċailleaċ marḃ. Ċuirfé splanc faoi an mbotán agus ḋóiġ sé é. Ṫáiniġ sé a baile ann sin, agus d'innis sé do'n fear beag go raiḃ an botán dóiġte. Ṫug an fear beag sgorán dó agus duḃairt, "Ni ḃéiḋ an sgorán sin folaṁ ċoṁ fad agus béiḋeas tu beó. Slán leat anois. Ni feicfiḋ tu mé níos mó, aċt bioḋ cuiṁne gnáṫaċ agad air an casóig. B'fhearr tosaċ agus príoṁ-áḋḃar do faiṫḃir."

Ṁair Páidín agus a ḃean bliaḋanta anḋiaiġ seó, ann san teaċ mór, agus nuair fuair sé bás d'fhág sé saiṫḃreas mór 'nna ḋiaiġ, agus muirġín mór le na ċaṫaḋ.

Sin cugaiḃ mo sgeul anois ó ṫús go deire, mar ċualaiḋ mise ó mo ṁáṫair ṁóir é.

UILLIAM O RUANAIĠ

Ann san aimsir i n-allód bí fear ann dar ab ainm Uilliam O Ruanaiġ, 'nna ċoṁnuiḋe i ngar do Ċláir-Ġailliṁ. Bí sé 'nna ḟeilméar. Aon lá aṁain ṫáinig an tiġearna-talṁan ċuige agus duḃairt. "Tá cíos trí bliaḋain agam ort, agus muna mbéiḋ sé agad dam faoi ċeann seaċtṁaine caiṫfiḋ mé amaċ air taoiḃ an bóṫair tu.

"Táim le dul go Gailliṁ amáraċ le h-ualaċ cruiṫneaċta do ḋíol, agus nuair a ġeoḃar mé a luaċ íocfaiḋ mé tu," ar Liam.

Air maidin, lá air na ṁáraċ, ċuir sé ualaċ cruiṫneaċta air an g-cairt agus bí sé dul go Gailliṁ leis.

" It is true for you," said Paudyeen. " She told me that she hadn't but a month to be on the world, and the month was up yesterday."

On the morning of the next day Paudyeen went to the hut and he found the hag dead. He put a coal under the hut and burned it. He came home and told the little man that the hut was burnt. The little man gave him a purse and said to him : " This purse will never be empty as long as you are alive. Now, you will never see me more ; but have a loving remembrance of the weasel. She was the beginning and the prime cause of your riches." Then he went away and Paudyeen never saw him again.

Paudyeen O'Kelly and his wife lived for years after this in the large house, and when he died he left great wealth behind him, and a large family to spend it.

There now is the story for you, from the first word to the last, as I heard it from my grandmother.

LEEAM O'ROONEY'S BURIAL.

IN the olden time there was once a man named William O'Rooney, living near Clare-Galway. He was a farmer. One day the landlord came to him and said : " I have three years' rent on you, and unless you have it for me within a week I'll throw you out on the side of the road."

" I'm going to Galway with a load of wheat to-morrow," said Leeam (William), " and when I get the price of it I'll pay you."

Next morning he put a load of wheat on the cart, and was going to Galway with it. When he was gone a

Nuair bi ré timċioll mile go leiṫ imṫiġṫe o'n teaċ, ṫáinig duine-uaṡal ċuige agus d'ḟiaḟruiġ ré ḋé "An cruiṫneaċt atá agad air an g-cairt?"

"Seaḋ," ar Liam, "tá mé dul 'ġá ḋiol le mo ċíor d'íoc."

"Cia méad atá ann?" ar ṡan duine uaṡal.

"Tá tonna cnearta ann," ar Liam.

"Ceannóċaiḋ mé uait é," ar ṡan duine uaṡal, agus ḃéaṟṟaiḋ mé an luaċ iṡ mó 'ṡa' margaḋ ḋuit. Nuair a ṟaċṟar tu ċom ṟaḋ leiṡ an mbóṫairín cáptaċ atá air do láiṁ ċlé, cas aṟteaċ agus bi ag imṫeaċt go dtagaiḋ tu go teaċ mór atá i ngleann, agus béiḋ mire ann ṡin ṟómaḋ le d'airgiou do ṫaḃairt duit.

Nuair ṫáinig Liam ċom ṟaḋa leiṡ an mbóṫairín ċar ṡé aṟteaċ, agus ḃí ṡé ag imṫeaċt go dtáinig ṡé ċom ṟaḋa le teaċ mór. Bi iongantaṡ air Liam nuair ċonnairc ṡé an teaċ mór, mar ṟugaḋ agus tógaḋ ann ṡan g-cómaṟṟanaċt é, agus ní ḟacaiḋ ṡé an teaċ mór ṡriaṁ roiṁe, cíu go raiḃ eólaṡ aige air uile teaċ i ḃroiġreaċt cúiġ ṁíle úḋ.

Nuair ṫáinig Liam i ngar do ṟgioból a ḃí anaice leiṡ an teaċ mór ṫáinig buaċaill beag amaċ agus duḃairt, "céad mile ḟáilte ṟómaḋ a Liaim Uí Ruanaiġ," cuir ṟac air a ṁuim agus ṫug aṟteaċ é. Ṫáinig buaċaill beag eile amaċ, cuir ḟáilte roiṁ Liam, cuir ṟac air a ṁuim, agus d'imṫiġ aṟteaċ leir. Bi buaċailliḋe ag teaċt, ag cuir ḟáilte roiṁ Liam, agus ag taḃairt ṟac leó, go raiḃ an tonna cruiṫneaċta imṫiġte. Ann ṡin ṫáinig iomlán na mbuaċaill i láṫair agus duḃairt Liam leó: "Tá eólaṡ agaiḃ uile orm-ṡa agus ní'l eólaṡ agam-ṡa orraiḃ-re." Ann ṡin duḃradar leir, "téiḋ aṟteaċ, agus iṫ do ḋinnéar, tá an máiġirtir ag ṟanaṁaint leat."

Ċuaiḋ Liam aṟteaċ agus ṟuiḋ ṡé ṟíoṡ ag an mbord. Ṃor iṫ ṡé an dara ġreim go dtáinig trom-ċodlaḋ air

couple of miles from the house a gentleman met him and asked him : " Is it wheat you've got on the cart ?"

" It is," says Leeam ; " I'm going to sell it to pay my rent."

" How much is there in it ?" said the gentleman.

" There's a ton, honest, in it," said Leeam.

" I'll buy it from you," said the gentleman, " and I'll give you the biggest price that's going in the market. When you'll go as far as the cart *boreen* (little road), that's on your left hand, turn down, and be going till you come to a big house in the valley. I'll be before you there to give you your money."

When Leeam came to the *boreen* he turned in, and was going until he came as far as the big house. Leeam wondered when he came as far as the big house, for he was born and raised (*i.e.*, reared) in the neighbourhood, and yet he had never seen the big house before, though he thought he knew every house within five miles of him.

When Leeam came near the barn that was close to the big house, a little lad came out and said : " A hundred thousand welcomes to you William O'Rooney," put a sack on his back and went in with it. Another little lad came out and welcomed Leeam, put a sack on his back, and went in with it. Lads were coming welcoming Leeam, and putting the sacks on their backs and carrying them in, until the ton of wheat was all gone. Then the whole of the lads came round him, and Leeam said : "Ye all know me, and I don't know ye !" Then they said to him : " Go in and eat your dinner ; the master's waiting for you."

Leeam went in and sat down at table ; but he had not the second mouthful taken till a heavy sleep came on him, and he fell down under the table. Then the aġus ċuit ré ꝼaoi an mbolͽ. Ann ꞅin ꞃinne an ꝺꞃaoiḋeaꝺóiꞃ ꝼeaꞃ-bꞃéiġe coꞃṁúil le Liam, aġus ċuiꞃ a baile cum mná Liaim é, leiꞃ an ᵹ-capoll, aġus leiꞃ an ᵹ-caiꞃt. Nuaiꞃ ᴛáiniᵹ ꞃé ᵹo ᴛeaċ Liaim ċuaiꝺ ꞃé ꞅuaꞅ ann ꞅan ᴛ-ꞅeompꞃa, luiꝺ aiꞃ leabuꝺ, aᵹuꞅ ꝼuaiꞃ báꞅ.

Níoꞃ bꝼaꝺa ᵹo nꝺeacaiꝺ an ᵹáiꞃ amaċ ᵹo ꞃaiḃ Liam O Ruanaiᵹ maꞃḃ. Ċuiꞃ an ᴛbean uiꞃᵹe ꞅíoꞃ aᵹuꞅ nuaiꞃ ḃí ꞅé ᴛeiṫ niᵹ ꞃí an coꞃp aᵹuꞅ ċuiꞃ oꞃ cionn cláiꞃ é. Ċáiniᵹ na cúṁaꞅꞃanna aᵹuꞅ ċaoineaꝺaꞃ ᵹo bꞃónaċ oꞃ cionn an ċuiꞃꞃ, aᵹuꞅ ḃí ᴛꞃuaᵹ ṁóꞃ ann ꝺo'n ṁnaoi ḃoiċᴛ, aċᴛ ni ꞃaiḃ móꞃán bꞃóin uiꞃꞃi ꝼéin, maꞃ ḃí Liam ꞅoꞃᴛa aᵹuꞅ i ꝼéin óᵹ. An lá aiꞃ na ṁáꞃaċ cuiꞃeaꝺ an coꞃp aᵹuꞅ ni ꞃaiḃ aon ċuiṁne níoꞃ mó aiꞃ Liam.

Ḃí buaċaill-aimꞅiꞃe aᵹ mnaoi Liaim aᵹuꞅ ꝺubaiꞃᴛ ꞅí leiꞃ, "buꝺ ċóiꞃ ꝺuiᴛ mé ꝼóꞅaꝺ, aᵹuꞅ áiᴛ Liaim ᵹlacaꝺ."

"ᴛá ꞅé ꞃó luaᴛ ꝼóꞃ, anꝺóiᵹ báꞃ ꝺo beiṫ ann ꞅan ᴛeaċ," aꞃ ꞅan buaċaill. "ꝼan ᵹo mbéiꝺ Liam cuꞃᴛa ꞅeaċᴛṁain."

Nuaiꞃ ḃí Liam ꞅeaċᴛ Lá aᵹuꞅ ꞅeaċᴛ n-oiꝺċe 'nna ċoꝺlaꝺ ᴛáiniᵹ buaċaill beaᵹ aᵹuꞅ ḋúiꞅiᵹ é. Ann ꞅin ꝺubaiꞃᴛ ꞃé leiꞃ, "ᴛáiꞃ ꞅeaċᴛṁain ꝺo ċoꝺlaꝺ. Cuiꞃeamaꞃ ꝺo ċapoll aᵹuꞅ ꝺo ċaiꞃᴛ aḃaile. Seó ḋuiᴛ ꝺo ċuiꝺ aiꞃᵹiꝺ, aᵹuꞅ imṫiᵹ."

ᴛáiniᵹ Liam a baile, aᵹuꞅ maꞃ ḃí ꞃé mall 'ꞅan oiꝺċe ni ꝼacaiꝺ aon ꝺuine é. Aiꞃ maꞃoin an laé ꞅin ċuaiꝺ bean Liaim aᵹuꞅ an buaċaill-aimꞅiꞃe ċum an ᴛ-ꞅaᵹaiꞃᴛ aᵹuꞅ ꝺ'iaꞃꞃ ꞃiaꝺ aiꞃ iaꝺ ꝺo ꝼóꞅaꝺ.

"Ḃꝼuil an ᴛ-aiꞃᵹioꝺ-póꞃᴛa aᵹaiḃ?"aꞃ ꞅan ꞅaᵹaiꞃᴛ.

"Níl," aꞃ ꞅan bean, "aċᴛ ᴛá ꞅᴛoꞃc muice aᵹam 'ꞅa' mbaile, aᵹuꞅ ᴛiᵹ leaᴛ i ḃeiṫ aᵹaꝺ i n-áiᴛ aiꞃᵹiꝺ.

Ꝼóꞃ an ꞅaᵹaiꞃᴛ iaꝺ, aᵹuꞅ ꝺubaiꞃᴛ, "cuiꞃꝼeaꝺ ꞅioꞃ aiꞃ an muic amáꞃaċ."

Nuaiꞃ ᴛáiniᵹ Liam ᵹo ꝺᴛí a ḃoꞃaꞅ ꝼéin, buail ꞃé buille

enchanter made a false man like William, and sent him
home to William's wife with the horse and cart. When
the false man came to Leeam's house, he went into the
room lay down on the bed and died.

It was not long till the cry went out that Leeam
O'Rooney was dead. The wife put down water, and
when it was hot she washed the body and put it over the
board (*i.e.*, laid it out). The neighbours came, and they
keened sorrowfully over the body, and there was great
pity for the poor wife, but there was not much grief on
herself, for Leeam was old and she was young. The
day on the morrow the body was buried, and there was
no more remembrance of Leeam.

Leeam's wife had a servant boy, and she said to him :
" You ought to marry me, and to take Leeam's place."

" It's too early yet, after there being a death in the
house," said the boy; " wait till Leeam is a week
buried."

When Leeam was seven days and seven nights asleep,
a little boy came to him and awoke him, and said:
" You've been asleep for a week; but we sent your horse
and cart home. Here's your money, and go."

Leeam came home, and as it was late at night nobody
saw him. On the morning of that same day Leeam's
wife and the servant lad went to the priest and asked
him to marry them.

" Have you the marriage money ? " said the priest.

" No," said the wife; " but I have a *sturk* of a pig at
home, and you can have her in place of money."

The priest married them, and said: " I'll send for the
pig to-morrow."

When Leeam came to his own door, he struck a blow
on it. The wife and the servant boy were going to bed,
and they asked : " Who's there ? "

aiṙ. Ḃí an ḃean aguṡ an buaċaill-aimṡiṙe aġ ḋul ċum
a leaḃuiḋ, aguṡ ḋ'ḟiaṙṙuiġ ṙiaḋ, "cia tá ann ṡin?"

"Miṡe," aṙ Liam, "foṡgail an ḋoṙaṡ ḋam."

Nuaiṙ ċualaḋaṙ an ġut ḃí fioṡ aca guṙ 'bé Liam ḋo
ḃí ann, aguṡ ḋuḃaiṙt a ḃean. "ní tiġ liom ḋo leigean
aṡteaċ, aguṡ iṡ móṙ an náiṙe ḋuit ḃeit teaċt aiṙ aiṙ anḋiaiġ tu ḃeit ṡeaċt lá ṙan uaiġ."

"An aiṙ miṙe atá tu?" aṙ Liam.

"Ní'lim aiṙ miṙe," aṙ ṡan ḃean, "tá fioṡ aġ an uile
ḋuine 'ṡa' bṙaṡáiṙte ġo bṙuaiṙ tu báṡ aguṡ guṙ ċuiṙ mé
ġo ġeanaṁail tu. Téiḋ aiṙ aiṙ ġo ḋ'uaiġ, aguṡ béiḋ
aiṡṙionn léiġte aġam aiṙ ṡon ḋ'anma ḃoiċt amáṙaċ."

"Fan ġo ḋtaġaiḋ ṡolaṡ an laé," aṙ Liam, "aguṡ
ḃéaṙṡaiḋ mé luaċ ḋo ṁaġaiḋ ḋuit."

Ann ṙin ċuaiḋ ṡé 'ṡan ṡtáḃla, 'n áit a ṙaiḃ a ċapall
aguṡ a ṁuc, ṡín ṡé ann ṡan tuiġe, aguṡ ṫuit ṡé 'nna
ċoḋlaḋ.

Aiṙ maiḋin, lá aiṙ na ṁáṙaċ, ḋuḃaiṙt an ṡaġaṙt le
buaċaill beaġ a ḃí aiġe, "Téiḋ ġo teaċ Liaim Ui Ruanaiġ
aguṡ ḃéaṙṡaiḋ an ḃean a ṗóṡ mé anḋé muc ḋuit le taḃ-
aiṙt a ḃaile leat."

Ṫáiniġ an buaċaill ġo ḋoṙaṡ an tiġe aguṡ ṫoṡuiġ 'ġá
ḃualaḋ le maiḋe a ḃí aiġe. Ḃí faitċioṡ aiṙ an mnaoi
an ḋoṙaṡ ḟoṡgailt, aċt ḋ'ḟiaṙṙuiġ ṙí, "cia tá ann ṡin?"

"Miṡe," aṙ ṡan buaċaill, "ċuiṙ an ṡaġaṙt mé le muc
ḋ'ḟáġail uait."

"Tá ṙí amuiġ 'ṡan ṡtáḃla," aṙ ṡan ḃean.

Cuaiḋ an buaċaill aṡteaċ 'ṡan ṡtáḃla aguṡ ṫoṡuiġ aġ
tiomáint na muice amaċ, nuaiṙ ḋ'éiṙiġ Liam aguṡ ḋuḃaiṙt,
"cá ḃfuil tu aġ ḋul le mo ṁuic?"

Nuaiṙ ċonnaiṙc an buaċaill Liam, aṙ ġo bṙát leiṡ,
aguṡ níoṙ ṙtop ġo nḋeacaiḋ ṡé ċum an tṡaġaiṙt aguṡ a
ċṙoiḋe aġ teaċt amaċ aiṙ a beul le faitċioṡ.

"Caḋ tá oṙt?" aṙ ṡan ṡaġaṙt.

"It's I," said Leeam; "open the door for me."

When they heard the voice, they knew that it was Leeam who was in it, and the wife said: "I can't let you in, and it's a great shame, you to be coming back again, after being seven days in your grave."

"Is it mad you are?" said Leeam.

"I'm not mad," said the wife; "doesn't every person in the parish know that you are dead, and that I buried you decently. Go back to your grave, and I'll have a mass read for your poor soul to-morrow."

"Wait till daylight comes," said Leeam, "and I'll give you the price of your joking!"

Then he went into the stable, where his horse and the pig were, stretched himself in the straw, and fell asleep.

Early on the morning of the next day, the priest said to a little lad that he had: "Get up, and go to Leeam O'Rooney's house, and the woman that I married yesterday will give you a pig to bring home with you."

The boy came to the door of the house, and began knocking at it with a stick. The wife was afraid to open the door, but she asked: "Who's there?"

"I," said the boy; "the priest sent me to get a pig from you."

"She's out in the stable," said the wife; "you can get her for yourself, and drive her back with you."

The lad went into the stable, and began driving out the pig, when Leeam rose up and said: "Where are you going with my pig?"

When the boy saw Leeam he never stopped to look again, but out with him as hard as he could, and he never stopped till he came back to the priest, and his heart coming out on his mouth with terror.

"What's on you?" says the priest.

D'innir an buaċaill dó go raiḃ Liam O Ruanaiġ ann ran ṛtáḃla, aguṛ naċ leigreaḋ ṛé ḋó an muc ṫaḃairt leiṛ.

" Ḃí do ṫoṛt, a ḃreugaḋóiṛ," aṛ ran ragaṛt, "tá Liam O'Ruanaiġ marḃ aguṛ ann ran uaiġ le reaċtṁain.

"Dá mbeiḋ' ṛé marḃ reaċt mbliaḋna connaṛic miṛe ann ran ṛtáḃla é ḃá ṁóimid ó ṛoin, aguṛ muna g-cṛeideann tu, taṛ, ṫu féin, aguṛ feicṛiḋ tu é."

Ann ṛin ṫáinig an ragaṛt aguṛ an buaċaill le ċéile go doṛaṛ an ṛtáḃla, aguṛ duḃairt an ragaṛt, "téiḋ aṛteaċ aguṛ cuiṛ an muc ṛin amaċ ċugam."

"Ní raċṛainn aṛteaċ aiṛ ran an méid iṛ ṛiú ṫu," aṛ ran buaċaill.

Cuaiḋ an ragaṛt aṛteaċ ann ṛin aguṛ ḃí ṛé ag tiomáint na muice amaċ, nuaiṛ d'éiṛiġ Liam ṛuaṛ aṛ an tuiġe aguṛ duḃairt, "cá ḃfuil tu dul le mo ṁuic, a aṫaiṛ Ṗádṛaig?"

Nuaiṛ a ċonnaiṛc an ragaṛt Liam ag éiṛiġe, aṛ go bṛáṫ leiṛ, ag ṛáḋ: "i n-ainm Dé orḋuiġim aiṛ aiṛ go dtí an uaiġ tu a Uilliaim Uí Ruanaiġ."

Ṫoṛuiġ Liam ag ṛit anḃiaiġ an trṛagaṛt, aguṛ ag ṛáḋ " A aṫaiṛ Ṗádṛaig ḃfuil tu aiṛ miṛe? ṛan aguṛ laḃaiṛ liom."

Níoṛ ṛan an ragaṛt aċt ċuaiḋ a ḃaile ċoṁ luaṫ aguṛ d'ḟeud a ċoṛa a iomċaṛ, aguṛ nuaiṛ ṫáinig ṛé aṛteaċ ḋún ṛé an doṛaṛ.   Ḃí Liam ag ḃualaḋ an doṛaiṛ go raiḃ ṛé ṛóṗuiġte, aċt ní leigṛeaḋ an ragaṛt aṛteaċ é.   Faoi ḋeiṛeaḋ ċuiṛ ṛé a ċeann amaċ aiṛ ḟuinneóiġ a ḃí aiṛ ḃáṛṛ an tiġe aguṛ duḃairt, "A Uilliam Uí Ruanaiġ téiḋ aiṛ aiṛ ċum d'uaiġe."

"Tá tu aiṛ miṛe a aṫaiṛ Ṗádṛaig, ní'l mé marḃ, aguṛ ní raiḃ mé ann aon uaiġ aṛiaṁ ó d'ḟág me bṛionn mo ṁáṫaiṛ," aṛ Liam.

"Ċonnaiṛc miṛe marḃ ṫu," aṛ ran ragaṛt, "ṛuaiṛ tu báṛ obann aguṛ ḃí mé i láṫaiṛ nuaiṛ cuiṛeaḋ tu 'ran uaiġ, aguṛ ṛinne mé ṛeanmóiṛ ḃṛeáġ oṛ do ċionn."

The lad told him that Leeam O'Rooney was in the stable, and would not let him drive out the pig.

"Hold your tongue, you liar!" said the priest; "Leeam O'Rooney's dead and in the grave this week."

"If he was in the grave this seven years, I saw him in the stable two moments ago; and if you don't believe me, come yourself, and you'll see him."

The priest and the boy then went together to the door of the stable, and the priest said: "Go in and turn me out that pig."

"I wouldn't go in for all ever you're worth," said the boy.

The priest went in, and began driving out the pig, when Leeam rose up out of the straw and said: "Where are you going with my pig, Father Patrick?"

When the priest saw Leeam, off and away with him, and he crying out: "In the name of God, I order you back to your grave, William O'Rooney."

Leeam began running after the priest, and saying, "Father Patrick, Father Patrick, are you mad? Wait and speak to me."

The priest would not wait for him, but made off home as fast as his feet could carry him, and when he got into the house, he shut the door. Leeam was knocking at the door till he was tired, but the priest would not let him in. At last, he put his head out of a window in the top of the house, and said: "William O'Rooney, go back to your grave."

"You're mad, Father Patrick! I'm not dead, and never was in a grave since I was born," said Leeam.

"I saw you dead," said the priest; "you died suddenly, and I was present when you were put into the grave, and made a fine sermon over you."

"Ðiaḃal uaim, ᵹo ḃfuil tu aiṙ miṙe cóṁ cinnte a'ṙ atá miṙe beó," aṙ Liam.

"Imtiġ aṙ m'aṁaṙc anoiṙ aᵹuṙ léiᵹ́ṙiḋ mé aifṙionn ḋuit amáṙaċ," aṙ ṙan ṙaᵹaṙt.

Ċuaiḋ Liam a ḃaile aᵹuṙ ḃuail ṙé a ḋoṙaṙ féin aċt ní leiᵹṙeaḋ an ḃean aṙteaċ é. Ann ṙin ḋuḃaiṙt ṙé leiṙ féin, "ṙaċfaḋ aᵹuṙ íocfaḋ mo ċíoṙ." Uile ḋuine a ċonnaiṙc Liam aiṙ a ḃealaċ ᵹo teaċ an tiᵹeaṙna ḃí ṙiaḋ aᵹ ṙit uaiḋ, maṙ faḋ i leaḃaṙ ᵹo ḃfuaiṙ ṙé báṙ. Nuaiṙ ċualaiḋ an tiᵹeaṙna talṁan ᵹo ṙaiḃ Liam O Ruanaiġ aᵹ teaċt ḋún ṙé na ḋoiṙṙe, aᵹuṙ ní leiᵹṙeaḋ ṙé aṙteaċ é. Ċoṙuiġ Liam aᵹ ḃualaḋ an ḋoṙaiṙ ṁóṙ ᵹuṙ faoil an tiᵹeaṙna ᵹo mbṙiṙfeaḋ ṙé aṙteaċ é. Ċáiniᵹ an tiᵹeaṙna ᵹo fuinneóiᵹ a ḃí aiṙ ḃáṙṙ an tiᵹe, aᵹuṙ ḋ'fiaṙṙuiᵹ, "caḋ tá tu aᵹ iaṙṙaiḋ?"

"Ċáiniᵹ mé le mo ċíoṙ íoc, maṙ feaṙ cneaṙta," aṙ Liam.

"Céiḋ aiṙ aiṙ ᵹo ḋtí ḃ'uaiġ, aᵹuṙ ḃéaṙṙaiḋ mé maiṫeaṁnaṙ ḋuit," aṙ ṙan Tiᵹeaṙna.

"Ní fáᵹṙaiḋ mé ṙeó, ᵹo ḃfáᵹ' mé ṙᵹṙíḃinn uait ᵹo ḃfuil mé íocta ṙuaṙ ᵹlan, ᵹo ḋtí an Ḃealtaine ṙeó ċuᵹainn.'

Ċuᵹ an Tiᵹeaṙna an ṙᵹṙíḃinn ḋó, aᵹuṙ ċáiniᵹ ṙé aḃaile. Ḃuail ṙé an ḋoṙaṙ, aċt ní leiᵹṙeaḋ an ḃean aṙteaċ é, aᵹ ṙáḋ leiṙ ᵹo ṙaiḃ Liam O Ruanaiġ maṙḃ aᵹuṙ euṙta, aᵹuṙ naċ ṙaiḃ ann ṙan ḃfeaṙ aᵹ an ḋoṙaṙ aċt fealltóiṙ.

"Ní fealltóiṙ mé," aṙ Liam, "tá mé anḋuaiġ cíoṙ tṙí ḃliaḋain ḃ'íoc le mo ṁáiᵹiṙtiṙ, aᵹuṙ ḃéiḋ ṙeilḃ mo tiᵹe féin aᵹam, no ḃéiḋ fioṙ aᵹam caḋ fáċ."

Ċuaiḋ ṙé ċum an ṙᵹioḃóil, aᵹuṙ fuaiṙ ṙé ḃaṙṙa móṙ iaṙainn aᵹuṙ níoṙ ḃṙaḋa ᵹuṙ ḃṙiṙ ṙé aṙteaċ an ḋoṙaṙ. Ḃí faitċioṙ móṙ aiṙ an mnaoi aᵹuṙ aiṙ an ḃfeaṙ nuaḋṙóṙta. Ṡaoileaḋaṙ ᵹo ṙaḃaḋaṙ i n-am an eiṙeiṙiġe, aᵹuṙ ᵹo ṙaiḃ ḋeiṙe an ḋoṁain aᵹ teaċt.

"Caḋ ċuiᵹe aiṙ faoil tu ᵹo ṙaiḃ miṙe maṙḃ?" aṙ Liam.

"The devil from me, but, as sure as I'm alive, you're mad!" said Leeam.

"Go out of my sight now," said the priest, "and I'll read a mass for you, to-morrow."

Leeam went home then, and knocked at his own door, but his wife would not let him in. Then he said to himself: "I may as well go and pay my rent now." On his way to the landlord's house every one who saw Leeam was running before him, for they thought he was dead. When the landlord heard that Leeam O'Rooney was coming, he shut the doors and would not let him in. Leeam began knocking at the hall-door till the lord thought he'd break it in. He came to a window in the top of the house, put out his head, and asked: "What are you wanting?"

"I'm come to pay my rent like an honest man," said Leeam.

"Go back to your grave, and I'll forgive you your rent," said the lord.

"I won't leave this," said Leeam, "till I get a writing from you that I'm paid up clean till next May."

The lord gave him the writing, and he came home and knocked at his own door, but the wife would not let him in. She said that Leeam O'Rooney was dead and buried, and that the man at the door was only a deceiver.

"I'm no deceiver," said William; "I'm after paying my master three years' rent, and I'll have possession of my own house, or else I'll know why."

He went to the barn and got a big bar of iron, and it wasn't long till he broke in the door. There was great fear on the wife, and the newly married husband. They thought they were in the time of the General Resurrection, and that the end of the world was coming.

"Naċ ḃfuil ḟios aġ uile ḋuine ann ṙan bṙaṗáiṙte ġo ḃfuil tu maṙḃ," aṙ ṙan ḃean.

"Do ċoṙp ó'n ḋiaḃal," aṙ Liam, "tá tu aġ maġaḋ ṙaḋa ġo leóṙ liom. Fáġ ḃuam niú le n-iṫe."

Ḃí eaġla ṁóṙ aiṙ ḟan mnaoi ḃoiċt aġur ġleur ṙí ḃiaḋ ḋó, aġur nuaiṙ ċonnaiṙc ṙí é aġ iṫe aġur aġ ól ḋuḃaiṙt ṙí, "tá mioṙḃúil ann."

Ann ṙin ḋ'innir Liam a ṙġeul ḋí, o ḃonn ġo ḃáṙṙ, aġur nuaiṙ ḋ'innir ṙé ġaċ níú, ḋuḃaiṙt ṙé, "ṙaċfaḋ ċum na n-uaiġe amáṙaċ ġo ḃfeicṙeaḋ an biṫeaṁnaċ ḋo ċuiṙ ṙiḃ-ṙe i m'áit-ṙé."

Lá aiṙ na ṁáṙaċ ṫuġ Liam ḋṙeam ḋaoine leiṙ, aġur ċuaiḋ ṙé ċum na ṙoiliġe, aġur ḋ'ḟoṙġail ṙiaḋ an uaiġ, aġur ḃíoḋaṙ ḋul an ċóṁṙa ḋ'ḟoṙġailt, aġur nuaiṙ a ḃí ṙiaḋ 'ġá tóġḃáil ṙuaṙ léim maḋaḋ móṙ ḋuḃ amaċ, aġur aṙ ġo ḃṙáċ leiṙ, aġur Liam aġur na ṙin eile 'nna ḋiaiġ. Ḃíoḋaṙ 'ġá leanaṁaint ġo ḃṙacaḋaṙ é aġ ḋul aṙteaċ ann ṙan teaċ a ṙaiḃ Liam 'nna ċoḋlaḋ ann. Ann ṙin ḋ'ḟoṙġail an talaṁ aġur ċuaiḋ an teaċ ṙíoṙ, aġur ní ḟacaiḋ aon ḋuine é ó ṙoin, aċt tá an poll móṙ le feicṙint ġo ḋtí an lá ṙo.

Nuaiṙ ḋ'imṫiġ Liam aġur na ṙin óga aḃaile ḋ'innir ṙiaḋ ġaċ níú ḋo ṙaġaiṙt na ṗaṙáiṙte, aġur ṙġaoil ṙé an ṗóṙaḋ a ḃi eiḋiṙ bean Liaim aġur an buaċaill-aimṙiṙe.

Do ṁaiṙ Liam bliaḋanta 'nna ḋiaiġ ṙeó, aġur ḋ'ḟáġ ṙé ṙaiḋḃṙeaṙ móṙ 'nna ḋiaiġ, aġur tá cuiṁne aiṙ i ġ-Cláṙ-Ġailliṁ ṙóṙ, aġur béiḋ ġo ḋeó, má ṫéiḋeann an ṙġeul ṙo ó na ṙean-ḋaoiniḃ ċum na nḋaoine óg.

"Why did you think I was dead?" said Leeam.

"Doesn't everybody in the parish know you're dead?" said the wife.

"Your body from the devil," said Leeam, "you're humbugging me long enough, and get me something to eat."

The poor woman was greatly afraid, and she dressed him some meat, and when she saw him eating and drinking, she said: "It's a miracle."

Then Leeam told her his story from first to last, and she told him each thing that happened, and then he said: "I'll go to the grave to-morrow, till I see the *behoonuck* ye buried in my place."

The day on the morrow Leeam brought a lot of men with him to the churchyard, and they dug open the grave, and were lifting up the coffin, when a big black dog jumped out of it, and made off, and Leeam and the men after it. They were following it till they saw it going into the house in which Leeam had been asleep, and then the ground opened, and the house went down, and nobody ever saw it from that out; but the big hole is to be seen till this day.

When Leeam and the men went home, they told everything to the priest of the parish, and he dissolved the marriage that was between Leeam's wife and the servant boy.

Leeam lived for years after that, and he left great wealth behind him, and they remember him in Clare-Galway still, and will remember him if this story goes down from the old people to the young.

GULEESH NA GUSS DHU.

THERE was once a boy in the County Mayo, and he never washed a foot from the day he was born. Guleesh was his name ; but as nobody could ever prevail on him to wash his feet, they used to call him Guleesh na guss dhu, or Guleesh Black-foot. It's often the father said to him : "Get up, you *stronc-sha* (lubber), and wash yourself," but the devil a foot would he get up, and the devil a foot would he wash. There was no use in talking to him. Every one used to be humbugging him on account of his dirty feet, but he paid them no heed nor attention. You might say anything at all to him, but in spite of it all he would have his own way afterwards.

One night the whole family were gathered in by the fire, telling stories and making fun for themselves, and he amongst them. The father said to him : " Guleesh, you are one and twenty years old to-night, and I believe you never washed a foot from the day you were born till to-day

" You lie," said Guleesh, " didn't I go a' swimming on May day last ? and I couldn't keep my feet out of the water."

" Well, they were as dirty as ever they were when you came to the shore," said the father.

" They were that, surely," said Guleesh.

" That's the thing I'm saying," says the father, " that it wasn't in you to wash your feet ever."

" And I never will wash them till the day of my death," said Guleesh.

" You miserable *bchovnugh !* you clown ! you tinker ! you good-for-nothing lubber ! what kind of answer is that ? " says the father ; " and with that he drew the hand

and struck him a hard fist on the jaw. "Be off with your-self," says he, "I can't stand you any longer."

Guleesh got up and put a hand to his jaw, where he got the fist. "Only that it's yourself that's in it, who gave me that blow," said he, "another blow you'd never strike till the day of your death." He went out of the house then and great anger on him.

There was the finest *lis*, or rath, in Ireland, a little way off from the gable of the house, and he was often in the habit of seating himself on the fine grass bank that was running round it. He stood, and he half leaning against the gable of the house, and looking up into the sky, and watching the beautiful white moon over his head. After him to be standing that way for a couple of hours, he said to himself: "My bitter grief that I am not gone away out of this place altogether. I'd sooner be any place in the world than here. Och, it's well for you, white moon," says he, "that's turning round, turning round, as you please yourself, and no man can put you back. I wish I was the same as you."

Hardly was the word out of his mouth when he heard a great noise coming like the sound of many people running together, and talking, and laughing, and making sport, and the sound went by him like a whirl of wind. and he was listening to it going into the rath. "Musha, by my soul, says he, "but ye're merry enough, and I'll follow ye.

What was in it but the fairy host, though he did not know at first that it was they who were in it, but he followed them into the rath. It's there he heard *the fulparnee, and the folpornee, the rap-lay-hoola, and the roolya-boolya,** that they had there, and every man of

---

* Untranslatable onomatopœic words expressive of noises.

them crying out as loud as he could: "My horse,
and bridle and saddle! My horse, and bridle, and
saddle!"

"By my hand," said Guleesh, "my boy, that's not
bad. I'll imitate ye," and he cried out as well as they:
"My horse, and bridle, and saddle! My horse, and
bridle, and saddle!" And on the moment there was a
fine horse with a bridle of gold, and a saddle of silver
standing before him. He leaped up on it, and the
moment he was on its back he saw clearly that the rath
was full of horses, and of little people going riding on
them.

Said a man of them to him: "Are you coming with
us to-night, Guleesh?"

"I am surely," said Guleesh.

"If you are, come along," said the little man, and out
with them altogether, riding like the wind, faster than
the fastest horse ever you saw a' hunting, and faster
than the fox and the hounds at his tail.

The cold winter's wind that was before them, they
overtook her, and the cold winter's wind that was behind
them, she did not overtake them. And stop nor stay of
that full race, did they make none, until they came to
the brink of the sea.

Then every one of them said: "Hie over cap! Hie
over cap!" and that moment they were up in the air,
and before Guleesh had time to remember where he
was, they were down on dry land again, and were going
like the wind. At last they stood, and a man of them
said to Guleesh: "Guleesh, do you know where you
are now?"

"Not a know," says Guleesh.

"You're in Rome, Guleesh," said he; "but we're going
further than that. The daughter of the king of France

is to be married to-night, the handsomest woman that
the sun ever saw, and we must do our best to bring her
with us, if we're only able to carry her off; and you
must come with us that we may be able to put the young
girl up behind you on the horse, when we'll be bringing
her away, for it's not lawful for us to put her sitting behind ourselves. But you're flesh and blood, and she can
take a good grip of you, so that she won't fall off the
horse. Are you satisfied, Guleesh, and will you do what
we're telling you?"

"Why shouldn't I be satisfied?" said Guleesh. "I m
satisfied, surely, and anything that ye will tell me to do
I'll do it without doubt; but where are we now?"

You're in Rome now, Guleesh," said the sheehogue
(fairy).

"In Rome, is it?" said Guleesh. "Indeed, and no lie,
I'm glad of that. The parish priest that we had he was
broken (suspended) and lost his parish some time ago;
I must go to the Pope till I get a bull from him that will
put him back in his own place again."

"Oh, Guleesh," said the sheehogue, "you can't do
that. You won't be let into the palace; and, anyhow,
we can't wait for you, for we're in a hurry."

"As much as a foot, I won't go with ye," says Guleesh,
"till I go to the Pope; but ye can go forward without
me, if ye wish. I won't stir till I go and get the pardon
of my parish priest."

"Guleesh, is it out of your senses you are? You can't
go; and there's your answer for you now. I tell you,
you can't go."

"Can't ye go on, and to leave me here after ye," said
Guleesh, "and when ye come back can't ye hoist the
girl up behind me?"

"But we want you at the palace of the king of

France," said the sheehogue, "and you must come with us now."

"The devil a foot," said Guleesh, "till I get the priest's pardon; the honestest and the pleasantest man that's in Ireland."

Another sheehogue spoke then, and said:

"Don't be so hard on Guleesh. The boy's a kind boy, and he has a good heart; and as he doesn't wish to come without the Pope's bull, we must do our best to get it for him. He and I will go in to the Pope, and ye can wait here."

"A thousand thanks to you," said Guleesh. "I'm ready to go with you; for this priest, he was the sportingest and the pleasantest man in the world."

"You have too much talk, Guleesh," said the sheehogue, "but come along now. Get off your horse and take my hand."

Guleesh dismounted, and took his hand; and then the little man said a couple of words he did not understand, and before he knew where he was he found himself in the room with the Pope.

The Pope was sitting up late that night reading a book that he liked. He was sitting on a big soft chair, and his two feet on the chimney-board. There was a fine fire in the grate, and a little table standing at his elbow, and a drop of ishka-baha (eau-de-vie) and sugar on the little table*en*; and he never felt till Guleesh came up behind him.

"Now Guleesh," said the sheehogue, "tell him that unless he gives you the bull you'll set the room on fire; and if he refuses it to you, I'll spurt fire round about out of my mouth, till he thinks the place is really in a blaze, and I'll go bail he'll be ready enough then to give you the pardon."

Guleesh went up to him and put his hand on his shoulder. The Pope turned round, and when he saw Guleesh standing behind him he frightened up.

"Don't be afraid," said Guleesh, "we have a parish priest at home, and some thief told your honour a lie about him, and he was broken; but he's the decentest man ever your honour saw, and there's not a man, woman, or child in Ballynatoothach but's in love with him.

"Hold your tongue, you *bodach*," said the Pope. "Where are you from, or what brought you here? Haven't I a lock on the door?"

"I came in on the keyhole," says Guleesh, "and I'd be very much obliged to your honour if you'd do what I'm asking."

The Pope cried out: "Where are all my people? Where are my servants? Shamus! Shawn! I'm killed; I'm robbed."

Guleesh put his back to the door, the way he could not get out, and he was afraid to go near Guleesh, so he had no help for it, but had to listen to Guleesh's story; and Guleesh could not tell it to him shortly and plainly, for he was slow and coarse in his speaking, and that angered the Pope; and when Guleesh finished his story, he vowed that he never would give the priest his pardon; and he threatened Guleesh himself that he would put him to death for his shamelessness in coming in upon him in the night; and he began again crying out for his servants. Whether the servants heard him or no, there was a lock on the inside of the door, so that they could not come in to him.

"Unless you give me a bull under your hand and seal, and the priest's pardon in it," said Guleesh; "I'll burn your house with fire."

The sheehogue, whom the Pope did not see, began to cast fire and flame out of his mouth, and the Pope thought that the room was all in a blaze. He cried out: "Oh, eternal destruction! I'll give you the pardon; I'll give you anything at all, only stop your fire, and don't burn me in my own house."

The sheehogue stopped the fire, and the Pope had to sit down and write a full pardon for the priest, and give him back his old place again, and when he had it ready written, he put his name under it on the paper, and put it into Guleesh's hand.

"Thank your honour," said Guleesh; "I never will come here again to you, and *bannacht lath* (good-bye.)

"Do not," said the Pope; "if you do I'll be ready before you, and you won't go from me so easily again. You will be shut up in a prison, and you won't get out for ever."

"Don't be afraid, I won't come again," said Guleesh. And before he could say any more the sheehogue spoke a couple of words, and caught Guleesh's hand again, and out with them. Guleesh found himself amongst the other sheehogues, and his horse waiting for him."

"Now, Guleesh," said they, "it's greatly you stopped us, and we in such a hurry; but come on now, and don't think of playing such a trick again, for we won't wait for you.

"I'm satisfied," said Guleesh, "and I'm thankful to ye; but tell me where are we going."

"We're to go to the palace of the king of France," said they; "and if we can at all, we're to carry off his daughter with us."

Every man of them then said, "Rise up, horse;" and the horses began leaping, and running, and prancing.

The cold wind of winter that was before them they overtook her, and the cold wind of winter that was behind them, she did not overtake them, and they never stopped of that race, till they came as far as the palace of the king of France.

They got off their horses there, and a man of them said a word that Guleesh did not understand, and on the moment they were lifted up, and Guleesh found himself and his companions in the palace. There was a great feast going on there, and there was not a nobleman or a gentleman in the kingdom but was gathered there, dressed in silk and satin, and gold and silver, and the night was as bright as the day with all the lamps and candles that were lit, and Guleesh had to shut his two eyes at the brightness. When he opened them again and looked from him, he thought he never saw anything as fine as all he saw there. There were a hundred tables spread out, and their full of meat and drink on each table of them, flesh-meat, and cakes and sweetmeats, and wine and ale, and every drink that ever a man saw. The musicians were at the two ends of the hall, and they playing the sweetest music that ever a man's ear heard, and there were young women and fine youths in the middle of the hall, dancing and turning, and going round so quickly and so lightly, that it put a *sooraun* in Guleesh's head to be looking at them. There were more there playing tricks, and more making fun and laughing, for such a feast as there was that day had not been in France for twenty years, because the old king had no children alive but only the one daughter, and she was to be married to the son of another king that night. Three days the feast was going on, and the third night she was to be married, and that was the night that Guleesh and the sheehogues came, hoping if they could, to carry off with them the king's young daughter.

Guleesh and his companions were standing together at the head of the hall, where there was a fine altar dressed up, and two bishops behind it waiting to marry the girl, as soon as the right time should come. Nobody could see the sheehogues, for they said a word as they came in, that made them all invisible, as if they had not been in it at all.

" Tell me which of them is the king's daughter," said Guleesh, when he was becoming a little used to the noise and the light.

" Don't you see her there from you ? " said the little man that he was talking to.

Guleesh looked where the little man was pointing with his finger, and there he saw the loveliest woman that was, he thought, upon the ridge of the world. The rose and the lily were fighting together in her face, and one could not tell which of them got the victory. Her arms and hands were like the lime, her mouth as red as a strawberry, when it is ripe, her foot was as small and as light as another one's hand, her form was smooth and slender, and her hair was falling down from her head in buckies of gold. Her garments and dress were woven with gold and silver, and the bright stone that was in the ring on her hand was as shining as the sun.

Guleesh was nearly blinded with all the loveliness and beauty that was in her; but when he looked again, he saw that she was crying, and that there was the trace of tears in her eyes. "It can't be," said Guleesh, "that there's grief on her, when everybody round her is so full of sport and merriment."

"Musha, then, she is grieved," said the little man; " for it's against her own will she's marrying, and she

has no love for the husband she is to marry. The king
was going to give her to him three years ago, when she
was only fifteen, but she said she was too young, and
requested him to leave her as she was yet. The king gave
her a year's grace, and when that year was up he gave
her another year's grace, and then another; but a week
or a day he would not give her longer, and she is
eighteen years old to-night, and it's time for her to
marry; but, indeed," says he, and he crooked his mouth
in an ugly way; "indeed, it's no king's son she'll marry,
if I can help it."

Guleesh pitied the handsome young lady greatly when
he heard that, and he was heart-broken to think that it
would be necessary for her to marry a man she did not
like, or what was worse, to take a nasty Sheehogue for
a husband. However, he did not say a word, though
he could not help giving many a curse to the ill-luck
that was laid out for himself, and he helping the people
that were to snatch her away from her home and from
her father.

He began thinking, then, what it was he ought to do
to save her, but he could think of nothing. "Oh, if I
could only give her some help and relief," said he, "I
wouldn't care whether I were alive or dead; but I see
nothing that I can do for her."

He was looking on when the king's son came up to
her and asked her for a kiss, but she turned her head
away from him. Guleesh had double pity for her then,
when he saw the lad taking her by the soft white hand,
and drawing her out to dance. They went round in
the dance near where Guleesh was, and he could plainly
see that there were tears in her eyes.

When the dancing was over, the old king, her father,
and her mother the queen, came up and said that this

9

was the right time to marry her, that the bishop was ready and the couch prepared, and it was time to put the wedding-ring on her and give her to her husband.

The old king put a laugh out of him: "Upon my honour," he said, "the night is nearly spent, but my son will make a night for himself. I'll go bail he won't rise early to-morrow."

"Musha, and maybe he would," said the Sheehogue in Guleesh's ear, "or not go to bed, perhaps, at all. Ha, ha, ha!"

Guleesh gave him no answer, for his two eyes were going out on his head watching to see what they would do then.

The king took the youth by the hand, and the queen took her daughter, and they went up together to the altar, with the lords and great people following them.

When they came near the altar, and were no more than about four yards from it, the little sheehogue stretched out his foot before the girl, and she fell. Before she was able to rise again he threw something that was in his hand upon her, said a couple of words, and upon the moment the maiden was gone from amongst them. Nobody could see her, for that word made her invisible. The little maneen seized her and raised her up behind Guleesh, and the king nor no one else saw them, but out with them through the hall till they came to the door.

Oro! dear Mary! it's there the pity was, and the trouble, and the crying, and the wonder, and the searching, and the rookawn, when that lady disappeared from their eyes, and without their seeing what did it. Out on the door of the palace with them, without being stopped or hindered, for nobody saw them, and, "My horse, my bridle, and saddle!" says every man of them.

"My horse, my bridle, and saddle!" says Guleesh; and on the moment the horse was standing ready caparisoned before him. "Now, jump up, Guleesh," said the little man, "and put the lady behind you, and we will be going; the morning is not far off from us now."

Guleesh raised her up on the horse's back, and leaped up himself before her, and, "Rise horse," said he; and his horse, and the other horses with him, went in a full race until they came to the sea.

"Highover, cap!" said every man of them.

"Highover, cap!" said Guleesh; and on the moment the horse rose under him, and cut a leap in the clouds, and came down in Erin.

They did not stop there, but went of a race to the place where was Guleesh's house and the rath. And when they came as far as that, Guleesh turned and caught the young girl in his two arms, and leaped off the horse.

"I call and cross you to myself, in the name of God!" said he; and on the spot, before the word was out of his mouth, the horse fell down, and what was in it but the beam of a plough, of which they had made a horse; and every other horse they had, it was that way they made it. Some of them were riding on an old besom, and some on a broken stick, and more on a *bohalawn* (rag weed), or a hemlock-stalk.

The good people called out together when they heard what Guleesh said:

"Oh, Guleesh, you clown, you thief, that no good may happen you, why did you play that trick on us?"

But they had no power at all to carry off the girl, after Guleesh had consecrated her to himself.

"Oh, Guleesh, isn't that a nice turn you did us, and we so kind to you? What good have we now out of

our journey to Rome and to France?. Never mind yet,
you clown, but you ll pay us another time for this. Believe us you'll repent it."

" He'll have no good to get out of the young girl," said
the little man that was t alking to him in the palace before that, and as he said the word he moved over to her
and struck her a slap on the side of the head. " Now,"
says he, " she'll be without talk any more ; now, Guleesh,
what good will she be to you when she'll be dumb? It's
time for us to go—but you'll remember us, Guleesh na
Guss Dhu ! "

When he said that he stretched out his two hands,
and before Guleesh was able to give an answer, he and
the rest of them were gone into the rath out of his sight,
and he saw them no more.

He turned to the young woman and said to her :
"Thanks be to God, they're gone. Would you not
sooner stay with me than with them ?". She gave him
no answer. " There's trouble and gri ef on her yet, said
Guleesh in his own mind, and he spoke to her again :
'I am afraid that you must spend this night in my
father's house, lady, and if there is anything that I can
do for you, tell me, and I'll be your servant."

The beautiful girl remained silent, but there were
tears in her eyes, and her face was white and red after
each other.

" Lady," said Guleesh, " tell me what you would like
me to do now. I never belonged at all to that lot of
sheehogues who carried you away with them. I am
the son of an honest farmer, and I went with them without knowing it. If I'll be able to send you back to your
father I'll do it, and I pray you make any use of me
now that you may wish."

He looked into her face, and he saw the mouth

moving as if she was going to speak, but there came no word from it.

"It cannot be," said Guleesh, "that you are dumb. Did I not hear you speaking to the king's son in the palace to-night?. Or has that devil made you really dumb, when he struck his nasty hand on your jaw?".

The girl raised her white smooth hand, and laid her finger on her tongue, to show him that she had lost her voice and power of speech, and the tears ran out of her two eyes like streams, and Guleesh's own eyes were not dry, for as rough as he was on the outside he had a soft heart, and could not stand the sight of the young girl, and she in that unhappy plight.

He began thinking with himself what he ought to do, and he did not like to bring her home with himself to his father's house, for he knew well that they would not believe him, that he had been in France and brought back with him the king of France's daughter, and he was afraid they might make a mock of the young lady or insult her.

As he was doubting what he ought to do, and hesitating, he chanced to put his hand in his pocket, and he found a paper in it. He pulled it up, and the moment he looked at it he remembered it was the Pope's bull. "Glory be to God," said he, "I know now what I'll do; I'll bring her to the priest's house, and as soon as he sees the pardon I have here, he won't refuse me to keep the lady and care her." He turned to the lady again and told her that he was loath to take her to his father's house, but that there was an excellent priest very friendly to himself, who would take good care of her, if she wished to remain in his house; but that if there was any other place she would rather go, he said he would bring her to it.

She bent her head, to show him she was obliged, and gave him to understand that she was ready to follow him any place he was going. "We will go to the priest's house, then," said he ; "he is under an obligation to me, and will do anything I ask him."

They went together accordingly to the priest's house, and the sun was just rising when they came to the door. Guleesh beat it hard, and as early as it was the priest was up, and opened the door himself. He wondered when he saw Guleesh and the girl, for he was certain that it was coming wanting to be married they were.

"Guleesh na Guss Dhu, isn't it the nice boy you are that you can't wait till ten o'clock or till twelve, but that you must be coming to me at this hour, looking for marriage, you and your *girshuch*. You ought to know that I'm broken, and that I can't marry you, or at all events, can't marry you lawfully. But ubbubboo ! " said he, suddenly, as he looked again at the young girl, " in the name of God, who have you here ?. Who is she, or how did you get her ? ".

"Father," said Guleesh, " you can marry me, or anybody else, any more, if you wish ; but it's not looking for marriage I came to you now, but to ask you, if you please, to give a lodging in your house to this young lady." And with that he drew out the Pope's bull, and gave it to the priest to read.

The priest took it, and read it, and looked sharply at the writing and seal, and he had no doubt but it was a right bull, from the hand of the Pope.

" Where did you get this ? " said he to Guleesh, and the hand he held the paper in, was trembling with wonder and joy.

" Oh, musha ! " said Guleesh, airily enough, " I got it last night in Rome ; I remained a couple of hours in the

city there, when I was on my way to bring this young
lady, daughter of the king of France, back with me."

The priest looked at him as though he had ten heads
on him; but without putting any other question to him,
he desired him to come in, himself and the maiden, and
when they came in, he shut the door, brought them into
the parlour, and put them sitting.

" Now, Guleesh," said he, " tell me truly where did you
get this bull, and who is this young lady, and whether
you're out of your senses really, or are only making a
joke of me?".

" I'm not telling a word of lie, nor making a joke of
you," said Guleesh; " but it was from the Pope himself
I got the paper, and it was from the palace of the king
of France I carried off this lady, and she is the daughter
of the king of France."

He began his story then, and told the whole to the
priest, and the priest was so much surprised that he
could not help calling out at times, or clapping his
hands together.

When Guleesh said from what he saw he thought the
girl was not satisfied with the marriage that was going
to take place in the palace before he and the sheehogues
broke it up, there came a red blush into the girl's cheek,
and he was more certain than ever that she had sooner be
as she was—badly as she was—than be the married wife
of the man she hated. When Guleesh said that he would
be very thankful to the priest if he would keep her in his
own house, the kind man said he would do that as long
as Guleesh pleased, but that he did not know what they
ought to do with her, because they had no means of
sending her back to her father again.

Guleesh answered that he was uneasy about the same
thing, and that he saw nothing to do but to keep quiet

until they should find some opportunity of doing something better.   They made it up then between themselves
that the priest should let on that it was his brother's
daughter he had, who was come on a visit to him from
another county, and that he should tell everybody that
she was dumb, and do his best to keep everyone away
from her.   They told the young girl what it was they in-
tended to do, and she showed by her eyes that she was
obliged to them.

Guleesh went home then, and when his people asked
him where he was, he said that he was asleep at the foot
of the ditch, and passed the night there.

There was great wonderment on the neighbours when
the honest priest showed them the Pope's bull, and got his
old place again, and everyone was rejoiced, for, indeed,
there was no fault at all in that honest man, except that
now and again he would have too much liking for a drop
of the bottle; but no one could say that he ever saw him
in a way that he could not utter "here's to your health," as
well as ever a man in the kingdom.   But if they wondered
to see the priest back again in his old place, much more
did they wonder at the girl who came so suddenly to his
house without anyone knowing where she was from, or
what business she had there.   Some of the people said that
everything was not as it ought to be, and others that it
was not possible that the Pope gave back his place to the
priest after taking it from him before, on account of the
complaints about his drinking.   And there were more of
them, too, who said that Guleesh na Guss Dhu was not like
the same man that was in it before, and that it was a great
story (i.e., a thing to wonder at) how he was drawing every
day to the priest's house, and that the priest had a wish
and a respect for him, a thing they could not clear up at
all.

That was true for them, indeed, for it was seldom the
day went by but Guleesh would go to the priest's house,
and have a talk with him, and as often as he would come
he used to hope to find the young lady well again, and
with leave to speak ; but, alas ! she remained dumb and
silent, without relief or cure. Since she had no other
means of talking she carried on a sort of conversation
between herself and himself, by moving her hand and
fingers, winking her eyes, opening and shutting her
mouth, laughing or smiling, and a thousand other
signs, so that it was not long until they understood each
other very well. Guleesh was always thinking how he
should send her back to her father ; butthere was no one
to go with her, and he himself did not know what road
to go, for he had never been out of his own country before the night he brought her away with him. Nor had
the priest any better knowledge than he ; but when
Guleesh asked him, he wrote three or four letters to the
king of France, and gave them to buyers and sellers of
wares, who used to be going from place to place across
the sea ; but they all went astray, and never one came to
the king's hand.

This was the way they were for many months, and
Guleesh was falling deeper and deeper in love with her
every day, and it was plain to himself and the priest that
she liked him. The boy feared greatly at last, lest the
king should really hear where his daughter was, and take
her back from himself, and he besought the priest to write
no more, but to leave the matter to God.

So they passed the time for a year, until there came a
day when Guleesh was lying by himself on the grass,
on the last day of the last month in autumn (*i.e.*, Octo-
ber), and he thinking over again in his own mind of
everything that happened to him from the day that he

went with the sheehogues across the sea. He remembered then, suddenly, that it was one November night that he was standing at the gable of the house, when the whirlwind came, and the sheehogues in it, and he said to himself: "We have November night again to-day, and I'll stand in the same place I was last year, until I see will the good people come again. Perhaps I might see or hear something that would be useful to me, and might bring back her talk again to Mary"—that was the name himself and the priest called the king's daughter, for neither of them knew her right name. He told his intention to the priest, and the priest gave him his blessing.

Guleesh accordingly went to the old rath when the night was darkening, and he stood with his bent elbow leaning on a gray old flag, waiting till the middle of the night should come. The moon rose slowly, and it was like a knob of fire behind him ; and there was a white fog which was raised up over the fields of grass and all damp places, through the coolness of the night after a great heat in the day. The night was calm as is a lake when there is not a breath of wind to move a wave on it, and there was no sound to be heard but the *cronawn* (hum) of the insects that would go by from time to time, or the hoarse sudden scream of the wild-geese, as they passed from lake to lake, half a mile up in the air over his head ; or the sharp whistle of the fadogues and flibeens (golden and green plover), rising and lying, lying and rising, as they do on a calm night. There were a thousand thousand bright stars shining over his head, and there was a little frost out, which left the grass under his foot white and crisp.

He stood there for an hour, for two hours, for three hours, and the frost increased greatly, so that he heard the breaking of the *trancens* under his foot as often as he moved. He was thinking, in his own mind, at last, that the sheehogues would not come that night, and that it was as good for him to return back again, when he heard a sound far away from him, coming towards him, and he recognised what it was at the first moment. The sound increased, and at first it was like the beating of waves on a stony shore, and then it was like the falling of a great waterfall, and at last it was like a loud storm in the tops of the trees, and then the whirlwind burst into the rath of one rout, and the sheeogues were in it.

It all went by him so suddenly that he lost his breath with it, but he came to himself on the spot, and put an ear on himself, listening to what they would say.

Scarcely had they gathered into the rath till they all began shouting, and screaming, and talking amongst themselves; and then each one of them cried out: " My horse, and bridle, and saddle ! My horse, and bridle, and saddle !" and Guleesh took courage, and called out as loudly as any of them : " My horse, and bridle and saddle ! My horse, and bridle and saddle." But before the word was well out of his mouth, another man cried out : " Ora ! Guleesh, my boy, are you here with us again ?. How are you coming on with your woman ?· There's no use in your calling for your horse to-night· I'll go bail you won't play on us again. It was a good trick you played on us last year !".

" It was," said another man, " he won't do it again."

" Isn't he a prime lad, the same lad ! to take a woman with him that never said as much to him as, ' how do you do ?' since this time last year !" says the third man.

" Perhaps he likes to be looking at her," said another voice.

" And if the *omadawn* only knew that there's an herb

growing up by his own door, and to boil it and give it
to her and she'd be well," said another voice.

"That's true for you."

"He is an omadawn."

"Don't bother your head with him, we'll be going."

"We'll leave the *bodach* as he is."

And with that they rose up into the air, and out with
them of one *roolya-boolya* the way they came; and they
left poor Guleesh standing where they found him, and
the two eyes going out of his head, looking after them
and wondering.

He did not stand long till he returned back, and he
thinking in his own mind on all he saw and heard, and
wondering whether there was really an herb at his own
door that would bring back the talk to the king's daughter. "It can't be," says he to himself, "that they would
tell it to me, if there was any virtue in it; but perhaps
the sheehogue didn't observe himself when he let the
word slip out of his mouth. I'll search well as soon as
the sun rises, whether there's any plant growing beside
the house except thistles and dockings."

He went home, and as tired as he was he did not sleep
a wink until the sun rose on the morrow. He got up
then, and it was the first thing he did to go out and search
well through the grass round about the house, trying
could he get any herb that he did not recognize. And,
indeed, he was not long searching till he observed a
large strange herb that was growing up just by the
gable of the house.

He went over to it, and observed it closely, and saw
that there were seven little branches coming out of
the stalk, and seven leaves growing on every branch*een*
of them, and that there was a white sap in the leaves.
"It's very wonderful," said he to himself, "that I never

noticed this herb before. If there's any virtue in an herb at all, it ought to be in such a strange one as this."

He drew out his knife, cut the plant, and carried it into his own house; stripped the leaves off it and cut up the stalk; and there came a thick, white juice out of it, as there comes out of the sow-thistle when it is bruised, except that the juice was more like oil.

He put it in a little pot and a little water in it, and laid it on the fire until the water was boiling, and then he took a cup, filled it half up with the juice, and put it to his own mouth. It came into his head then that perhaps it was poison that was in it, and that the good people were only tempting him that he might kill himself with that trick, or put the girl to death without meaning it. He put down the cup again, raised a couple of drops on the top of his finger, and put it to his mouth. It was not bitter, and, indeed, had a sweet, agreeable taste. He grew bolder then, and drank the full of a thimble of it, and then as much again, and he never stopped till he had half the cup drunk. He fell asleep after that, and did not wake till it was night, and there was great hunger and great thirst on him.

He had to wait, then, till the day rose; but he determined, as soon as he should wake in the morning, that he would go to the king's daughter and give her a drink of the juice of the herb.

As soon as he got up in the morning, he went over to the priest's house with the drink in his hand, and he never felt himself so bold and valiant, and spirited and light, as he was that day, and he was quite certain that it was the drink he drank which made him so hearty.

When he came to the house, he found the priest and the young lady within, and they were wondering greatly why he had not visited them for two days.

He told them all his news, and said that he was certain that there was great power in that herb, and that it would do the lady no hurt, for he tried it himself and got good from it, and then he made her taste it, for he vowed and swore that there was no harm in it.

Guleesh handed her the cup, and she drank half of it, and then fell back on her bed and a heavy sleep came on her, and she never woke out of that sleep till the day on the morrow.

Guleesh and the priest sat up the entire night with her, waiting till she should awake, and they between hope and unhope, between expectation of saving her and fear of hurting her.

She awoke at last when the sun had gone half its way through the heavens. She rubbed her eyes and looked like a person who did not know where she was. She was like one astonished when she saw Guleesh and the priest in the same room with her, and she sat up doing her best to collect her thoughts.

The two men were in great anxiety waiting to see would she speak, or would she not speak, and when they remained silent for a couple of minutes, the priest said to her: "Did you sleep well, Mary?".

And she answered him: "I slept, thank you."

No sooner did Guleesh hear her talking than he put a shout of joy out of him, and ran over to her and fell on his two knees, and said: "A thousand thanks to God, who has given you back the talk; lady of my heart, speak again to me."

The lady answered him that she understood it was he who boiled that drink for her, and gave it to her; that she was obliged to him from her heart for all the kindness he showed her since the day she first came to Ireland, and that he might be certain that she never would forget it.

Guleesh was ready to die with satisfaction and delight. Then they brought her food, and she eat with a good appetite, and was merry and joyous, and never left oft talking with the priest while she was eating.

After that Guleesh went home to his house, and stretched himself on the bed and fell asleep again, for the force of the herb was not all spent, and he passed another day and a night sleeping. When he woke up he went back to the priest's house, and found that the young lady was in the same state, and that she was asleep almost since the time that he left the house.

He went into her chamber with the priest, and they remained watching beside her till she awoke the second time, and she had her talk as well as ever, and Guleesh was greatly rejoiced. The priest put food on the table again, and they eat together, and Guleesh used after that to come to the house from day to day, and the friendship that was between him and the king's daughter increased, because she had no one to speak to except Guleesh and the priest, and she liked Guleesh best.

He had to tell her the way he was standing by the rath when the good people came, and how he went in to the Pope, and how the sheehogue blew fire out of his mouth, and every other thing that he did till the time the good people whipt her off with themselves; and when it would be all told he would have to begin it again out of the new, and she never was tired listening to him.

When they had been that way for another half year, she said that she could wait no longer without going back to her father and mother; that she was certain that they were greatly grieved for her; and that it was a shame for her to leave them in grief, when it was in her power to go as far as them. The priest did all he could to keep her with them for another while, but without effect, and Guleesh spoke every sweet word that came into his head, trying to get the victory over her, and to coax her and make her stay as she was, but it was no good for him. She determined that she would go, and no man alive would make her change her intention.

She had not much money, but only two rings that were on her hand, when the sheehogue carried her away, and a gold pin that was in her hair, and golden bluckles that were on her little shoes.

The priest took and sold them and gave her the money, and she said that she was ready to go.

She left her blessing and farewell with the priest and Guleesh, and departed. She was not long gone till there came such grief and melancholy over Guleesh that he knew he would not be long alive unless he were near her, and he followed her.

(The next 42 pages in the Leabhar Sgeuluigheachta are taken up with the adventures of Guleesh and the princess, on their way to the court of France. But this portion of the story is partly taken from other tales, and part is too much altered and amplified in the writing of it, so that I do not give it here, as not being genuine folk-lore, which the story, except for a very little embellishment, has been up to this point. The whole ends as follows, with the restoration of the princess and her marriage with Guleesh.)

It was well, and it was not ill. They married one another, and that was the fine wedding they had, and if I were to be there then, I would not be here now; but I heard it from a birdeen that there was neither cark nor care, sickness nor sorrow, mishap nor misfortune on them till the hour of their death, and that it may be the same with me, and with us all!

THE WELL OF D'YERREE-IN-DOWAN.

A LONG time ago—before St. Patrick's time—there was an old king in Connacht, and he had three sons. The king had a sore foot for many years, and he could get no cure. One day he sent for the Dall Glic (wise blind man) which he had, and said to him:

"I'm giving you wages this twenty years, and you can't tell me what will cure my foot."

"You never asked me that question before," said the Dall Glic; "but I tell you now that there is nothing in the world to cure you but a bottle of water from the Well of D'yerree-in-Dowan" (*i.e.*, end of the world).

In the morning, the day on the morrow, the king called his three sons, and he said to them:

"My foot will never be better until I get a bottle of water from the Well of D'yerree-in-Dowan, and whichever of you will bring me that, he has my kingdom to get."

"We will go in pursuit of it to-morrow," says the three. The names of the three were Art, Nart (*i.e.*, strength), and Cart* (*i.c.*, right).

On the morning of the day on the morrow, the king gave to each one of them a purse of gold, and they went on their way. When they came as far as the cross-roads, Art said:

"Each one of us ought to go a road for himself, and if one of us is back before a year and a day, let him wait till the other two come; or else let him set up a stone as a sign that he has come back safe."

They parted from one another after that, and Art and Nart went to an inn and began drinking; but Cart

---

* These names are not exactly pronounced as written. To pronounce them properly say *yart* first, and then *yart* with an *n* and a *c* before it, *n'yart* and *c'yart*

went on by himself. He walked all that day without
knowing where he was going. As the darkness of the
night came on he was entering a great wood, and he was
going forwards in the wood, until he came to a large
house. He went in and looked round him, but he saw
nobody, except a large white cat sitting beside the fire.
When the cat saw him she rose up and went into another
room. He was tired and sat beside the fire. It was
not long till the door of the chamber opened, and there
came out an old hag.

"One hundred thousand welcomes before you, son of
the king of Connacht," says the hag.

"How did you know me?" says the king's son.

"Oh, many's the good day I spent in your father's
castle in Bwee-sounee, and I know you since you were
born," said the hag.

Then she prepared him a fine supper, and gave it to
him. When he had eaten and drunk enough, she said
to him :

"You made a long journey to-day; come with me
until I show you a bed. Then she brought him to a fine
chamber, showed him a bed, and the king's son fell
asleep. He did not awake until the sun was coming in
on the windows the next morning.

Then he rose up, dressed himself, and was going out,
when the hag asked him where he was going.

"I don't know," said the king's son. "I left home to
find out the Well of D'yerree-in-Dowan."

"I'm after walking a good many places," said the hag,
"but I never heard talk of the Well of D'yerree-in-Dowan
before."

The king's son went out, and he was travelling till he
came to a cross-roads between two woods. He did not
know which road to take. He saw a seat under the

trunk of a great tree. When he went up to it he found it written: "This is the seat of travellers."

The king's son sat down, and after a minute he saw the most lovely woman in the world coming toward him, and she dressed in red silk, and she said to him:

"I often heard that it is better to go forward than back."

Then she went out of his sight as though the ground should swallow her.

The king's son rose up and went forward. He walked that day till the darkness of the night was coming on, and he did not know where to get lodgings. He saw a light in a wood, and he drew towards it. The light was in a little house. There was not as much as the end of a feather jutting up on the outside nor jutting down on the inside, but only one single feather that was keeping up the house. He knocked at the door, and an old hag opened it.

"God save all here," says the king's son.

"A hundred welcomes before you, son of the king of the castle of Bwee-sounee," said the hag.

"How did you know me?" said the king's son.

"It was my sister nursed you," said the hag, "and sit down till I get your supper ready."

When he ate and drank his enough, she put him to sleep till morning. When he rose up in the morning, he prayed to God to direct him on the road of his luck.

"How far will you go to-day?" said the hag.

"I don't know," said the king's son. "I'm in search of the Well of D'yerree-in-Dowan.

"I'm three hundred years here," said the hag, and I never heard of such a place before; but I have a sister older than myself, and, perhaps, she may know of it. Here is a ball of silver for you, and when you will go out upon the road throw it up before you, and follow it till you come to the house of my sister."

When he went out on the road he threw down the ball, and he was following it until the sun was going under the shadow of the hills. Then he went into a wood, and came to the door of a little house. When he struck the door, a hag opened it, and said:

"A hundred thousand welcomes before you, son of the king of the castle of Bwee-sounee, who were at my sister's house last night. You made a long journey to-day. Sit down; I have a supper ready for you."

When the king's son ate and drank his enough, the hag put him to sleep, and he did not wake up till the morning. Then the hag asked:

"Where are you going?".

"I don't rightly know," said the king's son. "I left home to find out the Well of D'yerree-in-Dowan."

"I am over five hundred years of age," said the hag, "and I never heard talk of that place before; but I have a brother, and if there is any such place in the world, he'll know of it. He is living seven hundred miles from here."

"It's a long journey," said the king's son.

"You'll be there to-night," said the hag.

Then she gave him a little garraun (nag, gelding) about the size of a goat.

"That little beast won't be able to carry me,' said the kings' son.

"Wait till you go riding on it," said the hag.

The king's son got on the garraun, and out for ever with him as fast as lightning.

When the sun was going under, that evening, he came to a little house in a wood. The king's son got off the garraun, went in, and it was not long till an old grey man came out, and said:

"A hundred thousand welcomes to you, son of the

king of the castle of Bwee-sounee.   You're in search of
the Well of D'yerree-in-Dowan."

"I am, indeed," said the king's son.

"Many's the good man went that way before you; but
not a man of them came back alive," said the old man;
"however, I'll do my best for you.   Stop here to-night,
and we'll have sport to-morrow."

Then he dressed a supper and gave it to the king's
son, and when he ate and drank, the old man put him
to sleep.

In the morning of the day on the morrow, the old man
said:

"I found out where the Well of D'yerree-in-Dowan is;
but it is difficult to go as far as it.   We must find out if
there's any good in you with the tight loop (bow?)."

Then he brought the king's son out into the wood,
gave him the loop, and put a mark on a tree two score
yards from him, and told him to strike it.   He drew the
loop and struck the mark.

"You'll do the business," said the old man.

They then went in, and spent the day telling stories
till the darkness of the night was come.

When the darkness of the night was come, the old
man gave him a loop (bow?) and a sheaf of sharp stings
(darts), and said:

"Come with me now."

They were going until they came to a great river.
Then the old man said:

"Go on my back, and I'll swim across the river with
you; but if you see a great bird coming, kill him, or we
shall be lost."

Then the king's son got on the old man's back, and
the old man began swimming.   When they were in the
middle of the river the king's son saw a great eagle

coming, and his gob (beak) open.   The king's son drew
the loop and wounded the eagle.

"Did you strike him?" said the old man.

"I struck him," said the king's son; "but here he
comes again."

He drew the loop the second time and the eagle fell
dead.

When they came to the land, the old man said:

"We are on the island of the Well of D'yerree-in-
Dowan.   The queen is asleep, and she will not waken
for a day and a year.   She never goes to sleep but once
in seven years.   There is a lion and a monster (uillphéist)
watching at the gate of the well, but they go to sleep
at the same time with the queen, and you will have no
difficulty in going to the well.   Here are two bottles for
you; fill one of them for yourself, and the other for me,
and it will make a young man of me."

The king's son went off, and when he came as far as
the castle he saw the lion and the monster sleeping on
each side of the gate.   Then he saw a great wheel
throwing up water out of the well, and he went and
filled the two bottles, and he was coming back when he
saw a shining light in the castle.   He looked in through
the window and saw a great table.   There was a loaf of
bread, with a knife, a bottle, and a glass on it.   He filled
the glass, but he did not diminish the bottle.   He observed that there was a writing on the bottle and on the
loaf; and he read on the bottle: "Water For the World,"
and on the loaf: "Bread For the World."   He cut a
piece off the loaf, but it only grew bigger.

"My grief! that we haven't that loaf and that bottle
at home," said the king's son, "and there'd be neither
hunger nor thirst on the poor people."

Then he went into a great chamber, and he saw the

queen and eleven waiting-maids asleep, and a sword of
light hung above the head of the queen.   It was it that
was giving light to the whole castle.

When he saw the queen, he said to himself: " It's a
pity to leave that pretty mouth without kissing it.   He
kissed the queen, and she never awoke; and after that
he did the same to the eleven maidens.   Then he got
the sword, the bottle, and the loaf, and came to the old
man, but he never told him that he had those things.

" How did you get on ? " said the old man.

" I got the thing I was in search of," said the king's son.

" Did you see any marvel since you left me ? " said the
old man.

The king's son told him that he had seen a wonderful
loaf, bottle, and sword.

" You did not touch them ? " said the old man ; shun
them, for they would bring trouble on you.   Come on
my back now till I bring you across the river."

When they went to the house of the old man, he put
water out of the bottle on himself, and made a young
man of himself.   Then he said to the king's son :

" My sisters and myself are now free from enchantment, and they are young women again."

The king's son remained there until most part of the
year and day were gone.   Then he began the journey
home ; but, my grief, he had not the little nag with him.
He walked the first day until the darkness of the night
was coming on.   He saw a large house.   He went to
the door, struck it, and the man of the house came out
to him.

" Can you give me lodgings ? " said he.

" I can," said the man of the house, " only I have no
light to light you."

" I have a light myself," said the king's son.

He went in then, drew the sword, and gave a fine light to them all, and to everybody that was in the island. They then gave him a good supper, and he went to sleep. When he was going away in the morning, the man of the house asked him for the honour of God, to leave the sword with them.

"Since you asked for it in the honour of God, you must have it," said the king's son.

He walked the second day till the darkness was coming. He went to another great house, beat the door, and it was not long till the woman of the house came to him, and he asked lodgings of her. The man of the house came and said :

"I can give you that; but I have not a drop of water to dress food for you."

"I have plenty of water myself," said the king's son.

He went in, drew out the bottle, and there was not a vessel in the house he did not fill, and still the bottle was full. Then a supper was dressed for him, and when he ate and drank his enough, he went to sleep. In the morning, when he was going, the woman asked of him, in the honour of God, to leave them the bottle.

"Since it has chanced that you ask it for the honour of God," said the king's son, "I cannot refuse you, for my mother put me under *gassa* (mystic obligations), before she died, never, if I could, to refuse anything that a person would ask of me for the honour of God."

Then he left the bottle to them.

He walked the third day until darkness was coming, and he reached a great house on the side of the road. He struck the door; the man of the house came out, and he asked lodgings of him.

"I can give you that, and welcome," said the man; "but I'm grieved that I have not a morsel of bread for you."

"I have plenty of bread myself," said the king's son.

He went in, got a knife, and began cutting the loaf, until the table was filled with pieces of bread, and yet the loaf was as big as it was when he began. Then they prepared a supper for him, and when he ate his enough, he went to sleep. When he was departing in the morning, they asked of him, for the honour of God, to leave the loaf with them, and he left it with them.

The three things were now gone from him.

He walked the fourth day until he came to a great river, and he had no way to get across it. He went upon his knees, and asked of God to send him help. After half a minute, he saw the beautiful woman he saw the day he left the house of the first hag. When she came near him, she said: "Son of the king of the castle of Bwee-sounnee, has it succeeded with you?"

"I got the thing I went in search of," said the king's son; "but I do not know how I shall pass over this river."

She drew out a thimble and said: "Bad is the day I would see your father's son without a boat."

Then she threw the thimble into the river, and made a splendid boat of it.

"Get into that boat now," said she; "and when you will come to the other side, there will be a steed before you to bring you as far as the cross-road, where you left your brothers."

The king's son stepped into the boat, and it was not long until he was at the other side, and there he found a white steed before him. He went riding on it, and it went off as swiftly as the wind. At about twelve o'clock on that day, he was at the cross-roads. The king's son looked round him, and he did not see his brothers, nor any stone set up, and he said to himself, "perhaps they

are at the inn." He went there, and found Art and
Nart, and they two-thirds drunk.

They asked him how he went on since he left them.

"I have found out the Well of D'yerree-in-Dowan, and
I have the bottle of water," said Cart.

Nart and Art were filled with jealousy, and they said
one to the other: "It's a great shame that the youngest
son should have the kingdom."

"We'll kill him, and bring the bottle of water to my
father," said Nart; "and we'll say that it was ourselves
who went to the Well of D'yerree-in-Dowan."

"I'm not with you there," said Art; "but we'll set
him drunk, and we'll take the bottle of (from) him. My
father will believe me and you, before he'll believe our
brother, because he has an idea that there's nothing in
him but a half *omadawn*."

"Then," he said to Cart, "since it has happened that
we have come home safe and sound we'll have a drink
before we go home."

They called for a quart of whiskey, and they made
Cart drink the most of it, and he fell drunk. Then
they took the bottle of water from him, went home themselves, and gave it to the king. He put a drop of the
water on his foot, and it made him as well as ever he
was.

Then they told him that they had great trouble to get
the bottle of water; that they had to fight giants, and
to go through great dangers.

"Did ye see Cart on your road?" said the king.

"He never went farther than the inn, since he left
us," said they; "and he's in it now, blind drunk."

"There never was any good in him," said the king;
but I cannot leave him there."

Then he sent six men to the inn, and they carried

Cart home. When he came to himself, the king made him into a servant to do all the dirty jobs about the castle.

*　　*　　*　　*　　*　　*　　*

When a year and a day had gone by, the queen of the Well of D'yerree-in-Dowan and her waiting-maidens woke up and the queen found a young son by her side, and the eleven maidens the same.

There was great anger on the queen, and she sent for the lion and the monster, and asked them what was become of the eagle that she left in charge of the castle.

"He must be dead, or he'd be here now, when you woke up," said they.

"I'm destroyed, myself, and the waiting-maidens ruined," said the queen; "and I never will stop till I find out the father of my son."

Then she got ready her enchanted coach, and two fawns under it. She was going till she came to the first house where the king's son got lodging, and she asked was there any stranger there lately. The man of the house said there was.

"Yes!" said the queen, "and he left the sword of light behind him; it is mine, and if you do not give it to me quickly I will throw your house upside down."

They gave her the sword, and she went on till she came to the second house, in which he had got lodging, and she asked was there any stranger there lately. They said that there was. "Yes," said she, "and he left a bottle after him. Give it to me quickly, or I'll throw the house on ye."

They gave her the bottle, and she went till she came to the third house, and she asked was there any stranger there lately. They said there was.

"Yes!" said she, "and he left the loaf of lasting

bread after him. That belongs to me, and if ye don't give it to me quickly I will kill ye all."

She got the loaf, and she was going, and never stopped till she came to the castle of Bwee-Sounee. She pulled the *cooalya-coric*, pole of combat and the king came out.

"Have you any son," said the queen.

"I have," said the king.

"Send him out here till I see him," said she.

The king sent out Art, and she asked him : "Were you at the Well of D'yerree-an-Dowan?"

"I was," said Art.

"And are you the father of my son ?" said she.

"I believe I am," said Art.

"I will know that soon," said she.

Then she drew two hairs out of her head, flung them against the wall, and they were made into a ladder that went up to the top of the castle. Then she said to Art : "If you were at the Well of Dyerree-in-Dowan, you can go up to the top of that ladder."

Art went up half way, then he fell, and his thigh was broken.

"You were never at the Well of D'yerree-in-Dowan," said the queen.

Then she asked the king : "Have you any other son."

"I have," said the king.

"Bring him out," said the queen.

Nart came out, and she asked him : "Were you ever at the Well of D'yerree-in-Dowan?"

"I was," said Nart.

"If you were, go up to the top of that ladder," said the queen.

He began going up, but he had not gone far till he fell and broke his foot.

" You were not at the Well of D'yerree-in-Dowan," said the queen.

Then she asked the king if he had any other son, and the king said he had. " But," said he, " it's a half fool he is, that never left home."

" Bring him here," said the queen.

When Cart came, she asked him : " Were you at the Well of D'yerree-in-Dowan ?".

" I was," said Cart, " and I saw you there."

" Go up to the top of that ladder," said the queen.

Cart went up like a cat, and when he came down she said : " You are the man who was at the Well of D'yerree-in-Dowan, and you are the father of my son."

Then Cart told the trick his brothers played on him, and the queen was going to slay them, until Cart asked pardon for them. Then the king said that Cart must get the kingdom.

Then the father dressed him out and put a chain of gold beneath his neck, and he got into the coach along with the queen, and they departed to the Well of D'yerree-in-Dowan.

The waiting-maidens gave a great welcome to the king's son, and they all of them came to him, each one asking him to marry herself.

He remained there for one-and-twenty years, until the queen died, and then he brought back with him his twelve sons, and came home to Galway. Each of them married a wife, and it is from them that the twelve tribes of Galway are descended.

THE COURT OF CRINNAWN.

A LONG time ago there came a lot of gentlemen to a river which is between the County Mee-òh (Mayo) and Roscommon, and they chose out a nice place for themselves on the brink of a river, and set up a court on it. Nobody at all in the little villages round about knew from what place these gentlemen came. MacDonnell was the name that was on them. The neighbours were for a long time without making friendship with them, until there came a great plague, and the people were getting death in their hundreds.

One day there was the only son of a poor widow dying from the destructive plague, and she had not a drop of milk to wet his tongue. She went to the court, and they asked her what she was looking for. She told them that the one son she had was dying of the plague, and that she had not a drop of milk to wet his tongue.

" Hard is your case," says a lady that was in the court to her. " I will give you milk and healing, and your son will be as well at the end of an hour as ever he was." Then she gave her a tin can, and said: " Go home now, this can will never be empty as long as you or your son is alive, if you keep the secret without telling anybody that you got it here. When you will go home put a morsel of the Mary's shamrock (four-leaved shamrock?) in the milk and give it to your son."

The widow went home. She put a bit of four-leaved shamrock in the milk, and gave it to her son to drink, and he rose up at the end of an hour as well as ever he was. Then the woman went through the villages round about with the can, and there was no one at all to whom she gave a drink that was not healed at the end of an hour.

It was not long till the fame of Maurya nec Keerachawn (Mary Kerrigan), that was the name of the widow, went through the country, and it was not long till she had the full of the bag of gold and silver.

One day Mary went to a *pattern* at Cultya Bronks, drank too much, fell on drunkenness, and let out the secret.

There came the heavy sleep of drunkenness on her, and when she awoke the can was gone. There was so much grief on her that she drowned herself in a place called Pull Bawn (the White Hole), within a mile of Cultya Bronks.

Everybody thought now that they had the can of healing to get at the Court of Crinnawn if they would go there. In the morning, the day on the morrow, there went plenty of people to the court, and they found every one who was in it dead. The shout went out, and the hundreds of people gathered together, but no man could go in, for the court was filled with smoke ; and lightning and thunder coming out of it.

They sent a message for the priest, who was in Ballaghadereen, but he said : "It is not in my parish, and I won't have anything to do with it." That night the people saw a great light in the court, and there was very great fear on them. The day on the morrow they sent word to the priest of Lisahull, but he would not come, as the place was not in his parish. Word was sent to the priest of Kilmovee, then, but he had the same excuse.

There were a lot of poor friars in Cultya Mawn, and when they heard the story they went to the court without a person with them but themselves.

When they went in they began saying prayers, but they saw no corpse. After a time the smoke went, the lightning and thunder ceased, a door opened, and there came out a great man. The friars noticed that he had only one eye, and that it was in his forehead.

"In the name of God, who are you?" said a man of the friars.

"I am Crinnawn, son of Belore, of the Evil Eye. Let there be no fear on ye, I shall do ye no damage, for ye are courageous, good men. The people who were here are gone to eternal rest, body and soul. I know that ye are poor, and that there are plenty of poor people round about ye. Here are two purses for ye, one of them for yourselves, and the other one to divide upon the poor; and when all that will be spent, do ye come again. Not of this world am I, but I shall do no damage to anyone unless he does it to me first, and do ye keep from me."

Then he gave them two purses, and said: "Go now on your good work." The friars went home; they gathered the poor people and they divided the money on them. The people questioned them as to what it was they saw in the court. "It is a secret each thing we saw in the court, and it is our advice to ye not to go near the court, and no harm will come upon ye."

The priests were covetous when they heard that the friars got plenty of money in the court, and the three of them went there with the hope that they would get some as the friars got it.

When they went in they began crying aloud: "Is there any person here? is there any person here?". Crinnawn came out of a chamber and asked: "What are ye looking for?". "We came to make friendship with you," said the priests. "I thought that priests were not given to telling lies," said Crinnawn; "ye came with a hope that ye would get money as the poor friars got. Ye were afraid to come when the people sent for ye, and now ye will not get a keenogue (mite ?) from me, for ye are not worth it."

" Don't you know that we have power to banish you out of this place," said the priests, "and we will make use of that power unless you will be more civil than you are."

" I don't care for your power," said Crinnawn, " I have more power myself than all the priests that are in Ireland."

" It's a lie you're speaking," said the priests.

" Ye will see a small share of my power to-night," said Crinnawn; " I will not leave a wattle over your heads that I will not sweep into yonder river, and I could kill ye with the sight of my eye, if I chose. Ye will find the roofs of your houses in the river to-morrow morning. Now put no other questions on me, and threaten me no more, or it will be worse for ye."

There came fear on the priests, and they went home ; but they did not believe that their houses would be without a roof before morning.

About midnight, that night, there came a blast of wind under the roof of the houses of the priests, and it swept them into the river forenent the court. There was not a bone of the priests but was shaken with terror, and they had to get shelter in the houses of the neighbours till morning.

In the morning, the day on the morrow, the priests came to the river opposite the court, and they saw the roofs that were on all their houses swimming in the water. They sent for the friars, and asked them to go to Crinnawn and proclaim a peace, and say to him that they would put no more trouble on him. The friars went to the court, and Crinnawn welcomed them, and asked them what they were seeking. " We come from the priests to proclaim a peace on you, they will trouble you no more." " That is well for them," said Crinnawn, " come with me now until ye see me putting back the roofs of the houses." They went with him as far as the river, and then he blew a blast out of each nostril. The roofs of the houses rose up as well as they were when they were first put on. There was wonder on the priests, and they said : " The power of enchantment is not yet dead, nor banished out of the country yet." From that day out neither priest nor anyone else would go near the Court of Crinnawn.

A year after the death of Mary Kerrigan, there was a pattern in Cultya Bronks. There were plenty of young men gathered in it, and amongst them was Paudyeen, the son of Mary Kerrigan. They drank whiskey till they were in madness. When they were going home, Paudyeen O'Kerrigan said : " There is money in plenty in the court up there, and if ye have courage we can get it." As the drink was in them, twelve of them said : " We have courage, and we will go to the court." When they came to the door, Paudyeen O'Kerrigan said: "Open the door, or we will break it." Crinnawn came out and said: " Unless ye go home I will put a month's sleep on ye." They thought to get a hold of Crinnawn, but he put a blast of wind out of his two nostrils that swept the young men to a *lis* (old circular rath) called Lisdrumneal, and put a heavy sleep on them, and a big cloud over them, and there is no name on the place from that out, but Lis-trum-nail (the fort of the heavy cloud).

On the morning, the day on the morrow, the young men were not to be found either backwards or forwards, and there was great grief amongst the people. That

day went by without any account from the young men.
People said that it was Crinnawn that killed them, fo
some saw them going to the court.   The fathers and
mothers of the young men went to the friars, and prayed
them to go to Crinnawn and to find out from him where
the young men were, dead or alive.

They went to Crinnawn, and Crinnawn told them the
trick the young men thought to do on him, and the thing
he did with them.   "If it be your will, bestow forgive-
ness on them this time," said the friars ; "they were mad
with whiskey, and they won't be guilty again."   "On
account of ye to ask it of me, I will loose them this time ;
but if they come again, I will put a sleep of seven years
on them.   Come with me now till you see them."

"It's bad walkers, we are," said the friars, "we would
be a long time going to the place where they are."

"Ye won't be two minutes going to it," said
Crinnawn, "and ye will be back at home in the same
time."

Then he brought them out, and put a blast of wind out
of his mouth, and swept them to Lisdrumneal, and he
himself was there as soon as they.

They saw the twelve young men asleep under a cloud
in the *lis*, and there was great wonder on them. "Now,"
said Crinnawn, " I will send them home." He blew
upon them, and they rose up like birds in the air, and it
was not long until each one of them was at home, and the
friars as well, and you may be certain that they did not
go to the Court of Crinnawn any more.

Crinnawn was living in the court years after that.
One day the friars went on a visit to him, but he was
not to be found. People say that the friars got great
riches after Crinnawn. At the end of a period of time
the roof fell off the court, as everyone was afraid

to go and live in it.   During many years after that, people would go round about a mile, before they would go near the old court.   There is only a portion of the walls to be found now; but there is no name on the old court from that day till this day, but Coort a Chrinnawn (Crinnawn's Court).

NEIL O'CARREE.

THERE was no nicety about him. He said to his wife that he would go to the forge to get a doctoring instrument. He went to the forge the next day. "Where are you going to to-day?" said the smith. "I am going till you make me an instrument for doctoring." "What is the instrument I shall make you?" "Make a *crumskeen* and a *galskecn* (crooked knife and white knife?) The smith made that for him. He came home.

When the day came—the day on the morrow—Neil OCarree rose up. He made ready to be going as a doctor. He went. He was walking away. A red lad met him on the side of the high road. He saluted Neil O'Carree; Neil saluted him. "Where are you going?" says the red man. "I am going till I be my (*i.c.*, a.) doctor. "It's a good trade," says the red man, "'twere best for you to hire me." "What's the wages you'll be looking for?" says Neil. "Half of what we shall earn till we shall be back again on this ground." "I'll give you that," says Neil. The couple walked on.

"There's a king's daughter," says the red man, with the (*i.e.*, near to) death; we will go as far as her, till we see will we heal her." They went as far as the gate. The porter came to them. He asked them where were they going. They said that it was coming to look at the king's daughter they were, to see would they do her good. The king desired to let them in. They went in.

They went to the place where the girl was lying. The red man went and took hold of her pulse. He said that if his master should get the price of his labour he would heal her. The king said that he would give his master whatever he should award himself. He said, "if he had the room to himself and his master, that it would be better." The king said he should have it.

He desired to bring down to him a skillet (little pot) of water. He put the skillet on the fire. He asked Neil O'Carree: "Where is the doctoring instrument?" "Here they are," says Neil, "a crumskeen and a galskeen."

He put the crumskeen on the neck of the girl. He took the head off her. He drew a green herb out of his pocket. He rubbed it to the neck. There did not come one drop of blood. He threw the head into the skillet. He knocked a boil out of it. He seized hold on the two ears. He took it out of the skillet. He struck it down on the neck. The head stuck as well as ever it was. "How do you feel yourself now." "I am as well as ever I was," said the king's daughter.

The big man shouted. The king came down. There was great joy on him. He would not let them go away for three days. When they were going he brought down a bag of money. He poured it out on the table. He asked of Neil O'Carree had he enough there. Neil said he had, and more than enough, that they would take but the half. The king desired them not to spare the money.

"There's the daughter of another king waiting for us to go and look at her." They bade farewell to the king and they went there.

They went looking at her. They went to the place where she was lying, looking at her in her bed, and it

was the same way this one was healed. The king was
grateful, and he said he did not mind how much money
Neil should take of him. He gave him three hundred
pounds of money. They went then, drawing on home.
" There's a king's son in such and such a place," said the
red man, " but we won't go to him, we will go home with
what we have."

They were drawing on home. The king (had)
bestowed half a score of heifers on them, to bring home
with them. They were walking away. When they
were in the place where Neil O'Carree hired the red
man, " I think," says the red man, " that this is the place
I met you the first time." " I think it is," says Neil
O'Carree. " Musha, how shall we divide the money ?"
" Two halves," says the red man, " that's the bargain was
in it." " I think it a great deal to give you a half," says
Neil O'Carree, " a third is big enough for you ; I have a
crumskeen and a galskeen (says Neil) and you have nothing." " I won't take anything," said the red man,
" unless I get the half." They fell out about the money.
The red man went and he left him.

Neil O'Carree was drawing home, riding on his beast.
He was driving his share of cattle. The day came hot.
The cattle went capering backwards and forwards. Neil
O'Carree was controlling them. When he would have
one or two caught the rest would be off when he used to
come back. He tied his garrawn (gelding) to a bit of a
tree. He was a-catching the cattle. At the last they
were all off and away. He did not know where they
went. He returned back to the place where he left his
garrawn and his money. Neither the garrawn nor the
money were to be got. He did not know then what he
should do. He thought he would go to the house of the
king whose son was ill.

He went along, drawing towards the house of the king. He went looking on the lad in the place where he was lying. He took a hold of his pulse. He said he thought he would heal him. "If you heal him," said the king' "I will give you three hundred pounds." "If I were to get the room to myself, for a little," says he. The king said that he should get that. He called down for a skillet of water. He put the skillet on the fire. He drew his crumskeen. He went to take the head off him as he saw the red man a-doing. He was a-sawing at the head, and it did not come with him to cut it off the neck. The blood was coming. He took the head off him at last. He threw it into the skillet. He knocked a boil out of it. When he considered the head to be boiled enough he made an attempt on the skillet. He got a hold of the two ears. The head fell in *gliggar* (a gurgling mass ?), and the two ears came with him. The blood was coming greatly. It was going down, and out of the door of the room. When the king saw it going down he knew that his son was dead. He desired to open the door. Neil O'Carree would not open the door. They broke the door. The man was dead. The floor was full of blood. They seized Neil O'Carree. He was to hang the next day. They gathered a guard till they should carry him to the place where he was to hang. They went the next day with him. They were walking away, drawing towards the tree where he should be hanged. They stopped his screaming. They see a man stripped making a running race. When they saw him there was a fog of water round him with all he was running. When he came as far as them (he cried), "what are ye doing to my master?" "If this man is your master, deny him, or you'll get the same treatment." "It's I that it's right should suffer; it's I who made the delay. He sent me for medicine, and I did not come in time, loose my master, perhaps we would heal the king's son yet."

They loosed him. They came to the king's house. The red man went to the place where the dead man was. He began gathering the bones that were in the skillet. He gathered them all but only the two ears.

"What did you do with the ears?"

"I don't know," said Neil O'Carree, "I was so much frightened."

The red man got the ears. He put them all together. He drew a green herb out of his pocket. He rubbed it round on the head. The skin grew on it, and the hair, as well as ever it was. He put the head in the skillet then. He knocked a boil out of it. He put the head back on the neck as well as ever it was. The king's son rose up in the bed.

"How are you now?" says the red man.

"I am well," says the king's son, "but that I'm weak."

The red man shouted again for the king. There was great joy on the king when he saw his son alive. They spent that night pleasantly.

The next day when they were going away, the king counted out three hundred pounds. He gave it to Neil O'Carree. He said to Neil that if he had not enough he would give him more. Neil O'Carree said he had enough, and that he would not take a penny more. He bade farewell and left his blessing, and struck out, drawing towards home.

When they saw that they were come to the place where they fell out with one another, "I think," says the red man, "that this is the place where we differed before." "It is, exactly," said Neil O'Carree. They sat down and they divided the money. He gave a half to the red man, and he kept another half himself. The red man bade him farewell, and he went. He was walking away for a while. He returned back. " I am here back again," said the red man, " I took another thought, to leave all your share of money with yourself. You yourself were open-handed. Do you mind the day you were going by past the churchyard. There were four inside in the churchyard, and a body with them in a coffin. There were a pair of them seeking to bury the body. There were debts on the body (*i.e.*, it owed debts). The two men who had the debts on it (*i.e.*, to whom it owed the debts), they were not satisfied for the body to be buried. They were arguing. You were listening to them. You went in. You asked how much they had on the body (*i.e.*, how were they owed by the body). The two men said that they had a pound on the body, and that they were not willing the body to be buried, until the people who were carrying it would promise to pay a portion of the debts. You said, " I have ten shillings, and I'll give it to ye, and let the body be buried." You gave the ten shillings, and the corpse was buried. " It's I who was in the coffin that day. When I saw you going a-doctoring, I knew that you would not do the business. When I saw you in a hobble, I came to you to save you. I bestow the money on you all entirely. You shall not see me until the last day, go home now. Don't do a single day's doctoring as long as you'll be alive. It's short you'll walk until you get your share of cattle and your garrawn."

Neil went, drawing towards home. Not far did he walk till his share of cattle and his nag met him. He went home and the whole with him. There is not a single day since that himself and his wife are not thriving on it.

I got the ford, they the stepping stones. They were drowned, and I came safe.

TRUNK-WITHOUT-HEAD.

LONG ago there was a widow woman living in the County Galway, and two sons with her, whose names were Dermod and Donal. Dermod was the eldest son, and he was the master over the house. They were large farmers, and they got a summons from the landlord to come and pay him a year's rent. They had not much money in the house, and Dermod said to Donal, "bring a load of oats to Galway, and sell it." Donal got ready a load, put two horses under the cart, and went to Galway. He sold the oats, and got a good price for it. When he was coming home, he stopped at the half-way house, as was his custom, to have a drink himself, and to give a drink and oats to the horses.

When he went in to get a drink for himself, he saw two boys playing cards. He looked at them for a while, and one of them said : "Will you have a game."? Donal began playing, and he did not stop till he lost every penny of the price of the oats. "What will I do now?," says Donal to himself, "Dermod will kill me. Anyhow, I'll go home and tell the truth."

When he came home, Dermod asked him : " Did you sell the oats ?." " I sold, and got a good price for it," says Donal. "Give me the money," says Dermod. " I haven't it," says Donal ; "I lost every penny of it playing cards at the house half-way." " My curse, and the curse of the four-and-twenty men on you," says Dermod. He went and told the mother the trick Donal did. " Give him his pardon this time," says the mother, "and he won't do it again." " You must sell another load to-morrow," says Dermod, "and if you lose the price, don't come here."

On the morning, the day on the morrow, Donal put another load on the cart, and he went to Galway. He sold the oats, and got a good price for it. When he was coming home, and near the half-way house, he said to himself: "I will shut my eyes till I go past that house, for fear there should be a temptation on me to go in." He shut his eyes; but when the horses came as far as the inn, they stood, and would not go a step further, for it was their custom to get oats and water in that place every time they would be coming out of Galway. He opened his eyes, gave oats and water to the horses, and went in himself to put a coal in his pipe.

When he went in he saw the boys playing cards. They asked him to play, and (said) that perhaps he might gain all that he lost the day before. As there is a temptation on the cards, Donal began playing, and he did not stop until he lost every penny of all that he had. "There is no good in my going home now," says Donal; "I'll stake the horses and the cart against all I lost." He played again, and he lost the horses and the cart. Then he did not know what he should do, but he thought and said: "Unless I go home, my poor mother will be anxious. I will go home and tell the truth to her. They can but banish me."

When he came home, Dermod asked him: "Did you sell the oats? or where are the horses and the cart?." "I lost the whole playing cards, and I would not come back except to leave ye my blessing before I go." "That you may not ever come back, or a penny of your price," said Dermod, "and I don't want your blessing."

He left his blessing with his mother then, and he went travelling, looking for service. When the darkness of the night was coming, there was thirst and hunger on him. He saw a poor man coming to him, and a bag on his back.   He recognised Donal, and said: "Donal, what brought you here, or where are you going?." "I don't know you," said Donal.

"It's many's the good night I spent in your father's house, may God have mercy upon him," said the poor man; "perhaps there's hunger on you, and that you would not be against eating something out of my bag?."

" It's a friend that would give it to me," says Donal. Then the poor man gave him beef and bread, and when he ate his enough, the poor man asked him: "Where are you going to-night?."

"Musha, then, I don't know," says Donal.

" There is a gentleman in the big house up there, and he gives lodging to anyone who comes to him after the darkness of night, and I'm going to him," says the poor man.

"Perhaps I would get lodgings with you," says Donal. "I have no doubt of it," says the poor man.

The pair went to the big house, and the poor man knocked at the door, and the servant opened it. " I want to see the master of this house," says Donal.

The servant went, and the master came.   "I am looking for a night's lodging," said Donal.

" I will give ye that, if ye wait.   Go up to the castle there above, and I will be after ye, and if ye wait in it till morning, each man of ye will get five score ten-penny pieces, and ye will have plenty to eat and drink as well; and a good bed to sleep on."

" That's a good offer," said they; "we will go there."

The pair came to the castle, went into a room, and put down a fire.   It was not long till the gentleman came, bringing beef, mutton, and other things to them.   "Come with me now till I show ye the cellar, there's plenty of wine and ale in it, and ye can draw your enough." When

he showed them the cellar, he went out, and he put a
lock on the door behind him.

Then Donal said to the poor man: " Put the things to
eat on the table, and I'll go for the ale." Then he got a
light, and a cruiskeen (jug), and went down into the cellar.
The first barrel he came to he stooped down to draw out
of it, when a voice said: "Stop, that barrel is mine."
Donal looked up, and he saw a little man without a head,
with his two legs spread straddle-wise on a barrel.

" If it is yours," says Donal, " I'll go to another." He
went to another; but when he stooped down to draw,
Trunk-without-head said: " That barrel is mine."
"They're not all yours," says Donal, " I'll go to another
one." He went to another one; but when he began
drawing out of it, Trunk-without-head said: " That's
mine." "I don't care," said Donal, "I'll fill my
cruiskeen." He did that, and came up to the poor man;
but he did not tell him that he saw Trunk-without-head.
Then they began eating and drinking till the jug was
empty. Then said Donal: " It's your turn to go down
and fill the jug. The poor man got the candle and the
cruiskeen, and went down into the cellar. He began
drawing out of a barrel, when he heard a voice saying:
" That barrel is mine." He looked up, and when he saw
Trunk-without-head, he let cruiskeen and candle fall, and
off and away with him to Donal. "Oh ! it's little but I'm
dead," says the poor man ; " I saw a man without a head,
and his two legs spread out on the barrel, and he said it
was his." " He would not do you any harm," said Donal,
" he was there when I went down ; get up and bring me
the jug and the candle." "Oh, I wouldn't go down again
if I were to get Ireland without a division," says the poor
man. Donal went down, and he brought up the jug filled.
" Did you see Trunk-without-head ?," says the poor man.

"I did," says Donal; "but he did not do me any harm."

They were drinking till they were half drunk, then said Donal : "It's time for us to be going to sleep, what place would you like best, the outside of the bed, or next the wall ?."

"I'll go next the wall," said the poor man. They went to bed leaving the candle lit.

They were not long in bed till they saw three men coming in, and a bladder (football) with them. They began beating *bayrees* (playing at ball) on the floor ; but there were two of them against one. Donal said to the poor man: "It is not right for two to be against one," and with that he leaped out and began helping the weak side, and he without a thread on him. Then they began laughing, and walked out.

Donal went to bed again, and he was not long there till there came in a piper playing sweet music. "Rise up," says Donal, "until we have a dance ; it's a great pity to let good music go to loss." "For your life, don't stir," says the poor man.

Donal gave a leap out of the bed, and he fell to dancing till he was tired. Then the piper began laughing, and walked out.

Donal went to bed again ; but he was not long there till there walked in two men, carrying a coffin. They left it down on the floor, and they walked out. "I don't know who's in the coffin, or whether it's for us it's meant," said Donal ; "I'll go till I see." He gave a leap out, raised the board of the coffin, and found a dead man in it. "By my conscience, it's the cold place you have," says Donal ; "if you were able to rise up, and sit at the fire, you would be better." The dead man rose up and warmed himself. Then said Donal, "the bed is wide enough for three." Donal went in the middle, the poor man next the wall, and the dead man on the outside. It was not long until the dead man began bruising Donal, and Donal bruising in on the poor man, until he was all as one as dead, and he had to give a leap out through the window, and to leave Donal and the dead man there. The dead man was crushing Donal then until he nearly put him out through the wall.

"Destruction on you," said Donal, then; "it's you're the ungrateful man; I let you out of the coffin; I gave you a heat at the fire, and a share of my bed; and now you won't keep quiet; but I'll put you out of the bed." Then the dead man spoke, and said: "You are a valiant man, and it stood you upon * to be so, or you would be dead." "Who would kill me?" said Donal. "I," says the dead man; "there never came any one here this twenty years back, that I did not kill. Do you know the man who paid you for remaining here?." He was a gentleman," said Donal. "He is my son," said the dead man, "and he thinks that you will be dead in the morning; but come with me now."

The dead man took him down into the cellar, and showed him a great flag. "Lift that flag. There are three pots under it, and they filled with gold. It is on account of the gold they killed me; but they did not get the gold. Let yourself have a pot, and a pot for my son, and the other one—divide it on the poor people. Then he opened a door in the wall, and drew out a paper, and said to Donal: "Give this to my son, and tell him that it was the butler who killed me, for my share of gold. I

---

* That means "It was well for yourself it was so. This old Elizabethan idiom is of frequent occurrence in Connacht English, having with many other Elizabethanisms, either filtered its way across the island from the Pale, or else been picked up by the people from the English peasantry with whom they have to associate when they go over to England to reap the harvest.

can get no rest until he'll be hanged; and if there is a
witness wanting I will come behind you in the court
without a head on me, so that everybody can see me.
When he will be hanged, you will marry my son's
daughter, and come to live in this castle. Let you have
no fear about me, for I shall have gone to eternal rest.
Farewell now."

Donal went to sleep, and he did not awake till the
gentleman came in the morning, and he asked him
did he sleep well, or where did the old man whom he
left with him go?. "I will tell you that another time;
I have a long story to tell you first." "Come to my
house with me," says the gentleman.

When they were going to the house, whom should they
see coming out of the bushes, but the poor man without
a thread on him, more than the night he was born,
and he shaking with the cold. The gentleman got him
his clothes, gave him his wages, and off for ever with him.

Donal went to the gentleman's house, and when he ate
and drank his enough, he said: "I have a story to tell
you." Then he told him everything that happened to
him the night before, until he came as far as the part
about the gold. "Come with me till I see the gold,"
said the gentleman. He went to the castle, he lifted the
flag, and when he saw the gold, he said: "I know now
that the story is true."

When he got the entire information from Donal, he
got a warrant against the butler; but concealed the crime
it was for. When the butler was brought before the
judge, Donal was there, and gave witness. Then the
judge read out of his papers, and said: "I cannot find
this man guilty without more evidence."

"I am here," said Trunk-without-head, coming behind
Donal. When the butler saw him, he said to the judge:

"Go no farther, I am guilty; I killed the man, and his head is under the hearth-stone in his own room." Then the judge gave order to hang the butler, and Trunk-without-head went away.

The day on the morrow, Donal was married to the gentleman's daughter, and got a great fortune with her, and went to live in the castle.

A short time after this, he got ready his coach and went on a visit to his mother.

When Dermod saw the coach coming, he did not know who the great man was who was in it. The mother came out and ran to him, saying: "Are not you my own Donal, the love of my heart you are? I was praying for you since you went." Then Dermod asked pardon of him, and got it. Then Donal gave him a purse of gold, saying at the same time: "There's the price of the two loads of oats, of the horses, and of the cart." Then he said to his mother: "You ought to come home with me. I have a fine castle without anybody in it but my wife and the servants." "I will go with you," said the mother; "and I will remain with you till I die."

Donal took his mother home, and they spent a prosperous life together in the castle.

THE HAGS OF THE LONG TEETH.

LONG ago, in the old time, there came a party of gentlemen from Dublin to Loch Glynn a-hunting and a-fishing. They put up in the priest's house, as there was no inn in the little village.

The first day they went a-hunting, they went into the Wood of Driminuch, and it was not long till they routed a hare. They fired many a ball after him, but they could not bring him down. They followed him till they saw him going into a little house in the wood.

When they came to the door, they saw a great black dog, and he would not let them in.

"Put a ball through the beggar," said a man of them. He let fly a ball, but the dog caught it in his mouth, chewed it, and flung it on the ground. They fired another ball, and another, but the dog did the same thing with them. Then he began barking as loud as he could, and it was not long till there came out a hag, and every tooth in her head as long as the tongs. "What are you doing to my pup?" says the hag.

"A hare went into your house, and this dog won't let us in after him," says a man of the hunters.

"Lie down, pup," said the hag. Then she said: "Ye can come in if ye wish." The hunters were afraid to go in, but a man of them asked: "Is there any person in the house with you ?."

"There are six sisters," said the old woman. "We should like to see them," said the hunters. No sooner had he said the word than the six old women came out, and each of them with teeth as long as the other. Such a sight the hunters had never seen before.

They went through the wood then, and they saw seven vultures on one tree, and they screeching. The hunters began cracking balls after them, but if they were in it ever since they would never bring down one of them.

There came a gray old man to them and said: "Those are the hags of the long tooth that are living in the little house over there. Do ye not know that they are under enchantment ?. They are there these hundreds of years, and they have a dog that never lets in anyone to the little house. They have a castle under the lake, and it is often the people saw them making seven swans of themselves, and going into the lake."

When the hunters came home that evening they told everything they heard and saw to the priest, but he did not believe the story.

On the day on the morrow, the priest went with the hunters, and when they came near the little house they saw the big black dog at the door. The priest put his conveniencies for blessing under his neck, and drew out a book and began reading prayers. The big dog began barking loudly. The hags came out, and when they saw the priest they let a screech out of them that was heard in every part of Ireland. When the priest was a while reading, the hags made vultures of themselves and flew up into a big tree that was over the house.

The priest began pressing in on the dog until he was within a couple of feet of him.

The dog gave a leap up, struck the priest with its four feet, and put him head over heels.

When the hunters took him up he was deaf and dumb, and the dog did not move from the door.

They brought the priest home and sent for the bishop. When he came and heard the story there was great grief on him. The people gathered together and asked of him to banish the hags of enchantment out of the wood. There was fright and shame on him, and he did not know what he would do, but he said to them : " I have no means of banishing them till I go home, but I will come at the end of a month and banish them."

The priest was too badly hurt to say anything. The big black dog was father of the hags, and his name was Dermod O'Muloony. His own son killed him, because he found him with his wife the day after their marriage, and killed the sisters for fear they should tell on him.

One night the bishop was in his chamber asleep, when one of the hags of the long tooth opened the door and came in. When the bishop wakened up he saw the hag standing by the side of his bed. He was so much afraid he was not able to speak a word until the hag spoke and said to him : " Let there be no fear on you ; I did not come to do you harm, but to give you advice. You promised the people of Loch Glynn that you would come to banish the hags of the long tooth out of the wood of Driminuch. If you come you will never go back alive."

His talk came to the bishop, and he said : " I cannot break my word."

" We have only a year and a day to be in the wood," said the hag, "and you can put off the people until then."

" Why are ye in the woods as ye are?" says the bishop.

" Our brother killed us," said the hag, " and when we went before the arch-judge, there was judgment passed on us, we to be as we are two hundred years. We have a castle under the lake, and be in it every night. We are suffering for the crime our father did." Then she told him the crime the father did.

" Hard is your case," said the bishop, " but we must put up with the will of the arch-judge, and I shall not trouble ye."

" You will get an account, when we are gone from the wood," said the hag. Then she went from him.

In the morning, the day on the morrow, the bishop came to Loch Glynn. He sent out notice and gathered the people. Then he said to them : " It is the will of the arch-king that the power of enchantment be not banished for another year and a day, and ye must keep out of the wood until then. It is a great wonder to me that ye never saw the hags of enchantment till the hunters came from Dublin.—It's a pity they did not remain at home."

About a week after that the priest was one day by himself in his chamber alone. The day was very fine and the window was open. The robin of the red breast came in and a little herb in its mouth. The priest stretched out his hand, and she laid the herb down on it. "Perhaps it was God sent me this herb," said the priest to himself, and he ate it. He had not eaten it one moment till he was as well as ever he was, and he said : "A thousand thanks to Him who has power stronger than the power of enchantment."

Then said the robin : "Do you remember the robin of the broken foot you had, two years this last winter."

"I remember her, indeed," said the priest, "but she went from me when the summer came."

"I am the same robin, and but for the good you did me I would not be alive now, and you would be deaf and dumb throughout your life. Take my advice now, and do not go near the hags of the long tooth any more, and do not tell to any person living that I gave you the herb." Then she flew from him.

When the house-keeper came she wondered to find that he had both his talk and his hearing. He sent word to the bishop and he came to Loch Glynn. He asked the priest how it was that he got better so suddenly. "It is a secret," said the priest, "but a certain friend gave me a little herb and it cured me."

Nothing else happened worth telling, till the year was gone. One night after that the bishop was in his chamber when the door opened, and the hag of the long tooth walked in, and said : "I come to give you notice that we will be leaving the wood a week from to-day. I have one thing to ask of you if you will do it for me."

"If it is in my power, and it not to be against the faith," said the bishop.

"A week from to-day," said the hag, "there will be seven vultures dead at the door of our house in the wood. Give orders to bury them in the quarry that is between the wood and Ballyglas; that is all I am asking of you."

"I shall do that if I am alive," said the bishop. Then she left him, and he was not sorry she to go from him.

A week after that day, the bishop came to Loch Glynn, and the day after he took men with him and went to the hags' house in the wood of Driminuch.

The big black dog was at the door, and when he saw the bishop he began running and never stoped until he went into the lake.

He saw the seven vultures dead at the door, and he said to the men: "Take them with you and follow me."

They took up the vultures and followed him to the brink of the quarry. Then he said to them: "Throw them into the quarry: There is an end to the hags of the enchantment."

As soon as the men threw them down to the bottom of the quarry, there rose from it seven swans as white as snow, and flew out of their sight. It was the opinion of the bishop and of every person who heard the story that it was up to heaven they flew, and that the big black dog went to the castle under the lake.

At any rate, nobody saw the hags of the long tooth or the big black dog from that out, any more.

WILLIAM OF THE TREE.

IN the time long ago there was a king in Erin. He was married to a beautiful queen, and they had but one only daughter. The queen was struck with sickness, and she knew that she would not be long alive. She put the king under *gassa* (mystical injunctions) that he should not marry again until the grass should be a foot high over her tomb. The daughter was cunning, and she used to go out every night with a scissors, and she used to cut the grass down to the ground.

The king had a great desire to have another wife, and he did not know why the grass was not growing over the grave of the queen. He said to himself: "There is somebody deceiving me."

That night he went to the churchyard, and he saw the daughter cutting the grass that was on the grave. There came great anger on him then, and he said : "I will marry the first woman I see, let she be old or young." When he went out on the road he saw an old hag. He brought her home and married her, as he would not break his word.

After marrying her, the daughter of the king was under bitter misery at (the hands of) the hag, and the hag put her under an oath not to tell anything at all to the king, and not to tell to any person anything she should see being done, except only to three who were never baptised.

The next morning on the morrow, the king went out a hunting, and when he was gone, the hag killed a fine hound the king had. When the king came home he asked the old hag "who killed my hound?"

"Your daughter killed it," says the old woman.

"Why did you kill my hound?" said the king.

" I did not kill your hound," says the daughter, " and
I cannot tell you who killed him."

" I will make you tell me," says the king.

He took the daughter with him to a great wood, and he
hanged her on a tree, and then he cut off the two hands
and the two feet off her, and left her in a state of death.
When he was going out of the wood there went a thorn
into his foot, and the daughter said: "That you may never
get better until I have hands and feet to cure you."

The king went home, and there grew a tree out of his
foot, and it was necessary for him to open the window,
to let the top of the tree out.

There was a gentleman going by near the wood, and
he heard the king's daughter a-screeching. He went to
the tree, and when he saw the state she was in, he took
pity on her, brought her home, and when she got better,
married her.

At the end of three quarters (of a year), the king's
daughter had three sons at one birth, and when they were
born, Granya Öi came and put hands and feet on the
king's daughter, and told her, " Don't let your children be
baptised until they are able to walk. There is a tree
growing out of your father's foot; it was cut often, but
it grows again, and it is with you lies his healing. You
are under an oath not to tell the things you saw your
stepmother doing to anyone but to three who were never
baptised, and God has sent you those three. When they
will be a year old bring them to your father's house, and
tell your story before your three sons, and rub your hand
on the stump of the tree, and your father will be as well
as he was the first day."

There was great wonderment on the gentleman when
he saw hands and feet on the king's daughter. She told
him then every word that Granya Oi said to her.

When the children were a year old, the mother took them with her, and went to the king's house.

There were doctors from every place in Erin attending on the king, but they were not able to do him any good.

When the daughter came in, the king did not recognise her. She sat down, and the three sons round her, and she told her story to them from top to bottom, and the king was listening to her telling it. Then she left her hand on the sole of the king's foot and the tree fell off it.

The day on the morrow he hanged the old hag, and he gave his estate to his daughter and to the gentleman.

THE OLD CROW & THE YOUNG CROW.

THERE was an old crow teaching a young crow one day, and he said to him, " Now my son," says he, " listen to the advice I'm going to give you. If you see a person coming near you and stooping, mind yourself, and be on your keeping ; he's stooping for a stone to throw at you."

" But tell me, says the young crow, " what should I do if he had a stone already down in his pocket ?"

"Musha, go 'long out of that," says the old crow, " you've learned enough ; the devil another learning I'm able to give you."

RIDDLES

A great great house it is,
A golden candlestick it is,
Guess it rightly,
Let it not go by thee.

       Heaven.

There's a garden that I ken,
Full of little gentlemen,
Little caps of blue they wear,
And green ribbons very fair.

       Flax.

I went up the boreen, I went down the boreen,
I brought the boreen with myself on my back.

     A Ladder.

He comes to ye amidst the brine
The butterfly of the sun,
The man of the coat so blue and fine,
With red thread his shirt is done.

      Lobster.

I threw it up as white as snow,
Like gold on a flag it fell below.

      Egg.

I ran and I got,
I sat and I searched,
If could get it I would not bring it with me,
And as I got it not I brought it.

     Thorn in the foot.

You see it come in on the shoulders of men,
Like a thread of the silk it will leave us again.

     Smoke.

He comes though the *lis** to me over the sward,
The man of the foot that is narrow and hard,
I would he were running the opposite way,
For o'er all that are living 'tis he who bears sway.

                              The Death.

In the garden's a castle with hundreds within,
Yet though stripped to my shirt I would never
    fit in.

                              Ant-hill.

From house to house he goes,
A messenger small and slight,
And whether it rains or snows,
He sleeps outside in the night.

                              Boreen.

Two feet on the ground,
And three feet overhead,
And the head of the living
In the mouth of the dead.

        Girl with (three-legged) pot on her head.

On the top of the tree
See the little man red,
A stone in his belly,
A cap on his head.

                              Haw.

There's a poor man at rest,
With a stick beneath his breast,
And he breaking his heart a-crying.

                    Lintel on a wet day.

*Rath or fort or circular moat.

As white as flour and it is not flour,
As green as grass and it is not grass,
As red as blood and it is not blood,
As black as ink and it is not ink.
                    Blackberry, from bud to fruit.

A bottomless barrel,
It's shaped like a hive,
It is filled full of flesh,
And the flesh is alive.
                    Tailor's thimble.

WHERE THE STORIES CAME FROM.

THE first three stories, namely, the "Tailor and the Three Beasts," "Bran," and "The King of Ireland's Son," I took down verbatim, without the alteration or addition of more than a word or two, from Seáġan O Cuinneaġáin (John Cunningham), who lives in the village of baile-an-puill (Ballinphuil), in the county Roscommon, some half mile from Mayo. He is between seventy and eighty years old, and is, I think, illiterate.

The story of "The Alp-luachra" is written down from notes made at the time I first heard the story. It was told me by Seumaſ o h-áiɲt (James Hart), a game-keeper, in the barony of Frenchpark, between sixty and seventy years old, and illiterate. The notes were not full ones, and I had to eke them out in writing down the story, the reciter, one of the best I ever met, having unfortunately died in the interval.

The stories of "Paudyeen O'Kelly," and of "Leeam O'Rooney's Burial," I got from Mr. Lynch Blake, near Ballinrobe, county Mayo, who took the trouble of writing them down for me in nearly phonetic Irish, for which I beg to return him my best thanks. I do not think that these particular stories underwent any additions at his hands while writing them down. I do not know from whom he heard the first, and cannot now find out, as he has left the locality. The second he told me he got from a man, eighty years old, named William Grady, who lived near Clare-Galway, but who for the last few years has been "carrying a bag."

The long story of "Guleesh na Guss dhu," was told by the same Shamus O'Hart, from whom I got the "Alp-luachra," but, as in the case of the "Alp-luachra" story, I had only taken notes of it, and not written down the whole as it fell from his lips. I have only met one other man since, Martin Brennan, the barony of Frenchpark, Roscommon, who knew the same story, and he told it to me—but in an abridged form—incident for incident up to the point where my translation leaves off.

There is a great deal more in the Irish version in the Leaḃaṛ Sgeului-ġeaċta, which I did not translate, not having been able to get it from Brennan, and having doctored it too much myself to give it as genuine folk-lore.

The rest of the stories in this volume are literally translated from my Leaḃaṛ Sgeuluiġeaċta. Neil O'Carre was taken down phonetically, by Mr. Larminie, from the recitation of a South Donegal peasant.

The Hags of the Long Teeth come from Ballinrobe, as also William of the Tree, the Court of Crinawn, and the Well of D'Yerree-in-Dowan. See pages 239-240 of the L. S.

NOTES.

———◆———

[*Notes in brackets signed A.N., by Alfred Nutt. The references to Arg. Tales are to "Waifs and Strays of Celtic Tradition; Argyllshire Series II.; Folk and Hero Tales from Argyllshire," collected, edited, and translated by the Rev. D. MacInnes, with Notes by the editor and Alfred Nutt. London, 1889.*]

———✝———

"THE TAILOR AND THE THREE BEASTS."

Page 1. In another variant of this tale, which I got from one Martin Brennan—more usually pronounced Brannan; in Irish, O'Braonáin—in Roscommon, the thing which the tailor kills is a swallow, which flew past him. He flung his needle at the bird, and it went through its eye and killed it. This success excites the tailor to further deeds of prowess. In this variant occurred also the widely-spread incident of the tailor's tricking the giant by pretending to squeeze water out of a stone.

Page 2. Garraun (ᵹeaṗṗán), is a common Anglicised Irish word in many parts of Ireland. It means properly a gelding or hack-horse; but in Donegal, strangely enough, it means a horse, and coppul (capall), the ordinary word for a horse elsewhere, means there a mare. The old English seem to have borrowed this word capal from the Irish, *cf.* Percy's version of "Robin Hood and Guy of Gisborne," where the latter is thus represented—

> " A sword and a dagger he wore by his side,
> Of manye a man the bane;
> And he was clad in his capull hyde,
> Topp and tayle and mayne."

Page 7, line 4. The modder-alla (maoṗa-alla, wild dog), is properly a wolf, not a lion ; but the reciter explained it thus, "ᵹᴀᴅᴀᴩ ᴀʟʟᴀ, ᴩᴎ ʟᴇó ᴍᴀᴎ," "modder álla, that's a l'yone," *i.e.*, "a lion," which I have accordingly translated it.

Page 9, line 18. The giant's shouting at night, or at dawn of day, is a common incident in these tales. In the story of "The Speckled Bull," not here given, there are three giants who each utter a shout every morning, "that the whole country hears them." The Irish for giant, in all these stories, is ᴩᴀᴄᴀᴄ̇ (pronounced fahuch), while the Scotch Gaelic word is *famhair*, a word which we have not got, but which is evidently the same as the Fomhor, or sea pirate of Irish mythical history, in whom Professor Rhys sees a kind of water god. The only place in Campbell's four volumes in which the word *fathach* occurs is in the "Lay of the Great Omadawn," which is a distinctly Irish piece, and of which MacLean remarks, "some of the phraseology is considered Irish.

Page 11. This incident appears to be a version of that in "Jack the Giant-Killer." It seems quite impossible to say whether it was always told in Ireland, or whether it may not have been borrowed from some English source. If it does come from an English source it is probably the only thing in these stories that does.

Page 13, line 6. "To take his wife off (pronounced *ov*) him again." The preposition "from" is not often used with take, etc., in Connacht English.

Page 15, line 12. These nonsense-endings are very common in Irish stories. It is remarkable that there seems little trace of them in Campbell. The only story in his volumes which ends with a piece of nonsense is the "Slender Grey Kerne," and it, as I tried to show in my Preface, is Irish. It ends thus : "I parted with them, and they gave me butter on a coal, and kail brose in a creel, and paper shoes, and they sent me away with a cannon-ball on a high-road of glass, till they left me sitting here." Why such endings seem to be stereotyped with some stories, and not used at all with others, I cannot guess. It seems to be the same amongst Slavonic Märchen, of which perhaps one in twenty has a nonsense-ending ; but the proportion is much larger in Ireland. Why the Highland tales, so excellent in themselves, and so closely related to the Irish ones, have lost this distinctive feature I cannot even conjecture, but certain it is that this is so.

[The incident of the king's court being destroyed at night is in the four-teenth-fifteenth century *Agallamh na Senorach*, where it is Finn who guards Tara against the wizard enemies.

I know nothing like the way in which the hero deals with the animals he meets, and cannot help thinking that the narrator forgot or mistold his story. Folk-tales are, as a rule, perfectly logical and sensible if their conditions be once accepted; but here the conduct of the hero is inexplicable, or at all events un-explained.—A. N.]

BRAN'S COLOUR.

Page 15. This stanza on Bran's colour is given by O'Flaherty, in 1808, in the "Gaelic Miscellany." The first two lines correspond with those of my shanachie, and the last two correspond *in sound*, if not in sense. O'Flaherty gave them thus—

> "Speckled back over the loins,
> Two ears scarlet, equal-red."

How the change came about is obvious. The old Irish ꞃuaıċne, "speckled," is not understood now in Connacht; so the word uaıċne, "green," which exactly rhymes with it, took its place. Though uaıċne generally means greenish, it evidently did not do so to the mind of my reciter, for, pointing to a mangy-looking cub of nondescript greyish colour in a corner of his cabin, he said, ꞃın uaıċne, "that's the colour oonya." The words uꞃ cıonn na Leıꞃge, "over the loins," have, for the same reason—namely, that Leaꞃg, "a loin," is obsolete now—been changed to word of the same sound. Aıꞃ baċ na ꞃeıLge, "of the colour of hunting," *i.e.*, the colour of the deer hunted. This, too, the reciter explained briefly by saying, ꞃeıLg ꞃın ꝼıaꝺ, "hunting, that's a deer." From the vivid colouring of Bran it would appear that she could have borne no resemblance whatever to the modern so-called Irish wolf-hound, and that she must in all probability have been short-haired, and not shaggy like them. Most of the Fenian poems contain words not in general use. I remember an old woman reciting me two lines of one of these old poems, and having to explain in current Irish the meaning of no less than five words in the two lines which were

> Aıċıꞃ ꝺam aguꞃ ná can ꞃo
> Cıonnaꞃ ꝼınneaꝺ Leó an tꞃeaLꞃ,

which she thus explained conversationally, ınnıꞃ ꝺam aguꞃ ná ꝺeun bꞃeug, cıa an ċaoı a noeaꞃnaıꝺ ꞃıaꝺ an ꝼıaꝺaċ.

Page 17, line 9. Pistrogue, or pishogue, is a common Anglo-Irish word for a charm or spell. Archbishop MacHale derived it from two words, fios siṫeóg, "knowledge of fairies," which seems hardly probable.

Page 19. "A fiery cloud out of her neck." Thus, in Dr. Atkinson's, Páis Partoloin, from the "Leabhar Breac," the devil appears in the form of an Ethiopian, and according to the Irish translator, ticed lassar borb as a bragait ocus as a shróin amal lassair shuirn tened. "There used to come a fierce flame out of his *neck* and nose, like the flame of a furnace of fire."

Page 19. According to another version of this story, the blind man was Ossian (whose name is in Ireland usually pronounced Essheen or Ussheen) himself, and he got Bran's pups hung up by their teeth to the skin of a newly-killed horse, and all the pups let go their hold except this black one, which clung to the skin and hung out of it. Then Ossian ordered the others to be drowned and kept this. In this other version, the coal which he throws at the infuriated pup was tuaġ no rud icéint, "a hatchet or something." There must be some confusion in this story, since Ossian was not blind during Bran's life-time, nor during the sway of the Fenians. The whole thing appears to be a bad version of Campbell's story, No. XXXI., Vol. II., p. 103. The story may, however, have some relation to the incident in that marvellous tale called "The Fort of little Red Yeoha" (Bruiġion Ċoċaiḋ big ḋeirg), in which we are told how Conan looked out of the fort, go bfacaiḋ sé aon óglaċ ag teaċt ċuige, agus cu ġearr ḋub air slabra iarainn aige, 'na láiṁ, agus is iongna naċ loisgeaḋ sí an bruiġion re gaċ caor teine d'á g-cuirfeaḋ sí tar a craos agus tar a cúbar-beul amaċ, *i.e.*, "he saw one youth coming to him, and he having a short black hound on an iron chain in his hand, and it is a wonder that it would not burn the fort with every ball of fire it would shoot out of its gullet, and out of its foam-mouth." This hound is eventually killed by Bran, but only after Conan had taken off "the shoe of refined silver that was on Bran's right paw" (an bróg airgid aiċ-leigṫe to bí air croiḃ ḋeis Brain). Bran figures largely in Fenian literature.

[I believe this is the only place in which Finn's *mother* is described as a fawn, though in the prose sequel to the "Lay of the Black Dog" (Leab. na Feinne, p. 91) it is stated that Bran, by glamour of the Lochlanners, is made to slay the Fenian women and children in the seeming of deer. That Finn enjoyed the favours of a princess bespelled as a fawn is well known; also that Oisin's mother was a fawn (see the reference in Arg. Tales, p. 470). The narrator may have jumbled these stories together in his memory.

The slaying of Bran's pup seems a variant of Oisin's " Blackbird Hunt " (*cf.* Kennedy, Fictions, 240), whilst the story, as a whole, seems to be mixed up with that of the " Fight of Bran with the Black Dog," of which there is a version translated by the Rev. D. Mac Innes—" Waifs and Strays of Celtic Tradition," Vol. I., p. 7, *et seq.*

It would seem from our text that the Black Dog was Bran's child, so that the fight is an animal variant of the father and son combat, as found in the Cuchullain saga. A good version of " Finn's Visit to Lochlann " (to be printed in Vol. III. of " Waifs and Strays of Celtic Tradition ") tells how Finn took with him Bran's leash; and how the Lochlanners sentenced him to be exposed in a desolate valley, where he was attacked by a savage dog whom he tamed by showing the leash. Vol. XII. of Campbell's " MSS. of Gaelic Stories " contains a poem entitled, " Bran's Colour." This should be compared with our text.—A. N.]

THE KING OF IRELAND'S SON.

Page 19. The king of Ireland's son. This title should properly be, " The son of a king in Ireland " (mac ꝛıġ ı n-Cꞃınn). As this name for the prince is rather cumbrous, I took advantage of having once heard him called the king of Ireland's son (mac ꝛıġ Cıꞃeann), and have so given it here. In another longer and more humorous version of this story, which I heard from Shamus O'Hart, but which I did not take down in writing, the short green man is the " Thin black man " (ꝼeaꞃ caol ꝺub); the gunman is ꝟunnéaꞃ, not ꝟunnaıꞃe; the ear-man is cluaꞃ-le-h-éıꞃꞇeacꞇ (ear for hearing), not cluaꞃaıꞃe; and the blowman is not Séıꝺꞇe, but pollaıꞃe-ꝼéꞃoꞇe (blowing nostril). This difference is the more curious, considering that the men lived only a couple of miles apart, and their families had lived in the same place for generations.

Page 27. This description of a house thatched with feathers is very common in Irish stories. On the present occasion the house is thatched with one single feather, so smooth that there was no projecting point or quill either above or below the feather-roof. For another instance, see the " Well of D'yerree in Dowan," page 131. In a poem from " The Dialogue of the Sages," the lady Credé's house is described thus :—

> " Of its sunny chamber the corner stones
> Are all of silver and precious gold,
> In faultless stripes its thatch is spread
> Of wings of brown and crimson red.
>
>   ✻   ✻   ✻   ✻

Its portico is covered, too,
With wings of birds both yellow and blue.

See O'Curry's " Man. Materials," p. 310.

Page 27. "He drew the cooalya-coric," *coolaya* in the text, is a misprint.
The cooalya-coric means "pole of combat." How it was "drawn" we have
no means of knowing. It was probably a pole meant to be drawn back and
let fall upon some sounding substance. The word ᴄᴀᴘᴘᴀɪɴᴦ, "draw," has,
however, in local, if not in literary use, the sense of drawing back one's arm
to make a blow. A peasant will say, "he drew the blow at me," or "he
drew the stick," in English; or "ᴄᴀᴘᴘᴀɪɴᴦ ᴘᴇ́ ᴀɴ buɪʟʟᴇ," in Irish, by which
he means, he made the blow and struck with the stick. This may be the case
in the phrase "drawing the cooalya-coric," which occurs so often in Irish
stories, and it may only mean, "he struck a blow with the pole of combat,"
either against something resonant, or against the door of the castle. I have come
across at least one allusion to it in the Fenian literature. In the story, called
ᴍᴀᴄᴀoᴍ ᴍóᴘ ᴍᴀᴄ ᴘɪᴦ ɴᴀ h-ᴄᴀᴘᴘáɪɴᴇ (the great man, the king of Spain's
son), the great man and Oscar fight all day, and when evening comes Oscar
grows faint and asks for a truce, and then takes Finn Mac Cool aside privately
and desires him to try to keep the great man awake all night, while he him
self sleeps; because he feels that if the great man, who had been already
three days and nights without rest, were to get some sleep on this night,
he himself would not be a match for him next morning. This is scarcely
agreeable to the character of Oscar, but the wiles which Finn employs to make
the great man relate to him his whole history, and so keep him from sleeping,
are very much in keeping with the shrewdness which all these stories attribute
to the Fenian king. The great man remains awake all night, sorely against
his will, telling Finn his extraordinary adventures; and whenever he tries
to stop, Finn incites him to begin again, and at last tells him not to be
afraid, because the Fenians never ask combat of any man until he
ask it of them first. At last, as the great man finished his adventures
ᴅo bí ᴀɴ ʟá ᴀᴦ ᴇ́ɪᴘɪᴦᴇ ᴀᴦᴜᴘ ᴅo ᴦᴀbᴀᴘ Oᴘᴦᴀᴘ ᴀᴦᴜᴘ ᴅo bᴜᴀɪʟ ᴀɴ
ᴄᴜᴀɪʟʟᴇ ᴄóᴍᴘᴀɪᴄ. ᴅo ᴇ́ᴜᴀʟᴀ ᴀɴ ᴘᴇᴀᴘ ᴍóᴘ ᴘɪɴ ᴀᴦᴜᴘ ᴀ ᴅᴜbᴀɪᴘᴄ, "ᴀ Pɪɴɴ
ʟɪᴍᴇ ᴄúᴍᴀɪʟ," ᴀᴘ ᴘᴇ́, "ᴅ'ᴘᴇᴀʟʟᴀɪᴘ oᴘᴍ," etc., *i.e.*, the day was rising, and
Oscar goes and struck (the word is not "drew" here) the pole of combat.
The great man heard that, and he said, "Oh, Finn Mac Cool, you have de-
ceived me," etc. Considering that they were all inside of Finn's palace at
Allan (co. Kildare) at this time, Oscar could hardly have struck the door.
It is more probable that the pole of combat stood outside the house, and it
seems to have been a regular institution. In Campbell's tale of "The Rider
of Grianag," there is mention made of a *slabhraidh comhrac*, "Chain of com-

bat,' which answers the same purpose as the pole, only not so conveniently, since the hero has to give it several hauls before he can "take a turn out of it." We find allusion to the same thing in the tale of ᴵollᴀn ᴀᵽm ᴅeᴀᵽᵹ Illan, the hero, comes to a castle in a solitude, and surprises a woman going to the well, and she points out to him the chain, and says, "ᵹᴀċ uᴀiᵽ ċᵽoiċᵽeᴀᵽ ᴄu ᴀn ᵽlᴀbᵽᴀ ᵽin ᴀᵽ ᴀn mbile, ᴅo ᵹeobᴀiᴅ ᴄu ᴄeuᴅ ᴄuᵽᴀᴅ ᴄᴀċ-ᴀᵽmᴀċ, ᴀᵹuᵽ ni ιᴀᵽᵽᵽᴀιᴅ oᵽᴄ ᴀċᴄ ᴀn ᴄóṁᵽᴀᴄ iᵽ ᴀil leᴀᴄ, mᴀᵽ ᴀᴄᴀ ᴅιᴀᵽ no ᴄᵽιúᵽ no ᴄeᴀċᵽᴀᵽ, no ᴄeuᴅ," i.e., "every time that you will shake yon chain (suspended) out of the tree, you will get (call forth) a hundred champions battle-armed, and they will only ask of thee the combat thou likest thyself, that is (combat with) two, or three, or four, or a hundred." Chains are continually mentioned in Irish stories. In the "Little Fort of Allan," a Fenian story, we read, ᴀnn ᵽin ᴅ'éiᵽiᵹ bollᵽᵹᴀiᵽe ᵹo bioċ-uᵽlᴀṁ ᴀᵹuᵽ ᴅo ċᵽoiċ ᵽlᴀbᵽᴀ éiᵽᴄeᴀċᴄᴀ nᴀ bᵽuiᵹne, ᴀᵹuᵽ ᴅ'éiᵽᴄeᴀᴅᴀᵽ uile ᵹo ᵽoiᵽᴄineᴀċ, i.e., "then there arose a herald with active readiness, and they shook the fort's chain of listening, and they all listened attentively;" and in the tale of "Illan, the Red-armed,' there are three chains in the palace, one of gold, one of silver, and one of findrinny (a kind of metal, perhaps bronze), which are shaken to seat the people at the banquet, and to secure their silence; but whoever spake after the gold chain had been shaken did it on pain of his head.

[In the story of Cuchullain's youthful feats it is related that, on his first expedition, he came to the court of the three Mac Nechtain, and, according to O'Curry's Summary ("Manners and Customs," II., p. 366), "sounded a challenge." The mode of this sounding is thus described by Prof. Zimmer, in his excellent summary of the *Tain bo Cualgne* (Zeit, f. vgl. Sprachforschung, 1887, p. 448). "On the lawn before the court stood a stone pillar, around which was a closed chain (or ring), upon which was written in Ogham, that every knight who passed thereby was bound, upon his knightly honour, to issue a challenge. Cuchullain took the stone pillar and threw it into a brook hard by." This is the nearest analogue I have been able to find to our passage in the old Irish literature (the *Tain*, it should be mentioned, goes back in its present form certainly to the tenth, and, probably, to the seventh century). As many of the Fenian romances assumed a fresh and quasi-definite shape in the twelfth-fourteenth centuries, it is natural to turn for a parallel to the mediæval romances of chivalry. In a twelfth century French romance, the Conte de Graal, which is in some way connected with the body of Gaelic Märchen (whether the connection be, as I think, due to the fact that the French poet worked up lays derived from Celtic sources, or, as Professor Zimmer thinks, that the French romances are the origin of much in current Gaelic folk-tales), when Perceval comes to the Castle of Maidens and enters therein, he finds a table of brass, and hanging from it by a chain of silver, a steel

hammer. With this he strikes three blows on the table, and forces the inmates
to come to him. Had they not done so the castle would have fallen into
ruins. Other parallels from the same romances are less close ; thus, when Perceval came to the castle of his enemy, Partinal, he defies him by throwing
down his shield, which hangs up on a tree outside the castle (v. 44,400,
et seq.). It is well known that the recognised method of challenging in
tournaments was for the challenger to touch his adversary's shield with the
lance. This may possibly be the origin of the "shield-clashing" challenge
which occurs several times in Conall Gulban ; or, on the other hand, the
mediæval practice may be a knightly transformation of an earlier custom·
In the thirteenth century prose Perceval le Gallois, when the hero comes
to the Turning Castle and finds the door shut, he strikes such a blow with
his sword that it enters three inches deep into a marble pillar (Potvin's edition,
p. 196). These mediæval instances do not seem sufficient to explain the
incident in our text, and I incline to think that our tale has preserved a genuine
trait of old Irish knightly life. In Kennedy's "Jack the Master, and Jack
the Servant" (Fictions, p. 32), the hero takes hold of a "club that hangs by
the door" and uses it as a knocker.—A. N.]

Page 29. They spent the night, &c. This brief run resembles very much
a passage in the story of Iollan Arm-dearg, which runs, ꝺo ꝑᵽᴉᴨᴨᴇᴀꝺᴀᴨ ꝩᴨᴉ
ꝯᴩᴇᴀᴨᴀ ꝺᴇ 'n oᴉꝺċᴇ, ᴀᴨ ċᴇᴜꝺ ꝯᴩᴉᴀᴨ ꝑᴇ h·ól ᴀᵹᴜᴩ ꝑᴇ h·ᴉᴍᴉᴩꝯ, ᴀᴨ ꝺᴀꝑᴀ
ꝯᴩᴉᴀᴨ ꝑᴇ ᴄᴇól ᴀᵹᴜᴩ ꝑᴇ h·oᴉꝑꝑᴉꝺᴇ ᴀᵹᴜᴩ ꝑᴇ h·ᴇᴀʟᴀꝺᴀᴨ, ᴀᵹᴜᴩ ᴀᴨ ꝯᴩᴇᴀꝩ
ꝯᴩᴉᴀᴨ ꝑᴇ ꝩᴜᴀᴨ ᴀᵹᴜᴩ ꝑᴇ ꝩᴀᵯ·ċooʟᴀꝺ, ᴀᵹᴜᴩ ꝺᴜ ᴨᴜᵹᴀꝺᴀᴨ ᴀꝩ ᴀᴨ oᴉꝺċᴇ ꝩᴉᴨ
i.e., they made three-thirds of the night ; the first third with drink and
play, the second third with music and melody and (feats of) science, and
the third third with slumber and gentle sleep, and they passed away that
night.

Page 33, line 28. This allusion to the horse and the docking is very ob-
scure and curious. The old fellow actually blushed at the absurdity of the
passage, yet he went through with it, though apparently unwillingly. He
could throw no light upon it, except to excuse himself by saying that "that
was how he heard it ever."

Page 37, line 4. The sword of *three* edges is curious ; the third edge would
seem to mean a rounded point, for it can hardly mean triangular like a bayo-
net. The sword that "never leaves the leavings of a blow behind it," is
common in Irish literature. In that affecting story of Deirdre, Naoise requests
to have his head struck off with such a sword, one that Mananan son of Lir,
had long before given to himself.

Page 47. The groundwork or motivating of this story is known to all European children, through Hans Andersen's tale of the "Travelling Companion."

[I have studied some of the features of this type of stories Arg. Tales, pp. 443-452.—A. N.]

THE ALP-LUACHRA.

Page 49. This legend of the alp-luachra is widely disseminated, and I have found traces of it in all parts of Ireland. The alp-luachra is really a newt, not a lizard, as is usually supposed. He is the lissotriton punctatus of naturalists, and is the only species of newt known in Ireland. The male has an orange belly, red-tipped tail, and olive back. It is in most parts of Ireland a rare reptile enough, and hence probably the superstitious fear with which it is regarded, on the principle of *omne ignotum pro terribli*. This reptile goes under a variety of names in the various counties. In speaking English the peasantry when they do not use the Irish name, call him a "mankeeper," a word which has probably some reference to the superstition related in our story. He is also called in some counties a "darklooker," a word which is probably, a corruption of an Irish name for him which I have heard the Kildare people use, dochi-luachair (ꝺꝍꝏ́ꝏ Luꝏꝏ́ꝑꝏ), a word not found in the dictionaries. In Waterford, again, he is called art-luachra, and the Irish MSS. call him arc-luachra (eꝏꝑꝏ-Luꝏꝏ́ꝑꝏ). The alt-pluachra of the text is a mispronunciation of the proper name, alp-luachra. In the Arran Islands they have another name, ꝏꝑꝏ-ėꝏꝏ́. I have frequently heard of people swallowing one while asleep. The symptoms, they say, are that the person swells enormously, and is afflicted with a thirst which makes him drink canfuls and pails of water or buttermilk, or anything else he can lay his hand on. In the south of Ireland it is believed that if something savoury is cooked on a pan, and the person's head held over it, the mankeeper will come out. A story very like the one here given is related in Waterford, but of a ꝺꝏꝑ ꝺꝏꝏL, or *daraga dheel*, as he is there called, a venomous insect, which has even more legends attached to him than the alp-luachra. In this county, too, they say that if you turn the alp-luachra over on its back, and lick it, it will cure burns. Keating, the Irish historian and theologian, alludes quaintly to this reptile in his Ꞇꝑꝏ bꞁꝍꝑꝏ́ꝏꝏꝏꝏꝏ ꝏꝏ bhꝏ́ꝑꝏ, so finely edited in the original the other day by Dr. Atkinson. "Since," says Keating, "prosperity or worldly store is the weapon of the adversary (the devil), what a man ought to do is to spend it in killing the adversary, that is, by bestowing it on God's poor. The thing which we read in Lactantius agrees with this, that if an airc-luachra were to inflict a wound on anyone, what he ought to do is to shake a pinchful of the ashes of the airc-luachra upon the wound, and he will be cured thereby; and so, if worldly prosperity wounds the conscience, what you ought to do is to put a poultice of the same prosperity to cure the wound which the covetousness by which you have amassed it has made in your conscience, by distributing upon the poor of God all that remains over your own necessity." The practice which the fourth-century Latin alludes to, is in Ireland to-day transferred to the dar-daol, or göevius olens of the naturalists, which is always burnt as soon as found. I have often heard people say:—" Kill a keerhogue (clock or little beetle); burn a dar-dael."

Page 59. Boccuch (bᴀcᴀċ), literally a lame man, is, or rather was, the name of a very common class of beggars about the beginning of this century. Many of these men were wealthy enough, and some used to go about with horses to collect the "alms" which the people unwillingly gave them. From all accounts they appear to have been regular black-mailers, and to have extorted charity partly through inspiring physical and partly moral terror, for the satire, at least of some of them, was as much dreaded as their cudgels. Here is a curious specimen of their truculence from a song called the bᴀcᴀċ buᴉ𝗈he, now nearly forgotten :—

ɪꞅ bᴀcᴀch mé ᴛᴀ́ ᴀ𝗂ꞃ ᴀon cho𝗂ꞃ, ꞃúbhᴀⱡꝼᴀᴉbh mé ᵹo ꞃpéᴉꞃeᴀᴛhᴀᴉⱡ,
Ceᴀnnóchᴀᴉbh mé bꞃéꝍᴉn ᴉ ᵹ-Cᴉⱡⱡ-Cᴀ𝗂nn𝗂ᵹh bo'n bhꞃᴀo𝗂ꞃ,
Cu𝗂ꞃꝼeᴀ𝗈 cóᴛᴀ cóꝑu𝗂ᵹᴛhe ᵹⱡeuꞃᴛᴀ, ᴀ'ꞃ búcⱡᴀ buᴉꝍhe ᴀ𝗂ꞃ m'ᴀon cho𝗂ꞃ,
ᴀ'ꞃ nᴀch mᴀᴉᴛh mo ꞃhⱡᴉᵹhe bᴉꝍh ᴀ'ꞃ cuꝍᴀᴉᵹh o chᴀᴉⱡⱡ mᴉo choꞃᴀ ꞃúbhᴀⱡ!
nᴉ'ⱡ bᴀcᴀch nᴀ́ ꝼeᴀꞃ-mᴀ́ⱡᴀ o Ṡⱡ𝗂ᵹeᴀch ᵹo Cᴉnn-ᴛꞃᴀ́ᴉⱡe
ᴀᵹuꞃ ó bheuⱡ-ᴀn-ᴀ́chᴀ ᵹo bᴀᴉⱡe-ᴛuᴉꝍhe nᴀ mᴉꝍhe,
nᴀch bhꞃuᴉⱡ ᴀᵹᴀm ꝼᴀoᴉ ᴀꝑꝍ-ch𝗂oꞃ, ᴀᵹuꞃ cꞃóᴉn ᴀuᴢᵹbᴀᴉꝍh nᴀ ꝑᴀ́ᴉᴛhe,
no mᴉneóchᴀᴉnn ᴀ ᵹ-cnᴀ́mhᴀ ⱡe bᴀᴛᴀ ᵹⱡᴀꞃ ꝍᴀꞃᴀᴉᵹh.

_i.e._,

I am a boccugh who goes on one foot, I will travel airily,
I will buy frize in Kilkenny for the breeches (?)
I will put a well-ordered prepared coat and yellow buckles on my one foot
And isn't it good, my way of getting food and clothes since my feet lost their walk.
There is no boccuch or bagman from Sligo to Kinsale
And from Ballina to Ballybwee (Athboy) in Meath,
That I have not under high rent to me—a crown every quarter from them—
Or I'd pound their bones small with a green oak stick.

The memory of these formidable guests is nearly vanished, and the boccuch in our story is only a feeble old beggarman. I fancy this tale of evicting the alt-pluachra family from their human abode is fathered upon a good many people as well as upon the father of the present MacDermot. [Is the peasant belief in the Alp-Luachra the originating idea of the well-known Irish Rabelaisian 14th century tale " The Vision of McConglinny?"—A.N.]

THE WEASEL.

Page 73. The weasel, like the cat, is an animal that has many legends and superstitions attaching to it. I remember hearing from an old shanachie, now unfortunately dead, a long and extraordinary story about the place called Chapelizod, a few miles from Dublin, which he said was Séipeul-easóg, the " weasel's chapel," in Irish, but which is usually supposed to have received its name from the Princess Iseult of Arthurian romance. The story was the account of how the place came by this name. How he, who was a Con-nachtman, and never left his native county except to reap the harvest in England, came by this story I do not know; but I imagine it must have been told him by some one in the neighbourhood, in whose house he spent the night, whilst walking across the island on his way to Dublin or Drogheda harbour. The weasel is a comical little animal, and one might very well think it was animated with a spirit. I have been assured by an old man, and one whom I have always found fairly veracious, that when watching for ducks beside a river one evening a kite swooped down and seized a weasel, with which it rose up again into the air. His brother fired, and the kite came down, the weasel still in its claws, and un-hurt. The little animal then came up, and stood in front of the two men where they sat, and nodded and bowed his head to them about twenty times over; "it was," said the old man, "thanking us he was." The weasel is a desperate fighter, and always makes for the throat. What, however, in Ire-land is called a weazel, is really a stoat, just as what is called a crow in Ireland is really a rook, and what is called a crane is really a heron.

Cáuher-na-mart, to which Paudyeen (diminutive of Paddy) was bound, means the "city of the beeves," but is now called in English Westport, one of the largest towns in Mayo. It was *apropos* of its long and desolate streets of ruined stores, with nothing in them, that some one remarked he saw Ireland's charac-teristics there in a nutshell—"an itch after greatness and nothingness;" a remark which was applicable enough to the squireocracy and bourgeoisie of the last century.

Page 79. The "big black dog" seems a favourite shape for the evil spirit to take. He appears three times in this volume.

Page 81. The little man, with his legs astride the barrel, appears to be akin to the south of Ireland spirit, the clooricaun, a being who is not known, at least by this name, in the north or west of the island. See Crofton Croker's "Haunted Cellar."

Page 87. "The green hill opened," etc. The fairies are still called Tuatha be Danann by the older peasantry, and all the early Irish literature agrees that the home of the Tuatha was in the hills, after the Milesians had taken to themselves the plains. Thus in the story of the "Piper and the Pooka," in the Leabhap Sgeulaigheachca, not translated here, a door opens in the hill of Croagh Patrick, and the pair walk in and find women dancing inside. Dónal, the name of the little piper, is now Anglicised into Daniel, except in one or two Irish families which retain the old form still. The *coash-t'ya bower*, in which the fairy consorts ride, means literally "the deaf coach," perhaps from the rumbling sound it is supposed to make, and the banshee is sometimes supposed to ride in it. It is an omen of ill to those who meet it. It seems rather out of place amongst the fairy population, being, as it is, a gloomy harbinger of death, which will pass even through a crowded town. Cnoc Matha, better Magha, the hill of the plain, is near the town of Tuam, in Galway. Finvara is the well-known king of the fairy host of Connacht. In Lady Wilde's "Ethna, the Bride," Finvara is said to have carried off a beautiful girl into his hill, whom her lover recovers with the greatest difficulty. When he gets her back at last, she lies on her bed for a year and a day as if dead. At the end of that time he hears voices saying that he may recover her by unloosing her girdle, burning it, and burying in the earth the enchanted pin that fastened it. This was, probably, the slumber-pin which we have met so often in the "King of Ireland's Son." Nuala, the name of the fairy queen, was a common female name amongst us until the last hundred years or so. The sister of the last O'Donnell, for whom Mac an Bhaird wrote his exquisite elegy, so well translated by Mangan—

> "Oh, woman of the piercing wail,
> That mournest o'er yon mound of clay"—

was Nuala. I do not think it is ever used now as a Christian name at all, having shared the unworthy fate of many beautiful Gaelic names of women common a hundred years ago, such as Mève, Una, Sheelah, Moreen, etc.

Slieve Belgadaun occurs also in another story which I heard, called the Bird
of Enchantment, in which a fairy desires some one to bring a sword of light
"from the King of the Firbolg, at the foot of Slieve Belgadaun." Nephin
is a high hill near Crossmolina, in North Mayo.

Page 89. Stongirya (ꞃꞇꜱnꞡꜱꞵ̇ꞃᵉ), a word not given in dictionaries, means, I
think, a "mean fellow." The dove's hole, near the village of Cong, in the
west of the county Mayo, is a deep cavity in the ground, and when a stone
is thrown down into it you hear it rumbling and crashing from side to side of
the rocky wall, as it descends, until the sound becomes too faint to hear. It
is the very place to be connected with the marvellous.

LEEAM O'ROONEY'S BURIAL.

Page 95. Might not Spenser have come across some Irish legend of an imi-
tation man made by enchantment, which gave him the idea of Archimago's imi-
tation of Una :

> " Who all this time, with charms and hidden artes,
>   Had made a lady of that other spright,
>   And framed of liquid ayre her tender partes,
>   So lively and so like in all men's sight
>   That weaker sence it could have ravished quite," etc.

I never remember meeting this easy *deus ex machinâ* for bringing about a
complication before.

Page 101. Leeam imprecates "the devil from me," thus skilfully turning a curse into a blessing, as the Irish peasantry invariably do, even when in
a passion. *Ḣonnam one d'ṙ᷎ud*—" my soul *from* the devil " is an ordinary
exclamation expressive of irritation or wonderment.

GULLEESH.

Page 104. When I first heard this story I thought that the name of the hero
was ꞡoꞁꞁꞃ, the pronunciation of which in English letters would be Gul-yeesh ;
but I have since heard the name pronounced more distinctly, and am sure that
it is ꞡꞁoꞁꞁꜱoꞃ, g'yulleesh, which is a corruption of the name ꞡꞁoꞁꞁꜱ-ioꞃꜱ,
a not uncommon Christian name amongst the seventeenth century Gaels. I
was, however, almost certain that the man (now dead) from whom I first got this

story, pronounced the word as Gulyeesh, anent which my friend Mr. Thomas Flannery furnished me at the time with the following interesting note :—Ní coriṁúil ʒuр ʒiolla-íoрa acá 'ɼan aiṁ ʒoillíр, níр b' ɼeioiр "ʒiolla-íoрa" do ḃul i n "ʒoillíр." Saoilim ʒuр b' ionann ʒoillíр aʒuр ʒoill-ʒéiр no ʒaill-ʒéiр, aʒuр iр ionann "ʒéiр" aʒuр "eala." Iр cuiṁne liom "muiрʒéiр" 'rna h-"annalaiḃ," aʒuр iр ioṁda aiṁ duine éiʒeaр o aniṁannaiḃ eun éoṁ maiṫ le ó aniṁannaiḃ beaṫaċ, maр aca bрan, ɼiaċ, lon, loinín, рeaḃac, ʒc. 'Sé ʒoillíр na ʒ-coр dub ɼóр. Naċ aiṫne duit ʒuр leaр-aiṁ an eala "coр-dub" i móрán d'áitiḃ i n-Ciрinn. Tá neiṫe eile 'ɼan рeeul рin do beiр oрm a ṁeaр ʒuр de na ɼʒeulcaiḃ a baineaр le h-ealaiḃ no ʒéiрiḃ é. Naċ aiрteaċ an ní ʒo dcuʒ bainpрíonṁɼa caiṫneaṁ do buaċaill coр-dub coр-рalaċ leiрceaṁuil maр é? Naċ ait an níḋ ɼóр naċ dcuʒċaр an leaр-aiṁ dó aрíр, caр éiр beaʒáin ɼocal aiр dcúр ó рin amaċ ʒo deiрeaḃ. Deaрmadcaр an leaр-aiṁ aʒuр an ɼáṫ ɼá bɼuaiр ɼé é. i.e., "It is not likely that the name Goillis is Giolla-iosa; the one could not be changed into the other. I think that Goillis is the same as Goill-ghéis, or Gaill-ghéis (i.e., foreign swan). Géis means swan. I remember a name Muirgheis (sea swan) in the Annals; and there is many a man's name that comes from the names of birds as well as from the names of animals, such as Bran (raven), Fiach (scald crow), Lon and Loinin (blackbird), Seabhac (falcon), etc. Moreover, he is Goillis *of the black feet*. Do you not know that the black-foot is a name for the swan in many parts of Ireland. There are other things in this story which make me believe that it is of those tales which treat of swans or géises. Is it not a strange thing that the princess should take a liking to a dirty-footed, black-footed, lazy boy like him? Is it not curious also that the nickname of black-foot is not given to him, after a few words at the beginning, from that out to the end? The nickname is forgotten, and the cause for which he got it."

This is certainly curious, as Mr. Flannery observes, and is probably due to the story being imperfectly remembered by the shanachie. In order to motivate the black feet at all, Guleesh should be made to say that he would never wash his feet till he made a princess fall in love with him, or something of that nature. This was probably the case originally, but these stories must be all greatly impaired during the last half century, since people ceased to take an interest in things Irish.

There are two stories in Lady Wilde's book that somewhat resemble this. "The Midnight Ride," a short story of four pages, in which the hero frightens the Pope by pretending to set his palace on fire; but the story ends thus, as do many of Crofton Croker's—"And from that hour to this his wife believed that he dreamt the whole story as he lay under the hayrick on his way home from a carouse with the boys." I take this, however, to be the sarcastic nineteenth century touch of an over-refined collector, for in all my experience I never knew a shanachie attribute the adventures of his hero to a dream. The other tale is called the "Stolen Bride," and is a story about the "kern of Querin," who saves a bride from the fairies on November Eve, but she will neither speak nor taste food. That day year he hears the fairies say that the way to cure her is to make her eat food off her father's table-cloth. She does this, and is cured. The trick which Gulleesh plays upon the Pope reminds us of the fifteenth century story of Dr. Faustus and his dealings with his Holiness.

[Cf. also the story of Michael Scott's journey to Rome, "Waifs and Strays of Celtic Tradition," Vol. I., p. 46. The disrespectful way in which the Pope is spoken of in these tales does not seem due to Protestantism, as is the case with the Faustus story, although, as I have pointed out, there are some curious points of contact between Michael Scott and Faustus. Guleesh seems to be an early Nationalist who thought more of his village and friend than of the head of his religion.—A.N.]

The description of the wedding is something like that in Crofton Croker's "Master and Man," only the scene in that story is laid at home.

The story of Gulleesh appears to be a very rare one. I have never been able to find a trace of it outside the locality (near where the counties of Sligo, Mayo, and Roscommon meet) in which I first heard it.

[It thus seems to be a very late working-up of certain old incidents with additions of new and incongruous ones.—A.N.]

Page 112. "The rose and the lily were fighting together in her face." This is a very common expression of the Irish bards. In one of Carolan's unpublished poems he says of Bridget Cruise, with whom he was in love in his youth :—" In her countenance there is the lily, the whitest and the brightest— a combat of the world—madly wrestling with the rose. Behold the conflict of the pair ; the goal—the rose will not lose it of her will ; victory—the lily cannot gain it ; oh, God ! is it not a hard struggle ! " etc.

Page 115. "I call and cross (or consecrate) you to myself," says Gulleesh. This is a phrase in constant use with Irish speakers, and proceeds from an underlying idea that certain phenomena are caused by fairy agency. If a child falls, if a cow kicks when being milked, if an animal is restless, I have often heard a woman cry, ᵹoᶌᵽᵻⱮ a'ᵽ caᵽcᵽaᵻcᶌⱮ ᶁu, "I call and cross you," often abbreviated into ᵹoᶌᵽᵻⱮ, ᵹoᶌᵽᵻⱮ, merely, i.e., "I call, I call."

14

The Well of D'Yerree-in-Dowan.

Page 129. There are two other versions of this story, one a rather evaporated one, filtered through English, told by Kennedy, in which the Dall Glic is a wise old hermit ; and another, and much better one, by Curtin. The Dall Glic, wise blind man, figures in several stories which I have got, as the king's counsellor. I do not remember ever meeting him in our literature. Bweesownee, the name of the king's castle, is, I think, a place in Mayo, and probably would be better written bᵘisᵉ-ᵉamnᵃiᵍ.

Page 131. This beautiful lady in red silk, who thus appears to the prince, and who comes again to him at the end of the story, is a curious creation of folk fancy. She may personify good fortune. There is nothing about her in the two parallel stories from Curtin and Kennedy.

Page 133. This "tight loop" (lúb ceann) can hardly be a bow, since the ordinary word for that is *bógha*; but it may, perhaps, be a name for a cross-bow.

Page 136. The story is thus invested with a moral, for it is the prince's piety in giving what was asked of him in the honour of God which enabled the queen to find him out, and eventually marry him.

Page 137. In the story of Caillᵉaᵈ nᵃ piᵃcᵃile ᵍᵃnᵃ, in my leᵃbhᵃp Sᵍeuluiᵍheᵃchtᵃ, not translated in this book, an old hag makes a boat out of a thimble, which she throws into the water, as the handsome lady does here.

Page 141. This incident of the ladder is not in Curtin's story, which makes the brothers mount the queen's horse and get thrown. There is a very curious account of a similar ladder in the story of the "Slender Grey Kerne," of which I possess a good MS., made by a northern scribe in 1763. The passage is of interest, because it represents a trick something almost identical with which I have heard Colonel Olcott, the celebrated American theosophist lecturer, say he saw Indian jugglers frequently performing. Colonel Olcott, who came over to examine Irish fairy lore in the light of theosophic science, was of opinion that these men could bring a person under their power so as to make him imagine that he saw whatever the juggler wished him to see. He especially mentioned this incident of making people see a man going up a ladder. The MS., of which I may as well give the original, runs thus:—

Iaɼ ɼin ċuʒ an ceiċeaɼnaċ mála amaċ ó na aɼʒoill, aʒuɼ ċuʒ ceiɼcle ɼíoda amaċ aɼ a ṁála, aʒuɼ do ċeilʒ ɼuaɼ i bɼɼiċiṁ na ɼioɼmaṁuince í, aʒaɼ do ɼinne dɼéimiɼe dí, aʒuɼ ċuʒ ʒeaɼɼɼiad amaċ aɼiɼ aʒuɼ do leiʒ ɼuaɼ ɼuaɼ dɼéimiɼe é. Ċuʒ ʒadaɼ cluaiɼ-deaɼʒ amaċ aɼiɼ aʒuɼ do leiʒ ɼuaɼ andiaiʒ an ʒeaɼɼɼiad é. Ċuʒ cu ɼaiceaċ ɼoluaimneaċ amaċ aʒuɼ do leiʒ ɼuaɼ andiaiʒ an ʒeaɼɼɼiad aʒuɼ an ʒadaɼ í, aʒuɼ a dubaiɼc, iɼ baoʒlaċ liom, aiɼ ɼé, ʒo n-íoɼɼaid an ʒadaɼ aʒuɼ an cú an ʒeaɼɼɼiad, aʒuɼ ni móɼ liom anaeal do ċuɼ aiɼ an ʒeaɼɼɼiad. Ċuʒ ann ɼin óʒánaċ deaɼ a n-eidead ɼó ṁaiċ amaċ aɼ an mála aʒuɼ do leiʒ ɼuaɼ andiaiʒ an ʒeaɼɼɼiad aʒuɼ an ʒadaɼ aʒuɼ na con é. Ċuʒ cailín áluind a n-eidead ɼó ċeaɼ amaċ aɼ an mála aʒuɼ do leiʒ ɼuaɼ andiaiʒ an ʒeaɼɼɼiad an ʒadaɼ an óʒánaiʒ aʒuɼ na con í.

Iɼ dona do éiɼiʒ daṁ anoiɼ, aɼ an Ceiċeaɼnaċ óiɼ acá an c-óʒanaċ aiʒ dul aʒ póʒad mo ṁná aʒuɼ an cú aiʒ cɼeim an ʒeaɼɼɼiad. Do ċaɼɼainʒ an Ceiċeaɼnaċ an dɼéimiɼe anuaɼ, aʒuɼ do ɼuaiɼ an c-óʒánaċ ɼaiɼɼe (?) an ṁnaoi aʒuɼ an cu aiʒ cɼeim an ʒeaɼɼɼiad aṁuil a dubaiɼc, i.e., after that the kerne took out a bag from under his arm-pit and he brought out a ball of silk from the bag, and he threw it up into the expanse (?) of the firmament, and it became a ladder; and again he took out a hare and let it up the ladder. Again he took out a red-eared hound and let it up after the hare. Again he took out a timid frisking dog, and he let her up after the hare and the hound, and said, "I am afraid," said he, "the hound and the dog will eat the hare, and I think I ought to send some relief to the hare." Then he took out of the bag a handsome youth in excellent apparel, and he let him up after the hare and the hound and the dog. He took out of the bag a lovely girl in beautiful attire, and he let her up after the hare the hound the youth and the dog.

"It's badly it happened to me now," says the kerne, "for the youth is going kissing my woman, and the dog gnawing the hare." The kerne drew down the ladder again and he found the youth "going along with the woman, and the dog gnawing the hare," as he said.

The English "Jack and the Beanstalk" is about the best-known ladder story.

Page 141. This story was not invented to explain the existence of the twelve tribes of Galway, as the absence of any allusion to them in all the

parallel versions proves ; but the application of it to them is evidently the brilliant afterthought of some Galwegian shanachie.

THE COURT OF CRINNAWN.

Page 142. The court of Crinnawn is an old ruin on the river Lung, which
divides the counties of Roscommon and Mayo, about a couple of miles from
the town of Ballaghadereen. I believe, despite the story, that it was built by
one of the Dillon family, and not so long ago either. There is an Irish pro-
phecy extant in these parts about the various great houses in Roscommon.
Clonalis, the seat of the O'Connor Donn—or Don, as they perversely insist on
spelling it ; Dungar, the seat of the De Freynes ; Loughlinn, of the Dillons,
etc. ; and amongst other verses, there is one which prophecies that "no roof
shall rise on Crinnawn," which the people say was fulfilled, the place having
never been inhabited or even roofed. In the face of this, how the story of
Crinnawn, son of Belore, sprang into being is to me quite incomprehensible, and
I confess I have been unable to discover any trace of this particular story on
the Roscommon side of the river, nor do I know from what source the shanachie, Mr. Lynch Blake, from whom I got it, became possessed of it. Balor of
the evil eye, who figures in the tale of "The Children of Tuireann," was not
Irish at all, but a "Fomorian." The *pattern*, accompanied with such funest
results for Mary Kerrigan, is a festival held in honour of the *patron* saint.
These patterns were common in many places half a century ago, and were
great scenes of revelry and amusement, and often, too, of hard fighting. But
these have been of late years stamped out, like everything else distinctively
Irish and lively.

[This story is a curious mixture of common peasant belief about haunted
raths and houses, with mythical matter probably derived from books. Balor
appears in the well-known tale of MacKineely, taken down by O'Donovan, in
1855, from Shane O'Dugan of Tory Island (Annals. I. 18, and cf. Rhys, Hibbert
Lect., p. 314), but I doubt whether in either case the appearance of the name
testifies to a genuine folk-belief in this mythological personage, one of the
principal representatives of the powers of darkness in the Irish god-saga.—
A.N.]

NEIL O'CARREE.

Page 148. The abrupt beginning of this story is no less curious than the short,
jerky sentences in which it is continued. Mr. Larminie, who took down this

story phonetically, and word for word, from a native of Glencolumkille, in Donegal, informed me that all the other stories of the same narrator were characterized by the same extraordinary style. I certainly have met nothing like it among any of my shanachies. The *crumskeen* and *galskeen* which Neil orders the smith to make for him. are instruments of which I never met or heard mention elsewhere. According to their etymology they appear to mean "stooping-knife" and "bright-knife," and were, probably, at one time, well-known names of Irish surgical instruments, of which no trace exists, unless it be in some of the mouldering and dust-covered medical MSS. from which Irish practitioners at one time drew their knowledge. The name of the hero, if written phonetically, would be more like Nee-al O Corrwy than Neil O Carree, but it is always difficult to convey Gaelic sounds in English letters. When Neil takes up the head out of the skillet (a good old Shaksperian word, by-the-by, old French, *escuellette*, in use all over Ireland, and adopted into Gaelic). it falls in a *gliggar* or *gluggar*. This Gaelic word is onomatopeic, and largely in vogue with the English-speaking population. Anything rattling or gurgling, like water in an india-rubber ball, makes a *gligger* ; hence, an egg that is no longer fresh is called a glugger, because it makes a noise when shaken. I came upon this word the other day. raised proudly aloft from its provincial obscurity, in O'Donovan Rossa's paper, the *United Irishman*, every copy of which is headed with this weighty *spruch*, indicative of his political faith :

" As soon will a goose sitting upon a glugger hatch goslings, as an Irishman, sitting in an English Parliament, will hatch an Irish Parliament."

This story is motivated like "The King of Ireland's Son." It is one of the many tales based upon an act of compassion shown to the dead.

Trunk-Without-Head.

Page 157. This description of the decapitated ghost sitting astride the beer-barrel, reminds one of Crofton Croker's "Clooricaun," and of the hag's son in the story of " Paudyeen O'Kelly and the Weasel." In Scotch Highland tradition, there is a " trunk-without-head," who infested a certain ford, and killed people who attempted to pass that way ; he is not the subject, however, of any regular story.

In a variant of this tale the hero's name is Labhras (Laurence) and the castle where the ghost appeared is called Baile-an-bhroin (Ballinvrone). It is also mentioned, that when the ghost appeared in court, he came in streaming with blood, as he was the day he was killed, and that the butler. on seeing him, fainted.

It is Donal's courage which saves him from the ghost, just as happens in another story which I got, and which is a close Gaelic parallel to Grimm's "Man who went out to learn to shake with fear." The ghost whom the hero lays explains that he had been for thirty years waiting to meet some one who would not be afraid of him. There is an evident moral in this.

THE HAGS OF THE LONG TEETH.

Page 162. Long teeth are a favourite adjunct to horrible personalities in folk-fancy. There is in my "Leabhar Sgeuluigheachta," another story of a hag of the long tooth; and in a story I got in Connacht, called the "Speckled Bull," there is a giant whose teeth are long enough to make a walking-staff for him, and who invites the hero to come to him "until I draw you under my long, cold teeth."

Loughlinn is a little village a few miles to the north-west of Castlerea, in the county Roscommon, not far from Mayo; and Drimnagh wood is a thick plantation close by. Ballyglas is the adjoining townland. There are two of the same name, upper and lower, and I do not know to which the story refers.

[In this very curious tale a family tradition seems to have got mixed up with the common belief about haunted raths and houses. It is not quite clear why the daughters should be bespelled for their father's sin. This conception could not easily be paralleled, I believe, from folk-belief in other parts of Ireland. I rather take it that in the original form of the story the sisters helped, or, at at all events, countenanced their father, or, perhaps, were punished because they countenanced the brother's parricide. The discomfiture of the priest is curious.—A. N.]

WILLIAM OF THE TREE.

Page 168. I have no idea who this Granya-Oi was. Her appearance in this story is very mysterious, for I have never met any trace of her elsewhere. The name appears to mean Granya the Virgin.

[Our story belongs to the group—the calumniated and exposed daughter or daughter-in-law. But in a German tale, belonging to the forbidden chamber series (Grimm's, No. 3, Marienkind), the Virgin Mary becomes god-mother to a child, whom she takes with her into heaven, forbidding her merely to open one particular door. The child does this, but denies it thrice. To punish her the Virgin banishes her from heaven into a thorny wood. Once, as she is sitting, clothed in her long hair solely, a king passes, sees her, loves and weds her, in spite of her being dumb. When she bears her first child, the Virgin appears, and promises to give her back her speech if she will confess her fault ; she refuses, whereupon the Virgin carries off the child. This happens thrice, and the queen, accused of devouring her children, is condemned to be burnt. She repents, the flames are extinguished, and the Virgin appears with the three children, whom she restores to the mother. Can there have been any similar form of the forbidden chamber current in Ireland, and can there have been substitution of Grainne, Finn's wife, for the Virgin Mary, or, *vice versa*, can the latter have taken the place of an older heathen goddess ?—A. N.]

Page 169. See Campbell s " Tales of the Western Highlands, vol. III., page 120, for a fable almost identical with this of the two crows.

NOTES ON THE IRISH TEXT.

Page 2, line 5, ábalta aip a ƌeunaṁ = able to do it, a word borrowed from English. There is a great diversity of words used in the various provinces for "able to," as ábalta aip (Mid Connacht); inneaṁuil ċum (Waterford); ionánn or i noán, with infinitive (West Galway); 'nimiḃ with infinitive (Donegal).

Page 4. line 18, ni leigeann riao oam = they don't allow me. Oam is pronounced in Mid Connacht *dumm*, but oaṁ-ṛa is pronounced *doo-sa*. Dr. Atkinson has clearly shown, in his fine edition of Keating's "Three Shafts of Death," that the "enclitic" form of the present tense, ending in (e)ann, should only be used in the singular. This was stringently observed a couple of hundred years ago, but now the rule seems to be no longer in force. One reason why the form of the present tense, which ends in (e)ann, has been substituted for the old present tense, in other words, why people say buaileann ṛé, "he strikes," instead of the correct buailiƌ ṛé, is, I think, though Dr Atkinson has not mentioned it, obvious to an Irish speaker. The change probably began at the same time that the ṛ in the future of regular verbs became quiescent, as it is now, I may say, all over Ireland. Anyone who uses the form buailiƌ ṛé would now be understood to say, "he will strike," not "he strikes," for buailṛiƌ ṛé, "he will strike," is now pronounced, in Connacht, at least, and I think elsewhere, buailiƌ ṛé. Some plain differentiation between the forms of the tenses was wanted, and this is probably the reason why the enclitic form in (e)ann has usurped the place of the old independent present, and is now used as an independent present itself. Line 30, maoṛa or maoaƌ alla = a wolf. Cuiṛ ṛoṛán aiṛ = salute him—a word common in Connacht and the Scotch Highlands, but not understood in the South. Line 34, ƌeiƌeaƌ ṛé = he would be, is pronounced in Connacht as a monosyllable, like beiċ (*vek* or *vugh*).

Page 6, line 8, eaṛball is pronounced *rubbal* not *arball*, in Connacht. 'ni and ṁioṇ are both used before ċáinig at the present day.

Page 8, line 18. go maṛbṛaƌ ṛé = that he would kill; another and commoner form is, go maṛóċaƌ ṛé, from maṛḃuig, the ḃ being quiescent in conversation. Line 31, anḃṛuiċ = broth, pronounced anċṛuiċ (*auhree*), the ḃ having the sound of an *h* only.

Page 12, line 27. an ċuma ṛaibṛó is more used, and is better. Sin é an ċuma a ḃí ṛé = "That's the way he was." It will be observed that this a before the past tense of a verb is only, as Dr. Atkinson remarks, a corruption of oo, which is the sign of the past tense. The oo is hardly ever used now, except as contracted into o' before a vowel, and this is a misfortune, because there is nothing more feeble or more tending to disintegrate the language than the constant use of this colourless vowel a. In these folk stories, however, I have kept the language as I found it. This a has already made much havoc in Scotch Gaelic, inserting itself into places where it means nothing. Thus, they say *tha 's again air a sin: Dinner a b fhearr na*

sin, etc. Even the preposition ᴅᴇ has with some people degenerated into this
ᴀ, thus ᴄᴀ ʀé ᴀ ᴠᴉᴄ oꞃᴍ, "I want it," for ᴅᴇ ᴠᴉᴄ.

Page 14, line 9. For ᴀɪʀ read ᴜꞃʀᴜ. Line 12. ꞃᴇɪᴌʒ means hunting, but the
reciter said, ꞃᴇɪᴌʒ, ꞃᴍ ꞃɪᴀᴠ, "Shellig, that's a deer," and thought that Bran's
back was the same colour as a deer's. ᴜᴀɪᴍᴇ, which usually means green, he
explained by turning to a mangy-looking cur of a dull nondescript colour, and
saying ᴄᴀ ᴀɴ ᴍᴀᴅᴀᴠ ꞃᴍ ᴜᴀɪᴍᴇ.

Page 16, line 30. ʙᴇᴀᴙᴍᴀ and ᴄᴇᴀɴʒᴀ, and some other substantives of the
same kind are losing, or have lost, their inflections throughout Connacht.
Line 31. ᴄɪʒᴇᴀᴄᴄ is used just as frequently and in the same breath as ᴄᴇᴀᴄᴄ,
without any difference of meaning. It is also spelt ᴄᴜɪᴅᴇᴀᴄᴄ, but in Mid-
Connacht the ᴄ is slender, that is ᴄɪʒᴇᴀᴄᴄ has the sound of *t'yee-ught*, not
tee-ught.

Dr. Atkinson has shown that it is incorrect to decline ᴄᴇᴀɴʒᴀ as an *-u*
stem: correct genitive is ᴄᴇᴀɴʒᴀᴠ. Rᴇᴀꞃᴄᴀ: see ᴘᴀʀᴄᴀ in O'Reilly. Used
in Arran thus: ɴɪ'ʟ ꞃé ᴍ ᴘᴀʀᴄᴀ ᴅᴜɪᴄ = you cannot venture to.

Page 18, line 15. ʒᴜᴀʟ means a coal; it must be here a corruption of some
other word. ᴍᴜɪᴅ is frequently used for ꞃᴍɴ, "we," both in Nom. and Acc.
all over Connacht, but especially in the West.

Page 20, line 3. ᴅᴇɪᴍᴜʒ (d'yemmool). This word puzzled me for a long
time until I met this verse in a song of Carolan's

ᴍᴏꞃ ᴄᴜɪᴌᴌ ꞃé ᴅɪᴏᴍᴜʒᴀᴠ ᴀᴏɴ ᴅᴜɪɴᴇ.

another MS. of which reads ᴠɪᴏᴍʙᴜᴀɪᴠ, *i.e.*, defeat, from ᴅɪ privitive, and
ʙᴜᴀɪᴠ "victory." ᴅᴇɪᴍᴜʒ or ᴅɪᴏᴍᴜʒ must be a slightly corrupt pronunciation of ᴠɪᴏᴍʙᴜᴀɪᴠ, and the meaning is, that the king's son put himself under
a wish that he might suffer defeat during the year, if he ate more than two
meals at one table, etc. Line 15. ᴘᴇᴀꞃᴄᴀ = a "writ," a word not in the
dictionaries—perhaps, from the English, "arrest." ᴄúɪʒ ᴘúɴᴄᴀ. The nume-
rals ᴄꞃɪ ᴄᴇɪᴛʀᴇ ᴄúɪʒ and ꞃé seem in Connacht to aspirate as often as not, and
always when the noun which follows them is in the singular, which it very
often is. Mr. Charles Bushe, B.L., tells me he has tested this rule over and
over again in West Mayo, and has found it invariable.

Page 22, line 2. ᴄᴀ = where, pronounced always cé (*kay*) in Central Connacht. Line 17, ᴍᴀ ʙꞃᴀʒ ᴍé If I get. In Mid-Connacht, ᴍᴀ eclipses
ꞃᴀʒ, as ᴍ eclipses ꞃᴜᴀꞃ.

Page 26, line 18. ɪ ᴅᴄᴇᴀᴄ ᴀɴ ꞃᴀᴄᴀɪʒ = In the giant's house. ᴄɪʒ, the
proper Dative of ᴄᴇᴀᴄ, is not much used now. Line 20. ᴄᴜᴀɪʟʟᴇ ᴄóᴍʀᴀɪᴄ =
the pole of battle.

Page 28, line 9. ᴄꞃɪᴀɴ ᴅɪ ʟᴇ ꞃɪᴀɴɴᴜɪʒᴇᴀᴄᴄ = one-third of it telling stories
about the Fenians. Line 10. This phrase ꞃᴏɪᴘᴍ ꞃᴀᴍ ꞃᴜᴀᴍ occurs in a poem
I heard from a man in the island of Achill—

"'Sí ɪꞃ ʙɪɴɴᴇ ᴍᴇᴜᴘᴀ ᴀʒ ꞃᴇɪɴᴍ ᴀɪꞃ ᴄᴇᴜᴅᴀɪᴠ,
ᴅᴏ ᴄᴜᴍꞃᴇᴀᴠ ɴᴀ ᴄᴇᴜᴅᴄᴀ 'ɴɴᴀ ʒ-ᴄᴏᴅʟᴀᴠ,
ʟᴇ ꞃᴏɪᴘᴍ ꞃᴀᴍ ꞃᴜᴀᴍ , ᴀ'ꞃ ɴᴀᴄ ᴍóꞃ é ᴀɴ ᴄ-éᴜᴄᴄ,
ʒᴀɴ ᴀᴏɴ ꞃᴇᴀꞃ ɪ ɴ-ᴄɪꞃɪɴɴ ᴅᴏ ᴅᴜʟ ɪ ɴ-ᴇᴜʒ
ʟᴇ ʒꞃᴀᴠ ᴅ'ᴀ ʒꞃᴜᴀᴠ."

I have never met this word ꞃᴏɪᴘᴍ elsewhere, but it may be another form of
ꞃᴏɪᴍʙᴇ, "gentleness." Line 18. ᴄᴏʟʙᴀ = a couch, pronounced colus (*cul-
loos*); here it means the head of the bed. ᴀɪꞃ ᴄᴏʟʙᴀ means, on the outside
of the bed, when two sleep in it. ʟᴇᴀʙᴜɪᴠ, or ʟᴇᴀʙᴀɪᴠ, "a bed," is unin-
flected; but ʟᴇᴀʙᴀ, gen. ʟᴇᴀᴘᴛᴀɴ, is another common form.

Page 30, line 30. ᴅᴀʙᴀᴄ, "a great vessel or vat;" used also, like ꞃᴏɪᴄᴇᴀᴄ,
for ship. The correct genitive is ᴠᴀɪʙᴄᴇ, but my reciter seemed not to inflect
it at all.

Page 32, line 14. háiᵹ-óıbıɾ—this is only the English word, "Hie-over.'
Line 21. Copóᵹ = a docking, a kind of a weed.

Page 36, line 2. Cloıbeaṁ na tɾı ɾaobaɾ, "the sword of three edges." In the last century both tɾı and the ɾaobaɾ would have been eclipsed. Cf. the song, "ᵹo péıb, a bean na btɾı mbo."

Page 40, line 33. ſoᵹſláınce = balsam. Line 25. buıtɾe, the English word "witch." The Scotch Gaels have also the word bhuitseachas = witchery. Gaelic organs of speech find it hard to pronounce the English tch, and make two syllables of it—it-sha.

Page 42, line 21. Sɾannɾapcaıᵹ = snoring.

Page 44, line 3, for ɾɾón read ſɾóın. Line 16. Cɾuaıbe = steel, as opposed to iron.

Page 46, line 21. Cɾap = to put hay together, or gather up crops.

Page 48, line 1, Sᵹeım = a stitch, sudden pain.

Page 52, line 15. "Súᵹ!" a common expression of disgust in central Connacht, both in Irish and in English. Line 18. uıle buıne. This word uıle is pronounced huıla in central Connacht, and it probably gets this h sound from the final é of ᵹaé, which used to be always put before it. Father Eugene O'Growney tells me that the guttural sound of this é is still heard before uıle in the Western islands, and would prefer to write the word 'é uıle. When uıle follows the noun, as na baome uıle, "all the people," it has the sound of ellik or elliᵹ, probably from the original phrase being uıle ᵹo léıɾ, contracted into uıleᵹ, or even, as in West Galway, into 'lıᵹ.

Page 54, line 9. ᵹoıle = "appetite," properly "stomach." Line 30. an cɾıoblóıb = the trouble, but better written an cɾıoblóıb, since feminine nouns, whose first letter is b or c, are seldom aspirated after the article. There is even a tendency to omit the aspiration from adjectives beginning with the letters b and c. Compare the celebrated song of bean bub an ᵹleanna, not bean búb.

Page 56, line 4. Aıcſo = a disease. Line 24. b'ſeıceál and b'ınɾeséc are usual Connacht infinitives of ſeıc and ınnıɾ. Line 21. Caıɾe = a stream. Line 26. Scɾácaılc = dragging along. Line 32. Luıbeaɾnaé, often pronounced like teffernugh = weeds.

Page 60, line 8. Tá beıɾeáb or bıɾeáb oɾm = "I am better;" tá ɾé ɾáᵹaıl beıɾıᵹ, more rightly, bıɾıᵹ = He's getting better. Line 22. Maıɾeab, pronounced musha, not mosha, as spelt, or often even mush in central Connacht. Line 28. Maɾéaın, infinitive of maıɾ, to live. Cuıblınc = striving, running a race with.

Page 64, line 4. Tıᵹ lıom = "it comes with me," "I can." This is a phrase in constant use in Connacht, but scarcely even known in parts of Munster. Line 15. Oıneab aᵹuɾ coınc uıbe = as much as the size of an egg. Line 23. Aɾ an nuab = de novo, over again.

Page 66, line 2. Aᵹ baınc léıɾ an uıɾᵹe = touching the water.

Page 66, line 15. Moéuıᵹ = "to feel." It is pronounced in central Connacht like maoıéıᵹ (mweehee), and is often used for "to hear;" ṁaoıéıᵹ mé ɾın ɾoıṁe ɾeo = I heard that before. Line 20. Sᵹannɾuıᵹ is either active or passive; it means colloquially either to frighten or to become frightened.

Page 68, line 12. ſan maɾ a bɾuıl cu = wait where you are, ſan maɾ cá cu = remain as you are. Line 17. Coɾ aıɾ bıé, short for aıɾ éoɾ aıɾ bıé, means "at all." In Munster they say aıɾ aon éoɾ.

Page 70, line 3. cab éuıᵹe = "why;" this is the usual word in Connacht, often contracted to cuıᵹe.

Page 72, line 13. Cáéaıɾ-na-maɾc = Westport.

Page 74, line 7. Lubaɾuıᵹ, a word not in the dictionaries; it means, I think, "gambolling." Line 20. Ceaɾab = seize, control. Line 22. Múlaé = black mud.

Page 76, line 2. Anaéaın = "damage," "harm." There are a great many synonyms for this word still in use in Connacht, such as damáiste, dolaiḋ, urċóid, doċar, etc. Line 16. Bréóiḋte = "destroyed."

Page 78, line 3. Coir, a crime; is pronounced like *quirrh*. Láiḋe = a loy, or narrow spade.

Page 80, line 5. Ar ḃ leis an teaċ mór = "who owned the big house." A raiḃ an teaċ mór aige = who had in his possession the big house. Line 21. Trusgán tiġe = house furniture. Line 26. 'Niḋ Dia ḋuit, short for go mbeannuiġ Dia ḋuit. Line 27. Go mbuḋ h-éḋuit = "the same to you," literally, "that it may be to you," the constant response to a salutation in Connacht.

Page 84, line 22. A gan fios dí = "without her knowing it," pronounced like *a gunyis dee*. I do not see what the force of this a is, but it is always used, and I have met it in MSS. of some antiquity.

Page 86, line 33. Dá 'r ḋéug, pronounced dá réug, short for dá fear déag, "twelve men." Stangaire = a mean fellow.

Page 92, line 10. Bóṫairín cárṫaċ = a cart road.

Page 94, line 22. Táir = tá tu, an uncommon form in Connacht now-a-days.

Page 66, line 13. Go dtagaiḋ another and very common form of go dtigiḋ.

Page 98, line 22. Níor ḟan an sagart aċt ċuaiḋ a baile, *i.e.*, ċuaiḋ sé abaile; the pronoun sé is, as the reader must have noticed, constantly left out in these stories, where it would be used in colloquial conversation.

Page 100, line 27. Seilḃ and seilg are the ordinary forms of sealḃ and sealg in Connacht.

INDEX OF INCIDENTS.

—•—

[I use the word " incident " as equivalent to the German *sagzug. i.e.*, as con-
noting not only the separate parts of an action, but also its pictorial
features.—A.N.]